I0822270

The First Assignment

By Billy Kramer

To my Parents.

Thank you for always pushing me to follow my dreams and to find what makes me happy.

Chapter 1

It wasn't the smell of decay that woke Shawn up. Nor was it the constant rocking motion that caused him to hit his knee on the door. He had already been up when he noticed these small annoyances.

An eerie quiet encompassed his body. Could someone be awoken by silence? Usually, when he slept, he tossed and turned. He'd tried three different mattresses in the past year alone. But last night, Shawn didn't even remember falling asleep. What he *did* remember was the size of his bed. He shouldn't be hitting his knee on anything. He sat straight up, knowing he wasn't in his bed.

He was right. The comfort of his grandmother's scratchy quilt was nowhere near him, and Shawn slept with it no matter how hot it was. Squinting, he surveyed his surroundings as his eyes adjusted. Across from him was a black leather bench that mirrored the seat underneath him. If he held his hands out, he could feel the stained wood walls. The whole enclosed compartment was tiny: about five feet by five feet.

The only other thing in the compartment seemed to be a door to his left. He could just make out the handle, which must have been what he bruised his knee on. Where was he?

Shawn wasn't supposed to be here; he was sure of it. He needed to think. Earlier, a sudden lurch in the compartment had almost caused Shawn to fall out of his seat. Whatever he was in, it was moving.

"What the..." he whispered. He struggled to recall the last thing he did. He'd been to the movies. Had sat through a God-awful turkey meatball dinner with his parents. But each time he got closer to what happened the day before, a wall came down in his mind.

Hair on the back of his neck came alive with the sudden flow of air.

"Ah, you're awake, are ya?" The voice came from behind.

Shawn jumped to the other side of the compartment, throwing himself against the wood. From this side, he could make out a tiny square hole where his head had been.

"What are you, mute, kid? Or can you move your tongue to make words?" The voice crackled.

As Shawn had no idea where he was or how he got there, he wasn't exactly keen on talking to some random voice coming through a hole in the wall.

"Name is Roddick. You got a name, kid?"

At least Shawn now had a name to tell the police when they apprehended his kidnapper. Well, Shawn wasn't in the mood for talking. He needed to get out of the damn box. He reached for the door and tried the handle. It moved about halfway before the lock engaged, stopping any further attempts. Great. Not only did he not know where he was, but he was trapped.

"They always try the door, eh Gracie? Never can just sit back and relax now, can they."

Shawn was going to hurl. A normal start to his day was apparently out of the question. At least Shawn learned that Roddick wasn't acting alone. His silent partner must take joy out of hearing Shawn squirm, because she remained tightlipped.

"Who the hell are you people?!" He yelled, unsure of where the bout of confidence came from. Hell, he might as well attempt to weasel information out of them. "Where am I?"

"Damn, mate. Don't need to shout. And I told you, the name is Roddick." He chuckled. "As to where you are, that might be a little harder to explain, but don't worry we're almost to the gate."

Confusion seemed to be the theme for today. "What are you talking about? Why am I locked in here? What freaking gate?" People say their minds move a hundred miles per hour in intense situations, but Shawn's brain felt like a turtle moving across a sewer of sludge. There was so much new random information being thrown at him that he wasn't sure what to grab onto.

Ignoring his questions, Roddick continued, "Ah, don't worry, kid. I see it now. You see it, Gracie?"

Why couldn't Shawn have just woken up passed out on a sidewalk or something? That would make more sense than whatever this was. "Maybe you want to help fill in a couple of gaps for me, uh, Gracie?"

"Ahhhhahaah, Gracie, he thinks *you* are going to talk to him." He giggled. "You certainly got a lot of questions, don't you, kid? What *is* your name by the way? Can't just call you 'kid' the whole time."

"Shawn. My name is Shawn." Figuring he was already trapped here; a name wouldn't do any damage. He felt a weird sense of calmness as he said it. Was that crazy? He was trapped, but at least his name was something he was confident about. "Now that we're on a first-name basis, Roddick, mind explaining why I'm not currently in my own bed?" Frustration leaked out of his voice.

The compartment jolted, and Shawn had to brace himself on the seat to avoid falling off. Looking up at the wall across from him, he saw that the hole in the wall had closed. Great. The guy wouldn't shut up, and as soon as Shawn opened his mouth, the conversation stopped.

With a sudden click, the wooden door to his right opened, and there stood a man who Shawn could only assume to be Roddick. "Well, Mister Turner, we seem to have arrived."

It didn't take long for Shawn's eyes to adjust to the dark world outside the door. It was as if someone had thrown a switch in his brain; in a matter of seconds, Shawn had a clear picture of the man in front of him.

The man stood across from him, looking like he'd come from an 1800s wedding. His blood-red tie seemed like it would stain his pearl dress shirt underneath. He even wore a jet-black vest to go along with his tailcoat, which wouldn't be complete without a top hat. The only thing he was missing to complete the tuxedo was a monocle.

"Before you hit me with more of the many bubbling questions boiling inside of your brain, why don't we wait for Mac?" The man offered his hand. Based on the way he talked, Shawn had assumed Roddick to be older, possibly even in his 80s, but the man who stood in front of him was in his early 40s at best.

Brushing off the gesture, Shawn stepped out on his own; he wasn't going to accept help from the man who'd trapped him in a box.

Shawn smelled the leaves before he noticed the trees surrounding him. Even in the dark, Shawn could make out the branches clotted with pumpkin-orange leaves. The forest seemed to take root everywhere he looked, with maple trees suddenly obscuring views in any direction he turned. Only one area was clear of the forest's clutches. Below Shawn's feet was a cobblestone path leading from the direction they traveled to the gate.

Turning back around, Shawn came face to face with a long snout. Before he knew it, Shawn felt the cobblestone make an imprint on his butt. Shaking his head, he almost wanted to laugh at the ridiculous scene he found himself in. In front of him stood an ash-gray-coated stallion. Two horses were pulling the carriage that he'd emerged from. An actual freaking carriage. Shawn worried that he'd stepped into another dimension. Either that or this guy had an itching to dress up.

Both horses held their heads straight, their blinders helping them resist any movement. Not that they needed them. When he was startled and yelling, they didn't even bat an eye. Shawn hated horses ever since he'd fallen off one during a family vacation. He'd cried about his sore ankle for ten minutes before his mother convinced him to get back on.

"Ah, I see you've met Gracie!" Roddick came over and patted her on the snout and winked at Shawn. "She and Timothy keep me in good company, ya know."

Shawn just stared at him. The wink threw Shawn off. What kind of kidnapper was he? "Mr. Roddick—"

"Nope. Just Roddick. 'Mr.' was my pops. He always taught me to show respect though."

"Right... Okay, Roddick, can you now tell me where I am?"

"Not my job, Mr. Shawn," he said with a bow, making sure to take his top hat off so it didn't fall.

Did someone slip him drugs last night? Shawn went up to the gate and gripped the rusted bars until his blood flow was almost cut off. Two stone ostriches sat perched on fire-scorched brick posts that framed the gate. On top of the entrance sat an iron-moon-shaped circle of swirls. The interweaving design stretched from post to post. Almost like a child had painstakingly traced swirls in different directions, only deciding at the end to sign their initials—evident by the gold "WA" saddled in the middle of the gate topper.

Leaning his head against the bars, he let his skin absorb the cool from the black metal as he tried to think clearly. Twenty-four hours ago, something had happened which caused him to wake up with basically no recollection of anything. Amnesia? Dream? Kidnapping? Any of these options could be the solution.

Turning around, he let his hand settle against the rough patch of brickwork. "Hey, Roddick?"

"Yes, Mr. Turner?" Roddick said without turning from his horses.

"Why don't I remember how I got here?" Be blunt. That's what his dad always said. One shouldn't beat around the bush. It was worth a shot to keep pestering the man. Shawn thought about running, but he wasn't intimidated by Roddick. Plus, he had no idea where he'd go.

Roddick continued stroking the silver mane of Gracie, or possibly Timothy—Shawn wasn't sure. "Ah, Mr. Turner, before we get into that, let me ask you a question."

"Are you joking?"

"Humor me." A large neigh erupted from Gracie with each pet from her master. "Hmm, well a young'un of your age should have a heartbeat of what?"

Sixty to a hundred for resting, Shawn thought, digging up the information he'd buried from health class. He shook his head, trying to shake off the grogginess. "What's the point of asking that? You need to tell me what's going on."

"And what is yours currently?" Roddick asked, as he continued to oblige the horse.

This time Shawn didn't need the grip of the gate to stop the blood flow in his body, because not only did Shawn not know where he was; he had no heartbeat.

Chapter 2

Footsteps echoed up the path, each one bouncing off Shawn and ricocheting around him. He stood in front of the gate, planted with anxiety. He wondered why he couldn't find his heartbeat. He checked his wrists and then his neck. He'd had problems finding it before, but even with a hand over his heart, he got the same thing: nothing.

"Roddick" the footsteps said.

Roddick finally stepped away from petting his horses to engage with the newcomer. "Ah, Mr. Mac! I have a delivery for you."

Shawn slouched out of the haze that engulfed him and sat against a tree. He didn't owe these people anything. He wasn't some package.

"There are supposed to be two today." Mac glanced at Shawn.

Digging his fingernails into the roots of the tree, Shawn met Mac's gaze.

"Now now, Mr. Mac. The other wasn't on my list. Ain't that right, Gracie? Only one today?"

Mac sighed and rubbed his head. "Lily bringing the other one then?"

"Like I said, not on my list. Not my job, Good Sir." He chuckled again and went back to petting his stallions.

Mac stared at Roddick, who tipped his hat in response. "You know, it wouldn't kill you to update your wardrobe, Rod."

A pair of leather boots appeared in front of Shawn's nose. Mac wore a long black sleeve pullover and a regular pair of blue jeans. One sleeve bore the roman numeral six, while the sleeve had a WA over the shoulder.

"Let's get going, Shawn."

Shawn was tempted to bash Mac's bald head in with the rock laying on the ground nearby, but then he saw what was in Mac's hand. A long-curved blade extended from his arm, as if it were part of him. A scythe. The man was carrying a freaking scythe! Shawn released the rock from his fingertips.

Noticing Shawn eye the weapon, Mac's eyebrows raised. "Orientation will explain most of the questions." The man turned on his heel and walked back towards the gate. Shawn assumed that he was supposed to follow.

"See ya around, Mr. Shawn!" Roddick called out to him as the horses trotted back.

Orientation? What were they going to do? Give him a PowerPoint presentation about why he was kidnapped? Shawn stood and followed Mac because, again, he had no choice. As he passed one of the stone ostriches, he had this feeling that being left in the dark carriage might not have been the worst thing in the world.

Walking down the cobblestone path revealed a rabbit-white brick building that seemed to spread two football fields across. At the center of the building was a six-story-high tower, with large arched windows. Shawn knew he should be taking in more of his surroundings, but the tower seemed to draw his attention like a candle on an ugly birthday cake. He could just make out the shape of a figure peering down from the top window. After a couple seconds, the image disappeared from sight.

Mac slowed down to a dull pace, which Shawn matched. Lights flickered in some of the windows, confirming that there were others here, but he couldn't gauge how many. The building seemed massive; it looked to hold perhaps around 2000 people. And this was only the front.

They made their way toward the center tower. An extravagant double-wide door welcomed them. Two knockers hung from the door. Both were a pair of marbled eyes that seemed to judge Shawn as he walked up.

"Are you going to let me know what I'm walking into?" Shawn asked.

A sigh was all he got in return. Mac knocked once on the cedar doors, completely ignoring the eye knockers. A man in a checkered blue tweed suit answered as if he'd been waiting all night for Shawn's arrival. But he gave a surprising glance down in Shawn's direction that suggested this wasn't necessarily the case.

Mac spoke before the man could finish formulating whatever words were still inside of his mouth. "Can you please take Mr. Turner up to the clubhouse, Franklin?"

"Uh, of course! Where is Mr. Musters?" Franklin replied.

"Delivery was a little late, but I'm going back out now to wait for his drop-off." Mac gestured to Shawn. "Now, can you take care of this one first?" He said this as if Shawn was just something to check off a list for the night.

"Of course, of course," said Franklin, smiling.

He seemed a little too energetic for Shawn at this time of night. Or morning? Shawn wasn't sure.

"Now this way, Mr. Turner." A path led Shawn to a door across the entryway. Inside the dome-shaped room, there wasn't much: three other doors, one on the east side of the foyer and one on the west. Franklin led Shawn to the third door. "WA" made another appearance on the wall closest to Shawn. But instead of gold, these large letters were painted in stark white paint.

If Shawn hadn't been completely terrified, he would have admired the room more. Walls that rounded into the ceiling were painted his favorite navy blue. A chair rail circled the room, with white wood paneling traced below it. Each wall had an out cove built into it that displayed a marble bust. Four busts sat for display, each with a face Shawn didn't recognize. In the middle of the room stood a single black marble table that held a glass vase of sunflowers. He was tempted to break the vase open and use the glass to fight his way out, but he put his hand back to his non-beating heart.

Shawn stood still on the checkered tile. "No offense, Franklin, but why in the world should I follow you?"

Without bothering to turn around, Franklin continued toward the door across the way. "That's because, Mr. Turner, as you're well aware, you have no memory of the last few nights."

This kind of response didn't make Shawn want to follow the man.

"And I have all the answers," Franklin added as he disappeared into the doorway.

Not exactly an inviting invitation, but choices were limited. Could he run out into the woods?

Franklin popped his head out from around the doorframe. "Also, all the doors are locked in here."

Just to satisfy the little sanity he still had left, Shawn tried the front door. To no avail. With no options, he followed the strange man through the doorway. It led into a stairwell.

"Come on, Mr. Turner. We haven't got all night." Franklin's voiced reverberated in the round chamber Shawn now found himself in.

"I take it you can't tell me what's going on either?" Shawn said.

"Well, you're at Wayward Academy. And you're a lucky one, much better than Free Eagle or Sandling."

Shawn soaked in this information, even though it meant absolutely nothing to him. At least the WA's plastered all over the walls finally made sense, but what sort of Academy has horse drawn carriages? Or kidnaps their students?

"Uh, sure... Does this mean WA is why my last couple days are missing?" Shawn grabbed the stone railing. The steps to the stairs kept spiraling endlessly upward.

Franklin sped up his speech. It was like he was at the climax of a movie and couldn't wait to see what came next. "Well, originally, back in the early days, memories were left intact. But then the shortage happened, and the council voted to go another way. The trauma was just too much for some individuals. Which seems strange at first, but it does make the transition much, much easier."

These people had taken away his memories to protect him from trauma? Shawn had Wayward Academy narrowed down to an insane asylum or a dream. His money was on the former. "Transition? What am I transitioning *to*? What trauma?"

"I don't think I need to explain the answer to the last question for you. Hmmm, do I, Mr. Turner?" Franklin responded as they passed another level. "As to the question of transition, that will be explained during orientation. But don't worry: you're in very good hands."

"Just to be clear, the Academy *didn't* cause me to wake up here?"

"Oh no, that would be impossible." Franklin stopped at the top of the stairs in front of a green wooden door. "Let's get you settled in the clubhouse... before you pass out."

Nothing made sense, which seemed to be a common theme around here. The guy must have eyes in the back of his head because Shawn's steps were becoming heavier as he made each landing. The marble staircase was now spiraling like a kaleidoscope.

"There are eighty-seven steps, including the top landing areas in the six stories," Franklin said, as if reading his mind.

"Well, I hope that door means we're at the last one," Shawn grunted. He wasn't out of shape–just purely exhausted. He swore he was more athletic than his raspy breath indicated.

"Now, if you would please be quiet when you enter the room so as to not disturb the others, that would be wonderful."

So, he wasn't the only one then. Were they planning on filling up the place up with confused seventeen-year-olds that had recollection issues? As Shawn stepped foot on the landing and through the door, his legs screamed out in joy.

The clubhouse seemed more like a military hospital wing; the room was scattered with rolling beds, accompanied by nightstands. Shawn could make out two figures underneath sheets. One seemed to be balled up completely underneath, while the other had long brown hair flowing across her pillow.

"There's some water on the table. Someone will be back to fetch you all in the morning for orientation."

Shawn wanted to let Franklin leave, but he also needed more information. He shuffled his way to a bed near the window. "What is this place?"

"Wayward Academy. I think we've gone over that."

Shawn let the water refresh his throat. His eyes started drooping. "No, I mean why am I here?"

Gripping the inside of his jacket, Franklin steadied himself. "I thought you figured that out by now."

"Mr. Turner."

Wait. This man had been calling him Mr. Turner? Shawn had never told him his last name.

"You're here because you're dead."

Chapter 3

Sitting on the edge of the bed, his body crumpled into the sheets before he had a chance to satisfy his thirst-quenched mouth. Luckily, Shawn hadn't felt like talking to anyone else in the looney bin anyway.

After being told he was dead—which Shawn found hard to believe, since his legs still held him up—he passed out for a couple hours. Just the thought of no heartbeat had his mind racing, yet he fell asleep easily. The outside world was still dark when he awoke, and there wasn't a clock hanging around anywhere. Another two beds had been filled while he'd been out, which meant he'd slept through two separate times when the door had opened.

For over two hours, he tried picking the lock with a long skinny nail that he'd dug up from the floorboards. He was determined to rush out that door the minute it opened. He'd take his chances in the woods. Eventually, he gave up and decided to wait for more information in the morning. Only the morning just brought more questions.

"So, how'd you die?" A boy asked, plopping into the bed next to Shawn's. Maybe not the strangest way to open a conversation, but it had to be up there. Shawn held a hand up to his chest, trying to find even the faintest of pulses. This boy, Shawn guessed, was in the same "life after death" boat.

Shawn couldn't help but laugh. "Great question, man." The boy seemed to take this answer in stride by giving Shawn a half-smile.

"Fucking cupcakes, man! I can't remember anything either. One day I was hitting aces over the net and then bam! I woke up in this room." He jumped off the bed as he said it. "Name's Quintin, but people call me Q." The boy stuck out his hand.

Shawn threw his body over the side of his bed, fully awake from this Quintin. "Name's Shawn, and people also call me Shawn?" He said as he met Q's hand.

Q's eyes widened. "Wait, you're *the* Shawn??"

Shawn had no idea what that even meant. It wasn't like he was the only person to ever be named Shawn. The most recognition he ever received was when he won an essay contest in third grade. “Uh, no clue what you’re talking about.”

“Oh yes, it all makes sense. You *are* him!” Closing his eyes, Q bowed to Shawn.

Shawn was leaning more toward this place being a hospital for the clinically insane with each passing moment.

“He did it to me too,” said a voice to his left.

Shawn turned to find the same flowing brown hair he saw the night before.

“So, I’m not royalty then?” He remarked sarcastically.

The girl was sitting cross-legged on top of her tossed sheets. “Well, maybe... Probably not, although the old thinker isn’t the most reliable at the moment.”

“Phew. I was worried I’d have to fire some servants.”

Both Q and the freckle-faced girl stared at Shawn in silence. If the window had been open, Shawn would’ve been tempted to escape the awkwardness through it.

Q suddenly burst out laughing. “Bloody brilliant. I like you, mate, and I’m... *dead* serious.”

The girl rolled her eyes at either the bad pun, Shawn, Q, or the combination of any of the three. She seemed unimpressed by both boys, which he couldn’t really blame her for.

“Do either of you have any idea where we are? And if someone says, ‘Wayward Academy’, I might flip.” Shawn said.

Q started pacing the room. “Nah, mate. No clue. Tried kicking the door down when I woke up in here. Didn’t wake you blokes up, surprisingly. I mean, I got some damn good whacks in. Thought either that or her snoring would wake you up.”

“I do *not* snore.” She glared at Q, who disagreed again, although this time under his breath. “And before you ask, yes, our memories also seem to be missing a couple of pieces as well. If I’d been awake when you arrived, I could’ve told you how much of a waste of time attempting to kick down that door was.”

“How long were you here before us then?” Shawn asked.

She paused. “Maybe a couple hours. I’m not sure honestly. When I arrived, I was the only one here, and I passed out quickly. I’m Maple by the way.”

"Would say it was nice to meet ya, but honestly, I would rather be anywhere else than here." Maple seemed to be staring at him, but Shawn followed Q as he continued pacing the room. Back and forth he went, as if he were trying to wear out the floorboards to escape.

"Who are the other two?" Shawn asked, hoping that the ball of sheets across the room might respond. Or that the guy passed out near the door might be of some help.

"Whoever that is," she said, motioning to the ball bunched up underneath the sheets, "hasn't moved since he came in right before you. As for that one," she said, turning toward the body by the door, "he came in last night a little after you."

"You were awake?" Shawn shook his head. "That guy, Mac, brought me in and told me there were supposed to be two deliveries. I'm guessing he must have been the second delivery then."

"Yes, I was awake. Who's Mac? I've only interacted with the guy in the tweed suit. Franklin, I think? Quintin, do you know who Mac is?"

Q didn't respond right away. It wasn't until he snapped out of the pacing trance that he realized he'd been asked a question. "Franklin? Yeah, strange cat that one. I mean, who tells kids they're dead? And before you ask, yes, I pinched myself to make sure I wasn't. Tests were inconclusive at best."

Just as Shawn thought the first two times: loony bin.

"You can't die in a dream." The bundle of sheets spoke quietly, his voice muffled as it was filtered through the fabric.

"See, that's where you're wrong, Sir Pile of Laundry. I'll have you know that I have died in a dream before! Came back as a ghost though, and instead of doing cool stuff, I just looked at old letters. Weird."

Q was an oddball, but Shawn decided he was mostly harmless.

A portion of the sheet slipped down to the boy's neck, framing it so it appeared that his head was floating. Parts of his mop of black hair stuck straight up, as if someone had glued them that way while he was deep in slumber. "I hope for your sake you're right then."

A knock at the door interrupted them. The door cracked open. Light from the window glinted off the metal that appeared at the doorway. Mac sauntered in, grasping his scythe.

"Hey, man, no need to kill us. We're apparently already dead." Q folded his hands on his lap and repeatedly blinked his eyes, trying to mask the deviance that Shawn was sure hid beneath.

"Mac," Shawn mouthed to the others.

"Clothes are underneath your bed. Please dress and be ready in three minutes." He turned and walked out without another word.

Maple had already pulled on a light sweatshirt similar to the one Mac was wearing. The only difference was hers was light gray and on her left sleeve was the roman numeral one. "Are you guys going to move or just ogle at me?"

Both Shawn and Q scrambled to put on their jeans and sweatshirts. Even the other boy removed himself from his hideaway underneath the sheets to get dressed. "Guess this is the uniform, eh?"

"Think so," Q replied. "Should we wake sleeping beauty over there?" Q glanced at the last remaining kid in the room.

Maple was already walking towards the door before Shawn had his pants pulled on. "Not our problem," she said. "I want information, and I'm not waiting around for him."

Q appeared at his side and leaned over. "Aww. She said, '*Our* problem. She likes us. She really does."

Mac was waiting on the steps outside the door, scythe in hand. All four sets of eyes were drawn toward the blade and then back to Mac. He shrugged, finally showing some emotion. "Never know how someone will react. Follow me."

"What about the other guy?" Shawn asked. They were all in this together, right?

"Yeah, probably best not to leave him all alone," Q piped in.

Maple rolled her eyes at this and followed Mac down the spiral staircase.

Mac called back over his shoulder, "he will join you later... Like I said, you never know how someone will react."

Shawn found the marble staircase a lot easier going down than up, and it wasn't just because of gravity. He felt more energetic than he had last night. But even with this newfound energy, he still had to half-jog to keep up with Maple and Mac.

Shawn had just caught up to her when his tongue acted on its own accord. "My name is Shawn by the way." Although he *did* need to stop referring to her as the girl in his head, he wasn't Captain Smooth.

Maple threw a sideways glance at him. "I know."

"Huh?"

"You introduced yourself earlier." With that, she ended the conversation and sped up her walk.

Shawn was not the definition of smooth.

"Don't worry, man. We'll figure that one out." Q threw him a wink as he said it, which made Shawn wonder if Q had figured *anything* out.

Mac led the group to the bottom of the stairwell, back to the tiled entryway. Both side doors were now propped open, revealing long hallways in which a few people were scattered about. Besides that, nothing had changed inside the dome. Shawn was tempted to bolt but figured information was key. As they crossed the front door threshold, Shawn stopped at the door knockers, placing one of the marble eyes in his hand. Someone had taken an incredible amount of time to detail the eye.

"Wow," Q muttered, pulling Shawn's attention away from the knocker.

Shawn had only known Q for what felt like ten minutes, so he was waiting for some type of sarcastic remark or joke, yet none came. Then Shawn noticed the roof above the trees. Yes, roof. A couple hundred feet up was a rock ceiling that stretched out in all directions in front of the Academy. Turning around to look at the building, Shawn could see the end of the cavern that they seemed to be in behind him, but as for how far it stretched, it could've been miles.

"What..." was all that Shawn could get out. Even the girl had nothing to say as she stopped to look at the ceiling and the strange light that emanated from it. Dotted across all areas of the cavern were tiny lights that the night before, Shawn had assumed were stars. Today, it was as if the dial had been turned up to full brightness. The strangest thing about the glowing roof wasn't even how big it was. It was how the light imitated sunlight but without any of his skin soaking up the warmth.

Mac seemed to have known this was going to happen, as he'd stopped up ahead, waiting for them to snap out of the glowing roof daze. Unsure of how long he'd been consumed with the ceiling, Shawn finally snapped out of it realizing he still had the knocker clutched in his hand.

Shawn dropped the eye and it banged against the door. Everyone turned.

"Sorry," Shawn apologized.

They continued on in their confused haze that grew worse every minute. Shawn took one last glance back at the knocker. He waited for something to happen because while he was gawking at the ceiling, he could have sworn he felt it move in his hand, as if it had blinked.

Mac led them past the face of the building onto a washed stone path that felt like it should be leading to a garden. Passing row after row of windows, they finally turned the corner. The path ended at a ridiculously large pit.

Shawn heard the people before he saw them. Built below ground level was a large stadium with an octangular stage in its center. Rows of people surrounded the stage at different levels. It made Shawn think of how a pebble creates ripples in the water when dropped straight down. He could see everyone inside of the stadium from his vantage point. It was as if a giant hole had been dug into the ground, and since it served no other purpose, someone thought it would make the perfect arena. Everything besides the stage was just rock. Even the rows people were sitting on were just rectangular slabs of stone.

"Find a seat. Headmaster Tyflin will address everyone in a moment," Mac said, stopping at the top of the stairs.

"Almost late, aren't you, Mac?" a woman sitting at the top said.

Mac sighed. "I don't need your sass, Krystal. Make sure these ones find a seat. I still have another in the tower that needs some *encouragement* to come down." With that Mac left, using the scythe as a walking stick like it was the most normal thing in the world.

The crowd of people sitting down were clearly divided into two groups. The first three rows were all talking to each other and fidgeting after any unexpected noise. These people, like Shawn, wore the roman numeral I on their sleeve. The other group left in the stadium were just sitting back and observing them. Some wore suits like they were on their way to a courtroom, while others wore the same attire as the first three rows, but with black sweatshirts that had roman numerals that ranged from II to V.

Feeling eyes coming from every direction, Shawn walked toward the safest place he evaluated to be: the front row. He'd never been one for sitting at the front of the class, but right now he didn't want to miss a beat. Maple had the same idea and was sitting on an empty slab of stone as Shawn and Q made their way down. The boy Q had called pile of laundry followed, but only after he was shoved forward by that Krystal woman.

Shawn sat between Q and Maple, while the boy with the bad case of bedhead, took a seat on the end of the aisle behind them. The hard surface flattened Shawn's ass and made him miss the bed back in the tower. At least he'd been comfortable there, scratchy wool sheets and all. He surveyed the arena, taking in the odd faces and hoping to recognize at least one person in the crowd. He didn't.

About six people sat per stone bench in the circular rows around the stage. There was a red-headed girl to Q's right, and a short blonde girl with a bob haircut that sat at the end of the row next to the redhead. Both girls were ignoring Shawn and the others.

The stage itself was empty and was about the only thing made of wood in the middle of the stone pit. Shawn fidgeted while he waited for, well, anything to happen really. The rest of the newcomers seemed to be in either a state of stunned silence or extreme anger. Some were yelling at others. A couple of people tried making a break for it by running up the stairs, only to be blocked by ten people in suits, who forced them to turn around.

If there had been a time to escape, that had passed. Noticing movement to his left, Shawn turned to see Mac pushing a boy with his scythe. It must have been the same boy who was passed out in the room. His short blond hair was perfectly well-kept. This contrasted with his eye, which had a nasty purple bruise swelling. Without saying a word, the boy was led to the last empty seat across the aisle from Shawn.

Shawn raised his right eyebrow out of curiosity. Mac ignored this gesture even when they made eye contact. Mac then turned and walked to the top of the staircase, where he planted himself for the remainder of the "orientation".

The boy from the room stared straight ahead, expressionless. He too wore the gray hoodie with the Roman numeral I on the sleeve.

Q gave Shawn a nudge, as someone walked onto the stage. The silence from the crowd formed in a wave, starting with the back and flowing to the front, until only one person was left yelling about his memory. Eventually, even he shut up to get some answers.

A woman in her mid-thirties took center stage. Her black hair hung over her crimson suit coat. Her matching vest was layered over a black button-down. The contrast made the jacket look like it came straight from Shawn's veins.

But the accessory that stood out most of all was the scythe she held horizontally while prowling the perimeter of the stage. No one seemed to want to move, let alone breathe.

"My name is Headmaster Tyflin, and this is Wayward Academy." She gestured to the building, as she slowly began twirling her scythe in a circle like a baton. "I know that you all are either confused, pissed off, worried, or a bit of all three." She spoke as she continued stalking the outer ring of the stage. "I know that you're all experiencing memory loss and have no idea how you ended up here, or what you are here for... I know, because I once sat in that very same seat wondering the same thing."

Maple stiffened next to Shawn. The woman on stage gestured to the room with her non-scythe-wielding hand. "Everyone in this stadium knows these feelings because they too have felt them." The woman stopped in front of Shawn's bench.

She slammed the end of her scythe into the floorboards. The sound vibrated across the arena. She hung her head. "We were all chosen to do a job here. One none of us chose or ever dreamt about. But the crowd you see around you wearing black has chosen to accept it, nonetheless." Lifting her chin as she spoke, she sighed and looked toward the ceiling.

A job that requires you to be dead? Shawn thought about his lack of a heartbeat and loss of memory and teetered more on the belief that he'd never graduate high school or have a family.

"Being here means you have one main responsibility, and it comes first, no matter what. Because in a way, this is your rebirth, just as it was for the people who sit behind you."

Shawn started observing the crowd around him in the black sweatshirts. Each person seemed to be looking directly at the woman on the stage—everyone that is, except Mac. Mac picked at his fingernails atop the entryway to one row, acting as its gatekeeper. Seemingly sensing Shawn's gaze, Mac looked up. Shawn held his gaze for a moment before returning his attention to the woman still speaking.

A snort came from the boy with the black eye across the aisle. It looked like Mac wasn't the only one who didn't care what this headmaster had to say. The boy clutched his hands into a fist and continued staring at the ground, lost in his own thoughts.

"While it wasn't your choice to be here, it wasn't our choice to put you in the position to be here either." The headmaster had her back turned to Shawn's area as she said this, so she didn't see the boy a couple of rows over from Shawn get up from his seat.

Nor did she see him run at a full sprint and then leap onto the stage. The gasp from the crowd came from only the first three rows. But even with this warning, she didn't turn around. Instead, she stopped speaking and waited. The boy was going to tackle her. Shawn waited for the thud of bodies to hit the ground.

As the boy got within three feet, Tyflin's left hand shifted from her side and she spun, bringing the scythe in a large arc. Shawn felt the blood on his face before he even processed what he was seeing.

Screams erupted from the front rows, while everyone else behind remained silent.

Touching his face, Shawn rubbed the blood between his fingers in shock. He turned and looked at the boy across the aisle. The boy with a black eye was paying attention now. It was hard not to when a severed head lay at his feet.

Up on the stage, the headless torso thumped to the ground and refused to snap anyone out of their hysteria. It was suddenly chaos in the first three rows, as people scrambled to get away.

"Silence!" the headmaster thundered. Everyone who wasn't already frozen to their seats sat back down for fear of being the next head to roll. The headmaster slowly rose from her crouch that she'd finished her swing in and casually wiped the blade on her jacket. Blood smeared across the lip of her crimson coat, where it went almost unnoticed.

Her voice remained level but boomed throughout the arena. "As most of you have come to hear, you've died. Yes, died, dead, deceased... passed on. Use whatever words you think will help, because while you may have been reborn..." she said, nudging the headless torso with her scythe, "it doesn't mean you can't experience death a second time."

Chapter 4

No one dared to move. Many were crying, while others were on the ground regurgitating whatever was in their system. The red-headed girl in his row had joined the latter and she was now familiar with her stomach contents. As he looked around, Shawn's nostrils filled with a mix of damp rocks and stomach acid.

Shawn remained sitting, not totally sure what to do. He just knew he didn't trust his legs. Maple had her head between her hands and didn't seem likely to move for a while. Across the aisle, the black-eyed boy was the only one who remained in his row. Everyone else had fled to other parts of the arena. Completely alone, the boy sat gripping the edge of the bench with shaky hands.

Silence snaked its way through the crowd until it had slithered all the way to Shawn's row. The headmaster waited until the screaming stopped and those puking cleaned themselves up. Back on stage, the headmaster stood over her newly decapitated torso, clutching a brown cloth bag.

At first, Shawn thought the bag was for the skull still sitting at the feet of bruised-cheek boy. Then he saw it. Gradually, teal-blue light spread like vines across the torso. It started from the fingertips and feet, pulsing its way toward the center of the chest, where it gathered. It then circled, hovering over the heart. A hazy orb grew as the pulsing teal vines retreated into it. Even in shock, Shawn was mesmerized by the beauty of it.

The glowing orb disappeared into the headmaster's bag. She crossed the stage and handed it over to a man waiting nearby. This man then sprinted up the steps toward the Academy.

"Ah, fuck this." Q stood up and turned like he was about to follow the man up the aisle when his pupils doubled in size. He sat back down in his seat and closed both eyes, shaking his head in disbelief.

At this point, Shawn wasn't sure he cared if he trusted his legs. He needed to get out of there. His chest was tightening. She'd killed the boy. Cleaned the body from the neck up and did brush strokes with the blood. Did he risk walking out? Whatever the costs? Who knew how long it was before his head was lying on the ground next? Then he glanced at what had forced Q to sit back down.

In the arena, eight main aisles separated the rows of benches that led to the exits. Coming down each one were horses. One came down the aisle closest to Shawn. It was a beautiful midnight stallion, with a mane that absorbed every color around it. Most people would think that such a beautiful coat was the reason the horse turned heads, yet this wasn't the case.

In contrast to the horse's dark coat were bones visible on the side of its face and yellowing with decay. Where the right eye should have been was an empty socket that had skin flaking off like a bad case of dandruff. Even the jaw and snout had visible bone fragments peeking through the face. Yet it wasn't this or the completely exposed bone from its front leg that had silenced everyone.

It was what rode on top of the freakshow animals. Although decaying, at least the horses had skin; the things riding on top of them weren't even human. Something resembling the shape of a man had jumped off a horse and strode down the aisle. Where his skin would be, looked like cracked gray stone. The thing's face was smooth and chiseled to look human-like. Shawn thought their movements were going to be slow and robotic, but they moved easily, like lava that hadn't cooled yet. What was even more odd were the ice-blue vein-like lines that webbed throughout the things' entire bodies.

Almost identical riders rode down each aisle on their half-skeleton horses, some resembling men, some women. Each rider wore a brown tunic outlined in black that reached down to their knees. A black strip of cloth was knotted around each thing's waist. When they reached the stage, they jumped off their horses. One landed next to Shawn, who expected to feel the impact, but the ground didn't shake. There wasn't even a thud.

The bald creatures walked toward the stage, surrounding it before turning their backs to stand at attention. Eyes with bright purple irises scanned the area, daring another attacker to make a move. Shawn rubbed his temples. Was this really happening?

"If reality hasn't set in yet for you, I hope that the greeting party sent by Sir Elder helps settle that issue." Tyflin addressed the jaw-dropped faces in the first three rows. "Don't fret. They're simply observers in the world above. But don't be mistaken. They can enforce the peace here as well."

This second sentence sent spasms up Shawn's back.

"We're underground," Maple whispered to herself. Once again, Shawn found his gaze drifting toward the ambient light source. He'd guessed a cave of some sort, but Tyflin made it seem like it was more than that. What exactly was above them?

The headmaster continued walking the circumference of the stage. "As I said before, we didn't choose for you to be here. But you're here for a reason." She paused, bending down near the torso, still leaking blood.

"What you saw happen here was unfortunate. We don't terminate someone's contract unless absolutely necessary." She said this with a tinge of sorrow. "A man ran out of here just a few moments ago with a bag that holds our very reason for existence. Our reason for a second chance. When this young man died, you might have seen something hovering over his chest. The orb that you saw is our job. We believe it to be the complete essence of a person: their soul. Our job is simple. We are merely messengers. Transporters, one may say. We make sure that this essence makes it to the next phase. Many of you will be familiar with our name; it is one of legend. I only hope you bring the honor and respect that those before you have brought it. Welcome, our new class of reapers, to Wayward Academy.

Chapter 5

Reapers? He pictured the angel of death known as the Grim Reaper. Did Shawn hear that correctly? He almost laughed at the absurdness of the image he kept conjuring in his head. These people wanted him to be a reaper of some sort? Shawn hated death. Well, maybe it wasn't so much hate, as fear. At the last funeral he went to, he almost fainted when the coffin was brought out. Thinking about death could pull him into a spiral of what-ifs. And yet here he was. Chosen to be a reaper. He wanted to throw up.

Franklin, wearing the same blue tweed jacket as the day before, stepped onto the stage, taking over for Headmaster Tyflin, who promptly left the pit. "Now this isn't easy to swallow. Which is why you will be assigned mentors and paired up with a partner for your first two years at the Academy." Bringing a glass to his lips, he took a gulp of water. "Patience, though, please, as you can see drastic actions will be met with consequences."

A partner? Shawn let out a breath. He didn't have to go through this alone. And two years meant that he probably wasn't dying anytime soon. At least, that's what he hoped.

"We know that many questions are bouncing around inside of you, and we will be more than happy to answer any in due time." Franklin's lips twitched into a smile as he mentioned giving answers. "As many of you can feel now, your body needs to adjust to the experience it has gone through. That's why you may be feeling exhaustion, even though you've just woken up."

Franklin kept his nervous smile as he spoke about some breakfast that had been prepared in the dining hall. He continued to ramble on, but Shawn was focusing on the stone people in front of him. Every so often, a head would turn and survey the crowd in the arena. The creature closest to Shawn was tall and thin. His uniform was identical to the others, except on the bottom left-hand side of his tunic were three gold dots. Leaning in, Shawn tried to see if there was any writing. That was when the head on top of this particular tunic turned in Shawn's direction. Purple irises locked onto his hazel ones, as though the stone creature had acquired its target. Finally, Shawn dropped his gaze.

He leaned over to Q. "What *are* those things?" he whispered.

"No bloody clue, and not sure I want to stay and find out," Q replied. "You feel me?"

Shawn nodded. But he wasn't sure he agreed. He didn't want to stay there, but maybe he shouldn't leave. That is if they'd even be allowed to leave. He rubbed his neck. There was still so much he didn't know, and he didn't want to end up like the guy on stage.

"Don't do it." Maple said, taking Shawn by surprise. Due to their last conversation, Shawn assumed she wasn't actually going to speak with him again.

"Now why shouldn't we, Sweetcakes?" Q whispered over Shawn.

She shook her head with annoyance. "Because, before we do that, we need to know exactly what we're escaping *from*." She gestured to Franklin on stage. "And what we're escaping *to*." This time she made eye contact with the rock creature nearest to the stage.

"Again, with the 'we' thing, I think she might be growing fond of us, Shawnie boy." Quintin managed to break him from his shock and draw a chuckle from Shawn.

Shawn looked at the skull to his left. For all he knew, just speaking about deserting would land them headless. In the seats around him, it didn't appear that anyone could hear them talking. Although he could have sworn that the kid across the aisle quickly turned his head away when Shawn looked over.

Franklin finished the rest of his speech and instructed the newcomers to go to the outdoor dining hall, near the pit. They filed out row by row, flanked by either scythes or stone fists. With the fear of punishment heavy in the air, no one dared make a run for it.

After reaching the top of the stone steps, Shawn could see the oblong tables. He smelled the food before he was even close.

There was a spread of bacon, eggs, waffles, breakfast burritos, hash browns–pretty much any breakfast food you could think of. It was all laid out when you first approached the "dining hall", which was really a rounded-out area in the woods that the trees fenced in.

In the middle of the clearing was a rounded table with other tables sprouting out from it like the hour markers on a watch. On autopilot, Shawn grabbed a plate full of bacon and hash browns and headed toward three o'clock, where Q was already sitting down.

"Apparently, we can go back and get as much as we want," Q said between mouthfuls of eggs.

Shawn picked up a piece of bacon and let the grease drip down his finger. "You want this? I'm actually not very hungry."

Q nodded like he was a bobblehead out of control, so Shawn dumped his plate onto Q's. "If we're dead, do we have to eat, or is it just habit?" Shawn asked.

Q stared blankly.

Shawn continued. "Like, what happens if I eat 50,000 pounds of this stuff? Could I have a heart attack and die again?"

"Wonderful question, Mr. Turner!" Franklin slipped around the corner of the table. "Actually, you can, in fact, 'get fat' or gain weight. Yet the wonderful thing about dying is it doesn't matter because most of your systems have already stopped working. So, in actuality, you don't have a heartbeat to stop." And as quickly as Franklin came in with an answer, he left, leaving only coat tails and shocked faces in his wake.

Across the room, Maple made her way toward Shawn and Q's table. She put her empty plate down as she sat.

"Not hungry?" Shawn asked while Q continued stuffing his face.

"After watching someone get their head sliced off in front of me? No, I'm not hungry," she said.

Q choked down the bits in his mouth.

At every table, the story seemed to be the same. It wasn't a very joyous lunch, as almost no one talked. From exhaustion or shock? Fear? It was tough to guess at this point. Some people nibbled on their food, while other plates remained untouched. Occasionally, a person would break down crying, but most stayed silent. Everyone now knew what happened to those who questioned their keepers.

While the new reapers kept together, so did the older reapers. At the central table sat six figures, including Franklin, Mac, and the headmaster. Spreading out to the surrounding tables were older reapers who remained silent.

One would think that finding out you're dead would consume your thoughts, but Shawn didn't even have the urge to focus on his past. The only thought going through his head was whether it was worth it to escape now. This place was a society of some sort, one which he didn't understand and which apparently beheaded people at whoever's wish, but a society, nevertheless. He wished he would wake up in his bed.

"What's next?" Maple interrupted his thoughts.

"What do you mean?" Shawn asked.

She sighed. "Well, I think that a lot more than 100 people die in a day. So, again, what's next?"

"Training will be your next step. And I'll be very interested in where you will land. Maple Collins, if I assume correctly?" Standing at the end of the table, wearing a gray suit with purple pinstripes, was a petite woman who spoke with a smile as tilted as the purple sun hat she wore.

"Why are you interested in *me*? Who are you exactly?" Maple sipped her water, seemingly unimpressed with the woman who'd called her out.

"I'm interested in everyone brought into the Academy, as well as Shawn and Quintin here." She nodded to the boys. "As for my name, it's Camren Fidler. Be careful who you challenge, Miss Collins. Not every council member is as forgiving as me."

Maple set down her glass calmly, trying not to disturb the water swashing inside. She almost convinced Shawn that these comments didn't affect her, but he saw the slight tremor in her fingertips. "May we help you, Camren?"

"It's Miss Fidler. But no. Actually, I'm here to tell you your room assignments," she said, taking out a clipboard.

"Uh, how long will we be here?" Shawn asked. Room assignments? What was this? Boarding school?

Camren Fidler leaned her hands against the table, showing that the fingernails on one hand were painted purple, while the other hand was left untouched.

"Well, that depends on you, Shawn. You may have noticed that some of our council members may be a little hot–well, mind my phrasing–headed."

Maple scrunched her eyebrows together, radiating anger. "How many–"

"Just trust me, and you'll do more than survive in this place, you'll flourish." Camren scooped up the clipboard. "Now, Miss Collins and Mr. Prodit: Room 324. And as for you Mr. Turner, Room 416."

Shawn looked at the only two people he'd spoken to so far, wondering how they got lucky enough to get paired together. "And who would *my* roommate be?"

"Mr. Musters will be accompanying you. Now, before I'm bombarded with more questions, I do have some other newcomers to inform." She turned to the next table, her gray and purple coat coattails trailing her.

Maple glared at the woman walking away and without even turning around to address Q, said to him, "Guess we have to make this work. I don't snore, and you better hope I never find out that you do."

Q's only response was to scarf down the last of his eggs.

Shawn had no idea who this Mr. Musters guy was, but honestly, he didn't really care. Or at least he shouldn't, since they were in the same situation. Shawn just wished he were a little closer to the only two people he knew.

"That must be the council," Maple said, as she continued to glare in Miss Fidler's direction.

Shawn followed her gaze and could see that Fidler was taking a seat at the rounded table in the middle. The company surrounding her gave them a snapshot of the council members. Apart from Camren, Mac was also seated at the table. Franklin sat to his left and was engaged in an enthusiastic conversation with another man that appeared to be nodding out of habit as he glanced around the room. One other woman kept looking around attempting to talk to people but couldn't find an audience. Lastly, of course, the headmaster herself sat at the table. Shawn didn't know the others, but in total, these people looked to make up most of the Wayward Academy council.

Shawn's room was similar to the room in the tower. It deserved to be featured in *Hospital Room Weekly*. It was simple and contained a sterile smell that infiltrated your nostrils. Inside were two beds with wooden trunks at the end, along with a nightstand. That was it. No designs or color on the walls. Just a white box.

Not caring where he slept, Shawn chose the bed closest to the wall, which, conveniently, didn't have a window for his escape.

He lay down on the only thing that splashed color into the whitewashed room: a navy-blue comforter. Shawn tried to imagine that this was his bed back in his old room. If he turned to the right, he might see his old posters, or the horse-shaped lamp that his parents refused to toss out. Just the thought of his parents made Shawn shiver. He was thankful that for the first time, he had a moment to himself. This lasted for about twenty seconds before he noticed a guy standing at his door. The boy, who couldn't have been much older than him, just stared at him. About thirty seconds passed before Shawn knew that the guy wasn't going to be moving anytime soon.

"Uh, hi there," Shawn said, convinced that this intellectual conversation starter would garner a response. Instead, all he got was a crooked smile from a boy with lopsided teeth. He wore the Roman numeral II on his shoulder, and his sweatshirt matched the color the crowd wore at the stadium. So, he wasn't a new reaper.

"Can I help you, man?... Are you my roommate?" Shawn wasn't sure if staring at someone creepily was normal for a school with beheadings, but he wouldn't be surprised if a couple eggs cracked after what he just witnessed.

The boy still refused to move. He didn't even blink. Shawn was beginning to wonder when the guy's eyes would dry out. A shove to the boys shoulder finally earned a reaction from the doorway watcher.

"Okay, move it along," said another boy, stepping in the doorway. He also wore the II on his sleeve. "Now, now. Let's leave the newbie alone."

The doorway watcher nodded but still didn't budge. This required one more shove from the other kid before the message was received and Shawn was left alone with the mystery pusher.

The new boy stepped into the room and made his way toward Shawn, hand outstretched. "Don't worry about Marvin there, he does that to everyone."

Shawn met the handshake while still sitting on his bed. He was never sure if he should get up for these kinds of things. "Thanks. Appreciate the help... I was getting a little creeped out there."

The boy laughed. "Oh, you have no idea, man."

Being completely focused on the watcher, Shawn only just noticed the boy had one eye. Trying not to stare, Shawn pretended to examine the rest of the room.

"So, what's your name?" Shawn asked, hoping that this was his new roommate.

He raised an eyebrow over his only currently-in-place eyeball. "Didn't they tell you?"

"Musters?" Shawn asked.

The boy threw his hands up. "Yes, Sir, roomie. Don't worry, I don't wet the bed. Much." He threw in a wink as he said it all. "I see you chose the bed closest to the wall, eh? Not a bad spot... I guess."

Shawn played with the blanket, trying to figure out this Musters guy. "Yeah, hope you're cool with that."

Musters threw himself down on the other bed. "Of course! I may be the first line of defense if someone tries to kill us, but I can also easily trap you if I want."

Immediately, Shawn looked for anything near the boy that might be a weapon. If it was a joke, it was poorly timed after the day he'd had. Normally, he'd assume he was just being messed with, but nothing was normal about this situation.

Musters threw his head back, laughing. "Ha, I love new reapers, man. You have that deer in the headlights look about you at all times. It's precious really, but that's Reaper Academy for you."

"Reaper Academy?" Shawn asked.

"While the uppity-ups like to call it Wayward Academy, you're at what we advanced students like to call Reaper Academy."

A knock at the door drew their attention. Shawn hadn't even seen Musters close it. Leading the way into the room, with his signature scythe, was Mac, who was surprised to see them both there. Gripping his scythe, he pointed to Musters. "Why are you here, Rupert?"

The boy—who was either Rupert or Musters or possibly Rupert Musters—was now the one who had the deer in the headlights look. "I..."

"Out," Mac said, as he sliced the air like it was muenster cheese. The boy got the hint, as he lept off the bed and bolted out the door without so much as a see-you-later.

Mac turned around and called out, "This is your stop. Your roommate assignment is with Mr. Turner." Mac said this like he was reading off a list, making check marks as he finished his sentence. Another figure walked in through the door, who Shawn recognized instantly. The bruise around his eye had become a deeper shade of purple.

"Turner and Musters," Mac said, again like he was double-checking his list, or possibly memorizing the pairing. "I'll be back for you later." Mac then left, closing the door behind him.

Shawn heard the click of the lock engage. Had he really expected them to be able walk around by themselves? No, but thinking something and knowing it were two very different things. He really hoped it wasn't going to be a last man standing kind of situation, because it wasn't going to end nicely for Shawn. He already knew that the other boy wouldn't back away from a punch.

"Are you actually Musters?" Shawn asked, not completely convinced he wasn't getting duped again.

The guy sat on the trunk at the foot of the bed, ignoring Shawn's question. He examined the room until his green eyes settled at the door.

"Yep, I'm pretty sure they locked us in again," Shawn said.

The boy stood up and examined the handle. "What do you mean 'again'?" He said with his back turned.

Shawn started fiddling with the edge of his worn blanket, running it over each knuckle. "Last night, they locked five of us in what they called the clubhouse. I tried for hours to open the door but with no luck. They brought you in, but you must have been passed out the entire time."

"Knocked out," he responded.

Shawn perked up. "Huh?"

The boy tried to turn the handle of the door, and to neither of their surprise, found it locked. "Doesn't matter."

"My name is Shawn by the way." Again, no response. Honestly, what was it with people here and not giving up their name? He was just going to have to start labeling people with numbers or something.

Boy 1/Musters/Roommate stayed in front of the door for some reason. Shawn wasn't sure if the guy thought it would magically open, or if he could unlock it with his mind, but neither the door nor him moved.

"Are you just going to stare at it until it opens?" Shawn finally asked, internally debating if the boy would keep planted right in front of it, and if it would hit him in the face when it actually did open.

The boy backed up about a foot from the door, his shoulders rising as he took a deep breath. Shawn knew what was coming next and, based on how the door was solid oak, didn't expect a good outcome for the boy's foot. "I don't think I'd do that."

The boy ignored Shawn. His leg shot out toward the middle of the door, missing the handle by centimeters. Shawn was impressed with the strike and had it been another door, it might have broken down. But, as he thought, solid oak.

The boy clenched his fists and went to his bed, turning his back on Shawn. He sat cross-legged on the bed, massaging his most likely bruised foot. At least it would match his face.

"Told ya," Shawn muttered as he continued fidgeting with his sheets. The creaking of mattress springs made him look up. Shawn had expected the boy to be glaring at him. Instead, the boy was flat-faced—a stark contrast from the angry, brooding vibe he'd been giving off before.

"Shawn, huh?"

"Yep, that would be me."

The boy half-snorted. "Well, you seem very accepting of your situation, *Shawn.*" He said the name as if it was a rotten piece of food in his mouth.

Shawn folded his arms across his body. "Maybe it's better to have more information before making rash decisions. Like trying to kick down a solid oak door. But hey, sue me."

The boy fluffed his pillow. "Good to know where you stand, man." He lay down, letting the bed conform to his body. "By the way, you have blood on the bridge of your nose."

Pins and needles may as well have been stabbing their way through Shawn's hand as he moved it underneath the pillow. Waking up disoriented, he realized he'd fallen asleep while staring at the ceiling. He looked over at the other bed and, by the gradual rising and falling of the sheet, figured his roommate had done the same. Thankfully, Shawn remained nightmare free. No stone men chasing after him, dark carriages to be trapped within, or heads rolling.

Quietly, he got up from his bed, inching forward to not disturb Mr. Personality. The two candle sconces sitting on the nightstands had gone out at some point during his slumber, so he felt around cautiously until he'd positioned himself with his back flat against the door. Closing his eyes, he listened. What for exactly? He wasn't too sure. But what he *was* sure about was that sooner or later someone would come to unlock this door. So, he sat there listening for the slightest hint of when that might be.

Without any clocks inside the room, Shawn didn't know how long he stayed in that position. A couple of times he had to stand up and stretch, working to get blood flow back into his legs. It was long enough to notice when the other boy altered his breathing and ruffled his sheets. Most likely awake now, they continued to ignore each other's presence. Which, at the moment, was perfectly fine with Shawn.

Every so often, Shawn could make out the footsteps echoing down the hallway. To him, it seemed that someone was patrolling it. Apparently to make sure no superhuman strength was lingering inside one of the newly dead teens.

"You're pretty fucking calm." Musters' voice broke through the trance.

Shawn cracked open an eye to see Musters sitting up, observing him.

"Outward appearances can be deceiving."

"Well, you were one of the few people on this floor that didn't start screaming bloody murder when we got locked in. So, that has to count for something".

Shawn scratched the itch on his nose. "Waste of breath doing that. Besides, Mac said he'd be back."

Musters reached up and felt the swelling around his eye. "Ah yes, Mac. He seems like a very reasonable person to listen to."

Shawn tried to ignore him. What right did this boy have to judge him? He wouldn't even give Shawn his first name. Curiosity got the best of him though. "Did you also wake up to a crazy top-hat-wearing carriage rider named Roddick?" Shawn asked.

Musters lay his head against the pillow again. "No, she wasn't wearing a top hat."

"Then before you start talking about who is reasonable or not, you should maybe wait to punch someone." The comment left them sitting in a thick air of awkwardness. Shawn worried he might have gone too far. Hell, he didn't know what this boy was capable of. With a couple of inches on Shawn, this Musters kid would be a problem if he wanted to be.

"A piece of advice for you, Shawn." Musters spoke with his head pointed to the ceiling.

"Yeah?"

"Maybe you should wait to recognize your situation before running off with your two pals. And, maybe, be quieter about it next time." As he finished his sentence, the bolt on the door clicked open.

Chapter 6

Two council members greeted them at the doorway. Franklin had added a green bow tie to his ensemble, while Miss Fidler continued sporting her violet sun hat, even inside the building. Shawn still hadn't seen anyone that looked over the age of fifty here. Even these two, the odd pair that they were, seemed to be in their early 30s. All the new reapers were teenagers, and the other Academy students appeared to be as well.

Shawn stood awaiting instructions, anxious to be doing something. Musters, on the other hand, threw an initial glance their way and laid his head back on his pillow. "Neither of you two look like Mac to me."

Like a toddler wanting to go to the bathroom, Franklin shifted his weight from right to left and back again, in clear discomfort.

Stepping forward into the room, Miss Fidler took charge. "Well, I'm most certainly thankful for that. All council members are on double duty tonight, so both Mr. Franklin and I will be leading you today." Moving further into the room, she stopped directly in front of Musters' bed, clasping her hands. "Besides, I thought I would let Mac *hit* some other rooms instead, right Mr. Musters?"

The eye contact between the two was that of two rival wolves circling each other. Sensing the tension, and visibly uneasy with it, Franklin cleared his throat and clapped his hands together. "Let's get this tour on the road then, shall we?"

"Yes, let's begin," Fidler said, making a sharp turn from Musters' bed and breezing out the door past Franklin. More than happy to leave his prison cell, Shawn wasn't going to wait around. He quickly followed into whatever awaited him.

Echoing off the black-stained hardwood, Miss Fidler's high heels sounded like a woodpecker repeatedly drilling into a tree. "No one knows exactly when this Academy was built or who decided to put us here," Fidler said as she made her way door by door to the end of the hallway. "But we do know our job once we've been called: save souls."

"Sorry, but how do we know this gassy blue orb is a soul?" Shawn felt his mouth moving before his brain could process the words.

"You have every right to question this, Mr. Turner," Fidler said. "I understand that most people must see before they believe, and you'll be provided many opportunities to see that what we're saying is true."

Musters snorted.

"After what you've witnessed yesterday, *this* is what you scoff at, Mr. Musters?"

Shawn watched his roommate search for a response, yet the doubt dissipated from Musters' eyes.

"Um, what exactly are we saving these souls *from*?" Shawn again found himself speaking before he knew it.

Miss Fidler turned a corner and made her way to a spiral stairwell. "Again, there'll be an opportunity for you to see what happens when an essence is not taken care of Mr. Turner."

"Wonderful." Musters' nostrils flared as he responded. "So here we are, basically kidnapped, but for a purpose!"

"You were *not* kidnapped, and I suggest you understand that soon. This is a new world for you, with new rules. But don't worry. We'll be here helping you along your new journey." The council member said this with a smile that gave Shawn no comfort.

They reached the landing of the first floor and paused. Franklin turned to them both. "Honestly, boys, this is hard. We won't pretend it isn't, but please remember, we've been there. Follow me." He said with a sigh and headed the opposite way Fidler was headed.

Speed walking to catch up, Fidler caught them right before Franklin reached the double doors at the end of the hallway. "Dirk Franklin, have you forgotten that this is not the correct procedure for newcomers?" She smiled at him like an old friend, yet her body went rigid, daring him to defy her.

"Lighten up, Camren. The world doesn't always need to be black and white." Franklin then motioned with his hands for her to step aside.

Fidler searched each face of the trio before she started chuckling. "Why of course! You boys are in for something special then, it seems." With that, she moved out of the way, allowing passage to the group.

This door led to the back of the Academy and opened to a courtyard. Although on the ground floor, the group had to walk down a wide set of stone steps that two other doors shared. It reminded Shawn of the museums he'd visited as a kid. He stepped carefully, not wanting to trip.

Wooden benches lined the outskirts of the courtyard, separated by groupings of tulips and daisies. The group followed a brick path toward the center of the rounded area, where a large birdbath-like sculpture rested. The midnight-blue marble of the sculpture was a stark contrast to the flame dancing above it.

Franklin paused at the torch nestled in the center. He said nothing. His eyes bore straight into the flame with either admiration or affection–Shawn wasn't sure which.

"An everlasting flame," Musters stated.

Franklin moved his hand to the flame and wavered around it. "Correct Mr. Musters, but also, very much wrong." He pulled his hand back. "This flame represents everything we stand for here at Wayward. You see, lives come and go. People live and die, but life moves on for everyone else." He turned to the rest of the group while leaning his hand lightly on the marble. "Fire consumes everything it touches and moves on to the next object, person, family, whatever is in its way. That's what we're about here: moving on."

"We *are* the fire," Shawn said softly.

"Until we become the fuel." Franklin stared into the flame. "That's what we do here. What you will do. We're the ones who carry souls after their death, making sure they're not extinguished. We don't determine who, where, and when. We're just simply put onto a path and follow it, reaping what comes our way."

Fidler stood beside Franklin, the flame illuminating their frames. "And that's what you two will become... if you so choose," said Fidler.

"Wait, are you saying there's a *choice* now?" said Musters. "Because I don't remember there being much of a choice when you locked us in a room, or for the kid whose head lay at my feet earlier." He stood with clenched fists, attempting to calm his anger before it was released.

Fidler wasn't fazed. It wasn't the first time, nor would it be the last time, a student challenged her. "You were locked into your rooms because waking up dead is a traumatizing experience. While most people can be confused and docile at first, others become bold, lacking the intellect to wait."

Ignoring the bickering, Shawn went to sit down on a bench to try and process everything. The wood beneath him felt cold against his flesh. He gripped the edges and raised his head. "Why do you want us?"

Franklin adjusted his bow tie and took the question before Fidler could. "Every so often, a reaper's retired and there's a need for a replacement. You two and the other couple hundred of students are those replacements."

"That's not what I asked," said Shawn.

Franklin scrunched his eyes, wrinkling the sides of his cheeks in confusion.

Shawn sighed. "Why do you want us? Why *us* of everyone who has died?"

Franklin looked over to Fidler. "Camren, I believe you can take it from here."

"Yes, I believe I can." Camren took off her sun hat and ran her fingers through her short chopped black hair. "We didn't choose you, Mr. Turner. In fact, we didn't choose either of you. You both have heard a bit about reapers in general, but I think it's time you heard about what *I* do."

"And what exactly is that?" Shawn asked.

Fidler smiled and quickly repositioned her hat at a tilt on her head. "My expertise, boys, would be as Head Talon."

Shawn followed the two Council members through a maze of corridors in the Academy, moving more and more into the center of the building. Judging by the look of glee on Fidler's face, he could tell they were getting close.

What he wasn't sure about was becoming a reaper. That was if it was really even a choice. Did he want to continuously be surrounded by death? Spending day after day in this afterlife, watching people take their last breath. The whole thing was insane. Shawn was waiting for someone to pop up and yell 'gotchya!' Even if this world was real, the idea of seeing someone unknowingly lose everything without any warning or inkling made him wish that he had food in his stomach that could be expunged.

Dropping back from the council members, he whispered to Musters, "Can you do this?"

"Don't think there's really much of a choice."

"What do you mean?"

Musters raised an eyebrow at him. "Don't be stupid. They didn't only behead the guy because he rushed the stage. They killed him because he wasn't fit to become a reaper. You saw how quickly the headmaster moved that blade."

Shawn gulped, wondering what he did in his past life that led him to become an agent of death. The blood drained from his face. He put his hand to his chest, willing himself to feel a beat.

Musters leaned over. "Might want to pull yourself together, ghost boy. Breathe."

Shawn took the advice and slowly filled his lungs and exhaled, "Thank you, Musters."

The boy rolled his eyes. "My name's Jay. Might as well know that before you get sliced up."

The group came to a halt before a set of double doors painted a dark shade of purple. Fidler pulled the golden-looped door handles, and they entered what was a puzzle piece of a room. The floor itself was separated into black octagons the size of a small dining room table. Each octagon was set at alternating heights, creating a confusing set of steps for the floor.

Shawn felt dizzy just looking at the set-up. He stepped onto the area. Filling up most of the space was a small round table. What he recognized next made him want to laugh. In the middle of the table was a ball of clear glass kept in place by three gold prongs. "A crystal ball? Really?"

Fidler laughed. "Yes, I see how ridiculous this can all seem. But we're not fortune tellers, Mr. Turner. More messengers. Almost telephone workers one can even say."

"I thought you said that you don't pick us to become reapers?" Shawn asked.

Fidler moved to join Shawn at the first octagon. "This isn't for picking reapers. That process isn't made public to even us I'm afraid. Our job is for non-reaper deaths. And we don't pick anyone: we wait for you to come to us."

Jay stepped into a lower quadrant next to theirs. "I'm sorry. What is this bullshit?"

"Watch Mr. Musters. Watch and see." Fidler grabbed the ball, but instead of peering into the glass like some cheap roadside fortune teller, she spun it. The crystal sphere twirled around in its three-pronged holder, never once veering or wobbling out.

Shawn's eyes almost couldn't keep up with the spin rate of the ball itself. Then something flashed. Shawn could almost make out an image as it went by. A dark image of some sort. He leaned in closer to get a better view.

Fidler waited patiently, not even looking at the ball anymore. Her hands crossed in front of her, delighted to watch the boys transfixed on her area of expertise.

Shawn was just about to give up, but instead of looking into the spinning glass itself, he just observed it. That was when the darkness formed an image he could make out. "It's an R."

Fidler clapped her hands. "Very good, Mr. Turner. It is indeed an R."

"Do you expect me to buy a vowel?" Jay remarked.

Fidler pulled a notebook out of her jacket pocket, ignoring Jay's sarcasm. "That completes the namesake."

"Name what now?" Shawn and Jay asked in unison.

"Pip Welmer," she said. Right as she finished speaking, the ball before her lit up bright purple, illuminating the rusted bronze walls. The ball then dimmed to reveal another image. But it wasn't whoever the hell Pip Welmer was. Instead, it was a date.

Fidler took a piece of parchment and wrote down both the name and the date in ink. She then carefully rolled it up and took a black string out of her pocket to tie it off. Satisfied, she looked at them both with glee before whistling three notes. Out of the rafters flew a black bird. It circled the table above them before diving down and snatching the parchment from the council member's outstretched arm and taking off down the corridor.

"As a talon, my job is to find the next soul ready for passage. Our ravens bring the name and date to the reaper responsible, and they take it from there. We talons are the messengers of death. We neither escort it through its last moments nor allow it safe passage. Those jobs are for blades and mustangs." Fidler jumped off the current quadrant and over to another. "This room is where fates are determined, and we're the readers who must simply pass along the message."

"Technology doesn't work down here, does it?" asked Jay.

His question threw Shawn off. He was just told how one's life is decided, and that's what he brings up?

Franklin came over and hesitated to put a hand on the table, looking uneasy as his hand slid along the stained wood. "That's correct, Mr. Musters. Many have tried using it, but those like us down here can't. It is why this place seems almost medieval."

"That doesn't make us primitive by any faction though," Fidler piped in. "This world you have entered is very different from the one above, and if you both agree to stay, there's so much more to discover." Fidler shifted her view as she said this to Shawn, making him feel uncomfortable. He didn't like the sudden attention, which made him feel like a science project.

"Unfortunately, we've already said what we can do. More than most will hear today, actually," Fidler said.

Jay moved back by the entrance with Shawn in tow. "What are you talking about?"

"Well, Mr. Musters, we can't say anything else until you've decided if you will sign your contracts."

Even as the words tumbled out of the council member's bow-tied throat, Shawn knew that Jay was right. There wasn't a choice in this matter: it was a test. They had to agree to whatever terms were set in front of them, no matter what. Shawn rubbed the back of his neck, not wanting to know what would happen if they didn't sign.

Chapter 7

The office was sparse and smelt like old cardboard. Shawn and Jay were directed to the checkered yellow and pink armchairs that reminded Shawn of marshmallow Peeps. Funny, Shawn thought. After everything he'd seen so far, he hadn't expected to be in a regular office to sign the contract. Especially not one that contained only armchairs and a desk.

"Council Member McLally will take it from here, boys. Miss Fidler and I will wait outside until you're done," Franklin said, closing the door behind him.

The woman behind the desk greeted them with a smile that almost reached the edges of her glasses. Her mint-green suit clashed against the armchairs. "Welcome, gentlemen. I deeply apologize for not giving you the tour myself. It's been a teensy bit hectic around here since I just moved in. Lucky for me, my fellow council members have already filled you in on the good bits." She rose to her feet and stuck out her hand. "Please do call me Carlin."

Jay didn't move an inch as her hand hovered in the air. Shawn contemplated matching Jay's defiance until he saw the look of pure disappointment on Carlin's face. Ignoring daggers from Jay, he got up and met her hand.

"You just moved in?" Shawn asked.

Carlin straightened her silver salamander brooch as she sat. "I'm the newbie on the council. This is actually my first year here at Wayward as well!" She gestured to her office. "As you can see, I haven't completely unpacked."

"What exactly is your job here?" Jay cut in, transferring his daggers to Carlin.

She nodded her head. "Yes, of course they didn't tell you. Technically, I'm in charge of the new incoming students."

"Technically?" Jay raised an eyebrow.

"I'm what they call the integration leader. But the timing of my hire was last minute, and, of course, this is one of the largest classes we've had in quite a while. Plus, I'm still finding my footing in this position. So, again, forgive me for not being able to give you the tour."

Jay leaned forward. "Ms. McLally?"

"Yes? And please do call me Carlin."

"Ms. McLally," Jay stated again, gripping the edge of the seat cushion. "Do you think we care that you didn't give us the fucking tour?"

Blood rushed to her cheeks. "Uh, no... I... well... I am sorry. Look, my main job here is to help guide you along as best as I can during your first year. Throughout the year, I'll give tours, lay out your duties, and try to make your adjustment to this new life as comfortable as possible."

Make our adjustment easier? Shawn almost felt bad for this Carlin person. Almost. She seemed eager to please, but so far, their adjustment had been anything but easy. Where was she when he woke alone in the carriage? Why weren't they given information sooner? While they were locked away in the tower clubhouse, she was moving in, worrying about her office set-up.

She slid across two pieces of parchment in front of them. "Look, I won't beat around the bush with you two any longer. What you see in front of you is your contracts, and if you decide to sign them, you will become a part of the reaper community for at least the next 25 years. After those 25 years are up, you can be released from your contracts and will be allowed to live out the rest of your second lives wherever you shall choose. Unless it disturbs the living, of course."

She said this as if it was the simplest thing in the world. "Can be released?" Shawn asked, not fond of the phrasing.

"Correct. One will either be released, or, if they chose to, can extend their contract for another quarter of a century. I'm currently in the middle of my second extension," she said, bouncing as she talked.

Jay sat up. "Wait. Are you telling us you've already served over thirty years here?"

That can't be right, Shawn thought. The woman across from him was in her mid-twenties, maybe twenty-five at most. He knew people try to make themselves look younger, but this was on a whole different level.

"I turned fifty-two last month!"

Shawn itched his forehead, waiting for a "gotcha" type moment. There was no way the woman in front of him could be that old.

"How?" Jay asked.

Carlin looked taken aback. "Has no one told you yet?" Receiving only blank stares in response, she continued. "Contracted reapers age at about one-fourth of the rate of regular humans. I was only fifteen when I became a reaper, which is why my body has stayed relatively the same throughout the years."

"That can't be possible," Shawn said. Had these people found the elixir of life or something? Then he thought back to Roddick and the odd language he used. He'd seemed to use words from another era, probably because he was from one.

"It's only possible while one is on contract actually. Otherwise, if the extension isn't signed, you will start to age at the normal rate. Many think this has to do with keeping reapers in their prime or something. Honestly, I'm not completely sure. That's more up council member Franklin's alley." She smiled.

This explained why Shawn hadn't seen any elderly around the Academy so far. He wondered how old Mac was, or the headmaster. It explained why people signed contract extensions: it was basically plastic surgery, only a thousand times better.

Carlin pointed to the bottom line of the contracts, which required a signature. She was like a dog at the pound, trying to keep potential owners interested. "After signing, there'll be an evaluation period. Each new student will be placed in one of three areas." She pointed to three images within the contract. The first was a black scythe. "A blade. They're the ones who go to the surface to collect the souls." She moved over to the next image: a purple ball sitting in the grasp of a raven's foot. "Talons. They uncover who's next for reaping." She stopped on the third image: a yellow stallion. "Mustangs, whom you both met when you awoke in this afterlife." Shawn knew instantly whom she was talking about. After all, it was hard to forget his first welcome in the afterlife, especially from someone in a tuxedo and top hat.

Shawn reached for the pen, but Jay shot forward just before he could lay a hand on it. Not even glancing Shawn's way, he clenched the pen between his fingers. "Twenty-five years and then we're free to do whatever we want?"

"Basically, ye—"

"What do you mean 'basically'?" Jay interrupted.

"Again, as long as you don't bother the living, you can go wherever you want. You can travel the world and live a new life. Many find family here at Wayward and choose to live in the village nearby; others sign on for extensions. If all the rules are followed, you have nothing to be worried about, Jay."

Shawn leaned back in his chair, feeling the checkered plush seep into his back. Twenty-five years of his life... in which he had no say, doing the world's bidding. Twenty-five years surrounded by death. "If we sign this contract, can you kill us?" Shawn asked, wondering whether this could guarantee his safety, at least temporarily.

Council member McLally shifted uncomfortably in her seat. "Reaper on reaper killings is a crime. Unless ordered by the Grand Council in the capital. Which very rarely happens." As soon as she finished speaking, Jay signed his contract and held out the pen to Shawn.

Shawn's hands were shaking. It felt like he was selling his soul right now. The whole thing was preposterous: he was basically becoming these lunatics' pawn for the next quarter of the century. It was supposed to be a noble duty, and one he was chosen to do for some godforsaken reason. His hand jerked a bit as he signed his name, causing a terrible "n" in Turner, but the deed was done.

"Congratulations, gentlemen. You're officially reapers!"

Chapter 8

After being escorted back up to their rooms, they were told dinner would be served in an hour and that they could explore the grounds at will. This time, the door remained unlocked. Shawn thought he'd feel less uneasy knowing that he wouldn't be locked in again; instead, he felt like the contract had now become the lock.

"Do you think we did the right thing?" He asked Jay.

Jay sat on the edge of his trunk, paying more attention to the floor beneath it than Shawn. "We did it to survive. Right? Wrong? What does it matter if they were going to kill us anyway?"

"These people don't seem like killers though. They actually seem, well, normal."

"Yeah, tell that to the guy whose head lay at my feet twenty-four hours ago."

Shawn knew Jay was right and that they couldn't fully trust them. At the same time, though, he almost felt guilty not doing that. With a job as important as being a reaper, there had to be reasons for them to be cautious about new reapers. "They haven't lied to us yet. Maybe we don't need to only go along with it. Maybe we should embrace it."

"Do whatever you want, dipstick. I'm going along with it because I don't want to end up like my buddy Headless Harry. Besides, tell me. Why didn't you ask about what happens if you don't sign the contract? Hmm?"

Shawn didn't reply.

"Yeah, that's what I thought." Jay walked to the door. "I doubt you'll see anyone walking around here who didn't sign." He left Shawn by himself.

Not wanting to be alone in his previous prison cell, Shawn made his way toward the staircase. Going down a floor, he walked until he saw "324" in white letters above the door. He didn't hear anything inside, but he knocked anyway. No answer. He waited a second before knocking again, feeling uncomfortable out in the hallway by himself. Finally, he tried the handle. Locked.

"They're out on the East side." A door opened a couple of rows down the hall, and Shawn turned to see a guy leaning up against the wooden frame. That unmistakable eyepatch on his face.

"Come on, newbie. I'll show ya."

Shawn stayed rooted in front of Room 324.

Rupert made his way over to Shawn. "Come on, Shawnie boy. I'm not playing games this time." With that, he walked past, not waiting around to see if Shawn followed him.

The East side of the Academy was full of new reapers milling around, not completely sure what to do next. "Sorry about earlier, by the way. Just trying to have a little fun." Rupert said over his shoulder.

"Not sure what fun it is confusing a newly dead person, but hey, it was hilarious." Shawn let the sarcasm drip out of his mouth. Jay was apparently rubbing off on him.

"Rupe, you screwing around with the new kids again?" a short stocky kid yelled across the field. A group of older reapers surrounded the kid, who wore a roman numeral III on his sleeve.

"Nah, just giving him the good old Welcome Dead tour!" Rupert shouted back, getting a chuckle from a couple of the surrounding reapers.

"You screw with a lot of people, don't you?" Shawn asked.

A smirk crept up on Rupert's face. "It's almost Halloween, so I'm just prepping myself."

Shawn gave Rupert a questioning look.

"Don't worry. You'll understand soon enough, Shawnie boy."

Up ahead, a large oak tree was just beginning to turn colors. Shawn could see the orange shades peeking through the leaves, waiting for a chance to escape the branches. Sitting underneath were the inhabitants of 324.

"See, told ya I wouldn't lead you astray."

"Thanks."

Rupert patted Shawn on the shoulder and walked back to the short stocky kid and the group of other non-newbies.

Q jumped up at the sight of Shawn and immediately pinned Shawn's arms to the side with a bear hug.

"So, dude, how's your day going?" Shawn choked out.

"I see you too made a deal with the Devil," Maple said, her back brushed up against the bark.

"Not sure I had a choice."

She nodded. "Smart man."

Legs suddenly dangled over Shawn's head, as Q clambered up the tree. "Knew you had brains the minute I laid eyes on ya."

Shawn looked around; the closest person was a guy about forty yards away. "I still have no idea if this is a place we should run from."

"Dunno, champ. Those stone people didn't exactly convince me to stay if you know what I mean," Q said.

"We wait," Maple said following his line of sight. "We gather information and try to figure out a plan, because I'm not waiting around for my throat to be slit."

"That's basically what my roommate said."

"Your roommate is right," Maple responded.

For the first time, Shawn allowed himself to think about the life he'd left behind. He wondered what friends mourned him, what the funeral was like, and even the color of the casket. "I miss them a lot, you know.

"Who?" Q asked.

"My parents."

Shawn locked eyes with Maple, getting lost for a moment in the brown waves of chocolate.

Maple shifted her gaze to the cavern ceiling, her shoulders drooping. The crystals embedded above them were growing dimmer by the minute. "They said that the crystals sense the location of the sun above ground. So, as the sun rises, they brighten. And as it sets, they dim." Maple spoke calmly, getting up from her seat. "Kind of beautiful really." She avoided Shawn's comment, choosing instead to walk to the dining hall. Her last words settled on Shawn like a blanket you put on someone with a fever: adding more heat to smother out the problem.

Shawn looked up, admiring the crystals that constantly reminded him he wasn't at home. If he didn't look up, he could pretend to be outside. He could pretend he was at the park in Roselle, waiting for his friends. Friends that he'd never see again.

"I miss them too." Q said as he stopped swinging his legs. "Especially my little brother."

"How old is he?"

"Seven." Q paused. His face then started lighting up with each word. "He's a little brat, you know. Always going through my crap, asking me to play, trying to scare me. Really, he doesn't shut the hell up." He grew more serious, "I miss him the most. Don't get me wrong, I love my parents. But I'd do anything for my brother Zander, that little bastard."

"Every summer, my mom made us go camping up north at Cable Lake," Shawn started, worried that bringing up old memories was doing more harm for him than good, he continued anyway. "My dad hates camping. Actually, I also hate camping." He laughed. "But we did it for Mom. She was big into it, making the fire, sleeping under the stars some nights–the whole shebang. One weekend, she wanted us to only eat what we caught from the lake. My dad snuck me doughnuts from Krispy Kreme the entire weekend to keep me happy. I think I'll miss times like those the most."

"Think they're doing okay without us?" Q asked.

"No," Shawn said bluntly. "But they'll survive. Just like we will."

On the west side of the Academy, Maple walked into the dining hall area. "Is she doing okay?" Shawn asked.

"Should she be?" Q shot back. Shawn didn't know how to answer this. He was still holding onto hope that he'd wake up next to his stupid horse lamp when he opened his eyes tomorrow morning.

Chimes rang out across the area and bounced off the trees, searching for open ears. None of the new first years in the field moved at first.

"I guess dinner's ready," Shawn said.

Q jumped down from the tree branch, landing with a soft pat next to Shawn. "Think we can trust any of these other bozos?"

Surveying the crowd headed for food, Shawn thought about that question. He spotted Jay as he wandered over to the clockwork of tables. Did he trust Jay? "No idea."

"Come on, mate" Q said, putting his hands on his stomach. "I'm starving."

Chapter 9

"Trevor Butcher," the man exclaimed as he pumped Shawn's and Jay's hands. Apparently, this was whom Shawn was going to be learning the ropes from in his first year. You could supposedly tell a lot from a handshake. A soft, weak handshake usually said the same thing about the person attached to it. From what Shawn could tell, Trevor was going to be extremely confident and enthusiastic.

Today was the first day of observation, and they happened to be learning from one of the Wayward Academy's famous married couples. At least, that was what Trevor kept telling them. "Honey, aren't you going to introduce yourself?" Trevor asked.

The woman sitting on the steps outside the entrance to the Academy slowly got up. "I think it's time we got going, don't you?"

Trevor looked at the boys and rolled his eyes "Ain't she a dream?" This comment swiftly earned him a punch in the arm from the woman with long, curly sea-black hair. "This is Adriana, the love of my deceased life."

"Did you call for a ride or should I?" Adriana asked.

The whistle from Trevor's lips echoed throughout the courtyard like an opera singer finding the right note.

"God, I hate it when you do that. You don't need to be so loud," Adriana said while her husband wrapped her into a bear hug that she had no choice but to accept.

A red blur fleeted in and out of the trees. Trevor perched his arm out, waiting patiently for the blur to find its mark. A cardinal suddenly emerged from the woods. Trevor took a yellow piece of parchment from his pocket and let the cardinal cradle it in its claws before flying out to the trees. "You guys will get your messengers soon too."

"They have to wait for testing to be completed," Adriana said, tightening her grip around her scythe.

Jay gently kicked a rock back and forth. "So, is this part of our testing then?"

Adriana snorted, opening her mouth to speak, only to have Trevor cut her off. "Don't worry. You guys will know when it's over."

Shawn heard the clacking of hooves before he saw the carriage appear from a path. Familiarity washed over him as the top hat of the mustang driving it bounced up and down. The carriage came to a halt right in front of Trevor.

Shawn stepped up and rubbed the horse's snout. "How ya doing, Gracie?"

"Gracie?? Ha, that's Timothy!" Roddick said, cackling.

Shawn smiled, knowing exactly what horse he was petting. "My mistake. How've you been, Roddick?"

"A lot better now that I have company on me next ride!" He said as he tipped his top hat to the Butchers. "Now everyone, hop in! I got me a schedule to stick to, and I'm not one for missing it."

Adriana wasted no time entering the carriage. Trevor, meanwhile, went over to Gracie with a peace offering. "You know I have to feed my favorite beast, Roddick."

Gracie eyed Trevor coming toward her, but when the carrot was within sight, she neighed, licking his outstretched palm.

"Ah, this is the famous Roddick." Jay stated as Trevor fed Gracie.

Shawn stepped back from Timothy. "Yep. Don't think I left much out about him."

"I like the top hat, adds class," Jay said, keeping his voice level, leaving no hint of sarcasm. Nodding to Roddick, he entered the carriage after Adriana.

Roddick was still in the same tuxedo the last time Shawn saw him. It seemed everyone either dressed like there was a royal ball to go to or in a pullover and jeans. Even Adriana and Trevor were dressed to the nines in their suits. Shawn rubbed the numeral between his fingers as he examined his pullover. His clothing was the most modern part of the whole place so far. Yet, it was also strangest. Here he was going to reap a soul, witnessing someone's last moments alive, and all he was wearing was a gray hoodie.

Shawn felt the grip on his shoulder. "I'm out of carrots, so let's get a move on before the old guy up there decides to let Gracie at us."

They rode off down one of the dirt paths leading to a cavern wall, the crystals illuminating the forest ahead. The four of them somehow squeezed inside the cabin. Shawn did have to contort his legs to make room for Trevor, so he was hoping it was a short ride.

Windows that had been blocked when Shawn rode last time remained open, allowing the cool cavern air to fill the last few crevices of the carriage. This time he was able to see the trees as they passed by, one by one, in a blur of orange and yellow.

"Now, let's go over the ground rules before we get out there, shall we?" Trevor began.

At dinner yesterday, they had a brief introduction to the rules of the ground, and they seemed pretty simple. So, while Trevor went on, Shawn zoned out while looking through the window, trying to prepare himself to watch someone die.

Rule 1: Don't interfere with the subject.

Rule 2: Don't affect surroundings in any way that can alert grounders of your presence.

Rule 3: Keep the subject within sight at all times.

Rule 4: Once a subject passes over, immediately send a messenger to grab a mustang.

Rule 5: Carry the essence to the entry point and wait for the mustang.

Rule 6: Do. Not. Be. Late.

To Shawn, these rules weren't going to be a problem. After all, this time around, they weren't doing much. Just observing. In such a large group, it would be easy to keep track of their subject. And probably a little boring as well.

"Save the foolishness for the holiday," Adriana said, interrupting Shawn's thought process.

Trevor grabbed his wife's hand and smiled. "Yes. Agreed, my love." Trevor turned his attention back to the boys. "Now, normally there's a one-week window in which we might observe a grounder, but sometimes there are special circumstances that give us a more accurate timeframe. Today would be one of those circumstances."

Roddick halted near an opening in the side of the cavern. "Okay. Everybody out and get a moving. Don't want to be late now."

Shawn froze when he recognized the creatures in front of him.

Standing on either side of the stone door were two of the stone men from orientation. Jay clambered out of the carriage after Shawn, missing the last step of the carriage. He had to use Shawn to stop his momentum; otherwise, he would have been having a date with the dirt.

Trevor ignored the balance issues and walked up to the stone creatures, presenting them the paper with the subject's name written down. Shawn thought he'd been close up during orientation, but now he was standing directly next to one of the stone creatures. The most fascinating thing about them was how they moved. Every motion seemed fluid, but Shawn could now see how certain parts of their bodies were moving. When one man grabbed the piece of parchment, his fingers were made up of thousands of tiny pebbles that shifted over each other as he moved. When his fingers gripped the paper, the pebbles settled into place, forming the seamless stone image from before.

"As I'm sure you gentlemen are well aware," said Trevor, "we have a training session today, and these two petrified boys behind us are the ones who'll be doing the observing."

The stone men both nodded and separated to each side of the gate. They put their right fists into tight slots that bookended the gate. Simultaneously, they turned their arms clockwise. From these holes, a purple light jettisoned along the wall, tracing every crack in the gate like a child coloring in a picture. Only once all the crevices were filled with this neon purple light did the gate start to lift.

Feeling eyes on him, Shawn looked over at Adriana and Trevor. They were watching both boys with amusement, obviously used to this spectacle.

"Honestly, it never gets old," Trevor said to them and walked through the doors.

On the other side of the gate was a small round chamber about the size of the bedroom back at the Academy. As soon as everyone was past the threshold, the gate lowered to the ground, sealing them in. Shawn sneezed. The room was bare, mostly filled with dust and cobwebs. Straight ahead was their only option out: a staircase.

"What are they?" Shawn asked.

Adriana went over and stroked Trevor's cardinal that sat perched on his shoulder. "Gargoyles," she said nonchalantly, as if he should have known.

"And?" Jay asked, his brow furling at her answer.

Adriana turned her back and sauntered over to the stairs. "They're the gatekeepers of our world." She started climbing.

Trevor followed quickly behind her. "Think of them as the police," he chimed in.

Shawn couldn't see where the stairs led, but he refused to be left alone in an empty room. "So, they keep us in line, and they guard the gate?"

"Basically, yes. They've existed for as long as reapers have. They are pretty much the eyes and ears above us. Sometimes, they hold us accountable and, as you saw, act as gatekeepers. No one has actually even heard of one dying..." Trevor said as they came to a corner and turned to an even steeper staircase.

Shawn grunted at the endless set of stairs in front of him. "You're telling me they're immortal?"

Trevor paused.

Adriana turned around. "Our records seem to indicate that those two gatekeepers have been at that post for at least 576 years."

Jay glanced at Shawn. "How far do the records go back?" he asked.

Adriana smiled. "As far back as reapers do."

After an endless number of stairs, a simple door awaited them at the top. Nothing out of the ordinary about it. For all Shawn knew, it could have led to someone's bedroom or garage. Trevor took a key out of his pocket and unlocked it from their side. He pushed it open, no glowing purple lights in sight.

Ahead of them was white marble. Nothing else. A breeze echoed throughout the chamber they entered.

"I promise not all the doorways are this... grim," Trevor said with a crooked smile.

Part of the wall closest to Shawn caught his eye. Once he leaned forward, he could make out small engravings. At first, Shawn thought the chamber was made from marble bricks. The outlines of squares were perfectly symmetrical to one another, giving him this illusion. Then he saw the flowers set upon the ground, withering from lack of care. This wasn't just a chamber: it was a burial chamber.

Jay squatted down next to him, picking up a shriveled petal. He examined it in the light before flicking it aside.

"Let's get going," Adriana said, breaking both boys from their trance.

The burial chamber was located near the back of a cemetery. Based on the shrubbery that had overgrown the iron fence behind it, this was a secluded area that didn't get many visitors. Shawn stepped over a crack in the ground and almost laughed at himself for worrying about superstitions at this point in his life.

Adriana led the way along the paved path.

"Where do you think we're going?" Shawn whispered to Jay.

Jay sighed. "Look around, I'm guessing not too far." He pointed a building out to Shawn across the way. One about eight stories tall that held a large red cross on the front, easily distinguishing it from anything around it.

"A hospital? That's where we're headed?" Shawn looked over to Trevor.

"I told you that this reaping was a special circumstance. It's easier to start out this way. Some of your peers may not get their first observation done for days. It's preferable to other reapings, as this is one where we can know exactly when a grounder is ready."

Shawn and Jay waited in silence for more of an explanation.

"It's like..." Trevor looked around as Adriana leaned against a tombstone. "Like this caterpillar."

"What?" Jay narrowed his eyes.

Trevor picked up the furry little caterpillar in one hand, and in the other he picked up a rock. "Sometimes, life is random, and you never know when you'll die. Other times, it could be determined by something like this rock." Trevor went on, knowing he still didn't have his audience. "If I intend to smash this rock in exactly one minute, then we would know the exact moment the caterpillar's life would come to an end."

The reality sunk in around Shawn. "This person has been scheduled to die."

"Good. You've got the full picture now. Lesson time. Stand to the side," Adriana said as she brushed off her pants. Right as they were about to keep walking, Shawn noticed a man on the path, headed straight for them.

Both Jay and Shawn did as they were told. The man was dressed casually, in jeans and a light jacket. He didn't carry flowers or look somber. He just simply whistled as he walked, like he'd been here a thousand times. He kept his head down, only paying attention to each footstep he took. He seemed to be lost in his own thoughts. Shawn could feel himself holding his breath. He worried that any air escaping his lungs would alert him to their presence. Everyone stayed quiet, observing the oblivious.

As soon as the man came within a foot of the group, Adriana brought her hands together swiftly, forcing a clap right beside the man's ear. Small hairs growing on top of his ear bristled from the force of the clap. Yet, the man kept walking. He brought his hand up to his ear, itching it. Then nothing. He just strolled past them, giving no other indication that he'd noticed the group of four. It was like nothing happened, and Shawn wondered for him... if anything had.

Chapter 10

"He barely reacted," Shawn said mystified.

The man kept along the path, leaving the group to stare after him.

"Correct, Shawn. If you wanted to, you could go over and scream in his face, wave to him–hell, even breakdance beside him. You name it, and he's not going to notice it," Trevor said.

"He did itch his ear," Shawn replied. The man may not have noticed him, but Adriana had generated some wind from that clap. Or it was a huge coincidence, but Shawn wasn't convinced of that.

"Ding ding ding, Mr. Turner," Trevor said as they moved toward the hospital. "We can affect them, but that doesn't mean we should. The Grand Council would find out and wouldn't be happy. Ain't that right, my love?"

"That's why I only clapped. If I'd gone over and pushed him, he would've moved. Which is why we have Rules One and Two: don't interfere and don't alert grounders to our presence. What I did was perfectly fine, but if I'd done anything to affect the grounder, that would have been a *huge* violation. And we must remain unnoticed. Got it?" She glared at both boys, daring them to speak.

"You keep using the term *grounders*. Is there a reason?" Shawn asked.

Adrianna looked annoyed at having to explain. "Because they live above ground. And a lot of people bury their dead below it. Now let's move."

The entrance to the hospital was nearly deserted. Only a few people stood milling around in the lobby, and none of them seemed to be in a hurry.

"Rule One, boys, Rule One," Trevor said as they walked down the hallway.

Never interfere. Shawn wasn't sure what he was about to see, but the small tremors in his hands weren't from the weather. He had just died. He didn't want to watch someone else suffer the same fate. Each footstep felt a little heavier as they passed the rooms. Many contained visiting family members waiting patiently at their loved one's bedside. Some rooms, though, were void of any visitors, leaving the patients alone in their final moments.

As the group moved throughout the hallway, they avoided any grounder closing in on them. Adriana and Trevor moved effortlessly, it was old hat to them. Jay avoided everyone pretty well too, only having to jump out the of way a few times. Shawn was the only one really struggling. He constantly had to remind himself they couldn't see him and that he needed to turn at any moment. Just as he started to get the hang of it, they slowed to a stop. Two people blocked the door they came to.

"It's about time, Maggie," a man with shaggy brown hair said, his eyes drooping, presumably from long nights. The woman across from him, who Shawn assumed was Maggie, tried to speak but couldn't get anything to come out. Instead, she moved to the door, opening it for themselves and their invisible guests.

Inside the room, the curtain had been pulled back from the bedside window, leaving a view to the cemetery across the road. A doctor and a nurse stood off to the side, waiting. Beneath the white-cotton sheets lay a man in a standard hospital gown. Tubes ran from his mouth to a machine on the side of the bed, forcing his chest to rise and fall systematically.

Shawn stayed near the back of the room, not wanting to be close for the man's final moments. Trevor stood at the front of the group with his head bowed respectfully; Adriana followed suit. Jay was the only one who held his head high, ready to be in full view of the reaping.

The doctor moved over to the machine, adjusting a couple of the switches before removing the tubes. Shawn had a fleeting thought that they were going to try and wake the man up one more time. Then the gown sitting on his chest gradually fell as the machine stopped pumping oxygen into his lungs. His heartbeat went the same way as the gown, slowly falling until the steady beep from another machine announced his fate.

Shawn leaned against the wall behind him, hoping that no one would notice him attempting to find support. His mind flashed to previous funerals, in which he looked down on the body of someone he knew. Shawn had never met this man, but the familiar feeling lingered. He reminded himself to breathe and to look at the scene before him. After all, this was going to be his job.

Blue light started pulsing from the man, traveling from vein to vein. Shawn looked to his mentors, who remained unphased and kept their heads bowed. Conflicted, knowing he should be respectful and keep his head down, Shawn copied Jay, staring at the body as the orb formed.

All the other grounders in the room were unaware of what was happening right before them, yet it resulted in the same outcome. Luckily, death was quick for the man. The woman from the hallway fell into a chair, shaking with tears. The man who had been consoling her earlier was off to the right, giving her space to grieve.

The swirling blue orb floated above the man's chest, waiting to be collected. Even under these circumstances, Shawn found the orb to be beautiful. Then, a sudden movement by Trevor surprised Shawn. The man moved swiftly, as he pulled a brown cloth bag out of the lining of his suit jacket. Carefully, he stepped forward, avoiding the grounders as he secured the orb inside the bag. At the same time, Adriana gave the cardinal a note, sending it speeding off through the hospital.

Adriana and Trevor made for the exit, with Shawn and Jay close behind. Once they were in the hallway, Trevor looked at them both. "Remember, this is why we're here." He held up the bag. "You guard this with your life and never miss an assignment. Otherwise, you're a waste of a second chance. Hear me?"

It was the first time Trevor had raised his voice to either of them. He may have been joking around before, but Shawn knew this man took his job seriously. Shawn was still a little uneasy after seeing another person die, but he was coherent enough to nod his head.

"Okay. Let's go. We're on a schedule," Trevor said, leading them away from the deceased.

Walking through the grounds of the cemetery had a slightly different meaning to Shawn now: purpose. The reapers didn't kill grounders: they were just watchers, harbingers of death. It made him almost rethink running. Where would he even go? Could he keep going through this for the next quarter of a century? He didn't think so. Sunlight reflected off Adriana's scythe, reminding him of the other reason he shouldn't run.

They walked the rest of the way in silence. Passing headstone after headstone, rotting body after rotting body, each one represented a completed assignment. The white marble gateway greeted them with about the same comfort as using a porcupine as a pillow. Shawn was unsure if his legs would lead him back down the endless staircase. He almost considered taking off, not knowing if he'd get a better chance.

He couldn't shake the image of the man's last moments. It wasn't some spectacle or all-knowing moment that ran through everyone in the room. It had been silent, eerily silent, like the sun setting. Such build-up throughout one's life for something that can happen instantly. He hoped his death had been the same. He hoped that his parents weren't witnesses to it. His heart tore apart just thinking about his parents finding him. But death was inevitable: it moved through everyone. Now he was supposed to be the one to come collect it.

Before he knew it, they'd made it back to the stone gate. Adriana put her scythe into a slot along the wall that Shawn hadn't noticed when they came in. It must have alerted the gargoyles because purple lights filled the crevices once again. After stepping through the lifted gate, both gargoyles removed their fists from the wall. Somehow the cardinal had gotten the message to Roddick, as he was waiting right outside the gate as well. Roddick gave a somber smile and threw his head toward the carriage for Shawn to enter. This time he didn't crack a joke: he was all business.

Shawn felt the pressure from a hand on his shoulder. "One step at a time, Shawn," Trevor quietly whispered as he passed Shawn and climbed into the carriage. Shawn felt like his feet were encased in concrete, and he refused to budge.

"Time is of the essence, Turner. Get in," Adriana barked. Her voice was stern, but her face gave away a little. It was like she was scolding a toddler when they shouldn't be doing something, but she also didn't completely blame them for doing it.

Shawn finally settled into the carriage next to Trevor, gladly accepting the hard bench beneath him. They took off at a fast pace back toward the Academy, the horses digging into the earth with each bound. Jay had his head down, staring at the floor. He was locked in, refusing to move while sitting next to Adriana's scythe.

Trevor leaned over and whispered to Shawn as they sped back with the newly released soul, "There's another reason we call them grounders. It's so we don't constantly remind ourselves we're truly dead. That we can't come back and that we won't enjoy the freeness of the life above. If we called them 'the living', our attitude might be different. I think we call them grounders to try and recapture a bit of the spirit of the living."

Chapter 11

Roddick halted in the back of the Academy. Several experienced reapers hung around, also back from recent reapings. Greeted by the everlasting flame, Shawn climbed out of the carriage.

"Thanks, Rod," Trevor said as they all exited. Roddick only tipped his hat before the reins slapped hard against the horses' backs, and he was off to his next pick-up.

The two lead reapers let the silence hang over Shawn and Jay like a weighted blanket. Shawn didn't know what he was supposed to do now. What does one usually do after they collect a human soul?

Adriana and Trevor stopped in front of the steps of the back entrance. Adriana took the bag from her husband. "Our next job is to bring the orb to a talon for them to process. I'm going to do this myself. Trevor thought you two have seen enough for today. You're both relieved and may go back to your dormitory." She started to go through the door and then hesitated, turning around. "Turner, Musters, good work today."

Unless Shawn had been completely out of it, he never heard Trevor mention anything about them seeing enough to Adriana. Then again, he wasn't going to complain about being dismissed. He needed a break to process everything.

"First time... Any thoughts?" Trevor asked. Jay kept his head down, not even glancing Trevor's way. Shawn wasn't sure what to think at first and followed Jay's silence. Trevor relaxed a bit, taking comfort in their nonexistent questions. "Good. It means you two aren't totally hopeless after all. Now go wash up and relax until dinner." Trevor grabbed each of the boy's shoulders. "It's a process, okay? Take your time with it." He smiled weakly.

Jay shook off Trevor's hand and walked toward the trees, hands clenched in his pockets.

Shawn thought about following but knew better of it. He nodded his thanks to Trevor and went up the marble steps, hoping that Room 324's occupants had returned from their observation as well.

It seemed that only a quarter of the hall had gotten back from their first observations. As Shawn passed each door, different attitudes were revealed. In one room, a girl slept comfortably in her bed, while her roommate sat in the middle of the floor crying. In another, one kid was hysterically laughing to himself and dancing to silence. Everyone was processing in their own way, but the last room he peeked into made the most sense to Shawn. In it, he could see two girls staring blankly at the wall in front of them. It seemed that neither one would be moving for quite a while.

He heard nothing coming from Q and Maple's room as he approached. Maybe they'd gone outside by the tree again? About to turn and walk out, he noticed a shadow underneath the door. He knocked lightly in case someone was sleeping.

"Come in," Maple said softly.

Inside, Q sat curled up in his bed, not even glancing at Shawn as he came in. Shawn was about to ask if they were alright, but Maple looked as though she might faint. And Q didn't look much better, judging from the mumbles he was making.

Whatever they saw on their outing made an impression. And not a good one. "Do you guys want to talk about it?" Shawn asked, hoping that they didn't.

"You know, I thought I'd handle this a bit better," Q said with a joyless chuckle from his corner.

Shawn raised an eyebrow. "None of us should be able to handle this."

Q's eyes seemed to burrow themselves into the wall, as if they were trying to escape what they'd just seen. "Have you ever seen a family get hit by a truck?"

A wave traveled from Shawn's fingertips to his shoulders. No goosebumps, no hairs sticking up: just one wave, coursing throughout his body.

Q refused to turn his head away from the wall. "Two kids by the way. Ages four and twelve, who'd just finished supporting their mother in some 5K run." He sniffed. "You know what the four-year-old said before he crossed the street?"

Shawn thought about saying something but bit his tongue.

In the corner of Q's eyes, tears formed where others had been seconds before. "When can I join Mama in one?" Q made no effort to wipe his eyes, choosing to let them fall onto his tear-stained shirt. "Right after that, a minivan blew its tire going fifty miles per hour, hitting them head-on.

"The dad was the only survivor," Maple added.

Q's chest rose and fell irregularly, as if it couldn't decide if it wanted to take in more air or not. Finally, he looked over to Shawn, "I'll never forget that sight, mate. Never."

Shawn reached out to Q and let him fall into his shoulder, releasing whatever tears he had left. Shawn thought about if *he'd* been the one to see that accident. Even just imagining it made him feel lightheaded.

Maple moved over to join them on the bed, a slight scent of rose petals wafting over her. The ringing of the dinner chimes echoed through the halls, but no one got up. "You know, for some reason I don't really have an appetite," Q said.

Maple and Shawn glanced at each other before bursting out laughing. Maple stopped at the door. "Come on, we need to get something else on our minds. Sitting around here listening to the others freak out does us no good. Let's go. I saw a place I wanted to check out."

The place she wanted to see was down a dirt path not far past the trees by the Academy where they had hung out. The castle-like structure was three stories tall, each corner containing a rounded tower that stretched one floor above the roof. It was as if the four towers had been built first, and then someone decided to connect them all. Entering through one of the corner towers, Shawn quickly found himself in a space just large enough for the brick staircase.

"Is this where we're holding up for the evening?" Shawn asked.

"Or for the rest of our afterlife?" Q asked, raising both hands to show his fingers crossed.

"Come on, at least there aren't people losing their minds in here," Maple said, waiting for someone to take the first step inside.

"Rude. You can't be sure about that," Q said, racing through the tower door and leaping up the steps two at a time.

"It's good to see him a bit back to normal," Maple said. Her eyes were still a bit puffy. Shawn guessed she must have tried washing them out with water, but the mark of what she saw still remained, even if she didn't wear it on her sleeve.

"I can't imagine what you two experienced," Shawn said.

She tugged at her sweatshirt. "Believe me, you don't even *want* to imagine."

"You still want to run from here?"

She moved into the stairwell, her hands lightly gripping the railing. "Now? Yes, although for different reasons."

"Second thoughts as well?"

"As well? So, Turner's having doubts about our original plan?"

Shawn looked down sheepishly. "I'm not sure I'm cut out for this stuff."

"Only one way to find out."

His eyes softened. "We better go find Q before he lights this place on fire."

White mats littered the floor of the first landing they came to. The air smelled of musk and salt, and it wasn't until Shawn saw the weapons on the wall that he knew why. "You want to get some sparring practice in?" He asked as he examined the wall. From left to right, scythes of different sizes hung on the wall.

"Don't think you'd want to, Turner." Maple grabbed a scythe and started twirling it expertly. The speed of the motions, as she spun the blade between her hands and then around her back, shocked Shawn. He was convinced that if he tried something similar, he would have cracked his skull.

"Uh, did you just happen to pick up this talent?" Shawn asked, taking a slight step backward.

Maple smiled. "No, idiot. I was on color guard."

"What the heck's that?"

"See, this is why I called you an idiot." Without breaking eye contact, she spun the blade around again. "Simply put, I was one of those people who spun flags around on the football field. Does that ring a bell?"

"Just be sure not to spin that right between my ribs. Okay?"

She laughed. "No promises."

Shawn picked a scythe off the wall. Its weight surprised him a bit. He expected it to be more top-heavy near the blade, but it was perfectly balanced in his hand.

Maple sat down on the mat and scrunched up her nose. "This is what I'm talking about—"

"There's so much we still don't know," Shawn said, finishing her thought.

"Exactly. Besides orientation, have you seen any reaper use a scythe?"

"No, I haven't." He thought back. Mac had carried one around before orientation, and Adriana had one during Shawn's first observation. But neither of them had used it except to open the gate again.

"Makes you wonder why they'd train us to use it. Doesn't it? You know, I felt a duty after that car crash. Almost like an obligation. I felt drawn to help the kids... even though they were already dead." She looked over at him. "Does that sound crazy?"

Shawn held out his hand, offering to pull her up. "Today, I saw a man get taken off life support with his family in the room."

Maple's hands clasped around her mouth.

"I don't know if it was an obligation necessarily, but while my mentors kept their heads bowed, I couldn't look away. I wanted to capture every detail in my head."

"Maybe it means we should stick around a little longer and find out," she said, shrugging.

Shawn wasn't sure he agreed. "Come on. Let's go find Q."

On the second landing, the door was locked, so they moved on to the third. The arc in the stairwell opened to a library. Maple stepped in, letting the smell of old paper fill her nostrils.

"If you think Q's in here, then you must have hit your head when you died," Shawn said. He studied the room, which was spread out into a jumble of bookcases. Q didn't seem like the type of person to stop in a library before venturing to the top of a tower.

They left the unread words sitting on their shelves. Maple looked slightly disappointed that they didn't dive into the sun-dried pages. Three windows awaited them at the top. Shawn and Maple came up through the middle of the floor as the tower circled around them. The roof, coming to a point in the middle, created an umbrella effect. Q was looking out one of the large open windows across to the other towers, and he wasn't alone.

"Roomie!"

"Um, I thought Jay was your roommate?" Maple asked, confused by the man with the eyepatch standing in front of them.

Rupert grabbed Maple's hand and kissed it, causing her to pull it back in disgust. "Fake roommates, of course! Just had some fun with our boy Shawnie here during his first day."

"Yeah... Maple, this is Rupert. Rupert, Maple."

"Nice to meet you, milady." Rupert put his arm around Shawn, it slanting upwards due to Shawn's height. Uncomfortable, but not trying to be rude, Shawn let him hang there, hoping he'd eventually break contact.

Maple's response was an icy glare at both boys.

The pressure was lifted from Shawn's shoulder as Rupert took a step down the stairs. Rupert patted him on the chest. "Wish I could stay and chat. Now, Quints, good boy, don't forget about the tradition." He turned to Maple and Shawn. "I expect to see both of you there as well."

Neither Shawn nor Maple could get a word out before Rupert popped down the staircase out of sight.

"Quints? Now that's a nickname I can get behind, 'good boy'," Maple said, smiling in spite of herself.

Q jumped up onto the windowsill, the crystal light causing his shadow to cast over Maple and Shawn. "Whatever you say, Mapleberry."

"Don't."

"I hope you enjoyed meeting the trickster of Wayward," Shawn said, moving between the two before Maple punched Q. Looking out, they had a view of the forest. How far did this place spread out? The trees appeared to stretch for miles. He could make out some of the paths that Roddick must ride near the mustang departure area. Squinting, Shawn thought he saw one of the carriages making its way back. Another reaping completed.

Whatever the so-called “tradition” was that Rupert mentioned, Shawn felt uneasy about it.

“Do you guys want to know what it is?” Q asked with a grin, which was a drastic improvement from a little bit ago. “I’m sorry. Let me rephrase. Do you guys want to know what we’re doing next week?”

“If we’re still here in a week,” Shawn mumbled, catching Maple’s eye.

She picked dirt out of her fingernails. “Out with it, boy.”

Her response only made Q happier. He jumped down from the windowsill, causing light to fill the space he left.

Shawn still thought it was weird how the light didn’t seem to emit any heat, at least none that he could feel.

“Well, if today’s October 25th, what’s next week?” Q asked.

Maple sighed. “What, are we going trick or treating?”

“Something like that. Don’t worry. I’ll let you know when it is happening.”

The fact that Q was this excited about it made Shawn nervous. Maple must have felt the same way because she gave Q the “Is your head screwed on straight?” look.

Q held his hands out cautiously. “Guys, I promise this will be a good little distraction. I don’t want to ruin the surprise.”

Shawn groaned. “No offense, but none of the surprises here have been good.”

“Trust me, this is a good one. And I’m not telling. I promised Rupert I wouldn’t tell any other first years.”

Maple glared at him again.

“Give me the evil eyes as much as you want. Didn’t work for the other guy either when he ventured up here.”

“What do you mean ‘the other guy’?” Maple asked, not remembering seeing anyone else on the way up.

Q pointed outside the window.

Maple and Shawn moved to see what lay on the other end of his finger and were surprised to see there was someone in almost every tower.

“I met your roomie! Who seems to have found another person to talk to instead of me.”

Opposite them, Jay and the redhead from the first row at orientation were in another tower. Jay appeared too enthralled in whatever he was discussing to notice the couple making out in the adjacent tower, or to notice the last tower, where another new reaper sat on the ledge, glossy-eyed.

"I'm going to check out the library. You knuckleheads have fun though." Maple left, leaving the boys to command the tower alone.

"You're really not going to tell me what this tradition is?" Shawn asked while studying Jay's body language, trying to see if his roommate showed any signs of trauma from the day's earlier events.

Q clapped his hands together. "Oh hell, no! It'll make it all the sweeter for you. Just trust me, okay?" His tone was energetic but felt forced. Occasionally, his eyes would glance down and express the morning's terror.

Shawn rolled his eyes. "Q, who else am I going to trust?"

"You're right, mate, you're stuck with me. So, when I lead you into a trap, don't be too shocked, okay?"

Q was certainly one for the dramatic, Shawn noted. "Okay. That's fair. Just nothing embarrassing. Deal?

"Now now, I make no guarantees."

Movement in one of the adjacent towers caught Shawn's attention. The kid who was sitting on the ledge of the window was now standing on the sill, peering out over the edge. The air suddenly felt heavy. Q continued talking, but Shawn wasn't listening.

Shawn's tongue refused to relay what his brain was telling him. He looked across to where Jay was sitting. Jay had also stopped his conversation, noticing the kid across from him. Shawn and Jay locked eyes, both realizing what was about to transpire.

The kid teetered closer to the edge, and the pounding in Shawn's head sped up. His brain could process that Jay was yelling something out, probably along the lines of "Don't do it!", but one look at the kid's face was enough to see that the decision was already made.

Four seconds later, the kid was airborne. Another three seconds was when the ground caught up to the new reaper. The sound of bones shattering was muffled by someone screaming. It was only while Shawn was racing down the staircase that he realized the person screaming was himself.

Chapter 12

Blood. That was the first thing that filled Shawn's vision. A mangled body of muscle and guts was spewed all over the ground. Bones sprouted out of the kid's joints, touching air for the first time, as they'd finally been released by the confines of his tissue. There was nothing left resembling the boy who'd been standing on the ledge. Shawn felt numb. He just kept staring at the mess splattered on the ground as the blue lights started to pulse from the remains.

A small group of students had gathered around, most likely drawn by Shawn's screams. Shawn recognized Miss McLally pushing her way to the front of the crowd. She took charge and talked to the couple that Shawn had seen making out at the top of the tower. "Matteo, Oliva, go get Mr. Peppertine immediately."

"Come on, Shawn. Let's go."

Shawn felt the presence of someone standing next to him. He didn't even realize he'd been knee-deep in the dirt, kneeling next to the body. Arms lifted him up unexpectedly, helping support him as he walked away from the scene.

"Let's get back to our room," Jay said.

Shawn said nothing. He tried searching for Maple and Q but didn't recognize them in the wall of people that formed around the body. He wasn't completely sure if he would have recognized them anyway; everything was moving in a haze for him.

The students surrounding the scene all wore black sweatshirts. First years had fled the area, while the remaining students didn't seem to bat an eye at their fellow reaper's insides that were sprinkled across the dirt. Had they really become so desensitized in their time here? Shawn had seen more people die in the last couple of days than he'd ever wanted to. Would he become one of those people soon?

Jay opened their door and led Shawn to his bed. The scratchy bedsheets between Shawn's fingers were a warm welcome from the experience at the tower.

"You need to pull yourself together," Jay said, sitting on the ground beside Shawn's bed.

Shawn continued rubbing the sheets between his thumb and index finger. "I thought I was doing a pretty good job." The lack of emotion in his voice barely convinced himself.

Sighing, Jay shook his head. "I told you, and you heard Trevor, we're being tested. Every reaction, every movement, and every word is being evaluated. They want us to be reapers, and it doesn't matter if we're ready or not. We have to perform until they think we are."

A knock at the door shut Jay up.

"Well, boys, it seems like you've had yourselves quite a day." The vein-red-colored suit coat of the headmaster looked recently ironed. "Why don't you both follow me." Thankfully, this time, she wasn't holding a scythe.

Jay got up instantly and started to follow, but he paused just long enough at the doorway to make sure he heard the creak of the bed behind him. They followed Headmaster Tyflin throughout the halls on the fourth floor and came to the back of the Academy, where they started descending.

This stairwell went past the ground floor, deeper into the Academy. A door made of mismatched wood finally stopped their descent. It looked like it was made out of the remaining pieces from a lumber yard. Different shades of brown, black, gray, and red wood mixed together to form the face of it.

Pulling a brass key out of her pocket, Tyflin unlocked and swung the door open to reveal another smaller curved set of stairs. She held the door open, waiting for the boys to go first. Neither Shawn nor Jay made a move to head down.

"Why should we go down there?" Shawn asked.

"One: it's only my office. Two: What other choice do you have?" Her arm held open the wooden puzzle of a door with ease. That was enough for Jay, so he went down, not looking back. To Shawn, it seemed like a stupid place to put the most important office, but he followed, letting the flicker from the torches on the walls guide his feet down.

They arrived at a long hallway, which had symbols painted on each side; the baby-blue paint made a stark contrast against the gray walls. On one side, he easily recognized each symbol. Talons, mustangs, blades, and the Wayward Academy initials lined this side. On the other wall sat four symbols that meant nothing to Shawn. He wanted to examine them more closely, but the end of the hallway opened into what he assumed was the headmaster's office.

Awaiting them were two stone stools; behind these stood a white marble desk. Shawn found the blue swirls running through the desk calming. It looked like a part of the ocean was trying to reach him through sea foam.

The rest of the room was bare. No photos hung on the walls. Just four torches providing light.

Headmaster Tyflin took a seat and motioned for them to do the same. Two bookcases, holding a minimal of books, were built into the wall behind her. Trinkets littered the spaces without books. A green glass sea turtle and metal scales were among the hodgepodge of items. A cabinet stood off in one corner. And in the opposite one was a giant globe. Shawn thought the globe was extremely old or at least very odd. It had the outlines of the continents, but the separations for the countries on it were completely wrong.

"They're the regions for reapers," Tyflin said, following Shawn's gaze.

"How many regions are there?" Jay asked.

Tyflin moved over to the wooden contraption that held the globe, spinning it 360 degrees. "America has about twenty-five zones. But Wayward's jurisdiction covers only forty percent of it."

"How many other academies are there?" Jay asked.

The flickering light from the candles made it hard to see the outlines on the globe. "Two other ones in North America," she said as she traced out the areas where the regions were divided. "You'll know more if you continue to grow here."

The weight of the "if" was not lost on either Jay or Shawn. Shawn wondered how many other students were brought into the office. No one had been here recently, as Shawn's seat was cold enough to frost the grass.

Tyflin poured a glass of brown liquid out of a decanter. "Either of you like whiskey?"

"I think I'll pass," Jay said, trying to maintain a clear head.

Shawn was curious about the liquor but decided not to add anything to the uneasiness already swirling around inside his stomach. He offered an awkward explanation. "No, thank you. I'm underage." Not captain smooth by any stretch.

Tyflin scoffed, amused. "If you haven't noticed, the rules are a little different here, but suit yourselves." She let the liquor swirl in the glass before taking a large gulp. She stayed silent, letting the seconds tick by with each swirl of liquor. Shawn usually felt uncomfortable in silence, but he needed it after the tower incident. He didn't want to talk and was completely fine letting the other two hash it out.

While Shawn was comfortable in the silence, Jay confronted it. He didn't seem to be blinking. He just faced forward, as emotional as a spotless chalkboard. Another thirty seconds passed before anyone spoke up. Jay finally budged, not interested in playing games: he wanted answers.

"Have we broken any rules?" Jay asked, quickly ending the cat-and-mouse game.

"No, you have not, Mr. Musters." She took another long drink of the whiskey she'd been toying with.

"Are we not learning quick enough?" Shawn made sure the annoyance in his voice was held back a bit, which wasn't hard because he was pretty sure he was still in shock.

"No." Another sip out of the glass.

Wonderful freaking answer. "Did we offend you or anyone else?" Shawn asked.

"No." Another sip.

Shawn could feel his face starting to get red from the anger rising within him. She wasn't giving away any information.

"Tell us why we're here then," Jay cut back in.

Tyflin stood up, grabbing a scroll and ink from the bookcase behind her. "The names of everyone in the tower you were in."

"Why?" Jay asked. Shawn didn't get why she wanted to know who was in the tower, but he didn't like where this was headed.

"Look, I'm not going to hurt anyone," she said, swirling her glass again. "I'm sorry for what you had to witness. But, most importantly... I'm sorry we failed the reaper that jumped. We should've been more aware of his circumstances. We should have done more." She sighed. "I need the names purely because you're all going on your dock walk a little earlier than expected."

Shawn squeezed his jeans between his fingers, needing to feel the pressure. "This is it. Right here: only us." Shawn didn't know what the dock walk was, but he didn't want Maple or Q to be a part of it. Jay went along with this deceit, writing down only his and Shawn's names across the piece of parchment.

Ink from the quill started pooling on the paper after neither boy moved the quill from its position. Shawn didn't even want to touch it; Tyflin should have given them a pen like McLally had.

"Very well. Tomorrow morning, you two will be going on the dock walk. Your mentors will meet you outside first thing in the morning."

Jay got up to leave, but Shawn stayed frozen to his seat. The look on Tyflin's face was replaced with curiosity.

Shawn wasn't moving until he got something. "Who was the boy that killed himself?"

Tyflin put down the glass of liquor. "His name was Paco, and he was also a first year in your class," she said, waiting for more questions.

"Does this happen often?"

"Kids jumping from the tower?"

"Killing kids. Reapers jumping from towers. Or, you know, cutting off their heads?" He bit his lip as he spat out the last words, feeling the daggers coming from Jay. Screw playing along right now.

The headmaster rose and straightened her suit jacket from the creases left by her chair. "Occasionally it does, yes. People come to conclusions about what this place is before they look to see what it could be. As for the incident at orientation, that only happens when hardheaded students decide their ending for themselves. Now, go get some dinner and rest up before tomorrow. The next couple weeks are going to be taxing." With that, Tyflin sat back down, waiting for them to exit.

A hand squeezed his shoulder, and Shawn took Jay's cue and started to exit Tyflin's office.

Just as they were about to enter the long hallway, Tyflin spoke again. "Oh, and boys, Maple Collins, Quintin Prodit and Sophia Trak will be joining you as well. Don't worry. I'll let them know." They took this answer in defeat and walked back to their room. The only solace Shawn took from the last exchange was that the whiskey glass was completely empty.

Chapter 13

Water lapped onto Shawn's bare feet. The five of them stood on the shore, wondering what the hell they were doing there. It was the end of October; the water should've been freezing, yet only lukewarm splashes came their way.

Maple and Q had been waiting at Shawn's door when he and Jay got back from their meeting. Tyflin had Maple's and Q's mentors deliver them notes, telling them to be ready first thing in the morning. No one understood what the dock walk meant. Q half-joked that it was like walking the plank—another way to get rid of the unwanted reapers. Something about Tyflin's face had told Shawn it wasn't a punishment, although he couldn't guess what else it might be.

As it was only six in the morning, the shore was mostly void of people. A few were out on the dock fishing, while others were watching the sunrise. Only the waves crashing against the rock walls of the dock made noise this early; everyone else seemed caught up in their own world.

Adriana cleared her throat. Trevor was out on a reaping assignment and couldn't be a part of their excursion. Sophia's mentor joined them instead; his name was Hamilton, and from what Shawn could tell, he was a quiet, no-nonsense kind of guy. Skinny as a toothpick. The sun shined off his bald head, making his dark skin look like it had been waxed on top.

Sophia, on the other hand, was the complete opposite. Shawn had only seen her at orientation and talking to Jay from afar. He learned very quickly she wouldn't shut up. "Are you going to tell us why we're here, or will we just have to drown ourselves?" She flipped her sunset red curls as she waited for Hamilton to respond. No shortage of confidence in her bones.

The only response Hamilton gave was a hard stare and a raised eyebrow. Sophia glared back but grew quickly uncomfortable when Hamilton didn't stop. Shawn thought Hamilton might get along with the gargoyles. Flustered, Sophia turned back to the shore, and Shawn saw a hint of a smile appear on her mentor.

"Walk to the end of the dock and back," Adriana instructed.

Q turned to Adriana, puzzled. "That's it? Walk to the end of the dock and back? You're not going to shove us in? Or drown us? Or have us hold our breath underwater?"

"That's it," Hamilton chimed in, unphased by Q's antics.

"Okay. No take-backs!" Q said, almost skipping onto the dock. Maple gave Shawn a shrug, echoing the continuing theme in their lives: that they had no choice.

Adriana rolled her eyes and gave Shawn a strong shove. Jay and Maple followed closely behind, not needing the same encouragement.

"I hate water. I better not get splashed by those waves," Sophia pouted as she followed.

Up ahead, Q continued to skip, ignoring the patrons on the dock.

"Anyone else smell something fishy about this?" Jay asked.

"Did you just make a pun?" Shawn asked. Jay barely spoke half the time, and here he was making puns?

"So, we shouldn't *tuna* round?" Jay responded, not even cracking a smile at his own joke.

Shawn stopped in his tracks.

Barely avoiding him, Maple had to sidestep his sudden roadblock. "Okay. We have a job to do. Can you stop fooling around?"

"It's not the joke." Shawn pointed to the end of the dock. "Look."

It was obvious this task wasn't going to be as simple as walking to the end of the dock and back. Shawn wasn't sure how Q had missed it either, as he kept skipping ahead, oblivious. It had to be hard to miss a gargoyle standing right off to the side of the dock, his purple eyes watching them as they approached. The sight of him even shut Sophia up.

Maple followed where he was pointing. "What's that thing doing here?"

"Doesn't matter. We still have to walk to the end of the dock and back." Jay gazed at the water, shaking his head. He then went ahead and stepped onto the dock, ignoring the gargoyle.

Shawn turned to Maple. "I don't like this."

"Jay's right. We still have to do this," Maple said.

Old wood, worn from years of people putting their weight on it, creaked underneath their feet. Shawn tried ignoring the gargoyle, but the guy in the brown tunic observed every move they made. It made him feel like a rat in a maze.

Now that he was on the dock, Shawn noticed that no one was actually fishing. Everyone appeared to just be looking out to the water, barely moving. A man in a white button-down shirt caught Shawn's attention. He looked like he was about to go into a meeting. Who had business on a dock at this hour? If Shawn were out here in a dress shirt, he'd be worried about getting it wet, or at the very least, getting sand in his shoes on the way back.

There was something off about the man. As Shawn approached, the man was fidgeting with his cuff links. His black bowler hat sat steadily on his head like it had been glued there. When was the last time someone wore a bowler hat? In the 1950s? The strangest part of the man's outfit was the hazy white outline surrounding every inch of clothing.

"Hey, do these people seem a little–"

Before Shawn could finish, the back of Maple's head rocketed off his chin. Shawn had been so distracted by bowler hat man that he hadn't even seen her stop a couple of feet ahead of him.

Maple didn't flinch after Shawn ran into her. Even Q had ceased his skipping, frozen to wooden planks below him. Jay had stopped in front of them as well, and Shawn wasn't hearing a peep from Sophia. That's when Shawn felt the eyes on him. Everyone on the dock had simultaneously changed the course of their gaze from the water to the group of reapers invading their space.

"Can they see us?" Sophia said, finally breaking her silence.

"Only one way to find out." Maple walked up to a woman wearing a sundress that shouldn't be worn in the fall. She avoided the woman's eyes as she walked up. Maple got so close to her, that under different circumstances he would have wondered if she knew the woman. Then Maple's arm shot out. She passed straight through the woman's midsection: no resistance.

Behind Shawn, Sophia let out a scream that perfectly summed up what he couldn't get out. Sophia fell to her knees, hyperventilating. Somewhere in his head, Shawn was conscious of Jay walking back to console her. The other part of his brain was fixated on the people on the dock, and all of the ghosts that happened to be right in front of him.

Shawn turned back to the businessman. A soft white glow formed the man's outline, making him slightly blurry around the edges. At first, Shawn thought it was because of the morning sun reflecting off the water, but no, the man would always be this way. He felt a ball of saliva slide down his throat as he forced himself to take another step forward. He needed to confront whatever was going on, even if he wanted to hightail it off the dock. The businessman appeared bored by the whole situation. As Shawn came closer, the man outstretched his hand. His initials engraved on his cufflinks had fake gold paint flaking off of them.

"Not even going to try?" The man said to him. A handshake—that was what was happening in front of him. Shawn reached out to meet the palm, knowing that it wouldn't connect. Passing through felt like waving his hand into a wall of mist. It wasn't like passing your hand through air, there was a slight pressure. Another sensation Shawn didn't expect was how the air was slightly warmer where the man appeared to be.

"When did it happen?" Shawn asked, resisting the urge to walk through him entirely.

The man went back to fidgeting with his cufflinks. "Oh, about eighty-four years ago."

Shawn absorbed this information. "All of you here? At the same time?"

"No no. There were about sixteen or so deaths in total from where our boat sank. Funny, isn't it?"

"Sorry?"

"Well, we were so close to shore. If only we'd learned how to swim."

Shawn didn't see the humor in the situation. "But how are you here? I mean..."

"Why am I a ghost?"

"Well, yes. Shouldn't you have been reaped?"

"We were unclaimed by reapers. So, we became this." He motioned to himself. "I'm sure your friends who brought you here have stressed how important it is to be quick in your new profession. *We* are the reason why." He said like it was a story he'd told a million times.

Shawn noticed him fidget with his cuff links again. "Are your initials GN?"

This seemed to strike a chord. If the man could lose color in his face, he would have. "They were my son's initials: Gordon."

"Did he... survive?" Shawn asked.

The man started rubbing the top of the cufflinks even harder, circling the G and N with the tip of his finger. "No."

Shawn looked around for a child but didn't see any when he glanced over the dock.

"A reaper did arrive when it happened. I begged her to take my son instead; luckily, she listened." If the lapel pin were made of real material, Shawn figured that the G and N would be worn away by now.

"I'm sorry." Shawn didn't know what else to say.

"Don't be. Just don't let other souls suffer the same fate," the businessman said before he absorbed Shawn for a split second and walked through him.

Shawn snapped around quickly, uncomfortable about being passed through. "Can I ask you one more thing?"

"Sure," he said with a sigh.

"Why haven't you left the dock?"

The man spread his arms wide. "We can only go so far from where we died. This dock. This stupid dock... is all I have." He brought down his arms and walked away from Shawn.

Shawn let out a breath he didn't know he was holding, letting the cool air expand his lungs. He heard a bustling, and suddenly footsteps took off at a running pace. Sophia had had enough and sprinted toward the beach where the mentors awaited.

"Guess we should finish our walk then?" A shaky Jay appeared at his side and, without waiting, walked onward.

Q was talking to what looked like a young fisherman, whose net would only catch air from now on. Maple had finished her conversation with the sundress woman and stood waiting at the center of the dock for him.

"Come on, let's finish this," Shawn said to her.

"All these people... stranded." She glanced from left to right, taking in each face. Turning towards Shawn, she gripped his forearm. "We can't let this happen to other people."

Whatever conversation took place between Maple and her ghost, it had left an impression. Shawn's skin started turning red from the pressure, each fingernail unwittingly leaving its mark.

A businessman, a mother, a fisherman, a teacher, a student, an engineer. Shawn spoke to some and counted the rest. Twelve souls were trapped on the dock. He reached the end and looked out over the water. More than ever, he got the reasoning for becoming a reaper. These people were the reason.

Afterward, they sat on the beach, everyone lost in the waves crashing into the rocks. Over and over, the water splashed. Just like they'd continue to splash for those trapped on the small plank of rotting wood.

"Can we leave?" Sophia kept her gaze at her feet as she said it.

"Once everyone has completed the walk," Adriana answered quickly.

"Get your eyes checked. We all walked on the bloody dock," Q said, squeezing a handful of sand between his fist.

"No, actually, not all of you have. Right, Miss Trak?" Adriana asked, not needing an answer.

"I walked on the damn dock!" Sophia stood up.

"You must walk the whole dock," Hamilton said without emotion. Shawn wasn't sure how he would be able to handle training someone like Sophia, She seemed to wear enough emotions on her sleeve for a small army.

Sophia bit her tongue and glanced at the dock, realizing that this wasn't up for debate.

Jay took a breath and stood as well. "Come on, I'll walk with you."

"You don't have to walk it again, Musters," Adriana reminded him.

Jay started walking anyway. "I know."

This seemed to be enough for Sophia, and she quickly followed in his footsteps.

Adriana squatted down near the three remaining reapers. "Do you all understand now?"

"I think he understands better than most of us," Q said while watching Jay lead the terrified redhead along the dock.

Adriana seemed satisfied with that answer and got up. "I'll take these three back," she told Hamilton, who nodded.

Maple and Shawn got up to follow Adriana, yet Q remained planted in the sand. "Come on, Q," Maple encouraged.

"I'd like to stay a bit longer if that's permitted." He said this with no sarcasm, never once taking his eyes off the two walking the dock.

"Suit yourself, Mr. Prodit."

Adriana sent a cardinal to come to collect them, and they made their way back down to the gargoyle gate. This time, Shawn didn't feel like running before he got back to the Academy.

Chapter 14

People strolled around on the grass, not knowing how close they were to death at any moment. The park was full of people blissfully unaware of the group that waited for one of them to perish. Everywhere Shawn looked, people went about their normal lives. A group of girls sat having a picnic. Runners pushed harder with every stride until they were out of breath. Dog walkers and the elderly strolled down dirt paths that circled the park. Shawn knew that was how he lived as well: ignoring death. Well, at least the possibility of it.

"Have you spotted the grounder yet?" Trevor asked as he picked at a piece of dirt that had landed on his mud-brown suit jacket.

Shawn looked from man to woman, from teenager to mom, and nothing gave him any inkling of who was going to be reaped next. Nothing distinguished one person from another in this park. This was their third day here, playing this game. The sun showered down on him, but he felt no warmth from it.

"The jogger in the red beanie," Jay said from the other side of the park bench.

"Why him?" Adriana asked, and Shawn wondered the same thing. How was Jay even able to take a stab at who was going to die? It wasn't like there was a big sign above the guy counting down the seconds.

Jay leaned his arms on his knees. "Why *not* him?"

That didn't clear things up for Shawn in the slightest.

"Follow him then," Trevor said, looking at Shawn.

"Me? The jogger? Is it even him?" Every day they'd come to this park, and their mentors asked them the same question, 'Have you spotted them yet?' How do you spot someone marked for death? Hint: you can't. At least Shawn couldn't. He wasn't about to go running alongside a jogger for no reason. He wasn't a fan of running and didn't know if he could even keep up with the guy.

"I guess we'll find out, won't we?" Trevor said through a toothy grin. Knowing it was pointless to argue, Shawn found himself trailing behind the red-beanie man, breathing heavily. Even without a heartbeat to pump blood throughout his veins, Shawn found it hard to keep up with the jogger. Everyone at Wayward said that you get used to it, and it was actually a lot easier to get in shape since the body didn't need as much to keep moving. Tell that to his burning lungs.

The two of them looped around the park six times, and based on the runner's routine from the other two days, Shawn knew that the seventh would be their last. Everyone has a routine and falls into habits. That was the one thing Shawn had realized when observing a park full of strangers. The older woman who fed the ducks arrived each day promptly at 2:15 pm. She walked three laps and sat on the bench waiting for the ducks to visit—which they always did. Even the ducks knew the routine. Another man came around 4 pm to chain smoke underneath a tree in the center of the park, smiling at the disgusted looks from the other parkgoers.

Shawn just had to make it one more lap. His legs burned with each step, begging for him to stop. He wished Jay had guessed the chain smoker, as getting secondhand smoke from the man under the tree sounded more enjoyable.

Thankfully, they came to a stop at a water fountain. The jogger never seemed to stay long at the fountain, so Shawn waited for his opportunity. Sure enough, after a couple of seconds, the grounder lifted his head from the spout. Shawn had to be quick. As the man released the button, Shawn shot his hand toward it, just barely grasping the edge to keep the thirst-quenching water flowing. If anyone was watching, they would assume the button got stuck for a couple extra seconds. This allowed Shawn to get a small drink. He wasn't sure if it was technically allowed, but it wasn't going to stop him from finding out.

A small breeze blew a few leaves to the ground as the red-beanie jogger set off down the winding path. Shawn thought that this whole exercise was pointless. He wondered how much Adriana and Trevor liked watching them make fools of themselves.

The girls who'd been picnicking in the grass walked past and said hello to the jogger, who smiled in return not hearing the girls over his music. Suddenly, red beanie broke into a sprint. Another freaking lap. Shawn hadn't been expecting that: he knew people had routines, but clearly, not everyone sticks to them.

Shawn raced through the group of girls, trying to catch up. Even knowing that grounders couldn't see him, he constantly forgot that he had to move out of their way. He only remembered at the last minute when the group converged on him. He was just able to avoid colliding fully with a girl, brushing only her shoulder. "Watch it," the girl said to her friend.

Shawn rushed forward, leaving the squabbling group of girls behind.

The jogger ended up doing two more laps. At the end, Shawn plopped down, breathless, on the bench next to Trevor. "How was your run?" Trevor said, laughing.

"So... that... wasn't... him?" Shawn said between breaths.

"Just keep watching," Adriana said. Her brown suit mirrored Trevor's, the only difference being her black lapels and cuffs.

Jay stood up and pointed to a tree in the center of the park. The chain-smoker was clutching his chest, gasping. "He's having a heart attack."

"Just watch," Adriana reiterated, holding her scythe out in front of Jay.

The elderly woman feeding the ducks screamed. Other grounders rushed around trying to find help. The man withered on the ground, gasping for air that wasn't coming. Somewhere in the distance, sirens called out. Someone had gotten hold of the paramedics quickly. But it wasn't going to help; they would be too late.

The man's body pulsed blue. The light traveled from each extremity towards the center and pulsed faster with each second. The all-too-familiar orb gathered at the center of the chain smoker. Every face that gathered around him contained a look of horror, as they realized he was gone.

If Shawn weren't already sitting down, he would have needed to. He wondered when he'd get used to getting a front-row view of death.

Jay brushed Adriana's scythe aside. "We have to collect the orb." Jay's voice was a bit strained as he tried to keep his frustration in check. While Shawn and Jay hadn't talked about the dock experience, they weren't going to forget it either.

"No," Trevor said.

"What do you mean 'no'?" Was this a test for them? To see how loyal they were to the process? Neither responded with words; instead, they kept looking at the orb.

"Fuck this," Jay said and walked toward the crowd.

Shawn was confused. Why wouldn't they want them to go collect the orb? He knew what happened if they didn't, so he forced his legs to stand and caught up to Jay.

Out of the tree line stepped two teenagers in suits. Not just two teenagers, though: two reapers. One wore a silver suit with a red and black striped tie.

The other wore a wide-brimmed top hat with a yellow ribbon tied around it to contrast with his black suit. They both ignored the two new reapers at the edge of the crowd and went to collect their assignment. After they collected the orb, they left the park without saying a word.

Shawn looked at Jay and asked, "What was that about?"

Jay shook his head. "Another test."

They walked back to the park bench where Adriana and Trevor hadn't moved.

Shawn thought about the people they'd observed the past few days and how each time they'd guessed someone, they were told to just watch. Jay had asked about the man under the tree before, but it wasn't ever confirmed. After three days of trying to figure out who was going to die and what made them different, they had come up with nothing... That's what finally clicked for Shawn. "We don't have an assignment, do we?"

Jay looked confused at this remark. But Adriana and Trevor smiled at each other.

"Very good, Mr. Turner. Now, why is that?" Trevor asked.

"We couldn't tell who was supposed to be reaped, because you aren't supposed to be able to tell." Trevor lightly clapped three times when Shawn had finished answering.

"Only part of the reason we're here," Adriana told them.

"The other reapers," Jay said.

"Correct, Musters." Adriana seemed pleased that they'd figured that portion out as well. "Reapers cross paths in the field all the time; sometimes, their assignments die together. Sometimes because a grounder is friends with another grounder scheduled for reaping. Never assume that your assignment is the only assignment."

"Most importantly, be aware of your surroundings," Trevor added. "You never know who else is around or what can happen in an environment. And not just above ground. Be careful below ground as well. Sometimes it pays off to learn about the environment you're in and to the other people you're with."

Chapter 15

"Duck," Mac shouted.

The reaper crouched into a power stance as the staff sliced the air right where she'd been seconds before.

"Roll." Mac brought the wooden blade down from the reaper's left, causing a temporary indent in the training mat.

The woman sprung up from the sweat-moistened mat, striking her right hand upward. She came to a stop mere inches before Mac.

"And strike. Very good, Ms. Harper."

Today was their first lesson from Mac, who was going to whip them into shape. At least that was what Trevor had told him. When Shawn looked around at the group of newbies, he knew that it wasn't going to be an easy job. Luckily, Maple was in his class. Since the tower could only hold so many reapers, Q and Jay were scheduled for later in the evening. Shawn didn't know a lot of the others but recognized Sophia blabbering to a couple of girls.

In the back of the sparring room were two other senior reapers, including Adriana. Apparently, she and Trevor were some of the best sparring reapers at the Academy. The rumor was that she knocked him out in their first year, and when he woke up in the infirmary, he immediately asked her out. Trevor denied the story, saying they were just rumors. But Adriana had a smirk when he denied it.

Adriana didn't even look Shawn's way as she waited for Mac's direction. Having twenty people sparring in the quad tower was going to be a little tight. Unless it was by accident, Shawn knew he had no chance of winning his sparring match.

"Now, I want you to remember, we're here to refine your skills." Mac surveyed the room, landing on Shawn. "Or, in some cases, create them."

Shawn felt his cheeks flush.

"You'll come to learn," Mac continued, "that not everywhere is safe for a reaper, and while the gargoyles act as protectors, we have to rely on ourselves sometimes." He spat out the last bit in disgust.

Protect ourselves from what? Shawn had been above ground a couple of times now, and nothing seemed remotely threatening. The only things he could think might be dangerous were gargoyles. And they were here to protect them.

Mac went to a barrel of wooden scythes and called out ten names, none of which were Shawn's. "Half of you will watch, while the other half spars. The senior reapers we have here today will help you with the basics, and we'll go from there." Mac handed everyone a wooden training scythe. "Now, everyone whose name was called, find your sparring partner and get onto the mat." He waited for the rush that didn't come as the new reapers sat grounded. "Now would be a good time."

Ten of the names called rushed forward, including Maple. Shawn and the other nine went near the back wall to sit down and observe. Mac went around to each pair, showing them the correct stances. When he got to Maple, Shawn's stomach tightened. Standing across from her was a bearded, six-foot-two boy, who looked like he'd eaten a whole Thanksgiving feast and then went to his neighbors to get seconds. Maple was going to get crushed, but she kept a good poker face. One of the senior reapers came up and instructed them how to start and what was or wasn't allowed.

Veins popped out in Maple's forearms from how tight she was holding onto the staff. She zeroed in on the mass of a human in front of her. The guy she faced licked his lips, apparently looking forward to his next meal. Or win. Whatever came first.

He charged like a bull in a coliseum. Maple awkwardly dove to the side of him as he charged, rolling a little before remembering she had to get up again. The guy grinned as he held the staff like a baseball bat. The giant oaf's ego was shooting through the roof, and Shawn hated watching it. He hoped that those color guard skills weren't just for show.

Maple held her staff out in front of her in a defensive stance, waiting for him to attack, which he did right away. He furiously swung the wooden pole in a wide arc at Maple's head. WHACK. A good block reverberated along Maple's staff. She winced, clasping her hand to her chest and trying to work feeling back into her fingers. The oaf took this as an opportunity to strike and attempted the same move. Maple dove again, almost losing the staff as she rolled. Sweat dripped from her ear onto the mat, like rain falling onto a house.

Once she bounced up, her face told it all. She looked like she wanted to bury the man across from her. She shifted her stance a bit, sliding her left foot slightly back while the staff pointed up in an attack pose. She lunged. The guy hadn't expected this from her, probably anticipating that the whole fight would be over quickly.

"Block," Adriana told the kid. Shawn had almost completely forgotten she was there. Honestly, he'd forgotten that anyone else was sparring. Gathering from the looks of the others sitting out, they seemed to have forgotten as well. Everyone was watching the battle Maple was putting on.

The guy got his staff up just in time to block Maple's attack, stumbling back as a result. His cheeks flushed at his mistake, and then his ears turned red. He charged again. Maple was ready. Attack. Block. Attack. Block. Each time he shot his staff out, she blocked it with her own. They seemed to be in a locked battle before Maple did something unexpected.

After another back-and-forth attack, the guy geared up to strike again. This time as he swung forward, instead of blocking, Maple ducked. The staff cleared the air where her head had just been. She didn't roll. Instead, she shot her staff out, hitting his kneecap straight on and then sweeping his legs. Instantly, he fell to the ground, dropping his staff, defeated. Shawn should have known better than to doubt her.

Maple smiled and then twirled her staff around her body before extending her hand. "Thanks for the workout."

The guy took it, but he wasn't smiling. He limped off to sit against the wall.

"Very good, Ms. Collins. You have potential," Adriana said as she went to observe another mat that still had a match going on.

Breathing heavily, Maple joined Shawn on the floor.

"Color guard? You sure that's it?"

"I have good reflexes. What can I say?" She said, smiling. "Oh, and I guess the boxing lessons may have helped with that as well."

Of course, Maple took boxing lessons. She had a few surprises up her sleeve. Shawn, unfortunately, did not.

"Everyone who hasn't matched up, stand," Mac told them as the last sparring session ended.

Shawn walked toward one of the matts. Across from him stood Sophia, or at least what resembled Sophia. She was pale and not talking again. Was she having flashbacks to the dock?

"You two can stand there gawking at each other, or you can pick up the damn staff," one of the senior reapers barked at them.

Picking up the wooden scythe, Shawn readied himself as best as he could. At least he didn't have to fight Maple. His ass would've been handed to him on a silver platter. He held the scythe out in a defensive stance and waited for Sophia. She bent down to pick up her staff, but her hand stopped, hovering over it. Her hair dangled down, hiding her from the rest of the room. Before he knew it, vomit leaked out onto the mat. It pooled right beneath her, seeping in between her toes as she hacked up more fluid.

Everyone had stopped to watch the disaster unfolding. Noticing this, Mac came over, put his hand on Sophia's back, and whispered into her ear. Her red curls shook as she nodded at whatever Mac said to her. Adriana came over and took Sophia's arm, walking her out of the room. Still, not a soul moved.

"Did anyone tell you to stop?" Mac yelled at the other sparring partners. His words seemed to snap everyone back to reality, and they all went back to their matches. Everyone except Shawn, who now had no partner.

Smells of acid wafted over Shawn's way, and he was worried that he might be adding to the pile on the mat soon.

"Turner," Mac called out.

Shawn walked over to the council member, trying to keep his composure.

"Guess we'll have to wait a bit to find out what you can do. Grab a mop and clean this up." Mac walked away, leaving Shawn with Sophia's mess and not a hint of where a mop might be.

Water spilled out from the bucket onto the mat; no matter how much Shawn scrubbed, the acid stench wouldn't go away. He stood up, taking a break from the scrubbing, and looked around the empty room. Empty except for Mac, who was cleaning the other mats with a mop of his own. Everyone else had left as soon as the last reaper hit the floor, dismissed for the evening.

Shawn's gaze drifted to the wall full of weapons. Shawn wondered when he'd get to try one out.

"Go grab one, Turner," Mac said without even looking up from his mop.

"I'm sorry. What, Sir?"

Mac sighed, standing the mop against the far wall. "Grab a weapon."

Shawn wasn't sure if this was a test or if Mac was just messing with him—even though Mac didn't seem like the kind of person to mess around. Shawn moved over to the wooden scythes.

"No. Grab a real scythe from the wall."

A real weapon? Was he nuts? "Um Sir, no offense, but why?"

"You mean besides the fact that you've been glancing at the wall every five seconds?" Mac went over to get it himself, throwing it onto the mat. "Take it."

Shawn walked over and twirled the scythe around in his hands, no doubt making a fool out of himself, but loving it. He might as well try and get used to it.

"Try not to cut yourself, Turner," Mac said as he went and grabbed a wooden staff.

"Isn't it a little unfair if I have a real scythe?" Shawn wasn't sure what the hell to make of this situation. About a minute ago, he was cleaning puke up, and now he was going to spar against a council member. With a real freaking blade. He might need that bucket again.

"Believe me, Turner, if I was scared of you with a real scythe, then I don't deserve to teach any of you. Let alone be a reaper." Mac walked over to the end of the mat and waited.

Should Shawn attack first? Wait on the defensive end? What happens if he accidentally killed Mac? Would they even believe that Mac allowed it?

"Any day, Turner."

Shawn didn't know anything about fighting. He avoided confrontation when he was alive, and it wasn't like he was extremely athletic either. He should've taken boxing lessons. Mac stood on the balls of his feet, examining Shawn, who stood flat-footed. If Mac had hair, there wouldn't have been one out of place. Meanwhile, the stains underneath Shawn's shirt were growing by the second.

There was no way Shawn was going to beat Mac hand-to-hand, even with the advantage of a real weapon. There was a reason Mac was teaching the new reapers. He was the best hand-to-hand fighter at Wayward.

Shawn bent down into a fighting stance, feet shoulder-width apart, scythe extended forward. Mac still hadn't moved: he just watched. Shawn charged, swinging the blade when he got within a couple of feet of the council member. He aimed for the largest part of Mac's body: his chest. He hit nothing but air.

Mac jumped out of the way, not even bothering to bring his scythe up to defend. Shawn turned to where he went and prepared himself to defend. Mac brought his wooden scythe behind his back, letting Shawn get any opening he wanted. Shawn took it, and he swung sporadically at him. Left arm. Right arm. Right knee. Right shoulder. Each time, Mac sidestepped Shawn without even bothering to block. Mac might as well not have been standing in front of him. Shawn stood no chance.

Taking a step back, Shawn surveyed his situation, gasping for breath. There was no way he could get close to Mac. That left only one move for him to try. He took a few more steps back, putting distance between himself and Mac. Again, Mac waited for him to make the move. Shawn lifted the scythe, acting like he was going to come down from above. Instead of trying to rush him, Shawn brought the blade back further over his shoulder, then snapped his arm forward. When the blade was at Mac's height, he let it fly.

It moved through the air with no spin, and the blade wasn't even facing the right way. But it was on track for his target. Brown wood flashed in front of Mac as he got his staff up in time to knock the scythe to the side. The blade buried itself into the mat next to them. Shawn gulped, knowing he was in serious trouble now. Mac wasn't even phased; he twirled the staff like a baton. Moving the wooden scythe behind his back, he bent the arm, holding it like a chicken wing. Then he took off straight towards Shawn.

Having almost no time to react and with nothing to defend himself, Shawn had no clue what to do. Mac surged and then slid on the mat, bringing the scythe out and taking Shawn's feet with it.

A cracked foam mat met the back of Shawn's head in a hurry. All presence of air left in Shawn's lungs dissipated. He gasped, trying to force air back in, like a child attempting to blow up a balloon that was taped shut. A shadow fell across Shawn's face.

"Not a terrible idea," Mac said. "Next time you try that move, throw the scythe and rush me at the same time. If you're quick enough, then while I'm distracted blocking, you might be able to get a hit in." He stuck his hand out to Shawn.

Shawn clasped it and pulled himself up.

"Also, work on your throwing. It had no rotation."

Feeling air reinflate his lungs, Shawn could finally form words. "What's the point of learning this? We're already dead."

Mac went over and picked up the scythe Shawn had thrown, brushing off the foam that had been pulled from the mat. Air whipped at Shawn's cheek, and a loud thud came from the wall behind him. Mac stood empty handed. Shawn turned and saw the blade embedded into a target on the wall: a perfect bullseye.

"That's how you throw it. Clean up those last two mats and put away the training tools," Mac said smirking as he walked out the door.

Chapter 16

"You sparred with Mac?" Q asked, putting down the chicken leg. He licked his fingers like he hadn't eaten in days.

Maple sat next to Shawn. "You know that Mac doesn't spar with anyone? No one even challenges him because he's unbeatable." She looked at Q chowing down on his dinner and crinkled her nose in disgust.

"That explains why he would have been able to take me down blindfolded."

The dining area was missing a lot of first years for dinner. Shawn kneaded a sore spot on his back and wondered how many others were nursing small injuries. The older reapers chatted loudly as they ate, and Shawn could feel the electricity in the air. "How did you do?"

Q slowly put down what was left of his chicken. "It was fine... I won... kinda."

"I'm so sorry for such unfortunate circumstances," Maple mocked. "What do you mean you 'kinda' won?"

Q pulled at his training hoodie. "Well, I won by default."

"Default?" Shawn asked.

"My partner refused to spar."

"Who was your partner?" Maple questioned.

"It was your roomie," he said, looking at Shawn.

"Jay?" Shawn was in disbelief. Black-eyed boy didn't want to fight? Hell, he tried kicking a door down the first day they were together. "Did he say why?"

Q shook his head no. "Just that he thought it was pointless, so he sat on the mat, refusing. Mac was not happy."

A hush suddenly fell upon the tables surrounding them. The three of them spun around to see Headmaster Tyflin standing at the center table. A rustling of leaves on the outer edge of the forest produced a gargoyle, a pumpkin cradled in his gray arms. Walking down the aisle, he made his way straight toward the headmaster. Once he reached the middle table, he carefully set the pumpkin down next to Tyflin. Within seconds, another gargoyle emerged from a different aisle. And another and another. Soon, each aisle had a gargoyle carrying a pumpkin to the council's center table.

Headmaster Tyflin couldn't contain her sly smile. Shawn wasn't sure what to make of the theatrics, but it *was* Halloween. Was this what Rupert had mentioned earlier? Even Q smirked, which meant that this couldn't be the only thing happening tonight. Shawn doubted Q would be excited just for this traditional display by their stone friends. The only question was, what was next?

Shawn examined the gargoyle in his aisle, still mesmerized by the fault lines spiderwebbed across its body. This one was the one with three gold dots on the bottom of its tunic. From what Shawn could tell, no one else had such dots. Why was he the only one with them?

Once the last gargoyle had placed its pumpkin, Tyflin held her arms out in a welcoming gesture. "Tonight begins a holiday as old as the reapers themselves. Many of the newcomers would know this as Halloween, but we here like to go by the more traditional name: All Hallows Eve. Thank you, friends, for coming this evening. As always, we're honored to have you as our guests."

Tyflin paused, glancing at the first gargoyle who walked down the aisle. The stone man took this as his cue and lifted a torch that had been strapped to his belt. Tyflin took one of the central candles from the table and ignited the torch; each gargoyle then came forward, lighting their own torches. The soft glow from the flames brightened the area as the cavern crystals above them dimmed.

"What we do here goes unnoticed by the world above. We live a complicated and intense life, a path we must follow. Let this evening serve as a reminder that while what we do goes unnoticed by everyone else, our fellow reapers know the fight." Tyflin reached down and grabbed her whiskey glass. "Our job is to *be* unnoticed... but not tonight. Tonight is All Hallows Eve."

Reapers around Shawn started drumming on the tables, a low rumbling that jumped from person to person.

The headmaster smiled. "Tonight," she shouted. "We will not go unnoticed. Our neighbors here will not be the only ones who see us. Tonight, the grounders will feel our presence!"

A roar erupted around the room as glasses were raised in celebration. "Enjoy your All Hallows Eve, and may your tricks be as sweet as your treats!" The headmaster shouted above the noise and then downed the whiskey left in her glass.

Flickers of orange started appearing in every window of the Academy, then areas along the mustang's paths, and finally in the forest. The glow of orange was unmistakable everywhere Shawn looked. As everyone was cheering, the gargoyles moved in sequence back down their respective rows. They made their way back into the forest, carrying their torches and officially starting All Hallows Eve.

Everyone seemed to be in the spirit now as word of the holiday spread throughout the Academy. Even the new reapers who hadn't been at dinner were finding out, becoming ecstatic about the chance at some freedom. Most were running back to their rooms to change quickly so they could get a jump on the night's festivities.

"Let me get this straight," Maple said, summing up Headmaster Tyflin. "One of the biggest rules just goes out the window on October thirty-first? All so we can go play tricks on the living?"

"Isn't it glorious!" said Q. "We get to wreak some havoc. All Hallows Eve is the only time we can impact the grounder's world. We have to take advantage!" He threw his arm around Shawn's shoulder.

"And there are no consequences?" Maple continued.

Q rolled his eyes. "Gosh, for someone given a free pass, you ask a lot of questions. We probably are fine as long as stay within reason."

Shawn laughed. "Who determines this reason, Q? The almighty Headmaster Tyflin?"

"Don't know! Rupert didn't mention specifics. Come on, we're burning pranking time. I told Rupert we'd meet him by the mustang circle soon."

Maple rolled her eyes "Yes, because the man who likes to play tricks on people here is the one we should be trusting."

Q tapped Shawn's chest with his free hand. "See, she gets it!"

"You two have fun scaring the helpless grounders. I'm going to explore that library a little more."

"Her loss," Q said as she walked away.

Black and orange striped blazers with tiny purple pocket squares littered the hallways of the Academy. Everyone was wearing the exact same thing.

"Guess we didn't get the memo?" Shawn said.

"No Shawnie boy, the question you should ask is, 'Where do we get ours from?'"

"Try your room," said a guy fiddling with his black bowtie. "At least that's where I found mine."

"Thanks, man. Wait, do I know you?" Shawn asked, thinking the voice sounded familiar.

"I think the last time you saw me, I was hiding from the world underneath a blanket." The boy with an unruly mop of black hair stuck out his hand. "Onyx."

Shawn shook his hand as he remembered the frightened boy from the clubhouse. "Nice to finally be introduced to you."

"Pile of laundry! Good to see you again, mate." Q pulled them both into a bear hug mid-handshake. "My day ones, ready to take on All Hallows Eve together?"

Perplexation spread across Onyx's face, making Shawn feel secondhand embarrassment.

Shawn maneuvered out of Q's grasp. "What my deranged friend here is trying to ask is if you want to join us on this exhibition?"

Onyx shrugged. "Sure, why not. Don't have any plans. I'd be down for a little mischief."

"We'll get along swimmingly then!" Q said. "I hope you're ready, because Rupes and I have a great plan mapped out for the night. We're going to get the full experience it seems."

"Um, full experience?" Onyx asked, looking to Shawn and seeming a bit taken aback by Q's energy.

"Ignore him. Just meet us in the mustang circle in ten minutes." Shawn grabbed Q by the arm, leading him away before he could scare off the poor guy.

Onyx was right. Lying on the bed were the traditional garments for the night. On top of the clothes was a piece of parchment paper. *Enjoy your first All Hallows Eve! -Carlin.* Shawn threw on the new clothes, surprised that they fit okay. He had to tighten the orange belt a little so his pants wouldn't fall off, but the jacket fit fine. He wasn't too keen on the orange socks and black dress shoes, but he liked the shirt.

"Nice jacket," said Jay, leaning in from the doorway.

"You have one too, you know."

Jay picked up the jacket and gave Shawn a 'You have to be kidding me' face.

"Well, if you can't beat them..." Shawn said.

"This isn't mandatory. Count me out." Jay said, putting down the jacket.

A knock at the door interrupted them. "Ding. Time to go, Shawnie boy." Q looked from Jay to Shawn, noticing that Jay hadn't changed. He sauntered into the room and grabbed the shirt off Jay's bed. "Let's go, pretty boy. Put this on and meet us outside in three minutes." He tossed the shirt at Jay's face.

Jay hesitated. "Fine. I'll go."

Q clapped. "Awesome! Now Shawn, let me see you in the proper hallway light, you dashing son of a bitch."

Chapter 17

The entire courtyard was adorned with decorations. In the small amount of time it had taken Shawn to change, Wayward Academy had been completely transformed. Whoever had decorated the area decided they only needed candles and pumpkins, and the effect was dazzling. Piles and piles of pumpkins were spread out in the dirt surrounding the Academy, illuminated by sconces that slowly dripped wax.

Most reapers were teaming up, deciding where to go. City, farmland, campgrounds–each group grinned at the possibilities. Shawn spotted Rupert by the eternal flame; he was gazing around, taking in the euphoric atmosphere.

Making eye contact with Shawn, Rupert meandered his way through the crowd. "Well, well, well. Looks like we have three joining us on this fine evening! You guys are in for a... treat."

The weak pun got a chuckle from Q. And even Jay cracked a smile.

Rupert looked at Jay. "Who's the sour face?"

"Sour face can talk for himself," Jay said.

"Rupert, this is my roommate, Jay." Shawn answered for him anyway, not needing a fight to start brewing. He had a feeling that these two wouldn't get along very well.

"Nice to meet ya, blackeye."

"You too, One-eyed Rupert."

Shawn took another opportunity to cut in. "What's the plan tonight, Rupert?"

"Yes, do tell! Is it to a graveyard or a haunted house?" Q asked, refraining from listing off every possibility.

"It's all about the clientele for tonight. You see these people around you?" Rupert asked as the crowd started to disperse in different directions. "Many will go wait hours in an empty cemetery, hoping that a grounder will show up. Others will go into the city, where it's crowded and hard to mess with anyone. And going to a haunted house is pointless: grounders go there *wanting* to be scared. No, I have something much better in mind." He let the comment hang to build suspense. "We're crashing a Halloween party."

"A party?" Jay chimed in. "That's the big plan?"

Rupert sighed and adjusted his eye patch. "We go to these parties, because they're full of naïve, drunk, scared grounders who'll take the 'supernatural' the most serious. You're welcome to go somewhere else on your own if you want."

No one had any arguments. Or anywhere else to go.

"That's what I thought. Let's get walking!" Rupert turned and starting down one of the mustang paths.

"Wait!" A voice called from behind them. Everyone turned to see Onyx jogging up the path. Shawn had completely forgotten about him.

"You are?" Rupert questioned, puzzled by the first year who was trying to join his party.

"Onyx. Sorry, I wasn't sure you were coming for a minute. Glad you could make it," Shawn said as Onyx introduced himself to Jay and Rupert.

"Welcome to the club, Ox boy. Anyone else joining us that I don't know about?" Rupert asked, slightly annoyed.

Everyone shook their heads.

"Good. Let's move it then."

They walked for about twenty minutes before they came to an open gate devoid of gargoyles.

"They leave the doors open most of the night and let us do our thing unsupervised," Rupert explained.

Unsupervised? Shawn glanced at Jay. If Jay was going to run, tonight would be the perfect opportunity.

Shawn expected another set of stairs. And he got them. It seemed that it was the only way up to the surface from the Academy. His legs were going to be in great shape in couple of months if he had to keep doing this. This time, though, the smell coming from above was nudging its way inside his nose.

"What is that?" Q asked as he pinched the bridge of his nose.

Rupert laughed. "Not every gate leads to pleasant places, gentlemen."

Pleasant places? A cemetery wasn't Shawn's idea of pleasant.

When they reached the door, Rupert unlocked it, unleashing a full wave of the smell. Shawn's eyes watered and Q gagged as he stepped through. Sewer water. They'd come up into a sewer. Everyone stayed as far away from the brown murky water as they could.

"That better be where we're going up," Jay said pointing to a ladder a short distance away.

"You newbies need to suck it up. This is our holiday. Enjoy it!" For emphasis, Rupert made it a point to take a large sniff of the air before ascending the ladder.

Streetlights greeted Shawn as he clambered out onto the street. They'd come up in the middle of a suburban area. All around them, children were walking with their candy bags open from house to house. Parents trailed slightly behind, waiting for the night to be over. The houses themselves were typical middle-class homes, complete with cheesy Halloween decorations and over-the-top lights.

"Gotta say, I didn't expect to be climbing out of a manhole cover tonight," Shawn said, grabbing Onyx's hand as helped him climb out. Shawn was happy to get out of the sewer system. But he had to wonder, where else did the gates lead to?

"Of all the things happening tonight, that might just be the most normal thing you do," Jay chided Shawn.

"You feel that boys? That's our future. Let it fill you up." Rupert spread his arms wide and howled at the moon. None of the trick or treaters reacted as his voice carried across the neighborhood.

"Is he okay?" Onyx asked.

Shawn shook his head. What exactly had he gotten himself into? "I think this is normal behavior."

"What's the plan?" Jay asked, clearly regretting his choice to join them tonight. A group of middle schoolers walked by in what might have been a modern take on vampires. The group of reapers had to split to make a path as they walked by in band t-shirts and fangs.

"The house is about two blocks from here, so stick close," Rupert said. He walked over to a young kid and grabbed a piece of candy from his bag, holding it in front of his face. The child's eyes widened at the candy that appeared to be floating in front of him. Rupert then unwrapped it, eating the chocolate and quickly put the wrapper in the child's bag. He ran away laughing as the kid stood petrified on the sidewalk, his mother trying to drag him along to the next house.

Q quickly ran after, cackling at the terror that spread across the child's face. Were these how ghost stories started? Should Shawn be messing with the people he passed by? Each time he passed someone, he did a double take, debating on pranking them. After seeing Rupert make another child cry, he opted to just observe the theatrics of the night.

Onyx handed him a flask. "Here this should help."

"With what exactly?" Shawn asked him as he took a sip anyway. Tequila coated his throat, burning its way down to his stomach. He coughed as he handed it back to Onyx.

"With pranking people tonight. Or the fact that we're dead. How we've seen people die in front of us. Take your pick." He said after taking a swig. Onyx didn't seem to be enjoying his newfound afterlife. He was shaking, and Shawn didn't think it was because of the alcohol.

"What was your first observation like?" Shawn wondered if Onyx had a nasty run-in like some of the other new reapers.

Sweat dripped down Onyx's face as he recalled his first time in the field. "I saw a teenager overdose."

Shawn didn't know what to say to that, so he let Onyx continue.

"I watched the father find him... It... it was the hardest thing I've ever seen." Onyx took another swig of his flask, letting the liquid wash away his memory. "But I guess that's our job, eh?"

Shawn took the flask back, taking another mouthful as the group approached their destination.

The music was barely audible from the outside as they came up to a typical two-story home. Nothing distinguished it from the rest of the cookie-cutter neighborhood. It even had tacky Halloween decorations that aimed for cute rather than scary. Without waiting for an invitation, Rupert walked in like he owned the place.

"How did he hear about a party?" Jay asked Shawn.

"No clue." Shawn shrugged. It was strange that Rupert knew of a grounder party miles away, but he wasn't going to question it.

Inside the house, the decorations spread out like sand in a desert; everywhere you looked, something was covered in a spiderweb or fake blood.

"Could use better decorations, eh Q?" Shawn looked over his shoulder at his friend, who'd stayed outside on the front porch, the door wide open. "Are you waiting for an invitation, man?"

"Wait for it," Q said, smiling.

"Huh? What do yo—"

"Kevin! Close the door next time you come in, man. Damn. Trying not to let the bugs in."

A kid in a superhero cape walked over and shut the door. He'd just started walking away when the front door was thrown open, crashing against the wall. His cape fluttered as he jumped and screamed "What da hell!?"

Q walked in giggling and immediately grabbed the door, slamming it shut.

The guy's jaw dropped like it had become unattached. He started backing up slowly. Jay was in the direct path of where the kid was headed. But instead of getting out of the way, like they'd been taught, he held his ground. Sure enough, the cape boy backed right into Jay, ruffling his new coat. The kid spun around, only to be met with air. There was no reason for him to have stopped: at least, nothing he could see. "Oh, fuck this," he whispered and then ran up the stairs.

Q keeled over in laughter. "Did you see the look on his face? That was fucking priceless, mate." Q grabbed Shawn's shoulder, laughing. "Now let's go scare some kiddies."

What Rupert had forgotten to mention was obvious the minute they looked around at the party attendees: there were no adults. Judging by the spread on the counter, someone's parents were going to come home to most of their liquor cabinet missing.

"He does know that we're about the same age as most of these grounders, right?" Jay rolled a cup between his hands and then looked around, wondering if anyone saw.

"At least they'll be easier to mess with," Onyx said.

"Why's that?" Shawn asked.

"Because drunk teenagers are gullible." Onyx shoved a glass off the counter for emphasis. The crashing alerted one of the cowboys attending the party.

"Dammit, Chad!" the tipsy cowboy yelled.

"See. Told ya," Onyx said, smirking.

Most of the party was in the basement, where the music was vibrating the walls. Shawn was concerned about being in such a tight space with a bunch of people around, but he had to keep reminding himself that it didn't matter if he bumped into one.

Q wandered upstairs, following a couple that was sneaking off. Poor souls had no idea what they were in for.

Shawn glanced up at the closed bedroom door. "We should probably go find Rupert. Did either of you two see where he went?"

Onyx pointed to the stairs. "Pretty sure he's down there."

Navigating the steps was tricky because they didn't want to alert everyone of their presence just yet. So, they couldn't shove someone, but they also couldn't let someone else catch up. Jay and Shawn waited for an opening and shot the gap as soon as it became available.

A group of zombie cheerleaders were headed up the stairs. Most had their hair in pigtails and blood dripping down their faces, staining their "uniforms". Shawn flattened against the wall as best as he could so they could pass. When the last one was on the step below Shawn, a partygoer ran into his back, causing Shawn to collide face-first into the undead cheer captain. Her body banged against the wall as drinks went flying. Shawn, meanwhile, tripped the last four steps down before ultimately landing square on his chest.

"Fucking asshole," the cheerleader called out.

"Sorry." The boy who ran into Shawn apologized, not realizing he wasn't the one who'd knocked her over.

Jay stood over Shawn, trying his best to hold in his laughter. The air blowing hard out his nostrils gave him away though.

"I don't want to hear it," Shawn croaked as he got up.

A voice called out at the top of the stairs. "Hey, Humpty Dumpty!" Q said, making his way down, apparently done messing with the couple.

"Nice of you to join us, Q," Jay said, smiling.

A waving hand called them over to the drink table. Onyx had found Rupert during Shawn's entrance. Spread out on the table were five shot glasses of various liquors. Warm sensations in Shawn's stomach reminded him that he was still processing the swigs he'd taken earlier.

"Pick your poison, gentlemen. Because the night is young, and there are talks about a Ouija board. Until it arrives, play lightly, because it's the grand prize. Happy first Hallows Eve, now let it be one you never forget!"

They all downed their shots. Jay looked unfazed, but Q looked like he was turning an odd shade of green.

Rupert went off to slowly mess with the partygoers, whether it was spiking the punch more, lifting wallets, or slowly levitating things out of the corner of people's view. Jay went off to observe from the corner, apparently not into the scene yet.

"How was upstairs?" Onyx asked Q.

This gave Q the perfect excuse to go into the lengthy story of how he'd put on the clothes of whoever had lived there to create an "invisible man look". The couple was so terrified that they ran out the door still in their underwear.

With Onyx completely captivated by the couple screaming down the street, Shawn explored the party. Lots of drunk kids, or kids pretending to be drunk, walking around gossiping. Someone shouted something about spin the bottle, and they all laughed. Shawn wondered how many moments like this he would now miss. While his grounder life friends moved on with their lives, he was stuck observing from the shadows.

" *When* I hit this with my eyes closed, you owe me." An arrogant statement made by a rich white male. Shawn wished he could say he was shocked. Maybe he should get into the All Hallows Eve spirit after all. He walked closer to the dart board.

The guy was winding up his arm like he was some major league baseball player; Shawn was betting the closest he would get would be dressing up like one. The guy covered his eyes with his hand and looked away, trying to make a show of it.

Shawn grabbed the corner of the dartboard, feeling the cracks in the cheap plastic. As soon as the dart was released from the boy's hand, Shawn yanked the dart board off the wall as hard as he could. A piece of the board broke off as the dart sailed past, embedding itself into the drywall.

"Shit! What the hell was that??" the baseball player screamed.

Even the girl he was with looked terrified. "The wind probably..."

"Yeah, the wind... inside a basement... with no windows. God, Cynthia, you're so dumb."

Shawn walked away, laughing as they continued bickering. Young love. A tap on Shawn's shoulder made him turn around.

"Looks like someone is finally participating!" Q was giddy with excitement.

Shawn's eyes shifted over to the corner where Jay had been. It was now empty as Jay walked around purposely hitting people's drinks up when they were taking sips to splash them in the face.

"Jay Musters having fun? Now I've seen everything," Shawn said, feigning shock.

Q took a bow. "You have yours truly to thank for that. No one can resist my charm."

Before Shawn had time to respond with a sarcastic remark, Rupert came down the stairs in a flurry. "It's show time, boys!" Following behind Rupert was a grounder with a box in his hand: the oh-so-powerful Ouija board. "Now everyone, go to a corner of the room and get ready to toss something. I'll build up the suspense."

"Wait. We're about to trash this party?" Onyx asked.

Rupert shook his head. "No no. Well, kind of. Just need to liven the party up a bit, dear lad. Now, places people!" He shooed everyone away as a crowd gathered in the middle of the room.

Everyone was joking about ghosts and the afterlife as they fooled around with the plastic triangle. Would this have been Shawn today if he hadn't died? Without a care in the world, joking about dead spirits?

"Oh, great powers beyond us, we welcome you into our home. Now, is there anyone out there?" A grounder in overalls with a straw hat asked.

The piece moved slightly, but Rupert stood by doing nothing.

"Hey Rupert, aren't you missing your chance?" Onyx called out.

"Just wait, young'un. Most of the time one of them is usually moving it. I'll get my opportunity."

This went on for a little bit, with the kids bickering back and forth about who was moving it. "This is stupid; it doesn't even work!" One said as he lifted his finger off the piece.

"Baby, get ready," Rupert said giddily. Shawn could now see how this was the kid who pretended to be his roommate that first day. He lived for these kinds of things.

Every kid participating slowly took their fingers off the triangle; that was when Rupert struck. He reached down and knocked the piece over. The party went silent, except for the music playing in the background.

"Ha. Okay, who did that?" someone asked.

Rupert picked the piece up and started moving it slowly across the board as people started screaming. Everyone backed up, and some grounders ran up the stairs. Rupert made sure each letter was painstakingly obvious as he settled on each one. "I. D.I.D." He dug the letters into the cardboard.

A girl in a dinosaur costume stuttered, "Wha... what do you want?"

Rupert was laughing as he moved the board to one single letter: U. Then he started widely moving around the plastic triangle over random letters. "Get ready," Rupert shouted. He settled on the part of the board that usually ends the 'game': Goodbye. He flipped the board up into the air, screaming, "Now!"

Q threw the chip bowl and cookie platter up, scattering the food across the group. Screams and feet headed for the staircase.

Shawn grabbed a lamp, lifted it above his head, and started running around the room. He could only imagine how a levitating lamp would look to these kids. Onyx grabbed decorations and ripped them off the walls. Even Jay was getting in on it as he knocked over chairs.

All the dressed-up grounders trampled each other to get out, and within two minutes, the basement had cleared. The five of them looked around the room at the destroyed party. They fell to the floor laughing.

"I guarantee you, this will be a night they'll never forget." Q wiped tears of laughter from his eyes.

Onyx responded in head nods, not able to get a breath in between laughs. It took about five minutes for them all to settle down. "I swear I thought one of them would pass out."

Walking over to the wall, Rupert started spelling out something in ketchup. "This should do it." He started spreading out his message across the entire wall in bright red ketchup.

"I am the future?" Shawn asked, puzzled.

Rupert snorted. "I don't know. Last year I put, "Check in aisle two."

They all looked at each other and broke down one more time.

The five of them went upstairs to see if anyone had bothered to stay after their little All Hallows Eve production. Most of the party had emptied out, but there were some partygoers milling around. Shawn figured these were the ones who'd stayed upstairs and didn't know about the basement scene.

A group of grounders were discussing barricading the door, while another group were playing drinking games behind them. Both groups just wanted to keep the party going. Shawn wouldn't argue with Rupert again: he'd chosen the perfect outing for their first reaper holiday.

"Their solution to stop a ghost was to barricade the door... and then party upstairs?" Onyx scratched his scalp.

Rupert threw his arms around him. "Ignorance is fucking bliss."

Shawn tapped Q on the shoulder and had to yell over the music, which was now causing frames to shake on the walls. "I'm going to head outside for a bit!"

Q threw Shawn the thumbs-up, most likely not hearing a word he'd said. Shawn needed fresh air.

Stepping outside, wind filled his jacket, making it flow behind him. Shawn took a deep breath and closed his eyes. Yes, this was much better. Streetlamps bathed the sidewalk in light and illuminated the trick or treaters still out.

A family was walking ahead with their two young children, and Shawn followed them for a couple houses. One of the kids turned around and seemed to stare straight through him. Shawn put his hands in his pockets and headed in another direction, leaving the kid on the sidewalk to watch empty air.

The music could now be heard from down the street. Someone had turned it up. Shawn was looking for the red and blue lights to come down the street at any second.

"Hey, jackass," one of the partiers called out.

No one was outside the house at least, but Shawn guessed that the neighbors weren't too pleased.

"Just going to ignore me, Stripes?" the voice called out again.

Turning to one of the areas between houses, Shawn squinted in the light. He could made out one of the zombie cheerleaders, who was glaring right at him. No one else was around.

Chapter 18

"Are you talking to me?" He asked softly, still expecting someone to pop up from behind a bush or tree.

The girl undid one of her pigtails and ran her fingers through her dreads like a rake. "Oh, shit. No. I was talking to that lamp post behind you. Please, by all means, carry on."

She could see him. She could hear him.

"You do understand English, correct?"

Shawn started freaking out. "I thought reapers were supposed to wear these suits on All Hallows Eve?"

"You blind too? I'm dressed up as a stupid zombie cheerleader. And that, Sir, isn't a Grim Reaper costume. Although the Grim Reaper would have been more my speed."

Saliva built up under his tongue, and Shawn stumbled forward. She didn't know what a reaper was. What the hell was the protocol for this? "Uhh..."

"I figured you came out here to apologize."

"Apologize?"

"Weren't you the one that ran into me on the stairs? Or was it another one of your striped friends?" She narrowed her eyes a bit more as Shawn got closer. "Wait, I remember you! You ran into me at the park the other day too. Stripes, are you stalking me?"

The park? Where the man had the heart attack? Oh, no. She was the one he'd bumped into, running after the jogger. He could now picture her sitting around with her friends, soaking up the sunshine. He needed to speak, yet no words were being communicated from his brain to his mouth.

"You don't look good, Stripes," she said, getting up off the porch. Pressure was building in his throat as more saliva pooled in his mouth. Suddenly, he darted for a bush and emptied the contents of his stomach, each heave causing him to shake like a rattle.

"Jeez, I can smell the liquor from here. Next time don't take so many shots with your barbershop quintet."

He wiped his mouth on the sleeve of his jacket. "You saw them? You haven't spoken to them, have you?" What in the world was going on? Adriana and Trevor never mentioned anything to him about grounders suddenly being able to see him. Was this a test?

She laughed. “Hard to miss those ensembles. And no, I’ve been out here since you bumped into me. But I can go get them if you want.”

“No!” He said too quickly.

She stared back.

“I can’t have them see me this way.”

“Don’t want them to know you’re a lightweight? Gotcha. Whatever you say, Stripes.”

“You’re not going back into the party?” he asked as he sat down on the curb, the concrete digging into his bottom. How much damage did he have to contain?

The girl thought for a second. “Hell no. Pretty sure the cops were called. A bunch of kids ran out screaming.”

At least that meant she hadn’t seen the Ouija board incident, and she wouldn’t interact with any of the other reapers.

“I’d offer you some water, but I got nothing,” she said.

“No problem. I’ll be fine.” He let the sentence hang, checking for other people. If she could see him, then it was possible others could too.

A man and his daughter walked by, but they were preoccupied. They continued past as the daughter complained about going to another house.

Zombie cheerleader pulled her dreadlocks to one side of her shoulder. “Did you just move here or something? Besides the park, I haven’t seen you around before.”

“College, actually.” Shawn hoped she wouldn’t ask a lot of questions. He had no idea what town he was in, let alone what colleges were nearby. He also looked way too young to be in college. The last time he went to a PG13 movie, he even got carded.

“Higher education has done wonders for your conversational skills.” She sized him up as he sat on the concrete steps of the empty house. “Not much of a partier, are you?”

Shawn glanced at the bush containing the regurgitated shots from earlier. "Not sure anything I said to you would convince you otherwise."

"Parties are overrated anyway. Everyone goes around pretending to be something they're not. I mean look at me." She gestured to the blood on her cheerleading uniform. "I wanted to be a zombie president."

"You're still a zombie at least." Shawn debated what he needed to do. Should he stay and try to figure out how she was able to see him? That would mean risk getting other reapers exposed... and if this was a test, then he'd fail. Although if he left before figuring it out, then he might fail as well.

"My friends modified my idea. Lupa wanted to impress some boy. So, that's why I got stuck in this stupid get-up. But I like the barbershop quintet idea: everyone else is too cliché around here."

As the girl kept talking, Shawn continued to freak out inside. "Your outfit might be cliché, but it could be worse. At least you're not getting huge pit stains from wearing a suit at a party."

She laughed at this, which felt like a win to Shawn. And it was true, the dampness under his arms was spreading. He needed to get out of here. "Well, it was nice meeting–"

"Cirie." She stuck out her hand, which Shawn's sweaty palms took.

"Shawn." Why didn't he give a fake name? He needed to get away and never see this girl again.

They unclasped hands and she immediately wiped hers off, not saying a word about the sweat.

"Well, nice meeting you, Shawn. Do me a favor next time, okay?"

"What's that?"

"Don't run into me," she joked. "I'll see you around, Stripes."

He stood up and shook off tiny bits of dirt from his pants. "Oh, I doubt it," he whispered under his breath as he waved. It took every nerve in his body not to sprint away.

The walk back seemed to take an eternity for Shawn. Each time the group went around the corner, he expected to see the girl with dreadlocks waiting, a blade in hand. Shawn couldn't shake Cirie from his head. Up ahead, Rupert and Q were bouncing from step to step, hyped up on the turmoil they had caused.

"What do you think?' Onyx asked, walking beside him and Jay.

"About tonight? It was fun. I can see why everyone was excited about it." Shawn didn't put enough enthusiasm in his voice because Onyx waited for more. Shawn smiled instead. All he wanted was to be back in his bed at the Academy.

"And... Wayward?" Onyx slowly shifted his head around when he said it.

"I think we do a necessary job. Maybe not one we ever wanted, but one where we're needed," Shawn answered automatically. His mind was still on the encounter. The woods around them seemed to eat whatever was said, the words shifting between the bark and into oblivion.

Onyx continued playing with his button. "I agree about the job. it's just—"

"Just what?" Jay jumped in.

"Do you really think we should have the power to decide who lives and who dies?"

"Remember we're *just* the messengers, not the executioner. We don't decide *anything*," Jay said sarcastically.

Onyx let go of a breath that he had been was holding. "You're right. I'm just in my own head. I think I just misunderstood."

Flickering orange specs dotted their vision, welcoming them back to the Academy grounds. Most reapers were making their way back to the dining hall. The crowd was gathering around the tables; everyone was celebrating their night of shenanigans against the grounders.

On the center table were pearl-colored goblets engraved with the Wayward initials. Every first-year grabbed one and had it filled as older reapers walked around dispersing wine. It looked like the second years had navy goblets, the thirds had maroon, and the fourth years had charcoal ones.

Shawn grabbed a cup and was surprised by how heavy the pearl goblet was.

"Every new class gets a different color," said Trevor, appearing out of nowhere, holding wine, and filling it to the brim. He then thrust a goblet into Onyx's hands and poured so much it almost overflowed. "This is the end of the celebration but the beginning of the work for you all. Big days ahead."

Rupert had disappeared within the crowd, but Shawn could see Q forcing Jay to clink his mug. Jay reluctantly did so, and they both took a sip.

"What do you mean?" Onyx asked.

"Soon, you'll all know who'll be mustangs, who'll be talons, and who'll be blades." On that note, Trevor left and filled up more pearl-colored cups.

Shawn and Onyx looked at each other. Shawn hoped that he was anything but a blade. That way he could get his first reaping over with and never have to reap another soul again.

"To figuring out who we are in this life," Onyx said, holding up his goblet. "And to not looking back."

They clinked, causing some of the wine to spill onto Shawn's coat, creating a dark wet circle around his wrist. The liquid was warm and soothed his throat, immediately relaxing Shawn. He hadn't realized how thirsty he'd been. After his time in the bushes, he didn't think he wanted any wine, but he was thirsty. The wine had a slight hint of pumpkin that lingered on his tongue. With each sip, he enjoyed it more and more, and after the Cirie encounter, he needed some liquid strength. By the third goblet, he couldn't taste anything.

"I'm heading back to the room," a stumbling Jay said.

Shawn thought about another goblet, but his bed was calling. With every step, his knees shook, teetering on the line between support or collapse.

"You look like an old man the way you're shaking."

"Shut up. You're one to talk, stumble stiltskin." They both chuckled at his horrible joke. "Did you ever get drunk when you were alive?"

"Oh, yeah." No hesitation from Jay.

"I never did." Shawn had a couple of drinks here and there, but never this much in one night. He felt funny. He fumbled for the doorknob, before finally finding it.

“You’ve punched that card now, dude,” Jay said, collapsing on his bed.

Shawn shut the door. “I don’t feel great.”

“I don’t feel great,” Jay mocked, his eyes fluttering closed.

Shawn laid down, letting the bed envelop his body and form around him like a cocoon. The wine sloshed inside him, but oddly, he didn’t feel sick. He went to lay his head on the pillow and was out before he made contact.

Chapter 19

Shawn woke up to darkness. He was worried that his head would be killing him, but it felt fine. His stomach didn't even hurt. His body, on the other hand, ached everywhere. The pain started in his legs and crawled its way up into his back, all the way to his arms. Was this what a hangover felt like?

He couldn't remember if he'd put water on his nightstand. He reached out, hoping for a miracle. He got about an inch before his fingers hit something. Something that wasn't supposed to be there. He felt up and down the wall. Wood. A pungent cedar smell was the only scent around him. His mind started racing. He reached out on the other side and felt the grooves of another wooden panel scratching along his fingertips. He took a deep breath to try and calm his nerves, blowing the air out of his mouth; warm air washed back over his face. He raised his arms to discover what he already feared: there was a wooden lid above him as well. This darkness wouldn't be fading away. Whatever had happened between falling asleep and now, he didn't know. What he did know was that he was trapped in a wooden box—or more accurately, a coffin.

"Help!" His voice cracked as he screamed out. Would anyone even hear him? He guessed it depended on how deep he was, or if anyone was looking for him. What terrified him the most was how much air he had. Control your breathing. Isn't that what they said? That one could lose a lot of air from panicking? Funny how things rushed to his mind as soon as there was danger.

Using his hands, he slowly felt around what was within arm's reach of his tiny box but found nothing. He had no idea what to do. He stopped moving for a second and listened. Wasting time screaming was only going to screw himself over, but if someone walked by, he might be able to hear them.

Shawn closed his eyes; he knew it made no difference, but it helped him concentrate solely on his hearing. A muffled noise was coming from nearby, although he couldn't place it. Turning his ear toward the ground, he waited for more sounds. After a couple more minutes of silence, he went back on his first thought and screamed. He didn't want whatever noise that he'd heard to get far away. Releasing everything he had, he let out a blood-freezing scream. One that he hoped would spread out of his box and into the dirt like the roots of a tree. He waited again.

Nothing. He screamed one more time, his throat agonizing over the lack of water. Did anyone even hear it? Could he be imagining this? The thought of dying, again, in a hole in the ground, with no reason made him angry.

Shawn picked up a muffled scream. This time, he put his head against the wall of his coffin, letting the wood soothe his ear. That's when he heard the noise again, and suddenly his coffin seemed a lot smaller. Because the muffled noise sounded a lot like a muffled cry for help, and that cry seemed to be coming from below ground, not above it. He wasn't the only one buried alive.

He had to get himself out. Simple as that. Each second that passed made Shawn more uncomfortable. His body was starting to freak out. His legs wanted to move, and knowing they were confined made him twitch. He. Had. To. Get. Out.

Running his hands along the wall, he felt the wood again. "Fuck!" His breath escaped his lips as a splinter entered his ring finger. Well, he definitely wasn't dreaming. His finger throbbed from the wood that had slithered its way into his skin. He laughed. Slowly at first, then he freed it. His whole body was shaking with laughter. Here he was, having died, forced into service in the afterlife, and stuck in a freaking coffin. Shawn's eyes leaked, and he was just able to maneuver his hands to wipe the sporadic tears.

No. He wouldn't die buried in some damn coffin. At least, not willingly. "Think," he whispered. He felt the marks on his arms he got when passing out on a mattress. He always woke up with the imprint all over his skin. That meant he hadn't been buried that long, as such marks went away after an hour or so. Okay, good. If he hadn't been buried long, then the dirt had just been dug up.

With all the force he could muster, Shawn threw his fist at the wood just below his chin. More splinters entered his hand, but Shawn barely felt these ones. Soon he was punching the same spot over and over again, jack-hammering his fists in the little space he had inside. He was screaming as he did it: fist, wood, fist, wood, fist, wood. It became therapeutic in a strange way.

He could feel the wood cracking as he pounded it, and soil slowly started filtering through the cracks he'd provided. After about five minutes of continuous pounding, he was gasping for breath, and Shawn feared that his stupid idea might have cost him all the air inside. But it was too late to do anything else.

Pieces of wood were loose enough that he was able to break some off. As soon as he broke off a piece, the dirt started filling in what little room was left in the coffin. It was difficult not to panic as it started to fall. The only thing he could hope for was that he wasn't buried deep. Otherwise, he was screwed.

He started shoving as much dirt as he could to the bottom of the coffin. Both eyes were stinging from where the dirt was falling. He broke a couple more pieces of wood off, desperately trying to form a circle through which he could push his body through. Soil started flowing with each piece that was broken off. He took one more big breath and then tore out a large chunk of the lid. Eyes still closed, he pushed up as soon as the piece was separated. He broke through the surface easily. Fresh air hit him from all sides.

He gasped for air. The rocks from the ceiling were too bright. He tried squinting, but the light mixed in with the dirt, stinging his eyes. He focused on getting air into his lungs while he tried to free the bottom portion of his body.

"Shawn!" Hands pulled him the rest of the way out of the ground. Shawn had to wipe more dirt from his eyes but was able to make out Jay's dirt-coated face. "Look, not a lot of time to talk. As soon as you're okay, we need to help the others." With that, Jay was gone. He walked a short distance away where two other kids were helping him dig.

Jay. Alive. Shawn was in shock, but he wasn't surprised that Jay had made it out of the coffin. He wheezed air back into his dirt-infested lungs. All around him, dots faded in and out of his vision from the lack of air. He could make out blobs of trees shifting into focus as he regained oxygen into his bloodstream. With each breath, more of the dots disappeared. His leg muscles ached as he stood up, a reminder of the confinement below.

Shawn looked around at his surroundings. Headstones were plotted in neat rows across the ground. He was in a graveyard. He looked back at his plot, examining the headstone for his hole. His full name was chiseled into the stone. A shiver went up his spine.

A gargoyle sat on a stump just outside the fencing of the cemetery, observing.

"Hey!" Shawn coughed out. "Hey, help us!"

The gargoyle cocked his head to the side, but that was the only response Shawn got out of him.

"Asshole," he whispered as he went over to where Jay and two others were furiously digging.

"None of those fucking gargoyles are a help. Don't waste your breath." Jay was drenched in sweat, his shirt becoming a wet rag. "You." He pointed to the kid with a buzzcut. "Go with Shawn and keep digging. I'm not sure how much longer any of them will have."

The kid nodded and took Shawn's arm to the plot one over. Lance Philon. That was the name engraved onto the headstone. Dirt stuffed itself underneath Shawn's nails as he scooped handful after handful. Almost like he was playing at the beach digging a moat, except in this case, it was to save someone's life.

"How many graves are there?" Shawn asked.

Buzzcut grunted. "Haven't had a chance to count. Too many for all of us to dig out," he said without looking up. Surrounding them were rows of graves, at least a couple dozen.

Buzzcut was right: they couldn't get to them in time. There was no way. Shawn could only hope that more would be able to dig themselves out.

It didn't take them long to reach the top of the coffin. The two of them put their hands on either side, desperately trying to get the lid off. Dirt tumbled off as they opened the lid. Lance lay there, eyes closed. Shawn leaned down, expecting the worst, but he could see the rise and fall of the boy's chest. Plus, no orb. Looks like Lance would escape this nightmare. He'd wake up confused but safe. Lucky him.

A couple of rows away, they could hear someone trying to dig their way out. Everyone immediately went over to assist. A hand poked out of the dirt, flailing around, trying to grasp anything within reach. Shawn nabbed it and pulled as the others dug around. A girl emerged and quickly clawed at her chest, trying to get dirt away from her. No one had time to explain a lot to her, so they moved on to the next grave.

The name on the grave stuck out to him: Onyx. "This one," Shawn said to his new grave-digging friend. He couldn't hear anything coming from the grave, but it seemed like a lot of the reapers were still affected by whatever had caused them to pass out.

Time slowed down during these digs. Each handful of dirt only took a second to grab, yet Shawn still felt he was going too slow. Finally, he scratched the top paneling of the coffin. They started brushing the top of the lid, and that was when Shawn noticed the blue hue coming from beneath the wood. No!

"Onyx!" Shawn squeaked out, barely recognizing his own depleted voice. Shawn's partner stopped digging when he saw the light. "Come on! Don't stop!" Shawn yelled. After getting enough of the dirt off, he struggled to lift the top. Wood splintered as he forced the lid off.

Onyx was lying still in his All Hallows Eve jacket, with a blue orb sitting in the middle of his chest.

Shawn was numb. He was just talking to Onyx hours ago. He barely got to know him, but that didn't matter to Shawn. Of all the deaths he'd seen so far, this hit him the hardest. "I'm sorry. I'm so sorry." He let a few tears drop. He then looked around at the other graves still to be dug up. No matter how he felt, there was more work to be done. Kneeling at the next grave, he started on another pile of dirt, handful after handful. Onyx may be dead, but that didn't mean the next person would be.

Shawn and his partner were able to dig up five more people. Every grave had been dug up—fifty in total. It became easier as more people got involved, but it still took them an hour. Shawn was thankful the graves hadn't been deep. Otherwise, the outcome would have been more disastrous than it already was. Almost everyone lived, but six blue orbs reminded Shawn that not everyone would be rejoining them.

The group of survivors had gathered at the edge of the cemetery. No one wanted to go near the graves they'd been trapped under. A bell rung out from further in the woods. Jay noticed it first and nudged Shawn. The ringing was far away, echoing through the forest. No one had uttered a word after the last person had been dug up, but now no one was moving. What were they supposed to do next?

Gargoyles started emerging from the forest like a bad game of hide and seek. Even the one from the stump got up and started walking toward the graves. He stopped in front of an orb as if he were guarding it. A handful of other gargoyles did the same thing until each lost soul had its own personal gargoyle watchdog.

Shawn had already scanned the group of survivors, but he did it again anyway. Maple and Q weren't part of them. But none of the grave markers were theirs either. So, where was everyone else?

The gargoyles herded everyone into a single file line, each survivor flanked on both sides by the stone men. The gargoyle from the stump took the lead. "Follow us." His voice boomed out over the group.

Shawn expected the voice to sound raspy or even monotonic, but if he'd closed his eyes, it could have been anyone.

Shawn maneuvered his way up the line to where Jay was. "Odds on us being led to the slaughterhouse?" He asked.

"If they wanted us to die, they would have left us in deeper graves. Although cattle never know they're about to be killed either."

"Where is everyone else?" Shawn asked.

"Who said this was the only cemetery?" Jay replied.

Shawn waited for him to go on. But movement up ahead caught his attention. Through the trees off to his right, Shawn could make out flashes of more gargoyles filtering between branches. Then he caught sight of another reaper covered in dirt. Shawn didn't need Jay to clarify anything, because another group of survivors were being led in the same direction.

Chapter 20

The entire time they were led through the forest, Shawn kept his eyes on the other group. He couldn't see anything past the gray wall of gargoyles. Desperate to make out any familiar face, he had to catch himself after overlooking a tree root on the forest floor. Unlike orientation, everyone remained quiet. There were no outbursts or even questions. No one had enough energy to speak after their experience in the cemetery. Jay even kept his head lowered, shuffling with every step.

They didn't have to walk far before a structure came into view. Peaking above the tree line were blades moving in unison: a windmill. The watcher from the stump halted the line a short distance away from the base of the structure. Green paint was chipping off the corners of the windmill tower, and it didn't look like the faded blue trim had been touched in years. There didn't seem to be a reason to keep up its appearance. It was basically abandoned.

Five gargoyles stood at the circular base of the windmill, each one standing in front of a small blue barn door. While the doors themselves were chipping from the lack of care, written in fresh gold paint were the Wayward Academy initials; the ends of the letters swirled around the door like vines. Shawn was starting to feel like the cattle Jay had mentioned.

"We'll open the doors to five people at a time. The front person of each line enters. No talking." Leaving no room for questions, the lead gargoyle from each line escorted the first reaper to the door.

Everyone could see the five going in, but due to the way the gargoyles had herded them, no one could get a good view of the other lines. Shawn was third in line, so he only had two more chances to see if Maple and Q were in this mess as well. He didn't want to think of the other possibility.

Twenty minutes passed before the doors opened again. They all opened at once, waiting to receive the next five. None of the reapers from before walked out. If waking up in a coffin wasn't enough to scare him, seeing five reapers enter and none exit just added more fuel to the fire. Did they leave out the back? Were they still inside?

Jay was next. Shawn wanted to wish him luck but remained silent out of fear. He strode toward the open door with his head held high, glaring at the gargoyles. The anger seeped off him like steam as he entered. He never once looked back.

Shawn was next, and he still hadn't seen Maple or Q. His body ached from dehydration and from being kept in a box. He wondered how everyone else felt after digging people out of their own graves. He wasn't sure if he'd ever get another good night's sleep back at the Academy. Who knew where he might wake up? Shifting from foot to foot, Shawn tried to keep his mind occupied with anything besides what was happening inside the windmill.

This round lasted only fifteen minutes: again, no one emerged. It was Shawn's turn. Walking forward, he immediately looked at the other four companions. Curly red hair stood out to his left. Sophia had made it. He tried to give her a friendly smile, but she was too terrified to look around.

He needed to focus back on the situation. For all he knew, he was entering a kill house. The stump watcher escorted him all the way to the open door. Shawn wanted to yell at him or hit him. The gargoyles refused to help, and six new reapers had perished. It made Shawn's blood boil. He never felt closer to Jay. But while Jay would lash out, Shawn remained quiet, still afraid of repercussions. Stepping inside the door, Shawn gave one last glance over his shoulder, hoping for a glimpse of Maple or Q. Instead, all he viewed was a mill door being slammed two inches from his face.

Inside, his bare feet curled up. The prickly hay-covered floor dug into his heels. Candles illuminated the mostly empty room. A black stone table was off in the corner, a notepad sitting on its surface. Shawn immediately recognized Franklin in his blue tweed suit sitting behind the table. Another gargoyle in a black tunic stood in the corner, observing. Franklin gave a soft smile and adjusted the rim of his glasses.

"Welcome, Shawn. Glad to see you've made it to the second stage of testing."

Shawn felt anything but welcome. These two could do whatever they wanted to him; he was easily outnumbered.

Another large barn door was opposite from where Shawn had entered. This one only had the chipped dark blue paint on it: there was no WA in sight. That must be where all the other reapers went. Did they walk out? Or were they dragged out?

Stepping forward, Shawn felt something wet between his toes. At the center of the room, part of the hay was darker, so Shawn knelt down to examine it. He touched the damp spot, and his fingers came up coated in red liquid. Blood. What could he do? Jay was nowhere to be seen. Was this Jay's blood? He shot daggers at Franklin. "Why?"

"You're through the worst of it, Shawn," Franklin said calmly.

Did he actually believe the crap he was saying?

"The first stage is always the hardest, but it's necessary."

Shawn scoffed. "Necessary? Having children buried alive, gasping for air, helpless... was necessary?" He clutched the blood-soaked straw between his fingers, letting the loose pieces snap in his grasp.

"To become a part of the living dead. You must have the will to live. Not die. It sounds like something out of a horror story, I know. It's a system that we employ and all hate. But it's one that works."

Shawn let the straws drop to the ground. "Tell that to the kids still lying in the graveyard."

Franklin twitched at Shawn's comment. Good. Shawn wanted him unnerved.

"It's time for Stage Two," the gargoyle said, breaking the tension. He walked to the other door in the room and opened it.

Shawn wasn't sure what to expect, but it wasn't what waddled in. A curly-tailed pig entered, sniffing the ground. Shawn was so shocked by its appearance, he didn't see what was beyond the door. It was quickly closed off, before he could take a glimpse.

"What in the actual hell?" Shawn asked out loud, no longer caring how anyone perceived him. The gargoyle said nothing but tossed something that landed at Shawn's feet.

An oink escaped the pig as it sniffed the object. After realizing it wasn't for consumption, the pig went back to sniffing hay. Shawn leaned over and picked up the knife, which was light in his hand. He glanced at the pig solving the mystery of the bloody hay.

Franklin cleared his throat. "Can you kill this animal, Shawn?"

The knife suddenly felt heavier. "Can I?" Shawn glanced at the pig who'd decided to lie down. "Do I have to?"

Neither of them said anything. Franklin sat at his table, paper in hand, waiting for Shawn to make a move. Stage Two. He had to remember he was being tested. He thought back to his observations. No reaper was asked to kill their subject. But was killing a pig supposed to show he was okay with watching death? Did experiencing it first-hand mean that Shawn had come to terms with his purpose? No. He was a messenger of death, not the cause of it. Shawn crossed one leg under the other and sat down, letting the blood seep into his pants. He hoped that this was the right answer.

Franklin started muttering to himself and scribbled on the parchment. They let Shawn sit in silence, making him wonder how long the charade would go on. The entire time Shawn ignored everyone but the pig. He wondered if everyone was facing the same situation in the other rooms, or if this was unique for him.

Movement from the gargoyle made Shawn wonder if the test was ending. The stone man stood in front of him with an open facepalm. "Knife."

Shawn handed over the knife instantly, thankful to get the weapon out of his own hands. Standing up, he walked over to the door that led inside the mill. It didn't open. "Isn't the test done?" he asked, turning to Franklin.

A pig squeal came from behind Shawn.

He spun around to see blood pooling out of the hog's neck, mixing with the hay on the ground once again.

Franklin went over to the door and removed the bar that had kept it locked. "Thank you, Shawn. Will you take the pig into the mill with you?"

Shawn stared back at him. Was he that exhausted, or did Franklin actually ask him to drag a pig's dead carcass? After the last twenty-four hours, Shawn was too stunned to argue. Leaning down, he grabbed the front leg and started dragging it to the middle of the mill. He stopped at the doorway and stared back at Franklin.

"Shawn, it's over. All the testing is over, okay? I promise you, there aren't any more surprises. You did well."

Did well? Shawn started dragging the pig again, and the door closed behind him. There were still kids lying in a cemetery in the woods, and now he was moving a pig corpse. Shawn wished he'd done more.

A room of blood-splattered first years greeted him. Before Shawn had a chance to sit down, an older reaper directed him to another room to drop off the pig. He felt pathetic dragging the thing along slowly, but he didn't have a lot of strength left. The smell of the room was full of iron, and pig corpses were being stacked in piles. It seemed that everyone else had the same test as him.

"I'll take it from here. You're good to join the other first years," another senior reaper told him.

Shawn nodded and dropped the leg, which plopped against the hay. Back in the main part of the mill, Shawn found Jay sitting by himself. He was only part of the third group, so it looked like they'd be waiting awhile for the test to be finished. About half the hands in the room were painted in red, like they'd all started finger-painting with the blood. Jay's hands were as clean as Shawn's. But blood was splattered across his face, red dots acting as newly created freckles. Shawn could only imagine what he looked like.

"You didn't kill it," he said to Shawn's bloodless hands.

"Reapers aren't supposed to kill," Shawn answered robotically.

Jay shook his head. "You may just survive this place after all."

Sophia was the last of Shawn's group to finish. She exited with tears streaming down her face as she dragged the lifeless body. Her hands dripped blood, and with each step, she left a trail of it in her wake. She huddled together with two other girls.

Shawn watched the three girls embrace. "Did you see Maple or Q?" Shawn asked, knowing that Jay didn't have any more of a chance of seeing their friends than he did.

"Couldn't see past the gargoyles in line," Jay said, seeming to sense Shawn's unease. "I'm sorry about Onyx. It shouldn't have happened." Jay's face remained blank; his forehead creased as he took in the room.

"None of this should have happened."

Another group must have entered the rooms because more gargoyles were leading pigs to each door. Shawn tried to catch a glimpse as the door opened, but it was of no use. He would just have to wait.

"Do you think there are more stages?" Shawn asked, keeping his eyes locked on the doors.

"Can't be many more. Otherwise, none of us will become reapers," Jay replied.

"Franklin told me it was over. But I don't know if I can believe him."

Jay stood up. "They can all go screw themselves." He walked over to where Sophia was huddling with her friends and squatted down.

It took a moment for her to recognize him, the trauma of her experience making her another victim of shock. As soon as she saw through the haze, she pulled him into a hug.

Each time the door opened, Shawn scoured over the first-year reapers exiting their test. Still, no Maple or Q. With every round of testing completed, Shawn's hopes were diminishing. It felt like ripping a band-aid off repeatedly, but he knew he wouldn't stop looking.

With the eleventh group, he finally got some relief. Drudging his way through the door was a sarcastic mop of dirty black hair. Q. He looked as if he'd tried tie-dyeing the white undershirt beneath his jacket. Blood was splattered across his whole front.

Q heaved the pig corpse into the next room, and Shawn gave him very little time after finishing before he embraced him. Q's eyes glistened when he recognized Shawn. "You're alive, mate," he said.

Shawn ignored the statement, squeezing his friend. "Have you seen..." He left the sentence unfinished, as if speaking it into existence would curse it.

"I was hoping she was in your group," Q replied. The wait wasn't over then.

"Wasn't in my group or among our dead." They both didn't state what that might mean for her.

"I'm assuming you talked your way out of that coffin?" Jay asked as he rejoined them.

Q gave a soft chuckle. "The dirt moves for you if you ask nicely, ya know".

"How many did you guys lose?" Jay asked Q.

"Four."

"We lost six," Shawn added. He thought back to the cemetery. To the lifeless bodies that looked like they were sleeping below ground. He thought back to Onyx. The blueish hue from the orb that had filtered through the wood panels of the coffin. Shawn's stomach tightened. "Onyx didn't make it."

Q closed his eyes and slowed his breathing, letting a couple more tears fall. No one said a word after that; instead, they let the squeals of dying pigs fill the void.

Shawn wasn't sure how many more times the doors opened and closed. But after a bit, some stopped closing. Some of the groups were finished. Still, there hadn't been a sign of Maple. Q had gone around asking, but no one knew. People were still processing the trauma they'd gone through, so Q and Shawn gave up that route. When there were only two doors left still testing, Shawn was losing hope. Then he spotted her.

The door had just opened, and she was teetering from exhaustion as she moved her pig. Shawn had never been so happy to see someone with blood speckled across their face. Not even waiting for her to finish moving her pig, Shawn plowed his way through the crowd. He grabbed her hand from behind. She turned around, throwing her fist right into the center of Shawn's chest, the force compelling him into the dirt.

"Maple," he wheezed.

"Shawn!" She dropped the pig and bent down. "I'm sorry. Of course, you'd grab someone from behind after they'd just experienced Hell."

"Yeah, that wasn't the brightest idea. Sorry, I just... wasn't sure if you made it."

"It's fine. I made sure I was the last one in my group. I saw you and Q walk through ages ago."

Shawn let her finish moving her pig, and then they went to maneuver their way through the crowded mill.

"I didn't think I was going to make it out of that box," Maple whispered.

"You did though. You got out. You didn't give up."

She pulled Shawn to a stop before they got over to Jay and Q. "No, Shawn. I did give up." She started shaking. "When I woke up in that box, I freaked. Completely lost it. I didn't even know I was claustrophobic. But in that coffin, underground, I screamed my head off." She paused. "Then I stopped screaming. I'd accepted my fate. The only reason I'm here is because someone else dug me out." She hung her head.

Not saying a word, Shawn pulled her into a hug. He wanted to tell her that everything was okay, but he wouldn't lie to her.

Nothing about this was okay. He let her compose herself and then they rejoined the others.

One more round later and every first-year reaper had been tested. Shawn wasn't sure how many in total they'd lost. He was afraid to know. Out of each barn door, a council member emerged. The crowd parted a bit as they let the council members walk out from the slaughtering rooms. Franklin, Mac, Camren, Carlin, and one he didn't recognize stood in front of their respective doors.

"Who's that?" Shawn asked, pointing towards an annoyed-looking man in a black suit with silver linings. His long brown hair draped across his shoulders.

The council member came from Q's door, so he answered. "Peppertine. Head of the mustangs apparently. Seems like a *real* joy to work with. Don't think he appreciated my joke about offering the pig a last meal before we slaughtered it."

One of the gargoyles made her way to the middle of the room, and the first years parted to make a path. Her voice boomed across the mill. "Phase Two is complete; everyone here will now move onto the last phase of testing before finding out their designations. Everyone will move in an orderly line out through the door of which they entered." She paused, scanning the crowd. "I will ask that the following five reapers remain behind." Shawn's blood went cold as she read the list of names. "Jay Musters, Quintin Prodit, Maple Collins, Shawn Turner, and Sophia Trak. You five, please remain in the mill."

Chapter 21

Everyone who knew the names gave a curious glance as they walked out. Shawn's stomach twisted as the inside of the mill slowly dissipated. With the lack of dirty bodies cluttering the place, fresh air filled the void. Occasionally, an odd waft of blood floated through that made Shawn want to run out.

Only one council member, Mac, remained behind after the others had led their groups out of the mill. Mac then turned his attention to the five remaining reapers. Shawn wished Franklin had remained behind: maybe he would've explained why he lied to Shawn, because this wasn't over.

Mac observed them all, taking in the dirt, cuts, and bruises. "Let's get going." That was it. No explanation why they were singled out or kept behind. Shawn expected Jay to speak up, but he kept his mouth shut with Mac standing in front of him.

They were led past the staircase leading to the top of the mill. Past where the pigs had been deposited. Blood was pooling in piles as older reapers were sorting the pigs. "All meat will be either preserved for use throughout the year or given to the villages nearby," Mac said as they walked through the room.

Villages? Shawn had heard about a retired reaper village nearby but didn't know that there were others.

Mac didn't mention anything else as he led the group back outside the mill. For a second, Shawn thought he had a heartbeat again. Mac grabbed the blade that he'd left waiting against the door. Shawn just hoped it wasn't waiting for them.

The woods were quiet again. The only noise was the breeze blowing through the branches. After so much time spent listening to squealing pigs, the calm was much needed. They headed toward the edge of the forest, near one of the walls of the cave. The ceiling started to slope down as the group approached the outer edge of the tree line.

Shawn spotted the cavern crystals that imitated light. They dotted the ceiling and spread down into the wall of the cavern—almost like a child putting up glow-in-the-dark stars in their bedroom. Each one was of a different shape and size. The only thing they had in common was that they were completely clear. Luckily, it was later in the day, so the light was diminishing from inside the crystals, allowing Shawn to view them.

Mac turned around abruptly. "You five completed Phase Three the other day. Which is why you were all asked to stay behind."

"What do you mean we completed Phase Three?" Q asked.

"You want me to repeat myself?" Mac said. "All your fellow first years will be completing a dock walk of their own today. Not necessarily the same one, but a dock walk, nonetheless. I was told to escort you to a couple of other areas instead."

Relief oozed off Shawn as he realized that the headmaster had told him the truth. She said that they were doing the dock walk early. Shawn just didn't know it was part of the testing.

"Wow! Just for us? I can't wait to see what's in store!" Q snarked back, but one look from Mac and Q went full tail between the legs.

They were led to an area that looked as if someone had ignited dynamite. Cracks spiraled down the wall of the cavern, and the end result was a pile of boulders that might as well have been stacked by a three-year-old. Shawn was too busy noticing the hole, so the kid sitting on the stump didn't register at first.

He wore the typical reaper gray hoodie with a Roman numeral I on the sleeve. Normal clothing–at least, it would have been had his clothes not been completely shredded. His sweatshirt was held together by strands clinging to their last bit of life. The same could not be said for the reaper in front of them.

"You're a ghost," Shawn said, unfiltered, as he examined the soft glow that encompassed the reaper's body.

The tattered kid jumped off the stump. "Real Sherlock we got here, eh Mac?"

Maple eyed Mac. "Do you two know each other?"

Mac said nothing.

"Oh, Mac Attack and I? We go *waaayyy* back." The dead reaper rolled his eyes. "He's the one that found my poor soul. Right Mac? What did you call me? A waste of time?"

Again, Mac remained silent.

"You died down here?" Q asked.

"Righto, boyo. Another thinker we got here. Anyone want to guess how it happened?"

Q looked ready to comment, but Maple grabbed his arm, tightening her fingers around his bicep until he got the hint.

"Oh, come on. None of you? Gotta be one in the bunch that has an idea." He sat back down on the stump, picking imaginary dirt from his palm.

"You fell down that." Jay pointed to the avalanche of boulders.

The kid gave Jay a smile, showing all teeth. "Finally, someone has cracked the code." He jumped again, exaggerating every movement. He was embracing the spotlight and his audience. "Yes, I was the reaper that came to a tragic end at the bottom of that pile." He walked over to the base of the rocks and his tone hardened. "I was alive for four days, you know." He looked straight at Mac as he spoke. "Pinned underneath the rubble. I eventually starved to death."

Mac didn't flinch. "What Rudy here doesn't tell you is that he murdered a fellow first year and tried to escape by climbing this opening in the wall." Mac traced the outline of his scythe as he spoke. "I was the one who found him because he was running from me."

"That was just a pure misunderstanding between good old Ingrid and I. My scythe slipped," Rudy said, nonchalantly waving his hand.

"Yes. Slipped right into her gut. As for the dismembered body parts?" Mac stepped forward. "Now Rudy, don't leave that out." He continued, turning his attention on the first-year reapers. "We take our job seriously here. You five have seen a lot during your first couple of weeks, but if there's one thing you should know, it's this. We respect the living. We respect the dead. But we also don't allow disrespect to our fellow reapers."

Maple stepped forward. "It seems that you deserved everything you got."

"Sometimes that's how the rock tumbles, baby." Rudy winked and looked her up and down.

Shawn's skin crawled. "How do you let someone like this become a reaper?" When he first saw Rudy, he felt sorry for him: a ghost trapped for eternity. But now, well, he agreed with Maple.

"Oh, honey, no one chooses," Rudy said, sniffling.

Shawn thought Mac would intercede, but he let Rudy carry on.

"The system isn't so different for those who become reaped. Except for once a year. You all just happened to strike one of the nights the black paper is sent out. So, don't think you're special, bucko."

“What do you mean black paper?” Maple asked.

“Instead of the usual parchment paper, reapers receive their assignments on black paper from the capital one day per year. These assignments determine who becomes a reaper. It’s just luck.”

“Yeah, I feel *real* lucky.” Jay snarked.

“We don’t handpick people. Otherwise, problems are created,” Mac said. While Mac pretended to be bored talking to Rudy, his whole body was tensed. He was letting the group in on a lesser-known secret. Wasn’t the process unknown?

Rudy slowly circled Mac. “Now, Mr. Mac. That isn’t totally true, is it?”

This time, Mac flinched slightly. “That was another time.”

“Care to explain?” Maple wanted answers and she wasn’t the only one.

“There was a short period of time when reapers were chosen. There was a shortage and mistakes were made. One of those mistakes will be sitting on this stump reminding us about that for a very very long time.”

A shortage of reapers? Shawn tried to imagine what the chaos would have been like. How many souls succumbed to the same fate as Rudy here?

“Always a pleasure, Rudy.” Mac walked away, knowing that the group would follow.

Just as they were about to be out of earshot, Rudy shouted, “See ya round, Mac Attack!” The laugh followed them through the forest.

Chapter 22

"Wanna give us all a little hint of what's coming next?" Q said, testing his limits. "Just one teeny tiny hint? Like if we're going to die, or slaughter a chicken nex–"

Stopping Q mid-sentence was the staff of the scythe that curled behind his legs. He was hit with such force that he went perpendicular in the air. His face landed first. He sat on the ground, stunned. Shawn thought back to his sparring lesson and knew that even then, without a real weapon, Mac had been going easy on him.

Mac spun the scythe back to his side and squatted next to Q. "Sometimes, Prodit, it's better to listen than yap like an uncontrolled puppy." He grabbed Q's arm and yanked him to his feet. "I want you to see the end of a cycle for a reaper. One who's given his whole time here and has done it honorably. If I hear a single word uttered, I'll move my blade quicker than you can get a second word out. Understood?"

After seeing what Mac did to Quintin, no one doubted this threat.

A bonfire illuminated a clearing in the distance. Flames leapt ten feet high, as if they were trying to reach out and touch the roof of the cavern. Besides the large piles of wood splintering underneath the fire, the clearing contained about twenty-five reapers, including the headmaster. She waved Mac over when the group emerged from the woods. "Stay here," Mac said.

He left everyone on the outer edge of the clearing, far enough away that they could observe but not be noticed.

Silhouetted in front of the fire was a wooden gurney. Ornate wooden vines danced around the sides of the gurney and connected to the wooden flowers carved into it. Shawn now understood what the end of a cycle for a reaper meant. Lying on top of the flowers was a man in a three-piece gray suit. Mac knelt down, putting his hand on the man's shoulder. He stayed there for a minute before making his way back to the group. Another reaper soon took his place by the gurney. Then, reaper after reaper did this routine until everyone but the first-years had gone up.

An elbow nudged into Shawn's side, and Maple mouthed something that he couldn't completely understand. The only word he could make out was "who". Who was the reaper? He wondered the same thing. Whoever he was, he was important enough for Mac to bring five fresh first years on a side exhibition to a funeral.

Examining the gurney, Shawn noticed that one thing was missing. There wasn't anything blue floating around near the body, so he assumed someone had already taken the orb. Another nudge from Maple brought Shawn's focus back. Realizing she couldn't be sly about it, she pointed. Shawn followed her finger and finally noticed three people dressed in dark brown pants and black polos. Two men and one woman all stood behind the fire with their hands behind their backs.

Shawn shrugged, also confused about who they were.

Headmaster Tyflin was the last one to go up to the gurney. After taking a moment to pay her respects, she gathered herself to address the group. "Today marks the end of a journey for one of the finest reapers I've had the pleasure of working alongside. One who brought a sense of duty to the job day in and day out. And one who could make a room erupt with a joke. I wish we had more years together, my friend. Two hundred doesn't seem like enough." Tyflin paused, holding onto the gurney to settle herself.

Two hundred years. Shawn gripped his knees, feeling lightheaded. Was this what he had to look forward to? Two hundred years of service?

Tyflin continued. "So many years ago, you signed your original contract. I remember how different you were back then from others who'd just become reapers. You were excited to be doing such a crucial job. A job that you would hold in the utmost regard every time you went out on assignment. I have that contract here with me now and figured you would have appreciated it going with you." She slid a rolled-up yellow piece of parchment with a black ribbon tied around it into the man's jacket pocket. "You were one of the most honorable men I ever met, and my only wish is that the reapers who come after you hold even a tenth of the spirit you brought to this place."

As the headmaster inched the wooden gurney into the fire, Shawn's throat felt raw. He knew what was happening and wanted to look away. Even now, he was reminded of the life he left behind. Did his father speak at his funeral? Could his mother have contained the tears that dripped down her face as she stood next to her son's lifeless body? Shawn knew the answers to those questions would haunt him for a long time.

Tyflin stood with the other reapers as three people in black polos stepped forward. Three loud pops rang through the clearing, like wood crackling from air pockets. The flames started inching higher after that.

"What in the..." Jay said.

With the people's hands stretched towards the gurney, flames crawled across their fingers. At first, Shawn thought they were putting their hands into the fire; he almost wished that was what he saw. Instead, the fire was being created by those three. It emanated from their hands, pouring onto the bonfire and increasing the heat tenfold.

No burn marks. No signs of sweat. Nothing. None of them seemed bothered by the growing flames or the heat that licked their skin. Each stayed focused as the man was engulfed. Shawn wasn't sure how, but the man's body started to crumble. Quickly.

Sophia let out a small gasp, hidden by the sounds of the gurney crackling. Within minutes, the man on the gurney had been reduced to ash. The three in the black polos stepped back. Their hands lacked scorch marks or any evidence of what they'd just accomplished.

"What you saw is an honor, so don't forget it," Mac said softly.

Honor. Shawn knew of the Viking funeral. The Vikings used to set the body adrift in a boat, and an archer would light the boat with a flaming arrow. This ritual was similar in a way—if one could consider people creating fire from their hands the same as a flaming arrow.

Sophia was shaking like a jackhammer that someone had walked away from. Shawn remembered her reaction at the dock walk and took off his dirt-infested blazer. She took the offering and clutched the remains of the jacket instead of putting it on.

"Who were those three..." Shawn didn't even know what to call them. Flame throwers? Hot hands? Were they even reapers?

"Welders. And before you ask, yes, they're able to produce fire from their hands," Mac said.

By this time, most of the crowd had cleared out. One of the last ones left was Tyflin, who gazed into the flames for a long while before disappearing into the woods.

Maple watched the three welders walk away in awe. "Wha—"

"I'm not here to answer your questions," Mac said. "Franklin can explain the rest to you at a later time. We have to get back to the Academy."

Two lines of reapers awaited them when they arrived back at Wayward. Usually gripping scythes, their hands now held torches. Mac stopped before the group entered the tunnel they formed. "This is the Walk of Flames. Every first year who passes testing is welcomed back this way. Follow the line to the dining hall." Immediately he left the group to make their walk alone.

Without waiting, Jay took the lead and started down the path.

Shawn wasn't sure what he expected. The silence from so many reapers outside was deafening. The torches illuminated the face of each reaper holding it. It felt like every senior reaper from the Academy was outside. Dots of light twisted their way across the grounds. He couldn't help appreciating how beautiful it was. Each time they passed by a reaper; they bowed their heads. Shawn imagined that each torch represented a reaper lost. He couldn't stop the image of Onyx's face from floating into his head as he walked.

Shawn had to remind himself that every one of these reapers had been through the same thing he had. They knew that reapers had been lost during this process because they had experienced such losses themselves.

A familiar face sporting an eye patch seemed relieved when he recognized the group walking toward him. Rupert let out a deep breath before bowing his head as well. The one next to him, however, did not. Shawn nudged Q, who looked up and saw the boy.

"That's Marvin Silver." Q whispered. "Strange lad. Apparently, he cut out his own tongue. Took a vow of silence for the dead.

The boy cocked his head as Shawn approached, refusing to blink or bow like his counterparts. After passing him, Shawn glanced back and found him continuing to examine them. He shivered

Their group was the last to arrive at the dining hall. Another feast had been laid out, but no one was eating. Exhausted, dirty, and hungry, everyone remained standing.

Headmaster Tyflin stood in the middle of the tables, giving no indication of what she'd witnessed only moments ago. "Today, we lost many new reapers to the testing process. You are still here though. After everything you've seen since being thrown into this world of the dead, I hope you remember that walk. I hope you remember those lost. This testing wasn't fair, and that's the point. Life was not fair for you, and it isn't for the grounders above us."

The tunnel of reapers disbanded and circled the newly tested reapers.

"Mustang, talon, blade," Tyflin continued. "In a day's time, you'll know what your future holds and how you can ensure that we won't have more areas filled with unreaped souls." She lifted her torch. "While we mourn those who didn't make it, we must carry on their torches."

As if a light had been flipped off, every flame was immediately blown out. The circle dissipated and the headmaster headed back into Wayward, leaving the survivors to eat their meal in the dark.

Chapter 23

"Look at this." Maple slammed a book down in front of Shawn.

He looked at the book Maple had grabbed from the library in the tower. *The Third Horseman: An Autobiography.* "Uh, what exactly am I supposed to be looking at?"

"Flip to the part about the formation of the test," she said, resisting making a snarky comment.

The tests have been the foundation for the reapers since they first began. I often wondered if there wasn't a better way to find the next reapers before I became a rider. I now know I must embrace history and uphold our traditions despite the integrity of the issues it causes.

Shawn pushed the book forward across the black-stained table. "Okay, so a reaper questioned the testing. So what?"

Maple sighed. "Not just any reaper: one of the Four Horsemen. Those busts you've seen in the foyer? He's one of them. That means he's a part of the Grand Council in the capital. We aren't crazy for thinking that the first portion of the test is crazy. And being one of the Four Horsemen, that means this guy has the highest authority."

"Or had," Q chimed in from his seat on the ground. He'd given up on reading the books hours ago. Instead he was repeatedly tossing a crumpled piece of paper up into the air. After the carnage of the past few days, Shawn understood the need.

"Glad you joined us today, Q," Maple scoffed.

Q looked up with sunken eyes that were attempting to crawl back into his skull. "Just because at one point he was a Four Horseman doesn't mean he is anymore."

They argued for a little bit, but Shawn also saw Q's point. Whomever this reaper was, even if he was a Four Horseman, nothing had changed. The system had been around since the beginning. It seemed the higher-ups acknowledged the flaws but decided to keep the system anyway.

He flipped through the book, not really comprehending anything else. Yesterday was chaos, but Shawn couldn't stop thinking about his interaction with Cirie. "Can you guys try and find something about grounders being able to see reapers?" Shawn asked.

"Any particular reason why, sweet cheeks?" Q asked, sitting up. Alerted from the random question, he put the paper down.

Shawn debated even mentioning the situation. He wasn't sure what happened that night. For all he knew, some reaper had pulled a prank on him. But he couldn't help but shake the thought that it was real. And if it was, then maybe that wasn't the only time it had happened. "A grounder saw me on All Hallows Eve," he spat out

Maple surveyed the library. "What do you mean 'saw' you?"

"Exactly that. She called me out when I was walking down the street." Shawn turned to Q. "She saw all of us at that party. Asked me if we were pretending to be a barbershop quintet."

"That's impossible," Q said.

"I mean we've all seen them, well, *not see* us," said Maple. "Hell, we've interacted with them, and they've been none the wiser. How would reapers do their jobs if some grounders could see us?" Maple rummaged through the shelves for something on the subject.

"It was the girl from that alley, wasn't it?" Q asked, not even attempting to search for a book on the matter.

Shawn nodded.

"I thought it was weird when you rushed us out of there," Q said.

"We had a brief conversation, but I didn't give any details on why I was there. I don't think she knows. No one else could see us. She called me out for bumping into her on the stairs." Shawn left out the park incident. He didn't want to share that it had happened multiple times. "What do you think it means?"

Maple stammered, "I ... I don't know. I barely know the rules of this place, let alone finding out a hidden mystery."

"But this can't be the first time it's happened, right? Did anyone else see it?" Q chimed in.

Shawn shook his head.

"There has to be something in here about it," Maple said, piling more books onto the desk.

A voice called out from the doorway, this time from someone dressed in blue tweed. "What exactly do you need help finding, Miss Collins?" Franklin entered the room sipping a cup of tea, his mustache moistening from the steam. "Thought I might find you all here."

"Information about the retirement ceremonies, Mr. Franklin." Maple silenced both Q and Shawn before they could speak. "We witnessed one during the testing and, well, we'd like to know more about their significance and traditions."

"Yes, the committee was aware of your special circumstances, provided by Headmaster Tyflin. It's curious: you're the first students she's done this with. She's usually a by-the-book kind of person." He took another sip of tea. "Oh well, this book should do the trick." Franklin went to a shelf and pulled a book from the rack.

Shawn wondered how long Franklin must have spent in the library to know exactly where to find a certain book by memory.

"Thanks, Franklin!" Q took the book and handed it over to Maple.

"My pleasure, Mr. Prodit." Franklin paused. "I must say, I was very relieved you three made it through the testing. I'll be interested in how you each do in your designations."

"When will we find that out?" Shawn asked.

Franklin moved around the library, examining the books as if they were long-lost relatives. "Tonight. The council will finish deliberating in a few hours." He picked up another book; its binding was cracked. "You know, not many first years come here. At least not right away."

Shawn understood that this was Franklin's arena, just as Mac's was the training room.

"Why the pig?" Maple asked, putting down a book.

Franklin chuckled. "Mostly for food purposes, but it's always been that way. A pig is supposed to represent good luck, but in our profession, luck isn't needed. We kill it because we must in some way not abide by the 'good fortunes' of life. At least that's what history says."

Maple seemed satisfied with the answer. "You already know our designations, don't you?"

Franklin searched the stacks, this time purposely looking for something of significance. "I have an inkling, but you'll have to wait until the unveiling." He finally found something. "Ah, here it is!" He tossed the book in front of Shawn. "Mac told me you had questions about our fiery friends."

Shawn examined the *History of Welders* book in front of him. "Thank you, sir. I appreciate you helping us out."

"Of course. It's no problem. But you three?" He stopped at the doorway. "You may have found more answers if you hadn't been searching in the grounder section of the library." He left down the stairs, leaving the group to a table piled with books and no answer to their real question.

Hundreds of birds sat perched in the middle of the stadium pit. It was a sea of red, yellow, and black feathers. With the amount of birds sharing the stage, Shawn was surprised that there wasn't any fighting. Each bird moved around a bit but mostly kept to themselves. Shawn sat next to Q and Maple as the rest of the first-year reapers trickled in.

Which bird would Shawn be receiving tonight? He didn't think he could handle being a blade. Seeing that much death would change a person, and he wasn't sure he wanted to see who he'd become. Mustangs, on the other hand, gave him anxiety. What if he got lost or didn't make it in time? Shawn shivered. Talons would be a safe bet. That was until he thought about seeing the name of a loved one come up. Even if he didn't see it, he would continually check their names to make sure. Was there a fourth option?

"Thank you all for your patience during this time." Headmaster Tyflin's voice echoed throughout the pit. "It's been a very long process for everyone here. But tonight, as you are well aware, is when you'll find out your designation. Our wonderful gargoyles have been gracious enough to help us score the tests and have been instrumental in this process. Thank you." She glanced at two gargoyle representatives sitting in one of the rows.

Shawn kept fidgeting in his seat. Most of the reapers around the room were transfixed on the birds, trying to figure out which one of them would be joining their side.

"With every new class comes their new messengers," said Tyflin.

Council member McLally bopped down one of the center rows, dragging a large silver bell on wheels behind her. "As new members of the Wayward Academy and part of this world, each one of you will receive your personal messenger bird." She arrived at the middle of the pit with a small silver hammer to accompany the bell.

Tyflin positioned herself next to McLally as the councilwoman continued. "Goldfinches for mustangs, ravens for talons, and cardinals for blades. The bird that settles on your shoulder determines your designation." McLally smiled, turning the hammer in her hand. "Well, I won't keep you all waiting any longer!" Three strikes of the bell later, the birds took off.

A tornado of colored feathers filled the air above the pit as the birds circled the stadium. Shawn felt dizzy. His future was up in the air, so he could only wait. One by one, the birds began to swoop out of the sky, dropping to their target. Raven, cardinal, goldfinch, cardinal, goldfinch, raven. There wasn't an order: just organized chaos.

Maple received her designation first. Black feathers settled onto her shoulder: talon. The raven gripped onto her like she was a newly grown tree branch. She reached up, trying to pet it, but it immediately tried to nip her finger. Q and Shawn both laughed at her shocked expression.

With every bird that found its new partner, the noise level rose. After so many uncertain days, there was a new kind of energy running through the first-year reapers. People were talking with one another as more birds found their partners. It was as if a bottleneck had finally been cleared in the arena. Each time a bird flew near, Shawn thought his heart might start beating again.

A flash of red to Shawn's left meant that Jay was a blade. Shawn couldn't say he was surprised; he didn't think the other two areas fit him. Sophia received a goldfinch, and the buzz-cut kid from the graveyard had a raven perched on his shoulder.

The flock was thinning as most of the birds had flown to their new homes, but Shawn saw two break away from the last of the pack. A cardinal and a goldfinch bolted toward where he sat. They circled each other before a pair of tiny claws found their way into Shawn's shoulder. The other bird sat on Q.

Shawn turned to Q, "Well, looks like I'm a blade." The cardinal attached to him whistled in response.

Chapter 24

Entering his room, Shawn was surprised to see a silver birdcage on both beds. "Well, little guy. Looks like this is your new home." He stroked the bird on top of its head and lowered it into the cage, double-checking that the locking mechanism was latched.

Jay closed the door as he walked in, examining the cardinal a bit before he put it in the cage.

"What are you naming yours?" Shawn asked.

"Streaker."

Shawn was about to ask why when he looked over. A silver streak of feathers ran down the bird's right wing. "Don't think I've ever seen a cardinal like that."

"Just like you haven't seen a horse with bones protruding, right?" He said sarcastically. Seeing the look on Shawn's face, he backtracked and sat on his bed. "Sorry. What's up?"

Crossing his arms, Shawn leaned up against the wall. He stared at his bird jumping from one part of the cage to another. "Funny how everyone was excited to find out their designations, don't you think?"

"What do you mean?"

"Everyone is happy now that a bird landed on their shoulder, when a day ago we were buried underground digging up our fellow reapers. This job may be crucial, but that doesn't make it any less cruel." He got up from his bed. "Come on. Let's go spar. I need to take my mind off of it all."

Shawn pictured the smiling faces at the ceremony. Almost everyone was excited to see what was next. Even Shawn had felt the energy. They had all ignored what the past held. Maybe that was how they were supposed to survive here. Or maybe they were all just birds trapped in cages. His cardinal whistled from his nightstand.

Sweat poured down Shawn's face and dripped onto the mat, where a puddle big enough to go swimming in was forming.

"Right, left, right." The staff came at him hard and fast. Jay was telling Shawn each move as it happened, yet he'd already received a couple of whacks to the head.

Shawn didn't love getting humiliated in front of others, but he needed the practice. What for? He still didn't know. But when he found out, he wanted to be prepared. The sparring floor wasn't too crowded. A couple of third years were stretching for a session, and a few fourth years were already going at it on the mats. One familiar senior reaper on the floor was shadowboxing in the corner. Adriana was there when they had arrived and, if Shawn had to guess, she'd still be there when they left.

Another whack smacked Shawn on his ear. "Okay. Timeout." He hunched over, rubbing the area. He knew that the pain would go away soon, but his lungs needed the break more. The dark areas under his armpits spread on his training shirt as he wiped the lingering sweat. Meanwhile, Jay looked like he'd just gone for a walk in the sun. Small beads of sweat on his forehead were the only evidence of the session.

"You're leaving your elbow down when you block. That's why it's taking longer for your staff to block my hits."

Hands on his knees, Shawn tried to take in what Jay was saying. "That's probably because I'm freaking exhausted." He took a deep breath and geared up for another attack.

"Your grip is wrong," Jay said from the side. He readjusted Shawn's grip so that his hands were even on the staff.

Adriana came over to their mat, sidestepping the puddle. "You also need to spread your feet shoulder-width apart." She kicked Shawn's left foot, scooting it up the mat a few inches. "If your balance is off, and the force is powerful enough, you'll be on your ass." She looked at Jay. "Move aside, Turner. Let's have Musters get some whacks at me."

Shawn gladly got out of the way. Although he wasn't sure Jay felt the same way. Adriana was one of the best at the Academy, almost on Mac's level. At least this time, he could observe someone else get their ass beat. The way these two looked at each other was like two wild animals about to fight over a meal.

Adriana pulled her ponytail back tighter and got into her stance. "Don't telegraph your moves either. I don't need a heads up."

Taking a couple of steps back, Shawn waited to see how this would turn out.

Jay lashed out immediately, trying to catch Adriana by surprise. Her staff went up in her defense just as quickly. Right, left, left, right. Each time Jay came at her, she easily swatted it away. Each of her movements were purposeful, setting up her next block. She seemed to be letting Jay wear himself out.

A sweat ring on Jay's chest grew larger with each thrust of his staff. Adriana never attacked. Only defended. Jay went at her for a while, but each time he was met with resistance. He tried faking a couple of hits, rolling on the ground, and sweeping the leg. Each move failed against the more agile reaper. Finally, Adriana did something unexpected: she dropped her staff.

"Um, what?" Jay stopped and looked at the staff on the ground.

"I didn't say we were done, Musters."

"How are you supposed to defend yourself?" he asked her. Shawn wondered the same thing. This was a little different from when Mac did it. Shawn was terrible with the staff, but Jay was skilled.

"Try me," she sneered.

Jay swung and made contact with the air as Adriana weaved and bobbed. She was extraordinarily quick, guessing where Jay was going to swing before the staff even moved. It was like watching a boxer dodge punches. Adriana couldn't be touched. She ducked and weaved through each pass.

"It's in the hips, Musters. Don't trust the eyes: they're misleading."

Jay was getting frustrated with each miss; he couldn't get close to her. On one swing, he missed so badly that his balance was thrown off and he stumbled on the mat. His nostrils started flaring as his anger festered. Jay tried to change tactics a bit. After Adriana weaved left, he continued the staff and tried to cut out her legs. She saw this coming and easily jumped over it, like skipping rope.

Frustrated, Jay continued the swing back on the other side. The sound of skin on staff reverberated throughout the training room. Adriana had barely got her forearm back up in time to block the staff. Shawn could tell it was going to leave a nasty bruise.

Adriana and Jay were breathing heavily, but Adriana was the one who was angry now. "Good hit. If you worked on misdirection more, you might have actually had it." Apparently finished, she picked up her staff and put it back in the rack. "As I said, it's all in the hips. Follow those and you won't get any more whacks. Tomorrow, we're taking you both into town to get fitted for your suits. Be ready after breakfast."

That meant that they were going to be getting their first assignment soon. Shawn had hoped for a couple more days of peace. He looked over at Jay, who was the one hunched over catching his breath this time.

"Stop smirking, Turner, and grab a fucking staff."

Shawn did, but this time he didn't get hit nearly as much.

Breakfast the next morning was pancakes of every type. Blueberry, chocolate chip, strawberry: no shortage of flavors. Shawn hadn't slept well. He'd expected his new cardinal to keep him up throughout the night, but the only thing that kept him awake was the fear of their first reaping.

"Are you going to grab something or just absorb the food through your eyes?" Jay asked him.

Shawn grabbed a couple of chocolate banana pancakes, thankful that there were plenty of his favorite left. He plopped down in his usual seat as saliva pooled under his tongue. He had to admit, one of the best things about Wayward was their food.

Jay sat down about a space away and, surprisingly, Sophia followed. Apparently, her posse wasn't around. She grabbed at the salt and knocked it over, her hands shaking as she cleaned up. She wasn't the cocky girl he'd met on orientation day. Now, she appeared more like a wounded animal. Her curly red hair spread out in all directions and hid half of her face. Unlike the chatterbox before, she didn't say a word.

"You made it through the wringer! I had my doubts about you, Turner, my man, but I knew Musters over here wouldn't have any trouble." Rupert came over and dumped his plate of breakfast meats on the table, grease splattering across the surface.

Shawn now noticed the lack of remorse. Another reaper ignoring the losses that was in front of his face. Shawn waited for Jay to jump in, but he was pushing around a stray piece of strawberry with his fork.

"Yeah, lucky us." Shawn stuffed another piece of pancake into his mouth, letting the flavor dance on his tongue to provide a bit of joy.

"Both of you blades too! Never would have guessed that one either. Ain't it wonderful, Marvin, dear boy?" Rupert's lackey was at his side as per usual. Shawn wondered how they'd become friends or if they'd ever even had a conversation.

Marvin answered with a tight-lipped smile.

Shawn lost his appetite. He turned to Jay. "I think Adriana and Trevor wanted to meet us by the flame." He got up from the table, leaving his plate half-untouched and knowing full well that the pancake was going to be one thing he regretted about the day. Jay gave him a nod but didn't move.

Calmly, Jay, put his fork down. "You slipped us something on All Hallows Eve."

Rupert shrugged. "Sorry, man. Don't worry. The next drink I spike will be with the good stuff!" He followed his statement with a salute.

"Did you spike all of our drinks?" Jay asked.

The question caught Shawn off guard. He had no idea where Jay was going with this. Why did it even matter at this point?

"I mean, I handed drinks to both you and Quints." He scratched his neck. "I'll admit I got a little lazy after that. Who wants to drug up all the first-years instead of partying on the best day of the year? Why?"

Jay leaned on the table, nostrils flaring. "Just wanted to know whom to blame."

It clicked for Shawn now. Jay blamed the lives lost on the fact that he and the other reapers at the party were drugged. If they hadn't been, would more reapers have survived? Shawn wasn't sure, but he knew it wouldn't help thinking of hypotheticals right now. He grabbed Jay's arm before things escalated. "Come on. Let's go. Adriana won't be happy if we're late."

Chapter 25

"Glad you two decided you could join us today." Trevor rolled his eyes. He and Adriana were waiting in front of the everlasting flame, annoyed that they were both late.

"It's a couple of miles to the town, so let's go." Without another word, Adriana started down the path.

Trevor grabbed at his chest. "Damn, I love that woman."

"Wait. We're not taking one of the carriages?" Shawn wasn't looking forward to a long walk through the woods with Adriana.

"Ha! Oh, no, sir," Trevor laughed. "Mustangs are not a taxi service, and you'd be best to remember that. If one of them had heard that, your cheek would have a nice little handprint. Come on. Let's go after my better half before she gets away."

"Are we going to meet any welders?" Shawn asked. He wanted to see them up close. *The History of Welders* mentioned how there was a community that lived near each Academy.

"You won't speak to them," Adriana said, her eyes narrowing. "Leave them be, and don't cause trouble. Understood?"

"Yes," both boys answered at the same time.

Kicking a couple of rocks as he went along, Trevor looked at the two first years. "Welders and reapers have very specific jobs down here." He glanced around. "And they don't always get along."

"What's that supposed to mean?" Jay asked, now interested in the conversation.

"There's a reason I always bring my scythe into town." Trevor spat on the ground. "Animals." Trevor dug his scythe into the cobblestone with each step. Shawn hadn't seen any reapers handle their scythes near the Academy unless they were going out for a reaping. What were these welders capable of?

"My husband is drastically over-exaggerating. There have been disagreements, but both sides know what we must do to coexist. If you don't cause trouble, neither will they."

Trevor didn't contradict Adriana's point, but he didn't agree with it either.

Walking in between the woods for an hour with nothing to see besides tree bark made Shawn's mind go numb. So, when houses started to pop up in his vision, he felt a burst of energy. The town itself was scrunched together; each building was built sandwiched next to another. Cobblestone continued into the maze of streets ahead, the roads barely wide enough for one carriage to pass through.

"Welcome to Allen Oak, boys," Trevor said, perking up. He pointed out a couple of places that were "hot spots" to eat around town, but from Adriana's expression, that might have been just his opinion. Small blue, red, and white pennants were strung up above the street, zigzagging across the brick buildings.

Adriana and Trevor led them to a white brick building with glass bay windows displaying mannequins. Cursive gold letters above the door spelled out "Drop Tailors". A bell chimed as they entered through the olive door. Inside was like someone exclusively bought all the furniture from an elegant antique shop. Plush forest green chairs and red cedar tables broke up the area. The whole store was made to feel like you were perusing a bookshop rather than at a tailor. Wooden cases that spread from floor to ceiling held the racks of suits, creating small alcoves in the labyrinth-like layout.

"Welcome, my new friends." A petite woman in a silver knee-length dress appeared from one of the stacks.

Trevor plopped himself down on one of the green chairs. "Boys, this is Sylvia. She runs the joint and will be able to get you squared away."

"Now, what can I do for you two gentlemen?" The woman smiled to reveal teeth as yellow as the pendant strung around her neck.

"Newbies, Sylvia. Need to be fitted for their first reaping," Adriana said as she examined a row of bow ties.

Sylvia clapped her hands together. "Wonderful. Let's start with you, then, shall we?" She pointed to Jay.

"Sure," Jay said in his usual tone of excitement.

As she took Jay to the back area, Shawn explored the aisles of suits. For such a small store, there had to be close to two thousand suits in the place. He didn't even know where to begin to look.

"Overwhelming, isn't it?" Trevor said, appearing at his side.

"I could be here for days just trying to choose a style."

Trevor laughed. "Ah, no no. She chooses your style. You just choose the colors."

That made things a little easier for Shawn. Fewer decisions. "That's it?"

"That's it."

"Does everyone come here for their suits?"

Trevor flipped through a stack of gray suit coats. "Mostly everyone. There used to be another shop, but good old Charlie retired. Sylvia has been doing it almost as long as anyone else. She has the knack for it."

"Is she a welder?" Shawn asked, thinking back to his earlier conversation.

"No," Trevor said a little too quickly. "She was a talon back in the day. Even before I was a reaper. She moved into town after everything was done, like most senior reapers."

So, there was a life after this. Shawn hadn't been sure it was true, but here he was standing in the proof. Reapers built careers and lives after their contracts. He thought about the life he was missing on earth and then thought about his future here. Maybe he could last the length of his contract if it meant he'd be free. "Most? But not all then?"

"No one has to stay around after their contract. We aren't a prison. You can go wherever you like once it's up. Some become roamers. They're usually the oddballs in my opinion. Others move into this town. Some settle in other towns of reapers. The capital. You name it. I'm glad everyone gets a choice because I couldn't live next to some reapers. Not totally sure all of them should be here, but hey, that's the system."

A striped suit caught Shawn's eye. The steel-gray coat had large black stripes, and Shawn felt like he could wear it for eternity. It had class. Shawn had never worn anything like it before. He couldn't have afforded anything close to it.

"Ah, the rope stripes. The young man has a good eye." Sylvia appeared behind him, examining the cloth. "Come with me, and I'll get you sorted."

Shawn followed her to a back room that contained a raised metal platform surrounded by mirrors.

Sylvia took out a measuring tape "Okay. Down to your skivvies."

"What?" Shawn blushed. He wasn't one to declothe himself in front of anyone, especially a woman who'd probably lived ten times his lifetime.

"No worries. Old Sylvia has no desire either, but the tape needs what it needs. And it must be exact."

Shawn reluctantly obeyed and stood on the pedestal in his briefs and t-shirt. She examined his arms, chest, and inner thigh with the measuring tape.

"Now what did you have in mind for your suit?" she asked.

His mind wandered back to the steel-gray suit, but something was missing. "I liked the suit color we were looking at earlier. But I feel like it was missing something."

Sylvia sat down on a stool in the corner, rubbing her shoulder. "How do you feel about your upcoming reaping?"

"Um, I guess I just want to do the right thing," Shawn answered. What did this have to do with his suit?

"You seem like a good kid." She cracked a bone. "What happens when things get complicated for you? Where do you turn to make a decision?" She crocked her head.

Shawn thought about the question. Where did he turn? He thought about Q and Maple. Would he turn to them? Yes. But that wasn't the answer. When he was a grounder, he never consulted his friends on important decisions. Heck, he didn't consult his family either. He never wanted to involve others in his decisions. He wanted each decision to be his own. "My gut. At least that way if things go wrong, there's no one to blame but myself."

"I know exactly what you need." Sylvia left the room, returning a couple of minutes later. "I think your eye was correct on those rope stripes, but I think you'll enjoy the small change from the one you looked at earlier."

Smiling, Shawn took hold of the suit and tried it on. Sylvia replaced the black stripes with a color a little more striking: lightning blue. It was everything he wanted. Classy, but with a little bit of flash. "I love it, Sylvia."

"Ah! Don't forget the tie now." She handed him a solid black tie.

"Wow. What can I do to thank you?" Shawn didn't know if he was ready for his first reaping, but he knew he'd at least look the part.

"Nothing. It's my pleasure, Shawn. My job is to take dashing men and polish them up a bit." She led him to the front of the store, where they were told that the suits would be sent to

Wayward by the following night. She would make the adjustments and send each one over immediately.

Shawn was the last one walking out the door, and out of habit, he thanked her again.

"Shawn," she said, stopping him. "Make sure you continue to follow that gut of yours." She smiled and shut the door.

Chapter 26

Wayward was mostly void of first-years when they arrived back. Many of the first years were out on training or even on their first assignment, so there weren't many Shawn recognized. There did happen to be one doofus waiting in the courtyard.

"Well, it is about bloody time." Q stood with his hands on his hips, grinning next to the tulips.

Trevor and Adriana gave each other a look before trotting off to their own business. They didn't have any training to do today, and Shawn was happy about that. His reaping was coming up soon, and he wanted to take advantage of the stress-free time while he could.

"It takes a long time to make Shawn look pretty in a suit," Jay smirked.

Q came up and purposely whispered loud enough to Jay for Shawn to hear, "Well, they *obviously* should've taken more time." They both laughed. The joke was lame, but Shawn was happy to see them both smile.

"You two are hilarious. Now, what are you doing waiting out here, Q?" Shawn asked.

"Oh, just looking to do some exploring if you two needle wads are in?" His eyes lit up with mischief.

"I think that's my cue to leave. Count me out for this adventure." Jay headed toward the stairway, patting Q's shoulder on the way out. "Good luck with this one, though."

"Ah, the two musketeers! Ready for some 'sploring!" Q said.

"I'll go with you, but you do know there were three, right? Speaking of which..." Shawn looked around for sight of a brown ponytail bobbing around.

"If Miss Maple is the one you're searching for, you won't find her. She's meeting with some talons. Which probably means I should meet up with the head of the mustangs, but I heard he was kind of an ass."

Shawn stopped scanning the area. Rumors were that Peppertine hated being a reaper. Shawn found it odd that he became a council member. Especially since he didn't want to oversee, well, anything. "I'm sure he'll be fine to work under," Shawn lied.

"I heard a rumor that he tried to fake his own retirement to get out of being on the council."

"That can't be even remotely close to the truth."

"No seriously! Roddick told me," Q continued. "Apparently, he sent his own goldfinch with a note about where to pick up his body. Roddick was on call that night and got the message. When he got to the clearing, he found a coffin and the Council member himself inside. So, he loaded the thing up and was riding back when he heard something coming from the back." Q paused for dramatic effect.

"Okay. I'll play along. What did he hear?"

"Peppertine was snoring! Apparently, he fell asleep waiting for someone to pick him up. He'd hoped to wake up in the retirement area to sneak out unscathed."

Shawn's side ached from laughing. It was as if all the tension that had built up from the last couple of weeks was being released like a balloon. He played along, knowing that none of this could be true. "Roddick must have had a field day with that one."

"He may have delivered Peppertine's coffin to the headmaster's office. Don't think my fearless mustang leader was happy about that one when he woke up!" Q wiped tears from the corners of his eyes. "Roddick spreads the story like wildfire too. He'll tell anyone that will listen."

Shawn took a breath, trying to calm down. "No wonder Peppertine still hates it here."

Q shrugged. "Okay. Let's move it, Shawnie boy. A little birdy told me about an area I want to check out."

Shawn had no choice but to follow as Q sprinted up the steps.

Past the dormitories and the talon room, Q led him to an area in the corner of the Academy. Most of Wayward was filled with dorms or small debriefing rooms. A few larger rooms for teaching purposes occupied the second floor, although Shawn had yet to use them.

Q led him to two double-arched doors on the first floor. "My birdy told me that there are some shiny toys behind these doors." He wiggled his eyebrows up and down.

Shawn shook his head. "You concern me sometimes. You know that?"

"Ta da!" Q exclaimed, channeling his inner magician. The same checkered marble tiles from the foyer spread throughout the space. A few chandeliers hung from the arched ceiling, their candle lights flickering off the items below like the sun on open water.

It was an armory. Racks of scythes lined the wall, waiting to be put to use. In the middle of the room was a box the size of a king bed, filled to the brim with metal helmets. Piles of armor packed the rest of the room. Chest plates, leg guards, arm guards, even lightweight chainmail. It felt like Shawn had walked into medieval times.

He picked up an arm guard and was surprised by how light it was. By the sheen and feel, they seemed to be metal, but Shawn wasn't sure what they were made from. He held up the arm guard in front of his face. His reflection stared back at him in a pool of black. "How did you hear about this?"

"Rupert told me to check it out."

"Why in the world would the Academy need an armory?"

"Do you really think everyone here is a boy scout?" Q put on a helmet and mocked a salute. "Because I think we've both seen enough deaths that would say otherwise. Makes you wonder why they're training us with those staffs too."

The thought had been bothering him since the first sparring lesson. What were they preparing for? "Q, do you remember the welders at the retirement ceremony?"

"The dudes with the fire spewing out of their palms? Nope. Not really ringing a bell."

Shawn ignored him. "Have you heard anything about the welders?"

"Read the same things from the book you did. Franklin should be giving us more information about them later. Why?"

One table had a white tablecloth thrown over it, with weaponry Shawn hadn't seen yet. A sickle lay on it, with a gold-encrusted WA on the handle. He hadn't seen anyone training with a sickle, so he was surprised that there was one here. Shawn toyed with the handle as he imagined how many reapers this armory could supply. "When I was going into town, I was warned not to cause any trouble: to not even interact with them. My mentor had this look on his face that was filled with anger. I'd never really seen him like that. Tension seems to be running high between the welders and reapers."

“These people could shoot fire at us if they wanted. That may be a reason why they don’t want you to interact with them. I’m sure tons of people would love to spew fire at my guts.”

“Yeah... Just seems like we might want to be cautious.” Shawn put the sickle back on the tablecloth, thankful that most of the things in here still had a fine layer of dust on them.

They spent a couple more minutes in the room going over the items before Shawn felt the itch to leave. “Q, let’s head out.” After no response, he turned around.

Q froze while trying to put on the leg guards.

“Are you saying I can’t try on the rest of the armor?” he asked, already wearing a chest plate.

Shawn crossed his arms.

“Okay. Point taken. Help me get this off.” After struggling to get his arms out of the chest plate for two minutes, they finally left the armory. “Where to next boss?” Q asked.

“I don’t know. You’re the one supposed to be leading this expedition.”

They walked around the corridors but found mostly the same thing. There were three other armories spread throughout the building. One near each corner of the Academy.

They stumbled upon purple doors to the talon room a little later and notice that they were cracked open as they passed by.

“—studying under our more senior talons to start. It’s vital that we read a name correctly and as quickly as possible.” Camren Fidler was lecturing a couple of new talons.

“How do reapers know exactly where to go if we only get the name?” Maple asked.

“It’s not like the location magically pops into their head,” another person chimed in.

“Pulling the name and date is only the first part. We send the name to the blades, and they get ready to go out into the field. We also have to take that name to the talon readers.” Fidler didn’t take her eyes off the two talons before her but motioned for Shawn and Q to enter the octangular room. Maple waved to them as they entered.

“What can I do for you two boys?” Fidler asked.

“We were just curious about the talon process,” Shawn jumped in.

"Very well. Follow me."

Fidler led them from platform to platform, and while she was used to the odd movements, Shawn certainly wasn't. He misjudged one of them and Maple just caught his arm before his face found out how hard the floor was.

"Graceful," she said, smirking.

Shawn rolled his eyes. He and Q followed Fidler until she reached a single door on the opposite side of the room.

She opened the door, revealing a short hallway that opened into a circular room. Exposed wooden beams ran across the vaulted ceiling in a crisscross pattern. Bookcases full of leather-bound books lined every wall. Four reapers, who Shawn assumed were talon readers, were sitting at purple stained-glass tables.

"Welcome to the reading room," Fidler said.

One of the talon readers noticed them and waved.

"Ah, Cassandra," said Fidler, "would you mind telling these new reapers what goes on in here?"

Smiling, Cassandra bounced over. "Of course! You see, our job here is to help manage all locations of every single human on Earth. Well... not exactly *everyone*. That would be impossible," she said, laughing. "Just the ones in our region. If we had to manage everyone on Earth, we'd be in a lot more trouble."

"Eh hem." Fidler made a circular motion with her fingers, telling Cassandra to reel it in a little bit.

"Yes, sorry. Here, we can look at what I'm currently working on." She brought forward a leather-bound book. "This is one of the J books and it contains the names and current locations of the grounders in our regions whose last names start with J. Well, specifically this is Ja to Jef."

Another look from Fidler brought Cassandra back to earth a bit.

"Anyway. See, my job right now is to go through our current completed reapings and strike their names from the book."

Maple squinted at the book. "How does this contain everyone in the region with these names though? As more people are born, shouldn't it be constantly changing?"

Her question made Cassandra's smile widen. "Exactly! Look at this name right here: Jacob Jeffrey. Here's his permanent location, but if you look to the right, his current coordinates are also shown."

Shawn could also see that Jacob Jeffrey was 73 and currently wearing blue jeans and a white t-shirt.

The numbers, which looked to be GPS coordinates, were written in faint black ink on the parchment. One of the numbers jumped from 7 to 8 and kept moving slowly, like seconds ticking on a clock. "It's a live document," Shawn muttered in bewilderment.

"You can see that name is also highlighted in red. Once a name has been read correctly by the talons, the name of the person being reaped is highlighted in the book," Fidler explained further.

Sure enough, Jacob's name was highlighted. Sometime in the next week or so, he'd be joining the ranks of the dead.

"What happens when they're reaped then? I don't see any names marked off," the other kid asked.

An ink pen sat on the table, and Cassandra picked it up. "I was actually just about to mark a reaping as completed. Watch this." She flipped to another page and found a name in red there. Dipping her pen in black ink, she looked at a list of names to her left and double-checked. She then dragged the pen across the name. As soon as she lifted her pen off the last letter, the name started disappearing. At first, Shawn thought the ink was just faded, but then it disappeared completely and the names below it jumped up, taking the place of the previous person.

"Thank you for the demonstration, Cassandra. We'll let you get back to your duties." Fidler led the group back into the main talon room, where eight reapers were currently pulling names. "Now, do you have any other questions?"

One of the talons must have finished pulling a name, because a raven down from the rafters collected the parchment. Shawn watched the bird fly back up to the ceiling and out a small circular window at the top. "Has a grounder ever been able to see their death coming?"

Fidler raised one of her eyebrows. "Are you talking about psychics?"

"Yeah, I guess that's probably what they'd be called.

"Grounders have never been able to see us coming. There are those who claim they're able to talk to spirits." Fidler air-quoted the last word. "But that's all hogwash. Many reapers go to psychics on All Hallows Eve, and they'll tell you the same thing." Fidler looked like she wanted to end the discussion. "Anything else?"

Debating whether to ask another question, Shawn dropped it for now. "No, Ma'am."

"Splendid. You all better get going. Tomorrow is going to be a big day for some of you." Fidler then addressed Shawn. "You'll be getting a message later on, but you'll be put into active rotation tomorrow morning. Congratulations."

Shawn felt his hands go numb. He'd hoped for a couple more days. He asked the next question, fully knowing the answer. "What do you mean: 'active rotation'?"

Fidler clasped her hands together. "You and Mr. Musters have your first reaping assignment tomorrow."

Chapter 27

Shawn skipped dinner, opting to spend his night underneath one of the oak trees. He took his cardinal out with him and let her fly around a bit. He felt bad that she'd been cooped up most of the day. Plus, he hadn't had a lot of time to get to know it.

"Missed out on dinner?" Maple sat down beside him, handing him a roll. "Eat this."

"Not really hungry to be honest."

She refused to move her hand, waiting until Shawn grabbed the bread roll. Now that he took it, he had to eat some of it.

"Did you name your cardinal?" She asked as Shawn nibbled on the food.

The cardinal was bouncing across the branches of the oak tree they were under. "Q told me to name her Mojo".

"Mojo?"

"That way when I call for her, I can tell people I'm getting my mojo back."

They both started chuckling. "My god. That's one of the worst jokes he's made yet."

"Yeah, just wait until you hear what he named his." Shawn smiled, but his gaze wandered to the Academy.

Following his eyesight, Maple tried to keep the conversation going. "You aren't going to be able to change it now."

Shawn whistled, causing the tree branch above him to vibrate as Mojo left to attach herself to his outstretched arm.

"Mojo it is." Shawn stroked the feathers on her head. "Are you avoiding asking me about tomorrow?"

Maple pulled her long gray sleeves over her hands, balling her fists in the material. "No clue what you're talking about."

Shawn appreciated that. She wasn't trying to pressure him to talk or even trying to leave him alone. She was just available if he needed her. He just wished that the tightening in his chest would go away. "I'm not ready for tomorrow."

"Did you receive a letter?"

"A goldfinch dropped off a note from McLally earlier. Have to be ready at 8 am."

The crystals embedded in the ceiling were starting to dim; Shawn didn't have much time left before tomorrow would arrive.

"Even got my suit just in time." He'd found it folded neatly on his bed when he arrived back at his room.

"No one is ready." She lifted her head up to the ceiling as well. "And if they say they are, then they're full of crap." Her fists stayed clenched inside her sweatshirt.

Night was setting in around them. The dark seemed to amplify sounds in the cavern, and the noise bounced around more than in the daytime. Still stroking Mojo's neck, Shawn felt the tightening in his chest loosen a little. "Do you think that all this death changes a person?"

"Yes," she said without hesitation. "I mean, look at us now. We haven't been here long, but we're different. How could we not change?"

"I miss my family," Shawn whispered.

Maple tensed her body at the mention of family. "My stepsister turns seven in a month. She won't get spoiled with gifts by me this year. We won't have our adventure days. She can't come annoy me to hang out with her anymore."

"What would you have gotten her this year?"

Maple's face brightened for a moment. "She wanted this stupid remote-control car. My dad had refused to buy it, but I was going to surprise her with it."

"You were a good sister."

"Now I need to be a good talon."

Shawn's mind drifted back to the dock, to the man who'd lost his child. He didn't want to let any grounder meet that same fate. He didn't want his parents, or Maple's sister, to end up like that. "And I need to be a good blade."

She squeezed his arm. "You're going to be fine tomorrow."

"Yeah, I think so too." Did Shawn believe it? He wasn't sure, but he didn't have any more time to be ready. Reaping day was here.

Chapter 28

"You can touch it. It's not dangerous." Jay motioned to the outfit laid out, having already put his suit on. Sylvia had decided on a black suit with crimson red flaps for him. He stood at the edge of his bed fiddling with his black tie, failing to form a knot.

"Neither is that tie you're manhandling. Give me it," Shawn responded.

Jay reluctantly handed it over.

Shawn couldn't believe he was about to go out for a reaping. He wished it was an observation. At least then he wouldn't feel as responsible. He pre-tied the knot like his father had taught him, leaving the loop large enough for Jay to put his head through. "Here."

"Thanks." Jay took the tie and tightened it around his neck. At least someone was ready for the day.

It's funny, Shawn thought. Here they were, dressing up like they were attending a wedding when only a funeral was guaranteed. Shawn couldn't let his suit remain folded on his nightstand, taunting him, so reluctantly he dressed. Ten minutes later, the two of them made their way down to a debriefing room.

The debriefing room on the first floor was mostly bare. Just a small oak table surrounded by a few chairs. It felt like one of the rooms at a hospital where you were told bad news. Adriana and Trevor were waiting for them, both in suits looking freshly cleaned.

"First Reaping Day boys. It'll be good to get it out of the way." Trevor said.

Adriana eyed the boys up and down, examining their outfits. She folded her hands, and seemingly approved. "We have no timetable on when you'll receive your assignment, but we do know that you were put high up in the rotation. So, I wouldn't get too comfortable."

"Try not to worry too much. Both Adriana and I will be there, helping you every step of the way. You'll appreciate it at first, but I'm sure you'll get really tired of us when a year rolls around." Trevor whistled for his cardinal so that Jay and Shawn would follow suit. He wanted them to be ready to go immediately.

Adriana leaned on the table. "When we get out there, remember your observations. The only difference now is that we could be out there for a while. Hopefully, your first one doesn't go seven days, but be prepared for it. Don't cause trouble."

"Who do you want to collect the essence?" Jay asked.

Adriana brought out one of the black cloth bags and lay it on the table. The golden rope was pulled closed for the moment, but Shawn knew it wouldn't stay that way. She looked at Trevor, and he gave her a smirk.

Trevor put a coin on the table. "Flip for it?"

One side of the copper coin displayed the Wayward Academy initials, and on the other side was a scythe. The images had a black outline that made it pop against the shimmering copper.

"Is this tradition?" Shawn asked, rolling the small piece of copper between his fingers.

"Not really." Trevor took his wife's hand. "It's *our* tradition. It was how we decided who retrieved the first soul when we were first-years."

"You two were paired together your first year?" Shawn asked.

"It's how we met. Poor gal had no idea what she was in for." He winked. "That little coin is also how I got her to go on a date. She's still a sore loser."

Blushing, Adriana took the coin. "Academy or scythe, Musters?"

"Scythe."

Adriana flipped the coin onto the table, where it wobbled like a drunk on a sidewalk. It spun to a stop, revealing the WA of Wayward Academy. Shawn felt that tightening in his chest again. He'd assumed Jay would take the first soul, but the coin face up on the table proved otherwise. He swallowed some saliva that had built up in his mouth, trying not to make a gulping sound. "Looks like I'm the lucky winner."

"Which means Jay can handle the map," Trevor said.

"Map?" Jay asked.

Reaching down, Trevor collected a rolled-up parchment paper. "How else do you think we can get around everywhere?"

Jay untied the black string that held the roll together. "This isn't a map," he said.

And he wasn't wrong: the whole piece was blank. In the middle of the paper was a small, raised rectangle, like a miniature frame. "I'm also not seeing a map," Shawn said.

"You will once we get the tracker." Trevor leaned back in his chair, balancing on two legs. "After we receive it from the talon, we just pop it in the middle there. After that bad boy is in, we'll have a route to the assignment."

Adriana rolled her eyes. "You can't expect reapers to know how to find someone immediately, even with coordinates."

They should've been practicing with the map. Now Shawn had to learn this part on the fly too? Well, Jay did, but still, they should've both been using it. "Why didn't you tell us earlier?" asked Shawn.

"It's a rite of passage for new reapers. Sink or swim," Adriana replied.

Trevor brought his wife's hand to his lips, kissing her knuckles. "Again, we're here to guide you through everything. It won't be that bad."

Shawn stared at the door, wondering when this debriefing would be over. His stomach was currently in his throat, and he was trying to think of the quickest route to one of the bathrooms.

Taking one look at Shawn, Jay cut in. "What should we do in the meantime?"

"Just stick with us," said Trevor. "We can go get breakfast. But just don't stray far. The assignment could come in five minutes, or it could come in five hours."

Only it wasn't hours or minutes. It was seconds. Wings flapping in the hallway signaled the arrival of the raven before they actually saw it. Soaring in the open half-moon window above the door, it landed in the middle of the table. The tracker parchment dropped from its beak in front of Jay before the raven took off again.

"Guess we're scrapping breakfast, boys," Trevor said, laughing.

Jay unfolded the tracker. "Let's go find this Ms. Zos."

"Now you can slide the tracker into the map," Trevor told them. "You put the assignment details facing the parchment as you put it in."

The tracker fit perfectly into the holder. As soon as it was in place in the middle of the map, lines started expanding out from the tracker. Black lines danced their way across the page, forming streets and parks. It was like watching slow-moving fireworks. Where the parchment paper had been inserted, a blinking dot appeared: their assignment.

"How do we know where we go?" Shawn asked, baffled.

Adriana pointed to another pulsing dot at the bottom of the page. This one had a number floating above it, like a point in a connect-the-dot picture. "That's the gate we must leave from. After we're through the gate, we'll make our way to the assignment. The map will automatically make adjustments as we go." Gate eleven. They had a starting point.

Jay whistled. Without waiting, or being prompted, he took out a piece of parchment he had stored in his jacket pocket. He wrote down the gate number, ready to give it to his cardinal. A moment later, Streaker flew in.

Shawn was glad Jay was handling this part, because he seemed like he knew exactly what to do.

Not wasting a moment, Jay gave the parchment to his bird. "Mustang," he told it.

Trevor grinned. "Off to the courtyard we go."

A carriage was already waiting for them when they arrived at the back circle. Shawn had hoped it would be Roddick taking them; he could use a familiar face at the moment. Instead, he didn't recognize the woman at the helm.

"Hey, Lil! Got some first-timers for you today," Trevor said, shaking her hand.

"Climb aboard. I'll take good care of ya. Gate eleven: correct?"

"Correct," Adriana said, stepping into the carriage. After they all crammed in, the carriage lurched forward, and soon they were flying down the path. The trees blurred by them. Not that Shawn noticed; he was too busy clutching the bag between his hands.

"You grip that thing any tighter, and you're going to tear the bag in two," Trevor said.

Taking a deep breath, Shawn loosened his grip on the bag but not the situation. He just had to get this one out of the way. If he could get through the first, maybe the rest would be easier.

Even though Shawn was peeling at the seams, Jay was business as usual. His face remained blank, barely even moving. Shawn squirmed in the carriage, attempting to find a comfortable position. But the only movement Shawn's partner made was the blinking of his eyelids. Jay remained laser focused. How did he keep it together?

A bump in the road threw Shawn forward. His hand shot out, grabbing the carriage wall.

“Sorry,” Lily called out.

From the looks on both of his mentors’ faces, Shawn decided to keep one hand braced against the wall.

“Where’s our assignment at?” Shawn asked.

Without looking at the map, Jay recited the location. “Shanowen Park.”

It was the same park in which Shawn had chased after the jogger. He didn’t think his legs could handle doing that again, so hopefully this woman didn’t pick up the same hobby.

“Can I take a look at the map for a second?” Shawn asked.

Jay handed it over. “Sure.”

Unfurling it, Shawn wanted to see how far gate eleven was from the assignment. He also thought he should get familiar with who this person was. At least he’d have a description to go off this time. It beat attempting to guess the assignment with no information. After he took the tracker out of the sleeve, the map dissipated immediately. “Woah,” Shawn said, not realizing he said it aloud.

“Yeah, the tracker must be in for it to work,” Trevor told him. “I’m glad you’re familiarizing yourself with your assignment. It will make it easier to spot her in the park.”

Shawn nodded and turned over the tracker. He froze. On the outside, it looked like he was memorizing the description or her outfit, but he wasn’t. Shawn was just trying not to have a panic attack in the carriage.

A nudge at his foot focused Shawn’s attention. Jay was studying him.

“You good?” Jay whispered.

Shawn attempted to speak but only ended up mouthing “yes”. In reality, Shawn was the furthest thing from good. Jay had left out the woman’s first name earlier. Or, rather, the girl’s first name. He wished they were going to a different park. But no, it just had to be the same one. If it was another park, then maybe there was a chance he was wrong. He reread the name, hoping it would change. It didn’t. Shawn slid the tracker back into the holder and handed the map back to Jay. He wasn’t sure what he was going to do. He couldn’t form a plan when her name was the only thing now consuming his thoughts: Cirie.

Chapter 29

A screeching halt meant that they'd arrived at the gate. "Sorry," Lily said again, more to herself than to anyone else.

Piling out of the carriage, Shawn felt unsteady. He recognized the two gargoyles standing where he'd last left last them. Did they ever leave their post?

Jay walked up to the first one. The gargoyle asked him a question that Shawn didn't even attempt to listen to. Jay handed over the parchment paper; the gargoyle read it and immediately gave it back. Both stonemen turned to the slot in the wall. Their moves synchronized as they inserted their fists in the slot at the same time.

As the purple light spread across the gate, Shawn could only think about Cirie. He wanted to turn back. Much to Shawn's dismay, the gate started lifting.

On the other side was the same unchanged round room. Without a word, Jay led them up the staircase as the gate closed behind them. Each step forward felt like a weight was being added to Shawn's shoes. Pretty soon, Jay was going to have to carry him out of here. Outside, the noise from the street engulfed them. It was singing with cars honking and people on their phones. Shawn hadn't realized how much he enjoyed the silence down at the Academy. He would give anything to be back in his room right now.

"She's still in the park," Jay said, checking the map.

Thankful yet again that Jay was carrying the map, Shawn followed on autopilot. He didn't look up as they left the cemetery and passed the hospital. Should he tell his mentors? Would they even believe him?

It was a short walk to the park. At least, it felt too short for Shawn. The Shanowen sign greeted him like a giant warning. All doubt of a mix-up was erased from Shawn's mind when he saw Cirie in the middle of the park. She had headphones on and was lying on a blanket with her eyes closed. Probably trying to enjoy some of the few pleasant days left before winter hit. She traded in the pigtails and zombie make-up for a sweatshirt and ripped jeans someone's grandmother would comment on.

Someone said his name. "Huh?"

"Where do you want to camp out?" Jay asked again.

Location. That was the control he needed to keep this whole thing going. If she couldn't see them, then he might get out of it unscathed. Shawn looked around at the bench they sat on last time and knew it was a no go. On a pathway? In the middle of everyone? That would be asking to be seen. A green pavilion rose into his vision, like it knew he needed it. The area was surrounded by trees but still had an opening where they could keep an eye on Cirie.

"The pavilion," Shawn replied. Even if Cirie spotted four people in suits, she might just think it was a business meeting. At least, he hoped.

The rust-covered picnic table creaked as they sat down. No one else was in the vicinity; it was still early in the day, so most park goers hadn't arrived yet. From their viewpoint, they could see the open area of the park where Cirie was planted. Shawn's only concern was that places like this got rented out. But it was November and early in the morning, so there was a low chance that it was going to be an issue.

Even in the cold fall air, Shawn was starting to sweat. Cirie just sat there, bopping her head to an unknown beat. People stared at her as they passed by, confused that a teenager was out so early in the morning. But she didn't mind, she was in her element. Shawn admired her for it and hoped that she got to be carefree for a little while longer. If only he knew what to do with her next.

"And now we wait," Trevor said, as if reading his mind.

An hour later, Cirie was asleep on her blanket. How long would it be before she was reaped? Minutes? Days? Hours? Shawn had to just sit there and wait for her to die. And he would have to do this repeatedly for the next twenty-five years.

"What's the longest you've ever waited?" Shawn asked, counting the seconds in his head.

"One almost went all seven days for me. Croaked with about nine hours left. At that point, I was happy to be going back," Trevor replied.

"Why?" Jay asked.

"Seven days is a long time to spend out here. You'll find that this isn't as exciting as it seems half the time."

Exciting wasn't the word Shawn would have used, but he understood. While he and Jay were running on adrenaline, Adriana and Trevor looked slightly bored. This was old hat for them, so they'd gotten used to the process. How long until Shawn felt that way? It was a strange feeling, waiting for someone to die, knowing that they were blissfully unaware. As Cirie sat there, Shawn wondered what grounders would do differently if they knew.

"Take a look at this." Jay passed the tracker to him. On it was an area that Shawn hadn't noticed the first time. Underneath Cirie's description was a countdown: "6 Days; 12 Hours; 41 Seconds". After each second, the time flickered to a new number, winding down as time went on. Six-and-a-half days of life left, at most.

The rest of the zombie cheerleading squad finally joined Cirie around midday. Shawn wished he could hear what they were saying, but he didn't want to get any closer. Unfortunately, the group of girls did not have the same idea. Cirie had packed up her blanket, and the group was walking straight to the pavilion. Shawn felt his throat shutting as the group closed the gap.

"Okay, boys," Trevor said yawning, stretching his hands above his head. "Looks like this show is on the move."

Shawn prayed that they didn't want to use the pavilion. Should he just tell everyone now that she would be able to see them? Odds were that neither mentor would believe him. They'd been doing this for years, and it hadn't happened. He decided to keep his mouth shut for now. Maybe she wouldn't notice the four well-dressed people following her every move.

"Want to hand that back?" Jay reached out for the tracker.

Without taking his eyes off Cirie, Shawn handed it over. The group was still headed right for them. Shawn bent down to tie his shoes—not that they needed tying. He fumbled with the laces as Cirie approached. He watched from underneath the table. She was going to spot him at any second. All she had to do was look to her left. Everything felt like it was moving in slow motion: Cirie chatting with friends, the group laughing, their steps, everything.

But they didn't stop at the pavilion. They headed to the park exit. Shawn let out a breath as she left the area. Then he realized he'd probably been under the table for too long. Sure enough, everyone was staring at him when he lifted his head.

"Do I even want to ask?" Adriana questioned.

"Sorry. Just got nervous when she approached." Which wasn't a lie. He was still freaking out and didn't know how he'd make it through the next couple of days. That was, if she lived that long.

"Took me a bit as well," encouraged Trevor. "I always thought someone would die right next to me. You'll get used to it."

Adriana didn't comment on this. "Let's get a move on."

Grounders packed the streets around the park. While the reapers had to weave in and out of the crowd behind the girls, it gave them a great smokescreen. At least that was how Shawn saw it. If they kept far enough back, then Cirie wouldn't notice them in the thick of it.

"Keep a close distance. You don't want to lose her in a city," Adriana instructed them.

Jay picked up his step a bit, but Shawn continued at his own pace. Where were they going? Where was she going? He needed the areas to stay crowded. Then he spotted the sign.

"She's headed to the subway." Shawn cut across the street, refusing to wait for anyone.

"Turner!" Trevor called after him.

Shawn was about halfway before he realized how bad of an idea this was. Here he was, so stressed about getting too close to Cirie that he wanted to cut across the road a street earlier, as if she wouldn't see that as odd. Shawn had gotten one foot on the other half of the road before he realized the other reason for his error. He'd been focusing so much on who could see him that he forgot who couldn't.

"Idiot!" Adriana shoved him from behind. The curb greeted him as a truck sped by, none the wiser.

Looking up from the curb, Shawn scratched the back of his neck. That truck had been right on top of him, almost close enough for him to brush his teeth in the mirror. "Thanks, Adriana."

"*Don't* do that again." She glared down at him.

Trevor and Jay waited a minute before they crossed as well. "What was that about?" Trevor reached out his hand.

Spotting his assignment, Shawn smirked a bit. At least he was right about that. "She's headed to the subway. I tried to take a shortcut, so we wouldn't be lost in the crowd."

"That was dumb," Trevor said. "You may have been right about the subway, but try to let us know of your harebrained plan next time."

Shawn nodded his agreement, and the group took off down the subway stairwell.

Each car was close to full capacity. The four of them managed to squeeze into the train at the last minute. There was room near a man in spandex playing the recorder. After listening for a minute, Shawn understood why there was space near him. No one around the train showed interest in his rendition of hot cross buns.

All the girls huddled together, sharing headphones and stories as the train left the station. Four stops later, Cirie and her group prepared to get off. Shawn nudged Jay to get ready because it looked like their stop was soon. Unlike the streets and subway car, it didn't look like a busy stop. Shawn was thankful she hadn't noticed his brilliant sprint across the street. It was lucky that her friends had distracted her on the ride. Coming to this stop was going to be like stepping into a spotlight though.

When the train lurched to a halt, the four of them braced for it. The drunk lady behind them did not. An elbow flew into Shawn's face as she came toppling forward. Disaster did not stop there, because this pushed Shawn into a man sitting down. His lunch toppled in the air, causing chips and lunch meat to rain down like confetti.

"What the fuck!" He shouted as his bread frisbeed a couple of feet away.

After a chaotic few seconds, Shawn found himself being pulled from a tangle of bodies. The man who lost his lunch was now arguing with the drunkard, blocking their exit. People had stepped off the platform when the doors chimed.

"Shit," Jay said.

Even with blood dripping from his nostril, Shawn's focus was the girl on the platform. None of the reapers could reach the door before it closed shut. Shawn heard comments behind him, but he didn't listen to them. His face was glued to the scene in front of him. His breath fogged the glass of the train window he looked out of. Grounders would only be able to see the misty-covered window, not him. At least, that was what most grounders should have been seeing. There happened to be one staring directly at him from the other side of the glass as the train pulled away.

Chapter 30

This was supposed to be the easy part of the job. Follow the grounder and monitor them until they pass on. Don't interact with anyone and keep them unaware of reapers. Simple. Only simple had stared him down until the train had left the station.

"Don't panic, boys. We still have her home address and her location," Trevor said.

Pulling out his map, Jay examined the route Cirie was taking. Her location coordinates were starting to line up with her home location. "She's going home."

Trevor smiled. "Guess girl time is over. Let's just get off at the next stop and head straight there." His answer seemed to cool Jay as they waited in front of the doors.

They didn't have far to go, just a couple of blocks over. As they drew nearer, Shawn held his breath. He could see on the map that they were close, but he couldn't find Cirie. If she spotted him, all hell would break loose.

"There she is!" Trevor said, pointing to the apartment building ahead.

Cirie guided her friends into the building like a dog walker wrangling her clients. All of them were on their phones, chatting away as the door closed. Shawn walked up to the handle and turned it. He felt the gears turning as he moved, but then about a quarter of the way through, he felt it jam. Locked.

"I was wrong. Guess it is girls' night," Trevor said.

"Now what?" Jay asked.

Apartment buildings littered the street. Shawn had lived in a small town, so the concrete playground was new to him. The area that Cirie lived in was a mishmash of development at the edge of the city. Her apartment building had gotten a facelift compared to the ones next to it. While her building had a fresh coat of paint, the one beside it had a few gutters swinging down from the roof.

"We can camp out there," Adriana said, pointing across the street at an abandoned house. A raccoon was attempting to crawl through its poorly boarded-up window.

"You've got to be kidding me," Jay said.

Roofing tiles were hanging by threads, and some areas had been duct taped like a jumbled puzzle. If anyone had lived in this house, it had been years ago. "Nope, it's perfect," Adriana said.

Putting one hand on the board over the front door, Trevor peeled the plywood back. The nails screeched as they were pulled away from their home to create an opening. Inside, the house was in better shape than Shawn expected. Trash heaps were still in every corner, and while there were broken bottles at their feet, the place still contained some furniture. A few chairs and a desk were downstairs. Plus, there was even a bed in one of the upstairs bedrooms, although Shawn itched from its color. Maybe a small family had lived here once. Shawn tried to imagine what the place looked like in its heyday but couldn't get past the grime covering the surface.

One room on the second floor had a desk in front of a cracked window that faced Cirie's apartment building. Astronaut wallpaper, although yellowing, was still clearly visible inside the former children's room.

"Good choice," Adriana said, joining him and dragged a chair over.

"Thanks. I thought it would be a good place to observe while we waited." Shawn also didn't want to be spotted, and the first floor didn't quell those fears.

"You have a good vantage point from here," Adriana told him. Across the street, Cirie was leaning out of the third-story window. Her hands were flapping out smoke that blended into the air.

Adriana brought over the other chair and offered it to him.

"Thanks. Can I ask you a question?" He took her silence as a yes. Knowing how finicky Adriana could be, he mulled over the question. "Why are we at this house instead of trying to get into the apartment?"

They watched the yellow glow of the sun bounce off the window. "Having the ability to be around someone in this type of moment doesn't mean you should use it. I've had times when I watched men and women spill their guts out, unloading all their secrets before they died the next day. And I've also seen people go along carefree just before biting the bullet." She paused and ran her hands along the astronaut wallpaper. "We have the power to be in these moments, but they aren't *our* moments. A reaper needs to stay close to their assignment, but I won't be their shadow."

An ambulance turned down the street, and sirens pierced through the walls of the home like they'd been invited in for coffee and cookies. Shawn poked his head out and followed the ambulance as it turned down the street, heading for another soul that a colleague may be meeting tonight. As he was about to pop his head back in, he spotted something fluttering down the street.

Black wings flapped closer and closer, the parchment paper dangling like a Christmas ornament from its talons. The paper soared up into the window and past Shawn. He turned to see it land on Adriana's shoulder. The raven released the note before exiting immediately. Adriana had apparently received a new assignment. While mentoring?

"Looks like Trevor will be guiding you guys from here on out." She read the parchment paper before stuffing it into her pocket.

The noise drew Trevor and Jay into the room after the raven was out of sight. "What's up?" Trevor asked, to which Adriana patted the pocket of her suit like she was hiding sweets in it.

"Ah shit, you're leaving me alone." Trevor frowned so forcefully that clowns would've been jealous.

"Duty calls. Unfortunately, I'll be on the other side of town. When I get done, though, I'll send a note. If you guys are still waiting, I'll rejoin."

Trevor kissed the top of her head. "Be free, my love. Leave me to my misery and training!"

Adriana rolled her eyes and turned to the two new blades. "You two are going to be fine. Remember the Academy Way."

"The *Adriana* Way!" Trevor injected.

She ignored her husband. "Don't screw it up." Cars barely traveled down this road, but Adriana walked along the sidewalk, still bound by the rules. They watched until the sight of her faded from their vision.

Trevor looked around the astronaut-styled room. "And then there were three."

Lettuce from the stolen sandwich fell to the ground as Shawn took a bite. He ignored the taste of rebellion that came with it. He made a mental note to try to bring food with him next time. Stealing didn't feel right to him. Then again, neither was dying so young.

"Try to make it into your mouth," Jay mocked. Trevor had given Shawn the first shift, but Jay hadn't even attempted to sleep. Instead, he'd planted himself in the other chair opposite Shawn. It was like he didn't trust Shawn to keep watch. Jay leaned back in his chair, its mismatched legs creaking under his weight. Someone had decided that the best way to fix the broken chair was to glue a random leg back onto it. The end result put the chair on a tilt. Not that Jay cared.

"Shouldn't you be sleeping?" Shawn continued with his sandwich as he kept an eye on the third-story window, worrying about anything that could happen.

"And why would I want to miss this?" he replied between creaks.

Jay glanced around the room, admiring the wallpaper. His gaze traveled the room and even examined the peeling parts in the corners. When his gaze shifted over to Shawn, Jay stared at him.

Shawn stared right back.

"Might want to keep an eye on the task, Turner."

Not wanting to wake Trevor in the next room, Shawn kept quiet as he walked towards the door.

Jay grabbed his arm before he got out the doorway. "What are you doing?"

"Going to keep a closer eye on it." He shook off Jay's grip and walked downstairs. Pausing, he took a deep breath. God, he needed this first reaping to be over. First one is always the hardest, right? An image of Cirie flashed in his head. The rest would be no problem... he hoped.

Scratching his back from the board on the front door, he slithered out from underneath it. Fresh air was a welcome change from the grungy stank of the abandoned house. Shawn crossed the street; the apartment building filled his entire vision.

What was he doing? He needed to get out from under Jay's constant supervision. Under his watch, Shawn couldn't breathe. Jay was bent on controlling everything so they wouldn't mess up. Shawn wasn't going to mess up. It couldn't happen. Shawn had to be at his best to ensure that everything went off without a hitch.

Walking the perimeter, Shawn let his fingers trail on the deteriorating brick walls of their safe house. Jay was most likely watching from the window. Good, let him watch. Shawn almost turned around and waved but resisted the urge to acknowledge him.

Instead, Shawn crossed the street to get closer to the apartment building. At ground level, he could peer into the rooms on the first floor. Only a few had their lights on. In one room, an elderly woman had a home workout video on, and to her credit was actually trying to go as fast as the instructors. She'd cleared out the whole room for her little late-night workout, making sure to get everything off the plush puke-green carpet. Another room had a man and his daughter playing cards on one of those folding tables that looked to double as their kitchen table. Their apartment was bare, but every time the young girl laid down a card, she smiled.

Every room had a story, but Shawn wasn't there for any of theirs. No, what he was there for was on the third floor. Light filtered through the blinds into the alley alongside the building, drawing Shawn to the side.

Night in the city escalated every sound. Everything seemed to be just nearby. Shawn's nerves were already on edge. He jumped at every siren, even knowing that he wouldn't be seen by anyone. Well, almost anyone. Barking echoed in the distance, and the sound danced between the bells of a TV game show set on the max volume. Wind blew debris off from the room that Shawn sidestepped. An ambulance flew down the street, rushing the occupants to the nearest hospital. Would Cirie be in that ambulance soon?

More debris dislodged from the roof, rattling the fire escape as it fell into the alley. Shawn looked up, expecting to get a glance at the full moon, but the figure climbing down the ladder blocked his sight. Now he understood why things were rattling around above him.

Cirie Zos slid down the ladder, dropping to the ground with a faint thud. Maybe she wouldn't turn his way: maybe she'd make her way across the street instead.

That thought lasted for two seconds, because she faced him immediately. "What the fuck?" She said aloud.

Shawn couldn't have agreed more with the statement.

Cirie squinted. "Wait. Stripes?"

If Shawn had a working heart, it would have been pounding against the inside of his rib cage. "Uh..." He thought for a second. "What are you doing here?" He went with his most common move: play dumb.

She shifted her hand out from behind her back, shoving something back in her pocket. "I live here." She gestured to the building she'd clambered down from. "Why are you creeping around my building like the night stalker?" A piece of her sweater snagged against the wall she leaned on.

Thinking on his feet, Shawn came up with the only story he could think of. "I got ditched."

Cirie fiddled with the object in her pocket, not taking her eyes off him. "And you decided, 'Hey, that alley looks like a good place to hang out?'"

The unknown object she hid made Shawn queasy. She was right though. It was completely strange that he was in the alleyway below her apartment. "It was the first quiet place I could find. Plus–"

A rumbling started in his stomach. Frantically, Shawn started searching around. He grabbed the trash can just as the stolen sandwich made a reappearance.

Cirie rubbed his back as he dry-heaved the last bits of food from his stomach. "Well, you are making a habit of that when I'm around."

Shawn's mind jumped to other patrons of the deli. He wasn't sure how anyone could become a regular at a place that produced this feeling in his stomach. Did they have iron stomachs? Either way, he was grateful for a diversion.

"Did you get it all out?"

"Yeah, I'm good now." They moved away from his dinner and slid down the alley wall. Dirt clouded the air near the ground, but it didn't bother either of them.

Cirie pulled on his lapel. "Getting a tiny bit of filth on your swanky clothes by sitting here."

"I'm sure some of my dinner is already on it," he said, laughing.

"Not wrong there, Stripes." She eyed the rest of his suit. "I gotta say, I do enjoy this version a lot better than the pumpkin guts you wore for Halloween."

"Can't argue with you there. Dirt and all, this is more my speed. Surprised to see you're not in pigtails though."

Cirie bumped his shoulder forcibly. "I'm never listening to my friends again. I'll do whatever I want next year. Go as a giant bookmark or something. All I know is, no more fucking pigtails. What kind of cheerleader puts their dreadlocks in a pigtail anyway?"

A piece of saliva caught in Shawn's throat as she mentioned her ideas for the future. He needed to change the subject. "So, why are you sneaking out the fire escape in the middle of the night?"

She tilted her head to the moon, examining it between the clouds that passed by. It was as if she was searching for an answer on the surface thousands of miles away. "For the ambience obviously."

Littered around them were fast food wrappers, scratched-off lotto tickets, and broken bottles. Shawn could have sworn he saw a cat walking around near the trash cans too. The smell was like a mixture of wet dog and rust, with a pinch of spoiled food.

"Obviously," Shawn agreed.

"Tell me about this fancy date of yours. Assuming it didn't start well, with you tripping on the subway."

"I thought you might have seen that," he said as he scratched his neck nervously.

"Hard to miss when you make a commotion that big. Downhill from there, eh?"

"It was all for some fundraiser. And before you ask, I have no idea what. My buddy had an extra ticket, so I just tagged along."

"Tagged along for a free meal? I don't blame you." She took a second to think. "Although next time you go to a fundraiser, at least make sure it isn't the same caterer as tonight."

Shawn chuckled. "I'll triple-check it if I have to."

He was starting to sweat now. Had he been gone too long? He didn't want Jay to come looking for him. He looked over at Cirie, but she was looking further down into the darkness. Shawn followed her eyes to a corner of the building that jutted out, forming a small L in the wall. "Are your parents going to come looking for you out here?"

She scrunched up her face. "My mom doesn't really notice much after work anymore. She usually passes out right about six. And since my dad is six feet under, I don't think he cares too much either."

"I'm sorry."

"Oh, now now. Don't be getting emotional on me, Stripes. It was couple years ago, so it ain't a big deal. Life happens."

Part of Shawn wished he could tell Cirie it would be okay, but he knew that wasn't going to be the case for her. Hell, it might not be okay in five minutes for all he knew.

A patch of yellow was shoved in the corner. The mustard-colored object was about six feet long and had a zipper on the side. Shawn wasn't going to say anything, but she notice him looking at the corner.

"I come down here to escape sometimes."

"Do you sleep out here?"

A money clip found its way into Cirie's hand. She moved it between her fingers mindlessly as she spoke. "Sometimes. I enjoy sleeping under the stars. Reminds me that not everything here is such a big deal. I mean, there's a whole galaxy out there."

The more he talked to Cirie, the more Shawn felt the guilt building up inside him. "Once the cloud coverage leaves, I'm sure it will make for a great view." Shawn left out how the temperature was going to drop. He didn't think she needed to be reminded of that. He lifted his head to the sky. Up above, the clouds covered it as if someone was holding a sheet over a new piece of art. He could barely make out stars through the small pockets of clear sky.

Another ambulance blasted down the street, piercing the darkness.

"A perfect night," Cirie scoffed under her breath, not realizing how loud she'd said it. She recomposed herself quickly and perked up again. "So, Stripes, what's your deal?"

"What do you mean?"

"I mean, what do you want in life?"

Shawn laughed. "That's a loaded question."

"Well, you're the one sitting outside my apartment in a suit, like we're in some kind of movie. So, I get to ask the questions right now."

Shawn thought, not about what he wanted out of life before, but what he wanted now. "I guess I want to make sure that I do something meaningful."

A car whizzed by and made him jump. He was really starting to push it with Jay. He only hoped that Jay decided to sleep before coming to look for him.

"Don't we all?" She reached into her pocket and put the money clip away. She put her arms behind her head and closed her eyes. A lot more at peace than she'd been moments ago.

"You ever think about what you'd do with your last couple days on earth?" Shawn asked, peaking over at the sleeping bag again.

"Maybe I'd grab a train ticket across the country and try to make friends in every car. Or maybe I wouldn't ever leave my apartment. I don't know, honestly."

Shawn sat forward. He didn't want her sitting in her apartment with a clock hanging above her head. "Come on. There isn't one thing you'd do if the world was going to end?"

She waited a couple seconds, contemplating telling the truth, before she responded. "I'd finally gain enough courage to play my violin in the park. If the world is ending, no one is going to care about some random violinist in the park. They might even find it soothing." Whatever had held her back from sharing this with Shawn dissipated as she talked more about it. "I used to go to lessons when I was younger. Stopped a while back, but I still play. Something about putting your heart and soul into a piece for the world to hear can be both terrifying and electrifying at the same time."

"You write your own stuff?"

She nodded, grinning as she continued. "The real reason I sit out underneath the stars is to compose. I obsessively tweak songs and try to make them better under the moonlight. It makes me feel like I enter a void when I composed something for myself. Nothing else feels important when I play."

"Not sure why you're waiting for the end of the world then. Why not just go out there and perform? What's the worst that could happen? A pigeon hates it so much they dive bomb you?" If Shawn could get her to perform just once, he would feel accomplished. He hated that her dreams would vanish before she took a chance. Even if she was terrible, at least she would have tried.

"Who knows? I could be at the park tomorrow because of you, Stripes." Her hand absentmindedly went to her pocket again, hovering over it. "What about your last day? What would you do?"

Chills came in waves throughout his body. His last day? What did he do on his last day as a grounder? He hoped that it was something worthwhile, but he didn't hold his breath. At first, he thought it was a curse to not remember his last week alive, but hearing Cirie's question made him think otherwise now. It was wasted. Of that, he was sure. Shawn stood up, brushing dirt from his slacks. "I guess I still have to figure that one out. Thanks for helping me out when I stumbled in here."

Cirie's laugh echoed down the alleyway. "Glad to be of assistance, Stripes. Thanks for being my stargazing partner."

"I'll see ya round, zombie." He walked away, refusing to look back. Shawn had stayed too long; he knew that. He just hoped that no one else knew.

Chapter 31

As soon as Shawn turned the corner, a hand gripped his forearm and pulled him out of Cirie's view. Fingers laced over his mouth and stifled his scream.

Jay.

His partner's ears were glowing a beat red, like someone had dumped food coloring over them. Using his other hand, Jay brought a finger up to his lips and then pointed down the street. Releasing his hand from Shawn's mouth, he kept a death grip on the arm as they hurried over a block.

As soon as they were out of hearing distance, Shawn spoke up. "Okay. I can explain."

The death grip was finally released as they stood at the end of the street. "You better talk, and you better talk fast."

Looking over to the abandoned house, Shawn expected to see Trevor waiting for him on the front steps. "Did you—"

"No, I didn't wake up Trevor. So, talk."

Flies buzzed around the streetlamp above them. "Okay. I know how it looks, but she can see us."

"I've caught that. How?"

Shawn felt himself unwinding as he rambled. "No clue. I can't find anything on it at the library. I tried to casually mention it to people, but no one has ever heard of it happening before. I'm at a complete loss. I thought the first couple times were a random chance. Thought that I wouldn't have to deal with it again. But of course, she's our first assignment. I've been trying to keep you guys away, so you wouldn't notice."

"A couple times? Dammit, Shawn. You should have at least warned me." Headlights from a car passing by cut through the conversation.

"And say what? Hey, that grounder we're reaping is able to see all of us? This is our first reaping, Jay. If I said anything about her, they would have thought I failed by alerting her to my presence somehow. You know how cruel this place can be for those who aren't committed. I wasn't going to end up like Onyx."

Jay squatted down and picked up a rock, throwing it down the street. "Gotta play the game."

"Exactly."

Pacing back and forth, Jay crossed the street multiple times, not looking or caring if a car was approaching. "This just made everything fifteen times harder. We're lucky Adriana was called away. At least we only have to worry about the grounder alerting Trevor then. We just need to wait for her to pass."

"Yes, and we can only hope it happens sooner rather than later," said Shawn wincing as soon as the words left his mouth.

"Hoping someone passes soon? That's a new side to you."

Color filled Shawn's cheeks. He didn't want her to die; he just knew she was going to. "You know what I mean."

Jay stopped pacing. "She knows nothing of us, right?"

Leaning against the light pole, Shawn thought back to all of their conversations. "Reapers? No, she just thinks that I'm a new student. And that I dressed up as part of a barbershop quintet on All Hallows Eve with my friends."

"Good. This is still salvageable. From now on, though, you tell me everything." Jay grabbed Shawn by his shoulders.

"Of course."

This satisfied Jay. At least they were in it together. "Okay, if we stick with each other we might make it out with our heads."

Based on the whisper of breathing coming from Trevor's room, he was still asleep when they got back. Jay took over for his scheduled watch, allowing Shawn to go into a troubled sleep. Shawn was in and out of it over the next couple hours. Never dreaming, but never fully awake.

Sunlight was the first thing to hit Shawn's face. Nature's alarm clock. He shot up in the bed, almost forgetting where he was. Shawn looked at the clock that was somehow still stuck up on the wall, the hands cemented in place from batteries that died a long time ago. He wasn't sure what time it was–only that nothing had happened, because the bag was still lying at the foot of his bed.

Throwing on his suit, Shawn went and joined his fellow blades.

"Well goooooood morning, sunshine!" Trevor was a little too giddy for Shawn's morning, but he let him have his fun. "Coffee and donuts over here."

A rumble inside of Shawn just confirmed what he already knew: he was starving. Taking one sip, the coffee fell down Shawn's throat, like it was a welcomed guest at a slip and slide. Except this guest was freezing cold. Shawn went over to the sink, or where there should have been a sink and spat the coffee out. "How old was that?"

"A few hours, give or take, your majesty. Don't worry. Next time I'll make sure to offer only the finest of our stolen goods at your time of choosing." Trevor got down on one knee and offered his scythe.

Shaking his head, Shawn went to the window. "Any changes?"

"Nope. She hasn't left the apartment," Jay answered, his coffee cup sitting empty on the windowsill.

The sound of wood scratching came from downstairs. Only Jay and Shawn remained in the room, so they made their way down; Trevor had dragged the wobbly table from the dining room into the middle of the house.

"What are you doing?" Jay asked, kicking a pile of crumpled-up newspapers off the stairs as he walked down, the stairs creaked with every step.

"Figured we might as well have a little fun while we wait. Lookie what I got." From his suit pocket, Trevor withdrew a pack of cards. He tossed the deck across the table to Jay, kicking up a cloud of dust as it went.

"Hey, Trevor." Shawn looked around the room. "You know we don't have chairs, right?"

"Shit. I got ahead of myself." He shrugged. "Well come over here, then." They all plopped on the floor, and Trevor spread out the cards. "Looks like we'll have some time on our hands, so Jay, just keep a watch on the coordinates. If she ends up kicking the bucket, the coordinates will turn red."

Jay put the parchment between him and Shawn, making sure the coordinates were in full view of them both.

"The name of the game is Welder's Hand," Trevor said. Shawn paid attention to only half of the rules as Trevor spoke. He didn't want to be in this house. He'd hoped he was going to be sitting in the park today. Did he really think that one small conversation had gotten through to Cirie, and he'd be hearing classical music fill the park? Yes, he actually did. The countdown on the parchment paper continued to tick. Cirie didn't have a lot of time left, and the more those numbers dwindled, the more Shawn doubted he'd be hearing any music.

"Do you think Adriana is coming back?" Jay asked as he won another hand.

Shawn's ears perked up at the question. Leave it to Jay to continue thinking ahead. If Adriana returned anytime soon, their little secret would be impossible to hide. Shawn couldn't even hide it from Jay after one day.

"My wife is a woman of her word. She wouldn't leave me all by my lonesome. I'm guessing her grounder hasn't bit the bullet yet either. Now stop distracting me. I have a reputation to uphold as the professor of poker."

Shawn let the comment go, since they were obviously not playing poker, and the only similarities Trevor and a professor had in common were fine clothing. The 'professor' delt out another hand.

"By the way," Trevor said, "I heard you almost got the best of my wife the other day on the mats."

Jay rearranged his cards, like he was organizing books at a library. "Not exactly. She handed me my ass."

"She said you had a lot of potential. You should count that as a win. She's one of the best at sparring, besides old Mac and myself, of course."

Shawn played a card, not knowing if it was correct or not. The scythe Trevor had brought leaned up against the wall menacingly.

"Really? You haven't mentioned it before." Shawn mocked.

"Now, Turner. I do have *some* talents, besides being handsome and charming that is." He brushed nonexistent long hair over his shoulder. "Mac took us both under his wing back in the day. Since then, Mac has been the only one to ever beat us."

"Are you really able to spar that often?" Jay asked.

Trevor looked like he was in another world as he spoke. "Oh yes, there are plenty of competitions, but the year-end event is the grand prize for you young bucks. All academies send their best to the capital for the event. Wayward Academy hasn't lost in 30 years."

This seemed to interest Jay a little more. "The capital? When do first years get to go?"

"They don't. Only second years and above. They want to make sure that first years are fully immersed before they head to it. Believe me, you're not missing out on much. Ah, I win!" Trevor scooped up the last pile of cards, leaving both Shawn and Jay empty-handed. "Want to play again?"

Shawn stared at the cards being laid out and had a feeling that this was going to be a long day.

It ended up being a long two days; Cirie didn't leave her apartment once in that time. Plenty of people came in and out, but none were the zombie cheerleader. It was on the third day when there was finally some movement.

"Food is served." Jay came into the room tossing a couple of cheeseburgers and fries around. He'd gone on a solo mission while Trevor and Shawn stayed back peering at shadows in the windows.

"No shake?" Saliva instantly filled Shawn's mouth, and he had to swallow before any drool escaped. He'd been craving a vanilla shake.

"Take it up with the manager," Jay replied, sitting on the splotchy, stained bed. Shawn didn't know how Jay could eat on that thing. The odor wafting up from it didn't add any flavor. But it seemed Jay's only concern was being comfortable.

One bite into the cheese-filled patty, and the location numbers started changing. Shawn froze mid-chew.

"Could just be going to one of the neighbors again," Jay said. He was watching the parchment like a hawk, his burger sitting untouched in its wrapper. A couple of false alarms had been raised, including one while the other two were sleeping, so no one was sure if anything was really happening. That was until Cirie strode out the front door, violin case in hand.

"Damn! They can never wait for me to finish my food, can they?" Trevor said to no one in particular.

Within seconds, they'd all thrown on their suit jackets. Thankfully, Jay made sure to take some extra time tying his shoes, letting Cirie gain some distance as she got further down the road. Jay's fumbling fingers gave them a two-block grace. At least from this distance, the group was less likely to be spotted.

Each block moved the group closer to the city center. And with each block, the streets became more alive. It was a Friday, so a lot of grounders were getting off work early. Schoolchildren were running rampant through the streets, excited for the weekend. One grounder nearly mowed down Shawn on a longboard.

"Any idea where she's headed, boys?" Trevor asked as they took the stairs into the train station.

“Not a clue.” There was a tiny part of Shawn that did know. Or at least hoped. Shawn hopped into the train car behind Cirie.

Surprisingly, Trevor didn’t say anything, but judging from his tensed shoulders, he obviously didn’t approve. Nodding, Jay said nothing but gripped the guard rail like it was his last day as a grounder. He wanted this to be over as much as Shawn did.

After each stop, the train filled with more grounders. At the fifth one, the group lost sight of Cirie.

“Well, what are we doing boys?” Trevor asked with a bit of judgment in his voice.

“Help me with this.” Jay thrust the map in front of him and unraveled the rest so they could see if Cirie had moved.

Shawn listened for the stop he was waiting for: Shanowen Park. A bell from the corner speaker alerted them that this stop was next. “This one!” Shawn exclaimed. Sure enough, Cirie was on the move.

The train lurched to a stop, almost causing Jay to fall this time. “Smooth,” Shawn said, smiling.

“Okay, Turner. Then maybe let’s move closer to the doors,” Jay said.

The train car was close to being at standing room only. They wouldn’t necessarily be noticed by anyone moving around, but they would have to weave their way through to the front. Another lurch forward and the train came to a complete stop.

No one fell this time. And Shawn didn’t have to worry about a pile-up of commuters trying to get out. He did take his time, though; he had to make sure that Cirie was already walking away.

“Doors closing,” the loudspeaker announced.

Crap. He’d misjudged the time and had to start bumping into people to get to the exit. Just as the door was starting to close, he reached out and shoved his hand against someone. This propelled him off the train like a fish jumping out of water. Jay caught his falling body. “Thanks,” Shawn whispered.

“Let me see the map,” Jay said, holding out his palm.

Shawn reached into his pocket, but it must’ve been in the other one. When he reached down the other side, he found it filled only with worry. The train doors had already closed, and the train started pulling away. He froze as the train sped off and with it their tracking parchment...

Chapter 32

Frantically, Shawn looked around him, hoping the tracker had just slipped out of the train alongside him. Debris lifted into the air as his last hope sped off. "We have a problem."

Jay sidestepped an over-eager teen on his way into the city. "Where are we going?"

"That's the problem," Shawn answered.

Without saying anything, Trevor whistled for his cardinal and scribbled feverishly on a piece of paper. It flew to his shoulder, nabbed the parchment out of his hand, and took off out of sight. "We need to move *now!* I just sent a note to Fidler. She or a senior talon will send us a new tracker immediately."

The blood inside of Shawn's veins felt like ice. How could he lose the tracker and the map? His head hung at his feet; he didn't want to look either of them in the eyes. "I'm sorry. It must have slipped as I tried to get off the train."

Hands appeared on either side of Shawn's shoulders. Trevor's voice seemed very much in control, but Shawn could sense the urgency with every word he spoke. "Both of you need to think. Do you have any idea where she might be going with that violin?"

Shanowen Park. That had to be where she was headed. Shawn wanted to think their conversation led her to scrounge up enough courage to perform there. There was no telling what was going to happen if he was wrong about this, but he didn't have any clue of where else she'd go. "Shanowen Park."

"Let's move then. My cardinal will find me."

The trio of reapers raced up the stairs into the city light, hoping not to be far behind their lost assignment. The sun beat down, but Shawn felt ice cold. Crowds awaited them at the top. The unwelcome sight of tourists and businesspeople flooded Shawn's vision. Trying to find Cirie was near impossible from their vantage point. Moving his way through the crowd, Shawn didn't even bother looking around for her. If she was on her way to the park, the best way to know was to actually go there. With all the training sessions he and Jay had gone through, Shawn was thankful that many had involved the little green safe haven in the city. At least he knew how to get there.

Each second that passed without Cirie in their sights was a second that could be lost collecting her essence. Without communicating, all three of them took off toward the park. Shawn pumped his legs one after the other, carving his way down the road until he was face-to-face with the gate.

"You better be right about this," Jay said as they entered the park.

Stopping, Shawn closed his eyes. He concentrated on the noise being produced around them. All he needed was one note to calm his nerves. One simple note.

"I don't hear anything," Trevor said. The blade of his scythe reflected the sunlight and Shawn's worries.

Was he wrong? This had to be the place. Yet no music was being played. Shawn was having trouble breathing now. He pictured the grave he'd dug himself out of and wondered if they'd use the same plot to bury him in. He could feel the dirt enclosing his body as it started to rot.

"You just got very lucky, Turner," Jay whispered.

"I knew it," Shawn replied, racing off through the trees separating the two sides of the park. A couple of notes floated their way to him and became clearer with each passing branch.

As he burst through to the sidewalk, he saw a girl standing in the middle of one of the pathways. Relief coursed through his veins: he hadn't lost her. Cirie wore ripped blue jeans, and a plain white t-shirt to go with a worn green leather jacket. She shuffled the music sheets on her stand as she put the violin up to her chin, just as she must have done thousands of times before. The three reapers stood at the tree line, mute, just waiting to become a part of the audience Cirie craved.

Random notes sprung from the strings at first. She tinkered with the strings as pedestrians walked past. No one even glanced at her. Cirie brought her arms down to her sides. Looking at the crowd in the park and shaking her head, she took a deep breath. Then the music started flowing.

It was soft at first, like she was afraid to make too much noise. Then a corner of her mouth lifted into a smirk. As soon as that happened, she became free. Shawn wasn't sure if she was playing her originals or not, but he knew what she meant when she said she went into a void. Strangers still walked past, but now they slowed. Parkgoers were used to street performers, but her music stopped quite a few. Change hit the bottom of her violin case from some people that appreciated her skill.

"Girl can play. I have to give her that," Trevor said as he swayed to the music like he was in the back row at a concert.

Shawn couldn't disagree. But Cirie wasn't going to become a world-class violinist. It was more likely that her career would end today with a mugger in the park. Or from falling down the large stone steps leading to the lower level. Or... or... Shawn's mind started racing. Suddenly, he felt like there was a spotlight on the three of them. Any moment, she could stop playing and glance up to see them standing there.

A smattering of applause came from a few bystanders as she finished her first piece. No, it wasn't a concert with a full house; nevertheless, the smile on her face was undeniable. Even if she didn't have much time left, Shawn felt a little solace in the fact that she'd gotten the courage to perform. He wasn't sure that she would after the other night. And who knew how have many chances she had left?

"Jay, send your cardinal to the talons and tell them that we have the grounder in sight," Trevor instructed.

Scribbling on spare parchment, Jay whistled for streaker. A pair of red wings darted from the sky and snatched the piece of paper out of his hand. It still shocked Shawn to see the cardinals in action. Both he and Jay had tested their cardinals out at the Academy. They'd gone to different areas of Wayward to see if their birds would still find them. Which they did without fail.

"How long until we get a new tracker and map?" Shawn asked, not taking his eyes off the violin.

Trevor sat down and patted the dying grass next to him. "Depends. Could be a couple of hours. It's contingent on the amount of souls being reaped, messages coming in, and the approval process. But they'll know to rush it through."

"Approval process?" Shawn asked.

"Mmmm, since we lost a tracker, it has to get approved by at least three Council members." Seeing the look of confusion on both first years, Trevor continued. "It's just so a few on the council are aware of the emergency. They then determine if a notice has to be sent to the capital to notify the Four Horseman of the situation."

Notice to the capital? These words froze the air inside Shawn's lungs. His chest refused to expand and contract. This could mean deep trouble and, based on the frustrated look Jay was throwing his way, Jay thought so too.

"But don't worry about that, you're both first years. It happens; believe me." The words did nothing to help alleviate the worry that had filled the tracker-sized space in Shawn's pockets.

Two hours straight. That was how long Cirie played for. She flirted with some classical music and stayed away from any kind of pop song renditions. But she mostly played her own work. As she packed up, she seemed more energetic. She collected the bundle of loose change from her case and swapped the earnings for her violin. She didn't bother counting the money; it wasn't about that for her. As she got up, the reapers followed.

Jay took the lead as they weaved their way through the park. With her headphones on, Cirie noticed nothing. Shoes untied, violin in hand, she was simply enjoying life. She led them through a portion of the park that was empty at this time of the day, dancing to whatever music was feeding her moves.

Those moves made their way back to the subway station. Musk filled Shawn's nostrils like a bathtub left on too long. It could be overwhelming, yet the city grounders ignored the sickly sweet scent. Each person that stood on the platform was caught up in their own little world and ignored their surroundings. No amount of pink and green graffiti would jolt them into reality. People were too concerned with going about their day.

Everyone except Cirie, that is. She stood near the edge of the platform, examining the passengers. It appeared that she was just bopping her head to some music, but her face was focused on examining everyone getting on and off. Her left hand remained clenched inside her jeans pocket.

Trains came and went like clockwork, the screeching announcing both arrivals and departures. As the station started emptying out, Shawn could feel invisible eyes settling on him. Just one turn from Cirie would expose everything. Only a handful of people were left in the station. They were too close. But there wasn't anything he could do at this point. Without a tracker, they had to be.

Thankfully, Cirie was starting to relax. Instead of eyeing her fellow passengers in the station, she started pacing along the edge of the landing. She put one foot in front of the other as if she were on a makeshift balance beam.

A light emerged far down in the tunnel as she continued her performance. Within seconds of the light illuminating the tunnel, a horn blasted, shattering the air in the station. Cirie twisted, drawn by the sound. Her feet overlapped like ribbon on a present. The sudden movement had broken her concentration and her balance. Her arms spread out, reaching for a railing that failed to appear.

The train ignored her panicked flailing and continued to move down the tunnel toward the station. People say that tragic things happen in slow motion. That adrenaline slows down one's perception. Maybe that was the case for Cirie. But for Shawn, it took mere seconds.

Like a bird failing to fly for the first time, Cirie dropped over the side of the landing. Her scream refused to be drowned out by the train's horn. Her violin case rattled against the tracks as it made contact. A collective scream was let out by the few remaining pedestrians in the station who stood, shell-shocked, in their spot.

Shawn's legs were moving before his mind was. Fueled by emotion and his moral compass, he rushed toward Cirie. Any reason besides helping her flew out the window. He couldn't watch another person die. Scratch that: he couldn't watch Cirie die. Not without trying to help.

"Shawn, wait." A voice called out from behind him.

Was it Trevor's or Jay's? He wasn't sure, and he didn't care. He wasn't thinking of the consequences if he helped her—only what happened if he didn't. He reached the edge of the landing in seconds. Cirie sat dazed on the tracks, a small cut above her eyebrow bleeding from her fall. The train's presence was getting heavier, with train cars replacing air as it screeched forward.

"Cirie!" Shawn screamed, extending his hand. The drop from the landing was about a couple feet down, and if Cirie hadn't bumped her head, she might have been fine to pull herself up, but she still sat there with a blank face. "Cirie, get up," Shawn yelled again, his voice breaking at the strain he put into it.

"Stripes?" Her fingers gripped the track and then it was as if she snapped back into reality. Her eyes widened when she gazed down the tunnel at her fate. The conductor must have seen what happened because he was laying down on the horn now. If she didn't move in moments, she was going to become a part of the train permanently, and Shawn's first assignment would be complete.

Breaks were shrieking as the conductor tried to stop, but it was of no use. No train is meant to stop on a dime.

Ignoring Shawn's outstretched hand, Cirie got up and hurled herself on top on the platform. She was halfway up when Shawn pulled her feet out of the danger zone, just as the train filled the space she'd just occupied. Violin pieces spilled into the station as the train blew up her case.

They both laid on the dirty ground staring at the flickering lights above them, breathing heavily from the near-death experience. "I... I..." was all she could get out.

"Are you okay?" Shawn asked.

Her fingers went to the cut above her eyebrow, coming back with a little blood. She nodded her head. "Yes, I'll be fine. Thank you."

A figure appeared above them as she spoke. Trevor's face flushed with an anger Shawn didn't know the man could contain. " *What* have you done?" It was at that moment that Shawn knew everything was not going to be fine.

Chapter 33

The scythe loomed over them like a dark cloud about to rain down pain. Trevor was fuming, his grip on the weapon tightening as he surveyed Cirie on the ground. When she met his gaze, confusion swept across his face. A grounder could see him. In all his years of reaping, this had never happened.

"Get the hell away from us," Cirie screamed at him as she pulled out a pocketknife from her pants. She had gone from one danger to another and was not about to go down without a fight.

Trevor stepped back. "You can see us?" He looked around the station, as if he'd suddenly appeared to all grounders. He expected to see them looking back, but instead, they looked at Cirie like she was a piece of trash in an alleyway. A woman who had started walking over to check on Cirie out of concern stopped in her tracks. The only thing they were seeing was a girl on the ground, pointing a pocket-knife at empty air. They thought she had lost it.

Trevor turned to Shawn and shook his head. "I thought you'd be a great blade. I was wrong."

Doors from the train hissed open as Trevor raised the scythe. Grounders scrambled out the cars, ignoring Cirie as they went about their lives. Cirie grabbed Shawn's hand and yanked him toward her as she tried to escape the arc of the scythe. Shawn knew it was no use: the length of the blade wouldn't miss from this distance. He'd saved Cirie from one disaster and led her into another. He closed his eyes.

A thud hit the floor. But when Shawn opened his eyes, it wasn't Cirie on the ground. There wasn't a blade sticking out of her back. There was no blood pooling around her body. Instead, Jay stood over Trevor's body with the lid of a trash can.

"Well, this has turned into a fucking mess," Jay said to them.

Cirie was speechless but still held her knife protectively. She didn't know Jay, and she wasn't sure if he was going to attack her next.

The metal lid clattered to the ground next to Trevor's unconscious body.

"You want to explain to the grounder that I'm not going to hurt her, so she can put down the knife?" Jay said.

Shawn snapped out of his daze and gripped Cirie's shoulder. "He's a friend. Jay's going to help us, okay?" Was he? Shawn almost didn't believe the words himself, but the body lying below him was proof enough.

This calmed Cirie, so she lowered her knife and put it back into her pocket. "What the hell is going on?"

Jay ignored the question. "We need to secure him." He pointed to Trevor and then started ripping at the lining of his suit. He tore the fabric, making two long pieces, and tossed one to Shawn. "Grab the feet."

Tie him up? Shawn held the fabric in his hands. They needed time to get away. If a cardinal was sent to alert the other reapers, they wouldn't have a chance. So, Shawn did what Jay told him to. Slipping the fabric around Trevor's feet, he knotted it, securing Trevor's legs and making sure it was tight.

"Someone better tell me what the hell is happening *now*!" demanded Cirie.

Shawn didn't know what to do. He didn't have a plan. He'd made a rash decision and now had to deal with the fallout.

"We can leave her. She's due soon anyway," Jay said to him. He wanted to run. Jay had always wanted to run. He didn't want to be a blade either. But he was, because he knew what happened to those that didn't follow the rules. And now they'd broken the biggest one of all.

Taking a deep breath, Shawn made his decision. It was the one he made when he went after Cirie. "No."

Jay froze mid-knot. "No?

"We can save her."

Jay glanced at Cirie, whose hand had returned into her pocket. The girl had almost died twice, and her two saviors were discussing leaving her for dead. Jay wouldn't even blame her if she attacked him. "Shawn... we need to get out of here."

"Then go ahead," Shawn snapped, turning his attention back to Cirie. "I owe you an explanation, but we need to get out of here first, okay?"

She released her grip on the knife in her pocket. "Damn right you owe me an explanation. Tell me one reason I shouldn't go to the police right now?"

Shawn went up to a random grounder waiting for the train. He pulled the man's wallet out of his pocket and held it in front of his face. The man was perplexed. The grounder stared at the wallet floating in front of him. Then Shawn tossed the wallet gently at his chest. The grounder turned white and looked around, wondering if anyone else had seen it.

Cirie just stared at him, still not comprehending.

"Oh hell." Jay went up to another and screamed, "You're all going to die!" into their faces. A woman Jay was closest to remained unphased, and Jay waved his hand in front of her.

It almost clicked then for Cirie. "What *are* you guys? Some kind of ghosts?"

"No," Shawn said, picking up Trevor's scythe. "We're reapers."

Chapter 34

"I think I should hold onto that," Jay said as he walked over.

Without hesitation, Shawn gave him the scythe. He knew that Jay would be better equipped than he was if they had to fight another reaper. Mac's lessons were still fresh in Shawn's mind.

Cirie put her head into her hands, taking slow deep breaths. "That's it. I've completely lost it."

Shawn knew that feeling. It was the one he had the first couple days—well, weeks—as a reaper. He extended his hand again. "Just give us a chance to explain, okay?"

The crowd continued to ignore Cirie on the ground as she hesitated. "Okay, Stripes. I'll come with you, but I'm not letting either of you hold that damn weapon."

"You want us to leave it here?" Jay asked, examining the station as if a reaper was going to jump out of the shadows.

"Hell no. I'm taking the damn thing. You two can move your buddy over there."

The two of them agreed to let Cirie take hold of the scythe, so they could end their game of hot potato. They moved their unconscious mentor away from the main part of the station and found a door leading to janitor supplies. Laying him down underneath the shelves, Trevor became another item lost in the dirt-covered closet.

"He's going to get out of there," Shawn said as Jay tightened the knots.

Cirie stood outside the cramped space, holding an invisible staff to anyone who looked her way.

"I know that," Jay said.

"Do you have a plan?" Shawn asked.

Jay's ears turned red. "Do I have a plan?" He tied another knot down at Trevor's feet, gripping the torn piece of fabric like it owed him a debt. "Do *you* have a plan, Shawn? In case you forgot, we're doing this because of you."

Shawn felt the anger emanating off Jay like steam from boiling water. Shawn rushed into things; he wasn't denying that. Still, he'd helped someone. He wasn't going to regret it. "We just need to buy time."

"There are other ways to buy time," Jay said, standing over Trevor.

Every muscle in Shawn's body tensed. He looked down at Trevor, his mentor: one of the few people helping this new world make sense to Shawn. "You don't mean–"

"No, Turner. I'm not *killing* the man. I'm not heartless. But I may have an idea."

"Hey, guys, I think you have mail," Cirie called from the hallway.

Both reapers poked their heads out of the room to see her stroking a tiny red bird. In her other hand, she gripped the blade and two pieces of rolled-up parchment that were tied together with black string.

Jay crept forward and, when he was close enough, snatched the bird from the ground.

Surprised by the sudden movement, Cirie jumped back. "What are you doing?"

"We can't let the cardinal go back." Shawn spoke for Jay, who let him continue. "It's how we communicate over long distances. If we let the bird go, Trevor will be able to get a message out quickly when he escapes. We have to trap it somewhere."

Spotting an empty box, Jay got up. "Any objections?" He motioned to the box.

"This seems like animal cruelty," Cirie protested.

"We'll poke holes in the box. Don't worry. Besides, this cardinal can't die like normal birds anyway."

Questions bounced across Cirie's face, but she remained quiet, letting Jay tape the box shut with the cardinal trapped inside. Air holes were punctured to Cirie's satisfaction, and the group stowed the box in an alley outside the station.

As they'd taken care of both Trevor and his cardinal, they could now focus on saving Cirie. At least, that was Shawn's priority. He wasn't sure what Jay wanted to do, and it wasn't like they could discuss it openly in front of their assignment.

Leaning against the wall, Cirie wanted answers. "Okay. Now please explain why a man with a blade was trying to decapitate me. And why we had to tie him up."

Shawn took the lead. "He did it because I interfered."

"Interfered?"

"Where we come from, we're only supposed to observe. We can't interfere with our assignment."

"And I'm that assignment," she stated, running her hands across the bricks. "And what would you be observing for your subject?" Disdain dripped out of her voice.

"Your death," Jay said blatantly.

Sensing the questions coming, Shawn tried to get ahead of them. "That's why they call us reapers. We get assigned someone, and once they pass away, we collect their essence so that they don't become trapped as ghosts."

Traffic from the city weaved its way out of the streets as silence spread over the group. Everything they were telling her was putting Jay and him at more risk. If they weren't going to be killed before, they most certainly would be now.

"Uh huh... and you two aren't ghosts?"

"We're both technically dead," Jay stated casually.

Slowly, her feet started inching backwards. "Well, this has been fun. But I've obviously suffered a psychotic break of some sort. You two Looney Tunes have fun reaping souls or whatever."

"Let me show you the parchment," Shawn pleaded.

Thinking it over, she ended up giving back the paper. The black string unfurled, letting the two pieces separate.

"I understand that this is all a lot, but if we weren't real, could you imagine this?" Shawn asked. The tracker slid into the middle pocket with ease. Slowly, the outline of the streets came into focus on the paper. Street names emerged onto it, while the timer on Cirie's life counted down.

"What is this?" she asked.

"It's a map," Shawn replied.

Leaning forward, Cirie tightened her grip on the scythe. "No shit, Sherlock. I understand that. What's that?" She pointed to the countdown on the tracker.

Shawn stared at the countdown, knowing that any second could bring a new challenge. "That would be how much time you have left to live."

Chapter 35

Leading them through a maze of streets, Cirie ignored the two reapers trying to keep up with her. After Shawn told her that she was going to die, she had turned and walked away. She hadn't looked or spoken to them for blocks.

"Cirie, talk to us!" Shawn pleaded. "Where are you going? If we don't come up with a plan, then they're going to kill us all."

Stalking behind them both, a brooding Jay kept pace. "It's no use. She's a lost cause. We have to leave before they come for us."

Cirie turned. "Who?" she steamed. "Are the other people in my head going to come and try to kill me? Please tell me who else knows I'm supposed to be killed?" A bystander gave her a curious glance, to which she sneered until he turned away.

"Not killed: reaped. Remember, we don't kill anyone. Although the gargoyles might be inclined to now," Jay said, too nonchalantly for this serious of a situation.

The last thing she needed was more craziness to fuel her idea of insanity. Shawn mouthed "stop" to Jay as Cirie charged forward.

"Ah, yes! How could I forget about the church-dwelling gargoyles!" She hit herself lightly on the side of her head. "Silly me." The walk signal went from green to red, yet Cirie continued on the path, daring the cars to hit her as she crossed.

Shawn wondered if Cirie now had a death wish. At this point, she was tempting fate.

"And about much time do I have left supposedly?"

Glancing at the tracker, Shawn wasn't thrilled about the results. How was he going to save her? "About two-and-a-half days." Realizing this did nothing to bring her back to reality, Shawn continued. "But that's why we're here."

"Right. To collect my essence or whatever. Gottttt it." The sarcasm in her voice was unmistakable.

This wasn't going to plan. Not that there was a plan. Shawn was starting to feel like he was trying to carry water in a fishing net. "No, we risked everything to make sure you survived past that date!"

This gave Cirie pause, and through all her disbelief, her hand still gripped the scythe. "You got a problem?" Cirie yelled at the strangers who were staring at her talking to thin air about souls and getting killed. The couple turned and went on their way. "If you both are so real, then why am I the only one that can see you?"

No book or person at the Academy that Shawn had consulted had given him an answer. So, he couldn't give her a reason. "We don't know."

"Is this real enough for ya?" Jay grabbed Cirie's jacket.

As if by instinct, she swatted his hand away, daring him to touch her. Whether she believed them to be real or fake, she wasn't going to let that happen again.

"Where are we going?" Shawn asked.

"Home," she stated flatly, like the answer had been obvious.

The look on Jay's face said everything. "You want to go to the most obvious location? You're brilliant."

The air seemed to thicken as she turned to face Jay. "Look, you don't get to make the rules. I do. And if you aren't a figment of my imagination, then go ahead and leave me the hell alone. Capeesh?"

"Let's go."

It took Shawn a second before he realized that Jay was talking to him. "What?"

"She doesn't want our help. We'll get ourselves killed if we stick with her."

Jay wasn't wrong. It didn't seem like she was going to believe them anytime soon. "You go," Shawn said. "I don't want to hold you back." Ever since they were reaped, Jay had been planning an escape. Shawn didn't want him to miss his chance.

Jay sighed. But didn't walk away. "I'm telling you, this isn't worth it. We don't have a good shot anyway."

"I'm not walking away from her." Shawn pointed to his left and realized their mistake because he was pointing to nothing. Cirie was gone.

Twirling around, Shawn couldn't spot her. While they were talking, she'd slipped into the crowd. They were near the pier market, so the crowd was dense with grounders trying to get a deal on fresh fish out of the harbor.

"Shawn, look at what's in your hand."

Of course. He was clenching the tracker and map she'd handed over. "Take it." He handed the map over to Jay, not trusting himself after everything that had happened.

"Looks like she's taking a stroll through the market. Must be going through it to get to her apartment. Not exactly a shortcut. Come on. Let's go find the grounder,"

Turning onto Fulton Ave, they were greeted with the wafting stench of dirty water secreting from the front of the market. Shops lined the pedestrian-only walkways. Lights hung between the shops, the calling sign of the market.

They sped past overpriced food stalls and novelty items, going straight into the small pathway full of pushy vendors, each one yelling at tourists and residents alike to buy one of their various trinkets. The tracker led the reapers deeper into this mess of grounders.

Turning a corner, Shawn came face to face with a man holding onto a small child. His eyes twitched back and forth like a supermarket scanner looking for the price on a barcode. Sidestepping away from them, Shawn called back to Jay. "Which way?"

Just ahead, they had three different options. They could continue straight like they had or go down the stairwell on the left that led to the end of the pier. The last option was the sloped hill of vendors to the right.

"What did you say?" Jay replied as he rounded the corner.

"Which way?" Shawn repeated while feeling the fear creep up into his fingertips. His clenched hands were shaking with each passing second.

A flash of brown leather drew Shawn's attention. Down the staircase, he found his target haggling with a vendor. With her last couple of days alive, she had decided to go shopping, of all things. Then he spotted something that froze the blood in his dead heart.

Next to the vendor was a plaque, but it wasn't this that terrified Shawn. It was what the plaque was referring to. Above it was a figure of a man yelling into a microphone, one hand in the air. A man made of stone.

Jay's face showed his dread. "Gargoyles," he whispered, like the word was crawling into his head.

A man made of gold was moving off a platform, walking in the direction they'd come from. "Meet me by the water," Jay said as he eyed the golden man. Without discussing his plan, Jay sped off toward the gargoyle, leaving Shawn to find Cirie before something else did.

Wasting no time, Shawn raced down the staircase. Taking the steps in groups of three, he attempted not to trip. He jumped through a fog of various scents as he passed a candle stand whose smells blended together. Cirie stood oblivious to the danger nearby, as she continued negotiating. Just a few feet away, the statue started shimmering at certain points. At the spot where the hand held the microphone, fingers were morphing out of it. Shawn had never seen anything like it. The hand came out of nothing: ripples of stone moved as it emerged like a hand from water, reaching out for help. Shawn hadn't seen the gargoyles on the surface yet and assumed the whole statue would move as one, but it seemed it was just a box for the deadly present inside.

"Italian beef!"

"Get your snapbacks! Two for one!"

"Picture frames! Come capture your time at the pier!"

Each vendor yelled as Shawn sprinted by, which caused his nerves to skyrocket as more of the gargoyle surfaced. An arm, then a leg. The thing was going to be on Cirie within moments.

"I think I'll take this one." Cirie pointed to a glass necklace encompassing what seemed to be a small purple flower.

The woman behind the counter grabbed the necklace and rang up the price on the cash register before handing over the item.

The gargoyle was standing just outside of its hiding place, glancing curiously at Cirie. It waited for a second, then started moving toward her.

With each breath, Shawn was cursing himself for not working out more when he was alive. His lungs burned, as he watched the hand inch toward the back of her neck.

Taking the necklace from the vendor, Cirie dropped the purchase into her pocket as the stand owner returned to her inventory. Cirie turned to face the stairway that Shawn was sprinting from. Her eyes went wide with fright at the sight of him barreling at her. In that instant, Shawn went airborne, tackling Cirie to the ground. The gargoyle snatched at the air where she'd just stood.

A scream escaped Cirie as the duo rolled on the brick pathway like a tumbleweed in the wind. The momentum of the roll produced bruises and scratches on their exposed skin.

"What the hell!" Cirie shouted.

"We don't have time!" Shawn screamed, pointing at the lug of rock walking at them.

The sight of the unknown creature making its way down the path stunned Cirie. "What in the world is that?"

Gasping, Shawn stood up. "That's what we were warning you about! Reapers aren't the only ones looking for you. That's a gargoyle!"

Chapter 36

Blue blood pulsed through the cracks in its skin. It stood with its head tilted, examining them both like a child learning the behavior of an adult. "Shawn Turner, you are in violation of multiple laws. Where is your mentor?" The voice came out flat but drove shivers up Shawn's spine. The Academy would definitely know now.

"It speaks," Cirie said from the ground, stunned.

The gargoyle took a step forward, drawn by her voice. "Blade, you have alerted a grounder?" He questioned. Not even the gargoyle could keep the surprise out of his voice. Shawn doubted he'd dealt with anything like this before.

Cirie stood. "I'm a damn human, pebble ass."

The gargoyle turned to Shawn, whose feet stayed frozen to the ground. "In accordance with the Watcher Society rules, I'm employing Section 8."

"Uh, Stripes, what's Section 8?"

Watcher Society rules? There was still so much Shawn didn't understand about this world, but he knew whatever Section 8 was, it wasn't going to be good. "We need to move. Now." He sprung up from the ground, and the two started sprinting past the gum-covered walls of the market. Daring a look behind him, Shawn's heart dropped into his stomach as the gargoyle easily kept pace. The stone man didn't even seem to be puffing.

"Surrender, or I will invoke Section 11," the gargoyle called from behind.

Shawn didn't plan on finding out what either Section 8 or 11 were. A pathway to his right came up, and he was taking it. Take sudden turns. That's what he had to do, confuse the poor stone face. As the turn came up, he grabbed Cirie's hand and pulled her with him.

"No, Shawn! Wait!" she screamed as he yanked her along. What was she talking about? Up ahead, he quickly found out. The gum wall expanded in this turn, but instead of a path to freedom, they were met with a wall. A dead end.

The gargoyle was now in front of their only way out. "Give me the scythe!" Shawn wasn't great, but maybe he could buy time for Cirie.

"Are you serious?" she asked.

Shawn looked over to her empty hands. How had he not noticed she didn't have it while running?

"I tossed it after I left you two arguing in the street. I didn't think it was real."

"Is it real now?" Shawn steamed. They had no weapons. The only thing this dead end contained was the trash that littered the ground.

"Blade. Turn the grounder in now."

On one of the walls was an outline of a heart made of red gum. Fitting really. His heart had stopped, and now Cirie's was about to join the club. Not seeing a way out, Shawn knew he was trapped. He considered surrendering, but then he caught a flash of crimson. "Not sure I want to do that, actually."

The gargoyle didn't react. "Response has been noted," he answered. He slowly shifted his stance so that his left foot was forward. He didn't want to be caught flat footed when Shawn and Cirie inevitably rushed him.

How strong was a gargoyle? Shawn had no idea, but the thing looked like it could dent his skull with a slap. If they weren't quick enough to escape his reach, they were going to find out the hard way. Cirie stretched her legs and got ready for the attempt. Did she see the crimson figure behind the creature as well? Shawn prayed that she did. There wasn't time to explain.

"Gotta agree with Stripes over here." She pointed to Shawn; a thin smile spread across her face. Apparently, she was starting to believe a bit. "I'm not feeling the whole 'hand me over' part either. Plus, I'm not really a fan of your whole outfit. Pretty trashy if you ask me, granite dick."

The sentence confused the gargoyle and would have confused Shawn too if he hadn't seen a large silver trashcan back in familiar hands as Jay crept behind the gargoyle. Tensing, Shawn prepared himself for the mad sprint forward.

"Now!" Shawn shouted as his legs sprung ahead. Contents of the trash flowed down the body of the gargoyle as Jay jammed the can over his head. Stone face swung his arms wildly, panicking like an animal caught in a trap. Freedom was on the other side of the fist coming Shawn's way. He ducked as Cirie went high to the right. Channeling her inner gymnast, she leaped off the wall as gray knuckles connected with the side. Shards of brick exploded from the punch. Pieces rained over Shawn as he went under the attack.

At least now he had an idea of how strong they were. Shawn's leg scraped along the ground. Parts of his flesh were sliced from the rough surface.

The gargoyle recovered quickly, yanking the garbage can off his head. He spotted the trio only a couple of feet away, scrambling to run. He bent down and it slowly dawned on Shawn what he was about to do.

"Cirie!" Shawn called out as he shoved her from the side, causing her to teeter off balance. At the same time, the gargoyle dove at the grounder. Instead of tackling Cirie, the force slammed into Shawn hard enough to cause a concussion. He went spiraling into the ground as the gargoyle missed his prey. Except it wasn't enough. Clutched between the gargoyle's fingers was Cirie's green leather jacket.

Cirie struggled against the grip, grimacing as the gargoyle pulled her up. She thrashed at his arm, but Shawn knew it was a battle she wasn't going to win. The gargoyle looked down at her. "Curious, you're not only able to see them, but me as well."

She scowled back at him.

Jay came over and motioned to the stone arm. He wasn't running this time. No, he didn't want to abandon Cirie either. Shawn saw the arm outstretched like a finish line or a bad game of red rover. And just like both of those, Shawn ran straight at it.

Making contact with the gargoyle's forearm was like trying to tackle a fire hydrant. Pain erupted throughout Shawn's chest as he broke through the grip. All air wheezed out of his lungs. He must have had a cracked rib or two. Spots filled his vision as he fought to gain back his breath. But Cirie was free.

Jay hurried over to pull Cirie out of reach, but, unlike Shawn, the gargoyle recovered instantly. The hands gripped her arm. A crack sounded as he snapped a bone. Cirie screamed in pain as the gargoyle threw her behind him. Her head snapped against the ground with a sick thud that rang through Shawn's ears. Her scream was cut short as she lay unconscious. Or worse.

Everything had happened in the span of seconds. Speechless, Shawn crawled away. Words were coming from behind him, but all he could focus on was Cirie's limp body. Was she dead?

Hands shook his shoulders. "Shawn, we gotta go." Jay was pulling him now.

All the commotion had drawn attention. The woman from the shop was checking on Cirie as a couple dialed 911 on their phone. There wasn't a way Shawn and Jay could get to her now.

"Let's get out of here," Shawn said. The words felt dirty leaving his mouth. After everything they'd done for Cirie, they had to leave her.

Chapter 37

Market stands became blurs as they raced away from the chaos. Rules were thrown out the window at this point, and they bumped into body after body; surprised yelps followed them every step of the way. Shawn was numb. Each step felt like one in the wrong direction. He shouldn't have left Cirie.

"We had no choice," Jay panted next to him.

No choice? There was always a choice. But the pain in Shawn's chest made it hard to breathe, let alone argue, so he stayed silent. As his feet pounded the pavement, pain shot across his rib cage.

Rumbling down the path, Shawn chanced a look behind him. No gargoyle. Stone face must have stayed by Cirie. Shawn slowed down to a walk. It took a couple of seconds before Jay even noticed that Shawn had stopped running.

"What are you doing?" Jay asked, jogging back.

"No one's following us." Shawn pointed at the path they'd just come from. Grounders still went about their shopping, oblivious to the reapers. Kids ran about from stall to stall, but there was no sign of the gargoyle.

"Doesn't mean we stop. You know more gargoyles could appear at any moment!" Jay couldn't keep the irritation out of his voice.

"We left her!" Shawn inhaled deeply and a shock wave of pain spread across his chest. "Like she was nothing."

Jay took a step forward, inches from Shawn's face. "What did you want to do? Keep fighting the gargoyle? Or maybe you just wanted to stick around and get caught by reapers!"

"It wasn't enough." Shawn's head drooped.

Jay ran a hand through his short hair. "I never said we were finished."

"What do you mean? She's been found out by the gargoyles. They'll just relay everything to Wayward."

Reaching into his jacket, Jay pulled out the tracker. "Look." He shoved the map into Shawn's hands. "She's alive. They aren't going to kill her. It's against the rules."

Time was still ticking down. She wasn't dead. Relief coursed through his body as her tracker started moving. "You're right. What's our next move?"

"Looks like she's being moved out of the market." Her ticker moved at a normal speed, then the locater dot inched closer to the front entrance. Once it reached the gates, her speed tripled. "Well, she isn't walking, that's for sure. Must be in a car or something."

A siren rose above the noise of the crowd and faded away just as quickly as it had come. The young reapers looked at each other. "Ambulance," they both said at once.

"Where's the nearest hospital?" Shawn said, scurrying over the map, wishing he was more familiar with the city.

Jay's finger came down a few blocks away on the map. "There. Doesn't look like there are any closer to the market. And the ambulance looks to be headed in that direction," Jay said as he looked up at Shawn. Then his whole body went rigid. Jay wasn't looking at Shawn anymore. He was looking past him.

Shawn spun around with the map gripped tight in his hands. "Okay. Time to get out of here."

Stone face wasn't making his way toward them, but two of his buddies were. These two gargoyles were shorter than the ones Shawn had seen. They looked to be about five feet tall, but that didn't stop their legs from propelling them forward with the speed of Olympic athletes.

"Follow me," Jay said, yanking Shawn's shirt and pulling him down the path. They didn't make it far before the two gargoyles were almost on top of them. It seemed like every step they took, the gargoyles gained two on them.

"There!" Jay shouted as they turned a corner on the path.

There? Shawn didn't know what Jay was talking about. They'd run out of track; the path they were on was leading straight to the water. "Where?" Shawn shouted between breaths.

"The water!" Jay yelled.

This statement did nothing to clarify Jay's intentions. Yet they were getting so close that Shawn could smell the water. Did he expect him to swim?

With a burst of speed, Jay separated himself from the group. If Jay had been a runner in his former life, he hadn't mentioned it. He was making a beeline for one of the boats. Boats! Finally, it clicked for Shawn. While he wasn't a great swimmer by any means, he at least didn't need floaties. He didn't think the same could be said for their heavy-footed friends following.

Jay leaped onto the deck, the wood thumping under each footstep. He was at a full sprint, aiming right for a small motorboat that a fisherman was attempting to start. The older man wiped sweat from his brow, cursing as he went to pull the handle again. Shawn almost shouted a warning, but even if the man had been able to hear him, it wouldn't have mattered. The fisherman released a grunt as Jay collided with the man's shoulder, sending him sprawling into the water.

"Hurry!" Jay pulled back the cord and got the engine started in one try. He raced to untangle the knots keeping the boat tethered to the dock.

Shawn glanced behind him and wished he hadn't. The two gargoyles were running in unison. Both arms were at rigid right angles, pumping in perfect robot-like motion. Their faces showed no sign of emotion or strain, as their tight-lipped mouths didn't even open for air. Shawn's legs ached as he tried to reach the boat. He knew he should have joined the track team like his mother had wanted him to. His foot felt the ground change beneath him as he entered the dock. He could see Jay still struggling with rope as he approached. The pounding from behind him had gotten closer as the two mini gargoyles made up more ground.

The last of the knots came undone just as Shawn approached. Jay shoved off the side, trying to distance himself from the dock as the two gargoyles raced toward them. It was now or never. Shawn went airborne. Leaping from the side of the dock, he hoped he'd judged the distance correctly.

If Shawn had joined the track team, he never would have competed in the long jump. Friends joked about barely being able to slip a piece of paper under his feet when he jumped. Shawn had always laughed along, knowing they were joking. But as he was barreling down midair to the side of the boat, he couldn't help but think they'd been right. His feet splashed in the water, as his midsection landed on the railing of the boat. All the air was forced out of his lungs again, and if he didn't have a broken rib before, he most certainly did now.

Jay's hands pulled him the rest of the way into the boat, where Shawn let his body slump onto the floor. Shawn could hear the motor running and felt the movement as they pulled even further away from the dock. Everything hurt, and he could barely breathe, but Shawn lifted his head to glance back. The two mini gargoyles looked like something out of a horror film, as they stood staring at the two rogue reapers driving away.

It was a tale that the fisherman knew n -one would believe. His own boat driving away, after he got knocked into the water by... wind? Not that it was any of Shawn's concern, although a smile crept onto his face as he saw the man pull himself out of the water. The smile felt hollow, though. Even with adrenaline coursing through his body, Shawn felt defeated. Waves leapt at the boat as he and Jay continued to pull away from the dock, water splashing into the bottom.

"We left her," Shawn muttered again to himself.

Steering with white knuckles, Jay responded without looking. "We had to." His words rang with a bit of truth, but the truth felt as hollow as Shawn's smile. "Shawn," Jay said. "She'll be okay."

"I know." Unlike Jay's words, the lie sat burning on his lips. Shawn kept his head down, afraid his eyes would betray his voice. He let Jay focus on getting them out of the gargoyles' sight.

Traveling across the lake, neither reaper spoke. Only the sound of waves lapping against the bow filled the air between the two. The radio silence suited Shawn fine. Here he was, wondering if this was all a giant mistake. Why did he have to become a reaper? Why couldn't they have picked someone else—someone more suited for this job?

"Let's dock over there." After checking the tracker, Jay pointed to an area of a beach where there wasn't anyone in sight. He steered toward it. As they pulled up, he cut the engine. Not that it mattered if there had been people on the beach who could hear the engine. They'd blown way past the need for following reaper rules. Nevertheless, Shawn remained quiet as they glided into shore.

As soon as his foot hit solid land, Shawn collapsed into the sand. Everything hurt from his encounter with the gargoyles, but his ribs were making it extra clear that they wanted to be heard above everything else. He let the sand filter through his fingers as he wheezed like a slowly deflating balloon.

Jay fiddled with the boat as Shawn remained motionless. It wasn't that Shawn wouldn't help, but he couldn't find the strength to. After a minute of tinkering, the engine roared to life again. Shawn laughed, which garnered a quizzical look from Jay.

"Sorry," Shawn said with a chuckle. From his aching ribs to letting Cirie get caught, he couldn't help but laugh through the pain. Another laugh escaped. What was the point in cutting the freaking engine when they were just going to start it up again?

Pushing the motor into the forward position, Jay let go of the stern. Without a latch to the land, their stolen vehicle pumped forward in the water, away from the city. Away from the problems that Jay and Shawn carried with them. Shawn couldn't help but wish that he could trade places.

"It's best not to leave a trace of where we went," Jay explained as if Shawn had questioned him out loud.

He was right. Shawn knew this, but he also didn't care too much anymore. "Being conspicuous isn't really at the top of my priority list right now."

Jay bent down. Sand poured out between his fingers when he tried to clench it. "Really? So, you've just blown everything up and now we are, what, done, is it?"

Shawn gazed into the sky, wondering how much longer that would be up over his head instead of the cavern ceiling... or a coffin lid. "We've already broken rule number one. It doesn't matter anymore; we just need to survive."

Jay jerked back up, his ears glowing. "Wake up, Shawn." Taking what was left of the sand he'd been clenching; Jay threw the remains down at him. Bits of sand pelted Shawn across his body like a target being shot at.

"What the hell?" Shawn said, spitting out stray bits of sand.

Anger steamed out of Jay's voice. "What do you think I'm doing? You think I just sent the boat off into the middle of the water for shits and gigs? *Think!* By now, word's being sent back to the Academy and probably being spread amongst gargoyles as well. I sent the boat out, so a reaper doesn't spot it. I sent it out so a gargoyle can't come after us after finding our trail. I sent it out to help us survive!" After the last the sentence he paused, closing his eyes. Inhaling, he calmed himself. "Tell me, even now, why don't we want grounders alerted to our presence?"

Jay was scary when he was angry but was downright terrifying when he was moments away from releasing that rage. But he was right. Shawn wasn't thinking, he was just sulking. And sulking at a time like this would get a coffin lid over his head. "Because if grounders become alerted, then it will be easy for a watching gargoyle to find out."

Satisfied with the answer, Jay extended his hand. "We leave as little of a trace as we can." He helped Shawn up from the sand. "The quieter we move through the grounder world, the harder it will be for them to find us. Even the tiniest clues can come back to haunt us."

Nodding, Shawn was thankful not to be alone in this mess. "Then we're wasting time. Let's get moving."

The coordinates on the tracker had stopped changing drastically. It looked like her ambulance ride was over.

"Told you we weren't finished," Jay said, smirking.

Cirie's location was a single building on the map. Jay had been right: she was taken to a hospital. But what Jay was smirking at wasn't being right about the ambulance ride or the destination. He was smirking at where he'd taken them on their little boat ride. The hospital in question was only a couple blocks away from their beach. While the ambulance wound through the streets like a kid-friendly maze, Jay had cut across the obstacles and taken a shortcut on the water. Now Shawn couldn't help but grin.

"So, are you going to stay on this beach and wallow? Or are you coming with me?"

"Which way?"

Jay folded up the tracker and put it back in his suit pocket. "Follow me."

Chapter 38

Ambulances streamed in and out of the hospital, each one bringing the possibility of a reaper. Every time a stretcher went past, Shawn couldn't help himself to see if one was Cirie. "If she came by ambulance, then she must already have a bed," he said, eyeing the waiting area.

"Agreed. She would have beat us by five minutes at least. Let's try our luck on one of the computers near the front desk." With another stretcher coming up to the entrance, the young reapers stood back. Automatic doors hissed open to allow the EMTs through. Following close behind, Jay and Shawn tagged along into the hospital as silent passengers.

Stale air pumped into the hallway from hospital vents that formed a white noise throughout the building. A waiting room filled with concerned family members sat left of the front desk. Shawn thought back to his first reaping observation. He thought of the woman who couldn't speak, while the life support of someone she loved was turned off. Many of these people would go through the same range of emotions as they found out about the loss of a loved one. Shawn was here to make sure Cirie wasn't one of those losses. He just hoped that they hadn't traveled all this way for his first reaping assignment to mirror his first observation.

They made their way to the reception desk, where a man was trying to calm down a father and his screaming child. Ignoring the squeals about a pea being stuck up a nose, the reapers looked over at the unattended computer.

Looking up where Cirie was staying was great in theory. Not knowing how to work the software program in the hospital was the reality. Shawn hoped that Jay might have some idea at least. "What do we do?"

"No idea."

There went that hope.

Careful to avoid as much noise as possible, Shawn slowly typed Cirie's name into whatever front desk software program they used at the entrance. Thankfully, the screaming child covered up the clack of the keys, but Shawn knew he was on borrowed time. He hit "Enter" and watched the circle, indicating his search, spin round and round.

Invalid search.

Shit.

"According to our tracker, she's definitely here." Jay held out the parchment so that Shawn could see the coordinates. The tracker showed a zoomed-in view of the streets around the hospital, and in a corner of the building were her coordinates.

"I wish we had the layout of the hospital on here too," Shawn said. Would it have been too much to ask if they could see what room she was in?

Jay walked away from the front desk, holding out the tracker. "Well, at least the tracker zeroes in when we move closer to her coordinates."

Something about this problem reminded Shawn of his childhood. "Can I see the tracker?" Taking it from Jay, he watched the map zoom out of the square building the further away from Cirie's coordinates he got. The whole thing felt similar to an old children's game he used to play. "Hot or Cold!" he exclaimed.

Jay walked over. "What are you talking about?"

"That's how we can find her!" He told Jay as if it was the most obvious thing in the world. During family parties, Shawn's cousins used to steal his favorite dinosaur toy and force him to play a game to get it back: Hot or Cold. It was a simple game where they'd hide the toy somewhere in the house and Shawn had to find it. The only clues to the toy's whereabouts were his cousins shouting "hot" or "cold" as he stumbled around looking for it. The closer he got, the "hotter" he would be. This whole problem was just one large game of hot or cold.

"Come with me," Shawn said.

The reapers took off down the sterile disinfectant-coated hallways, watching the tracker coordinates change as the map slowly moved in on the building. Shawn kept his eyes glued to the parchment as Jay made sure he avoided any patients or workers. One wrong turn zoomed out the map but gave them the right direction to go next.

"Shawn, stop." Jay's voice came out as a whisper, one which Shawn almost tuned out. Then he looked up.

Walking up ahead of them was a woman in an all-white suit, which normally would have been fine, but normally people aren't walking around carrying scythes. A hospital blade.

As if someone had started a lawnmower in his hands, Shawn trembled while holding the corners of the tracker. They couldn't play dumb this time: the gargoyle told them that he'd alerted other reapers.

"Where?" Shawn asked.

Knowing that Shawn wasn't asking where the reaper was, Jay grabbed Shawn's jacket and pulled him into an open room to their right. Two beds sat empty, waiting for new patients to fill them. If Shawn had looked around, he would have thought about how depressing these rooms were. How hospital rooms and hotel rooms shopped at the same tacky art stores, where cheery came across as thoughtless.

"She was turned when we walked into the hallway, so it doesn't seem like she spotted us," Jay said as he peeked out the tiny window in the door.

"We have to go that same direction," Shawn said, staring at the vibrating piece of parchment in his hands.

Without taking his eyes off the hallway, Jay made their decision. "Then we wait it out for a second."

Not a second. Shawn waited a painstaking four minutes and thirty-seven seconds. He knew the exact timing from watching Cirie's clock countdown on the tracker. A countdown that could end at any minute. "I think we need to keep moving. We still need to figure out a room."

"What happens if she isn't in the room?"

"Then we were cold." Shawn took as deep of a breath as he could, the pain squeezing at his side, before opening the door. "Come on. We have some distance between her and us now. So as long as we don't draw attention, we should be okay. Either she's here for Cirie, and we're on the right floor, or she has another assignment."

"She might not be the only one," Jay stated.

The thought of turning a corner and coming face to face with a blade ran rampant in Shawn's head. They had to be careful. There was no telling how many assignments would end up at the hospital. Which meant there was no telling how many reapers there would be. Each step now took considerably more effort for Shawn. It felt as if his legs felt a different kind of gravity than the rest of his body after seeing the reaper. Step by step, he forced himself forward.

Too terrified to lift his eyes from the tracker, Shawn let Jay be his guide again. They found their way into the emergency ward, another step closer. She was in this hallway. She had to be. Even though he wasn't looking, Shawn was attuned to each noise around him. The intercom in the hallway kept going off, spouting out names that never ended up being Cirie's. The constant messages for the staff became more white noise as they gained more ground on Cirie's location.

Tick by tick, they got closer until the coordinates matched up almost perfectly with their position.

"Hot," Shawn said. Room 1118. Turning the handle with ease, the two reapers made their way into the room.

"Cir—" Shawn didn't finish her name, because no one was there to answer them. Both beds were empty.

"Where is she?" Jay asked. Checking the bathrooms, he made sure no one was hiding. He found nothing. She wasn't there. Jay looked over the tracker, "Our coordinates are right on top of each other."

He was right: the coordinates were exactly the same.

Something was off. What was Shawn missing? He thought back to the game of Hot and Cold. Back when his cousins kept laughing at him, calling out "Hot, hot, burning hot!" as he spun around in circles in the living room. He did the same thing now as he did then: he looked up. "That's why!"

"What are you talking about?" Jay said, scrambling after Shawn into the hallway.

"Where is it, where is it, where is it?" Shawn mumbled, looking up and down the hallway. Then, just like the tiny green tail of a stegosaurus peeking out over a ceiling fan, he spotted it. "There!" He pointed to one of the walls near a door where the outline of a stick figure walking up a zigzag hung.

"Stairs?" Jay asked.

"Stairs indeed. We had the right room." Shawn chuckled, thinking of that tiny green toy. "Just the wrong floor."

Chapter 39

How many floors were in this hospital? Five? Six? Seven? Shawn had no idea. Putting a hand to his forehead, he worked out a plan. "Okay, Jay. You need to go to 3118. I'll take 2118 and the rest of the even floors. Once you find her, bring her to the stairwell. That way, we'll know if the other one finds her first."

"Let's go then. We'll have to hurry. Remember to keep your eyes peeled. At any point, you might run into a gargoyle or reapers." Jay let his hand hover above the doorknob for a second before he turned around. "This is a good plan. Be careful, Shawn."

A rare compliment from Jay gave new energy to Shawn's steps. Exiting the room, their heads were spinning both ways, as if they had to make sure it was safe to cross the street. Except instead of a bus, it would be a steel blade hitting them. After seeing no sign of stone men or suited angels of death, they beelined it for the stairwell.

Shawn tilted his head up and felt slightly defeated by the long set of stairs in front of him. There were a lot more than seven floors. Probably twelve. And with each step, he wasn't sure if he was getting closer to Cirie or just another empty room.

Jay took the stairs two at a time. Shawn thought about doing the same, but the image of tripping and crashing into the stairs played in his head. The last thing he needed was a broken arm to go with his ribs. Upon reaching the second-floor landing, he hesitated to open the door. Just the possibility of a reaper being on the other side was paralyzing him. Here he was already dead, but still afraid of death. Shaking off the jitters, he ignored the thoughts and pushed open the door to make his way into the hallway.

No blade was waiting for him on the other side. Not wanting to draw attention to himself, in case a reaper was on assignment in one of the rooms, he speed-walked down the hallway. Perhaps Jay was wrong. Maybe if Shawn was found by one, they'd just think he was on an assignment as well. They should be looking for *two* young reapers, right? Not one. The speed-walking lasted about halfway to room 2118 before Shawn thought *screw it* and sprinted the last bit.

Through the window in the door, he could make out one of the curtains drawn. Jackpot. She was there. Not bothering to check his surroundings, he rushed towards the curtain. Without hesitating, he pulled it back to reveal someone who was most definitely not Cirie. A sleeping pregnant woman lay in the bed.

At least she *had* been sleeping. Confusion spread across her face at the loss of privacy. The metal rings on the curtain rod had disturbed her slumber. "Doctor?" she called out.

Her eyes stared straight through Shawn.

He rubbed his neck; he still wasn't used to not being seen. "Sorry," he whispered, the words falling on deaf ears. Strike two. Hopefully, he had more than three.

Back in the stairwell, hoping that there'd been better luck on the third floor, he called out, "Jay!" A stretch of silence was his answer, and he moved up to the fourth floor.

This time, he showed a little more caution in opening the door. The fourth-floor hallway was bustling with people. From nurses to family members holding flowers, the floor was flooded with reaper opportunities. Shawn was convinced someone would spot him.

Rooms 4110, 4112, 4114, and 4116 slid past his vision as he approached another roomful of dwindling hope. As he approached, a voice drifted out from underneath the door.

"You have a slight concussion, but otherwise, you should be okay. I suggest holding you here for observation for the night just to be safe."

"Yeah Doc, thanks and all. But I think I'll probably be heading out. Pretty sure this is the last place I should be."

It took all of Shawn's willpower not to barge his way inside after hearing the voice. It was one he recognized. He'd found Cirie.

The squeak of gurney wheels circled past Shawn as he waited for the doctor to leave. If the room had been empty, they would have already been on their way to the stairwell to meet Jay. More people walked past him, some with tears streaming down their faces. Others attempted to put on a brave appearance for whatever fate awaited their loved one. The elevator at the end of the hallway beeped as a nurse in blue scrubs and another doctor got off.

Except it wasn't a doctor.

Shawn did a double-take and saw the glint of the steel blade. Screw protocol. There wasn't time to wait around. Slowly, he popped open the door, trying to make it seem inconspicuous. He squeezed through the small gap he made and wondered if the reaper had seen him.

Inside, the doctor only saw empty space when he looked over at the doorway: not Shawn's frazzled look. Cirie's eyes grew wide with recognition. Shawn held up a finger to his lips, praying that she'd stay quiet. Otherwise, more company was about to join them.

The doctor walked over while continuing to make marks on his clipboard. "Sorry about that. Sometimes these doors stick a bit and don't close all the way." He shut it.

Standing at the edge of the bed, Shawn frantically filled Cirie in. "Look, we have a reaper on the floor headed our way." He looked around frantically. "There could be more here as well. We aren't sure. This time, they should be focused on me and Jay. Just play dumb when they walk in."

Intercom speakers squawked from the hallway as Cirie processed everything Shawn threw at her. Looking down at her in the rolling bed, Shawn was thankful he'd gotten there in time. Yet he couldn't shake the image of a clock when the countdown on her life was still happening.

"Where's Jay?" Cirie asked.

"Hmm, what was that?" The doctor looked up from his clipboard. "Ma'am, did you hear me?"

Cirie focused her attention back on the doctor. "Yes, sorry. I think you might be right. What could my other symptoms be again? I think I may be feeling a little woozy."

The doctor, satisfied with this response, continued to rant about symptoms and what she should avoid. Cirie ignored every single word coming out of his mouth and winked at Shawn. Her hand slowly reached over to her side table. Maneuvering around the TV remote and food brochure, she found the lid of her cup. Without breaking eye contact with the doctor, she removed the lid and brought the cup up to her lips.

"Ow!"

Suddenly, her hands flew up to her head, flinging the cup in the air. Red liquid escaped from the lidless cup like it was on a jail break. Red dots splattered across the doctor's white jacket.

"Ah, crap!" The doctor jumped back, not even close to avoiding the spill.

"Oh, God! I am so so sorry! I had a sharp pain all of the sudden." She squinted and kept one hand up near her ear.

Flustered, it was clear the man hadn't had this particular problem happen to him at work. "It's, uh, fine. It... happens. I'm just going to change. I'll be right back."

Once the door shut, Cirie burst into action. "Is Jay on this floor?" She poked her head into the tiny window.

"No, we split up. We weren't sure what floor you were on."

She turned her head back toward Shawn, not hiding the annoyance in her voice. "Isn't that what your little tracking map is for?"

"Doesn't work like that. But that doesn't matter. We need to find Jay and get out now. I wasn't even sure we'd have *this* chance." He wasn't even sure she'd be alive. Shawn thought he'd blown it in the alley. He didn't want to waste his second chance.

The pain in Cirie's head throbbed. "Yeah, believe me, that dude knocked me out like some MMA fighter. I thought the darkness was going to be forever." Seeing the worry spread across Shawn's face like a delicate spiderweb, she backtracked. "But I knew as soon as I woke up here that you and Jay would come. Thanks for not making me a liar to myself."

There were so many apologies Shawn wanted to make, but all he could muster was, "Sorry."

Eyes wide, Cirie sprinted back to the bed. "Jacket off!"

What was she talking about?

"Now!"

Following her instructions, Shawn took off his jacket and handed it over to her. She took it and stuffed it underneath her like she needed a pillow to help fluff her up. A calm panic was suddenly in every word she spoke. "You're going to be an intern." Looking around, she grabbed the clipboard and flung it to him. "Looks like your reaper friend is about to pay me a visit."

Thankfully, Shawn had enough coordination to catch the clipboard full of hospital jargon. Understanding the gravity of what was about to happen, Shawn started rubbing his neck. "Don't make eye contact or alert her in any way. Just keep talking to me."

"Understood." Cirie looked like she was about to say more, but the door slowly creaked open. A scythe led the way into the room.

Holding the clipboard gave Shawn some sense of stability to grip onto. He knew that he couldn't give the reaper the slimmest chance of recognizing him. He had to follow his own advice and talk to Cirie. He did what he'd seen doctors on TV do: he flipped through her chart. Except he couldn't focus. All the fear inside his veins was spreading, paralyzing him. Behind him at that very moment, a reaper was sulking her way through the room to decapitate him.

"Thanks again for the meds. I'm already starting to feel better." Cirie smiled at him. Calming the spread of fear.

A future doctor, Shawn reminded himself. "Just my job, Ma'am. Hoping this internship will help push me into a good medical program." Pushing through his own fear paralysis, Shawn turned and scuttled to the door like he was annoyed. "Damn doors in this place never latch when they close. Sorry about that."

"No worries. Can you tell me how long until I'm back up and running at 100%?"

Out of the corner of his eye, Shawn saw flashes of white as the reaper sauntered around the room. "Hmm, based on the test results, I'd say give it about two weeks before you do anything active. And just keep drinking fluids."

"So, this is who the commotion is all about," the reaper said aloud to herself.

Shawn almost stumbled, caught off guard by the reaper talking to herself. He had to focus intensely on talking to Cirie, trying to hold a smile that was faltering by the second.

Seemingly on the complete opposite spectrum, Cirie was casual. Her life was in imminent danger, but her eyes gave nothing away. "You know, I hate to admit it sir, but I'm not sure about my insurance coverage for a place like this."

The white-suited reaper stood at the foot of the bed and stroked the blanket that lay there. "Doesn't seem like much to me." She glanced up and down at Cirie. "Idiot reapers falling in love on a job," she scoffed as she moved in even closer.

With his feet molded to the spot, Shawn tried to keep his cool, but he could feel a bead of sweat sitting on his forehead. Falling in love on the job? That's how they were spinning this? "To me, your vitals look great, but I'll check with the doc. Honestly, I'm betting you should be able to go home soon. Just make sure to be a little more careful out on those steps next time." No one even noticed the janky conversation turn Shawn had caused. Cirie just went along with it.

The reaper was half-listening as she leaned in closer toward Cirie's face. Mere inches were between their two heads, yet Cirie remained unfazed. Shawn knew he had to keep talking, read results, make suggestions, something. Only he couldn't get his eyes off the scene unfolding before him. A harbinger of death was standing nose to nose with her, but Cirie kept her eyes locked on Shawn. If he were in her shoes, he knew he wouldn't be nearly as calm.

"I'm a bit of a klutz at times, but I'll do my best," she said, sniffing. "Question. Do head injuries have anything to do with my sense of smell?"

"Uh, well, there has been some history with these symptoms." Shawn panicked, not understanding why she'd bring this up. Sweaty hands now gripped the clipboard tightly. "From the doctor's notes on your CAT scan, it doesn't look like you have long-term effects."

Cirie crinkled her nose. "Ah, okay. It's just... I noticed it kind of smells like wet cat in here lately."

The white-coat reaper jerked her head up at the comment.

"Must just be the hospital," Cirie said, shrugging.

"Stupid little..." The reaper's hands gripped the scythe tighter.

Shawn prayed Cirie hadn't gone too far. Now wasn't the time to piss someone off. Leaning forward, the reaper hovered the tip of the scythe over Cirie's throat. Any movement wouldn't kill her; the only damage would be a small nick. The reaper was daring Cirie to move. Seems the white-coat reaper decided rules could be bent outside of All Hallows Eve. Shawn filed that information away. Breaking the rules like this was idiotic.

Through all of this, Cirie kept smiling at him. Never once giving the indication that a blade was pointed at her neck. She had absolutely no fear.

Shawn had to try and get the reaper to back off a bit. "So sorry about that. I'm sure as soon as you're out of here, you'll be smell free. But I'll see if we can do something about the musk in the room."

The reaper leaned in until she was about to brush noses with Cirie. "Can't wait for you to expire. I'll gladly bag your soul." She said the last comment with a cackle before backing off. After smoothing out her lapels, she headed to the door.

She hadn't recognized him. Shawn was almost in the clear. He wished he could turn and watch to make sure she left, but he didn't want to give himself away. Cirie's desperate plan had worked. Shawn could feel the muscles in his shoulders relax.

It happened quickly. Shawn had relaxed too much. As soon as he thought he was home free, the clipboard slipped through his fingers and clattered onto the tile floor. Shawn froze. The door hadn't creaked open. She hadn't left the room. Which meant she was staring right at him.

If he'd been facing the door, she would've seen fear expand in his pupils. He would have given himself away. Instead, the reaper watched him bend down and pick up the chart.

"Seems that I'm a bit of a klutz myself," he said, laughing awkwardly.

"Probably caught my bad juju. Careful, man. Don't want to end up in the room next to me." Again, no hint of fear was expressed through her smile.

A small creak came from the door behind him, dropping Cirie's smile in the process. "Um, it seems that door popped open again. Can you close it? Want to make sure my headache doesn't get worse with all the commotion outside."

Shawn was still shaken from the clipboard fiasco but was able to take this cue from Cirie and closed the door.

"That was too close for comfort. We need to get the hell out of here." Cirie jumped out of the bed, tossing Shawn's jacket at him.

He exhaled after holding the breath inside his chest hostage during the exchange. "Thanks. I don't know how you kept your cool." He put the clipboard back in its spot. "I obviously couldn't."

"Thank my cousin Hal," she said as she threw on her jeans and leather jacket. "That dude used to pretend to punch me. If I flinched, I got three hard pinches."

"Doesn't sound like a great game to be honest."

"It wasn't for him. I was way better at it," she said, laughing.

Shawn looked through the window in the door, trying to see how far the reaper had gone, but she wasn't within view. "We have to make it to the stairwell. Hopefully, Jay didn't run into any trouble."

"Stairwell, right. Let's get moving then." The door slowly swung open as Cirie escaped into the hallway, Shawn right behind her.

A few patients were out of their rooms as well. One young girl waved to Cirie while supporting her mother, who was struggling to use a walker. Another patient was calling out to a nurse about needing pancakes. The annoyance emanated from the nurse, who was in the middle of speaking with another patient as they walked past.

Flashes of white made Shawn's head spin as doctors made their way out of rooms. Each time a door opened, Shawn felt like a spring compressing with fear. Sooner or later, it would be a blade in a white suit coming out of those doors instead of a white jacket.

"Ms. Zos?"

Cirie spun around at the mention of her voice.

Wearing a fresh non-stained coat, her doctor stood behind the nurse's station, wondering what the heck his patient was doing out of bed. Instead of responding, Cirie turned back around and kept walking to the stairwell.

"Should we say something?" Shawn asked, speed-walking next to Cirie while keeping an eye out for a sliver of steel.

"Ma'am, you need to stop! You haven't been discharged," he called out after her, causing patients and nurses alike to gaze in their direction.

Blood drained from Cirie's face. But she wasn't looking at the nurse's station. No, that wasn't her concern. Her fear was at the end of the hall. The one person in the hallway holding a scythe. "Run."

They bolted. Cirie spun into a doctor, causing him to topple to the ground hard.

"Security!" someone yelled from behind. Great. Another obstacle to maneuver, Shawn thought.

"Scum. Stop there, reaper!" No one needed to turn around to know who shouted that one.

People say that running in hotel hallways makes them feel like they're running faster, but the opposite must have been true for hospitals. As Shawn sprinted down the hall, he passed room after room like he was in quicksand: it felt as if they were never going to reach the end.

Intercom speakers buzzed to life with an announcement about security, but he'd stopped listening.

"Stop her!" A nurse yelled.

Behind them, the reaper had made up a bit of ground. "Oh, I will," she snarled. Her suit remained static, as if it were afraid of getting wrinkles as she ran. Even her tie wasn't moving as she pounded down the hallway.

The exit sign hung above the doorway a couple of feet away, waiting for them like an unused safety net. It was going to be a battle once they got to the stairwell. The best-case scenario would be Jay waiting on the other side of that door, and Shawn didn't want to think about the worst-case scenario. He was focused on the door a few feet away as the sound of the blade closing the gap haunted him.

In an instant, they both ran through the doorway. Their bodies tumbled into the stairwell railing. "Close it!" Shawn screamed.

Rage erupted across the reaper's face as she threw herself at the gap. Things slowed down for Shawn in that moment. He could see the crack closing centimeter by centimeter. Next to him, Cirie bit her bottom lip as her arm muscles strained with the force. Loudspeakers were still blaring a call to security. The last thing he noticed gave him hope. It was the sound of someone rushing down the stairwell.

Jay's feet slapped into the landing beside Shawn. Throwing his shoulder into the door, Jay tried to force it closed.

"You idiots!" The hospital reaper yelled. She was frantic, pushing against the three of them with a flurry of strength. "Do you even understand the ramifications of what you're doing? This isn't something you want to see through."

Her words gave Shawn reason to pause. Was this a mistake? Should he just let go of the door now? He really didn't know what he'd gotten himself into; he was thrown into this world and barely knew the rules, let alone what was right. These thoughts lasted all of two seconds.

"You really just like hearing yourself talk, don't you, slimeball?" Cirie asked.

Shawn was amazed. There she stood shoulder to shoulder with the reaper, fighting for her life, and she was calling her names. For someone whose family wouldn't see her again, someone whose dreams would be taken away, she was fearless. She had no other options. Which meant neither did Shawn.

The blade discovered her mistake. "So you can see me?" The realization almost stopped the woman in her tracks. The door was so close to being shut. "They weren't lying," she mumbled. But a few seconds later, she was back at full force; perhaps she remembered the wet cat smell comment.

"You bitch!" Taking her scythe, the reaper thrust it through the opening, trying to get a slice of anyone.

"I have an idea," Shawn grunted.

Jay gave him a look that screamed, 'Well, fucking say it then.'

"Let's pull the chair."

"What?" Cirie and Jay both barked.

All their arms were in agony from preventing the door from being opened any further. The reaper had almost gargoyle-like strength and was determined to barge into the stairwell. Even the door seemed to be struggling. It appeared to warp around where the reaper was thrusting herself. They were at a standstill, but how long could they keep it up? They couldn't run, and if they stayed here, reinforcements would be on their way. They'd been lucky not to see any yet.

Taking his voice down to a whisper, Shawn said, "On my mark, let go of the door and move out of the way. Okay?"

It seemed as if Jay was about to argue, but before he could say anything, Shawn started the countdown.

"Three." Shawn planted his foot behind him.

"Two." He took a deep breath.

"One." All three of them let go.

Pulling the chair was a basketball term Shawn had learned. It was used when defending against a larger player, one who clearly had more strength than you. The goal was to make them rely on you pushing against their back. Once they fell into that expectation, you used the player's own strength against them. Instead of keeping the pressure, you moved out of the way quickly, which caused them to tumble backward. It was the same idea as pulling the chair out from underneath someone as they sat down. If done correctly, the stronger player's own strength becomes their undoing.

With the opposing pressure suddenly gone, the door swung open. The reaper burst through the doorway like a football team tearing through a paper banner at the start of a game. White fabric went sideways as the reaper fell forward. No one saw the look on the reaper's face as she toppled. What stood out was the clang of the metal guard rail that collided with her head on the way down.

The reaper crumbled to the ground in front of them.

"Shit. Good job, Shawn," Jay said, standing over the limp body.

"She's not..." Shawn refused to finish the question.

Cirie bent down to feel the woman's pulse, her hands trembling as she reached toward her neck. Shawn intercepted before she got there.

"Even if she wasn't..." Shawn didn't even know the right word for the passing of a reaper. "Gone, she wouldn't have a pulse."

"Are you guys done? We need to leave," Jay said as he looked through the tiny window that led into the hallway.

Shawn didn't know what Jay saw, but he didn't want to stick around to find out. They took the steps two, sometimes three at a time, trying to just get out of the building. Hospital workers yelled at Cirie to slow down as she raced past.

Reaching the bottom of the steps felt like the three of them had conquered something noticeable only to themselves. The nurses' station passed by in a blur as they arrived at the automatic doors that swung open with no issues, thanks to Cirie.

Adrenaline bubbled inside Shawn's body. They'd escaped the hospital, but now there was a bigger issue. Where would they go from here?

Chapter 40

"They'll always know where we are," Shawn said, tapping his suit pocket.

It took a second for Cirie to remember the tracker. "Is there *any place* where they can't track us?"

"Anywhere we go, they'll be able to follow," Shawn said.

"So, I'm screwed."

"Yes," Jay answered, much to Shawn's horror.

"Shut up," Shawn said before turning to Cirie. "No. We're not screwed." He took a deep breath. "Look, obviously we're new to this, but we'll save you. Okay?"

Taking in his words, Cirie's voice softened, and Shawn thought he even saw tears in her eyes. "Don't make a promise you can't keep."

"I think I have a safe place we can go. It isn't far from here," Jay interrupted.

Shawn was skeptical. What place could be safe when they had blades or gargoyles on their tail? Shawn wanted a further explanation but knew they needed to keep moving. And at this point, he'd take any idea. "Lead the way," he said.

The way ended up being back toward the beach. Cirie took her shoes off the instant she touched the sand, and the others followed suit. "Can I see the tracker again?" She asked.

Shawn handed it over to her but kept watching as she unfurled the parchment and gazed down at the map. Her eyes drifted to the countdown, soaking in the waning moments of her life: "3 Days, 4 hours, 14 minutes."

"Hot or cold," Jay said.

Shawn wasn't sure what Jay was going on about and gave him a raised eyebrow.

"Hot or cold," Jay repeated. Again, radio silence. He rolled his eyes. "That's how you found Cirie, correct?"

"Yes?"

"Then that's what we do. We play that game, but on a more extreme scale than a couple of floors."

Cirie turned to Shawn. "What's he talking about?"

Jay pressed on. "What I'm suggesting is that we don't keep running. We let them know our coordinates. Or at least we don't care if they know. They can't change. But what can?"

A lightbulb finally flipped on for Shawn. "Our level."

"There you go. So, where's one place they'd never expect to look?"

Cirie turned her head to the sky as a plane passed overhead. "Not sure being in a tin box in the sky is the best place for me right now."

"What do they say? Hide in the least suspected place?"

"Which would be?" Cirie asked.

Jay smirked as the opening of a cave came into vision. "Where we live: Wayward Academy."

"You live *here?*" Cirie said, not trying to conceal the disappointment in her voice.

"We don't, no... Jay, there isn't a door here." Years of erosion from the lake had carved up the land near the beach. The pitch-black opening stood as an open invitation into the unknown they were 'living' in. Such a small entrance was barely visible from the beach. "Even if there was, we wouldn't be able to get past the gargoyles."

Jay kept walking into the cave. "If we went to a gate, they'd know. Just follow me."

"Yeah, this definitely seems like the place where I'm going to die," Cirie said, brushing against Shawn as they entered the mouth of the cave.

Stalagmites—or was it stalactites? Shawn could never remember—towered above them, waiting to pin Shawn like a cushion. Night had fallen, and it was as if the darkness from the cave had seeped out into the world.

Further and further into the cave, they trudged. Shawn knew Cirie had no other choice, but he was still surprised she'd even stayed with them. If he was the one being led into a cave by two strangers, telling him he was going to die, he would have taken the first bus out of town.

"I barely spent any time in our room, and you never asked me where I went," Jay said.

Cirie squinted back and forth from Jay to Shawn, trying to force her eyes to adjust. "You guys live together?"

"Yep. We share a room at the Academy," Shawn said. He thought back to all the nights there and couldn't put a finger on what Jay was talking about. "I hadn't, but honestly, if you weren't usually around, I thought you were just meeting up with Sophia." It wasn't as if Shawn kept tabs on him all the time.

'Mmmm, Sophia. Interesting," said Cirie.

"That's what you thought I was doing?" Jay said, laughing. "Oh god no. Not even close. I'm not going around with Sophia of all people, believe me."

Pitch black. They'd reached the point where Shawn couldn't even see the outlines in front of him. Pure darkness surrounded the trio as they kept walking. Shawn flashed back to the inside of the coffin. How the air had become thinner. The uncertainty of what was going to happen next. He took a deep breath in, holding it for a few seconds before letting it out. Instinctively, his hand went to the back of his neck as he tried to get a hold of himself.

"I went to talk to Rudy one night."

Shawn thought back to the boy in the tattered clothes. No, not boy—the murderer in those tattered clothes. "Why would you even want to speak to that psychopath?"

"Because he almost got out," Jay said as if it was the most logical answer. "It's not much further, but there are some turns, so just grab on."

A hand patted his chest. Shawn grabbed it tightly and offered his other one to Cirie.

"I'm more of a shirt clutcher," she said, ignoring Shawn's hand and death-gripped the back of Shawn's collar, causing him to choke a bit.

"My bad." She readjusted her grip a little lower on his shirt, freeing his throat.

"This way." Jay led, pulling them both behind him. It was slow-moving as Jay traced the wall of the cave with his free hand. Shawn again felt like one of those rats in a maze. He didn't know where the end was or where he was going, he just had to figure it out. Or at least, let Jay figure it out. How does someone know their way around a cave by feel after one day? Shawn had no clue.

"Are you going to tell us which deathtrap you're leading us to? Or should I just guess?" Cirie said, dripping with sarcasm.

"When I got to Wayward Academy, we weren't allowed to leave. So, I looked, unsuccessfully, for a way out." He paused as he felt around another corner. "Then I met Rudy."

"A psychopathic killer reaper," Shawn added.

Cirie's hand clutched Shawn's shirt a little tighter at the mention of a killer. "Excuse me?"

"Shawn is correct. Rudy killed a fellow reaper and went on the run."

"And this helps us how?" Cirie asked. "Because, no offense, I don't think I want help from a murderer."

Jay continued, unphased by Cirie's concern. "It helps because he tried escaping through a tunnel in the Academy."

"Yeah, now you've lost me. This Academy has tunnels? Stripes, can you translate?"

That confusion that Cirie felt must have been the same as when Shawn felt when he first woke up in the carriage.

"The only way in and out of the Academy is through gates," said Shawn. "Gates that are guarded by gargoyles. Ones that, let me remind you, Jay, we won't be able to get through. As for the tunnels... well, the Academy is underground."

"We aren't going through a gate."

"Then where the hell are we going?" Cirie's voice echoed throughout the cave, her frustration leaking into the darkest corners.

"When Rudy tried to escape, he hadn't just picked a spot in the cavern that had a crack. He had scouted up top."

The realization of where they were headed started to dawn on Shawn.

"He wasn't just a stupid reaper looking to dig his way up," Jay said. "He'd already found a way down. In this cave."

Sweat pooled in Shawn's hand. "Are you telling me he'd already made it down to the Academy? Without using a gate?"

"A hundred percent. And that's the way we're going to get back to the Academy." Jay stopped and knelt in the dirt.

"This is a joke," Cirie said from behind Shawn.

"Yeah... I don't think he's kidding," Shawn said, kneeling down next to Jay and curling his fingers around a jagged edge of rock. There was no floor in front of him. Just an abyss.

"Let me get this straight," Cirie said. "You want to follow the direction of a killer, so we can take his secret underground route into a den of reapers. Reapers who not only want me dead but want you dead as well?"

Jay sighed. "Pretty much. Unless you have a better plan, it's our only option."

"Nope. I'm out." Cirie released the back of Shawn's jacket, ready to leave. But doubt crept into her mind as she tried to think of a way back.

"Then you're both dead."

"You're doing an awesome job at convincing us to go down your death hole man," Shawn said. He couldn't see Jay get tense, but the air felt a little thicker from where Jay was squatted.

"You think I'm joking? Both of you will be dead if you go back out into the grounder world. Cirie, you have a time limit right now, so anything you do could kill you in the next three days. And Shawn, do you really think they're just going to let you walk away after what you've done? You've seen what happens."

Shivers traveled up and down Shawn's spine like cars on a freeway. He thought back to Onyx. He was dead and he didn't even do anything wrong.

Jay continued. "Why wouldn't we risk going down this tunnel that could lead us to not only a place no one will be looking but also one that may save you, Cirie."

"Save her? What do you mean?" Playing an extreme game of hot or cold made sense to Shawn. But that was a band-aid. While his goal had been to save Cirie, he still had no idea how he was supposed to do that. Jay lost him at that part of the plan.

"I've been thinking about the tracker," Jay continued. "And we know it works when she's up here. But what happens when she's in our world? A world where no grounder is supposed to be."

Cirie walked a little closer. "This is just a theory."

"No shit. But as of right now, it's the only theory that might save your life."

Within minutes, Shawn could quickly be on his way to joining Rudy at the bottom of the cavern. But Jay was right. "Let's do it then."

"Well?" Jay asked Cirie.

"If I die here, you bet your ass I'm going to haunt you for eternity."

Chapter 41

Inching their way down the sloped tunnel, they went painstakingly slow. Shawn worried that at any moment, the floor would fall out beneath him. He didn't need a second death so soon. The memory of the first one still tugged at his brain; every time he tried to recall it, it was like he was trying to navigate through fog. He was caught between wanting to know and thankful he didn't have the memory.

"Why didn't you guys try to escape earlier?" Cirie's voice floated from behind Shawn as they crawled on.

The shuffling ahead of Shawn went away for a second. "Being a reaper is complicated... To you, they must seem like enemies, but in reality, it's an important job. But that doesn't mean they do everything right. Or that there aren't scumbags carrying scythes around."

They crawled along for another two hours. Shawn didn't even feel the rocks anymore. His knees had gone numb an hour ago. All he could focus on was getting out of there.

A light would be perfect right now. Or a torch. Shawn wasn't picky. He just wanted to see. The walls felt closer than they'd been before. It was like he was in a trash compactor, slowly being squeezed. This plan felt more idiotic by the minute. "I don't know if I can keep crawling."

"What's up, Stripes?" Cirie squeezed the top of his suit.

Shawn breathed only short and shallow breaths. "I just..." Worried that at any second, he could run out, Shawn gulped in large amounts of air. "Rudy made it down. Allegedly." He spit the last word out like it was trying to dig a hole in his cheek. "But he never made it back up."

"Shawn... this is the best option. This is the only thing that might save us all," said Jay.

"Excuse me?" Concern crept back into Cirie's voice. "What do you mean back up?"

If Shawn had any light, he was sure that Jay would be glaring at him. He just wanted to get out of this tunnel. Out of the dark. Is this how Maple felt while trapped?

"Rudy tried climbing back up," Jay said, shuffling forward. "The tunnel collapsed on him."

"Dammit," a muffled Cirie exclaimed as her head rammed straight into Shawn's behind. "Are you telling me we're crawling down a collapsed tunnel?"

Jay stopped shuffling forward.

"What's up, Jay?" Shawn asked.

"I'm not sure..."

This wasn't good. If they did all of this just to have to turn around, Shawn might lose it. Odds are there'd be a couple of blades waiting to roll heads if they emerged back that way. "What do you mean you're not sure?" He asked.

"Come feel this. I think there's enough room for both of us to be side by side right now." Jay squeezed against the wall, allowing Shawn to fit alongside him. "Reach out."

Shawn cautiously felt around in the darkness. Everything may have been hidden from his sight, but the groves of rocks prickled his skin as he felt the wall of rock impeding their path. "Shit."

"You guys want to inform me what's going on up there?"

"No! No! No! We didn't do all of this to be stopped by some tunnel collapse!" Shawn started clawing at the wall. Was it getting harder to breathe? How much oxygen did they have?

"Shawn, stop! It's no use." Jay made a grab at his arm, but Shawn shook him off.

Dirt tumbled down with each hit. They'd found the other end of the collapsed tunnel. With each rock Shawn furiously scraped at the wall, he grew more intense. This was for the stage jumper, the kid in the tower, the ones in the graves, Onyx. No way in hell was he going to add Jay and Cirie to that list.

"Wait, Shawn. Stop! I think–"

And just like that, Shawn's other fear came to fruition: the floor dropped out.

Side to side. Shawn was thrown, ricocheting off one rock and into another. His ribs screamed with each impact. Reflexively, his hands went to his head and ribs as he tried to shield himself from each impact. He wasn't even sure if Jay and Cirie were with him, as the echoing sound of falling rocks blocked out any screams that would have filled the spaces between.

Bounce after bounce, Shawn felt himself losing consciousness. Jagged pieces tore at his suit. At one point pain, fear, and the unknown all collided. Shawn could only think of Rudy. Were these how his last moments played out too? In an endless landslide of pain? It almost made him feel sorry for his death.

He wasn't sure how long they'd been falling; it could have been seconds or minutes. All sense of time was pointless to the rocks, and it was pointless to him. Gradually, he hit the sides of the tunnel less and less. The avalanche of rocks was funneling to one spot. Only the occasional jagged piece now caught him as he started to slide down the tunnel rather than fall.

Then it all came to a jarring stop.

Dots floated above Shawn's vision, but he was alive. At least he thought he was; he hadn't exactly watched YouTube videos on how to become a ghost. But he had to have a concussion. He didn't dare move, afraid of the state of his body. His blurred vision slowly cleared as he blinked. Those dots he'd seen weren't actually dots, they were crystals. Crystals that had gone mostly dark with the setting sun. He'd landed on his back, staring up at the cavern ceiling. He made it.

A muffled voice came from somewhere over to his left. "Guys?"

Without any hesitation, Shawn jumped up, rubble falling off all around him. He immediately regretted that action. His chest felt like an elephant had used it repeatedly as a soccer ball. His body was aching and sore all over, but the adrenaline helped for now.

"Cirie!" Shawn shouted. About ten feet away, Cirie lay half-covered in rubble, pieces of rock embedded into her face.

"I'm okay, I'm okay. At least, I think. Where's Jay?"

Mounds of rock had formed out of the rubble, coating everything nearby in a layer of dirt. Where was he? Stumbling around, he couldn't focus. Then over at a tree, he spotted an outline of a human, face down. Rushing over, Shawn feared the worst. *Please be alive, please be alive*, he pleaded. But Jay wasn't moving as Shawn got closer.

"Jay, wake up. Jay!" Shawn shook him.

"Oh god. Is he..." Cirie let the words trail off.

No, he wasn't. He couldn't be. Shawn turned him over. Blood matted down his crew cut like he'd showered in it. Shawn cradled Jay's head in his hands, willing him to wake up.

"Feel for a pulse. We can do CPR," Cirie offered.

"We don't have a pulse; we don't even have a freaking heartbeat! Okay?"

Movement from between Shawn's hands released a flood of relief.

"Take that Rudy," Jay whimpered.

Gently laying down Jay's head, Shawn and Cirie collapsed next to him. All of them were bleeding and hurt. But alive.

After being surrounded by darkness and rocks for so long, it was strange for Shawn to be surrounded by trees. Luckily, Rudy was off somewhere else, so he wouldn't discover his spot, a little altered, until later.

Cirie looked around. "Where are we?"

Shawn chuckled. "Welcome to Wayward Academy."

Chapter 42

Each of them looked like they'd stumbled out of a collapsed building. Jay was missing one of his pants legs; Shawn's sleeves were shredded; Cirie had tears down her jeans that Shawn could swear weren't there before. They'd become human ragdolls that the landslide decided to play with.

"Now what?" Cirie asked, echoing Shawn's feelings.

"The tracker!" Shawn shouted as he rummaged through his jacket pockets, which miraculously hadn't torn apart in the fall. His fingers caught the corner of the parchment. He took a deep breath and thanked whatever guardian angel he had that they'd arrived in one piece. They hadn't lost the tracker.

Holding the parchment in his hands, Shawn hesitated to open it. Cirie and Jay waited for him to gather himself. Their stares locked onto the paper. Unfurling the corner of the tracker meant answers to questions Shawn wasn't sure he wanted answered. The usual info was there: Cirie's name and description and at the bottom, he could see the time she had left still counting down. "Oh no."

Cirie lifted her head to the ceiling, her voice carrying no emotion. "Was that all for nothing?"

"Wait," Jay said. "Look at the location."

And they did. The GPS coordinates that were supposed to be there were replaced by dashes. The realization swept across Shawn: they had no location. They were safe.

"What does this mean exactly for me? Am I safe?"

Jay and Shawn exchanged a glance. Was she? They sure as hell didn't know, but at least she wasn't a beacon to the reapers anymore.

"We aren't sure." Jay took the lead. "All we know is that they can't track you down here. We're not entirely sure that at the end of that countdown, you'll be alive."

Cirie seemed to mull over this a bit. "Okay. At least my location isn't being broadcast everywhere then."

A snapping twig caught Shawn's attention, but two seconds later a bird flew out of one of the trees surrounding them. Shawn wasn't sure if he would ever see this underground forest again. "We probably shouldn't stay here and wait for Rudy to wander back." Shawn tried standing up, ready to get out of there in a hurry. "Ah!"

he yelped. Pain erupted across his abdomen, forcing him back into a squat.

"Your ribs," Cirie said, sounding worried.

As she was riddled with concern for Shawn's ribs, Cirie failed to speak about her own injury. Either due to adrenaline or shock, she'd only just noticed her left arm. Bloody red gashes ran up and down her forearm, forming a river of blood and dirt. The worst part was how the arm curved in an unnatural way.

"Huh? That doesn't look right," Cirie said. She gingerly touched her forearm and winced.

"We should make a sling," Shawn said.

"Here, use this." Jay unbuttoned his shirt, leaving him bare-chested under what was left of his suit coat.

"Cheers," Cirie said through gritted cheeks as her arm fell snuggly into the makeshift sling.

"We should make our way to the windmill. I doubt there'll be anyone there," Jay said as he stood up.

No one argued with him. Not that Cirie could: she was completely lost. "I've never seen anything like this," Cirie said, laughing at the underground forest. "I thought the craziest thing that could happen today was someone discovering my music." She held her head up to the top of the cave. "If only."

Shawn followed her gaze and saw the crystals. "Kind of beautiful, right?" As he spoke, he almost tripped over a root in the ground. "They mimic the light above ground."

"But the sun's already set?"

Jay stared up at the ceiling with them. "It also mimics the moonlight. I don't like it down here, but I will admit it's stunning."

Thankfully, they didn't have far to walk to get to the windmill. If anyone spotted them in this state, they'd be sure to ask questions. Each step through the woods felt like walking through a memory. Shawn looked left and right, expecting to see a group of gargoyles leading dirt-coated reapers to their next test.

"Are we sure I'm not dead yet?" Cirie asked.

Jay and Shawn gave each other a look.

Cirie was the first to speak. "I'm in an underground cavern with magical crystal lights and Jim and Slim Reaper, but sure, look at each other like *I'm* the lunatic."

This was what they needed to break the tension. They all laughed.

"Fair call," Jay said. It was a lot to take in. He'd also been thrown into the deep end, but it was like Cirie had been thrown into the water with weights around her ankles.

When the chipped green paint of the windmill came into sight, so did the memories that haunted Shawn. The gold WA was still freshly painted, reminding him that it hadn't been that long since their testing. The windmill blades slowly turned through the air, almost mocking the trio for how slow they were moving.

"You both wait here. I'll go in and scope it out." Jay sprinted off before anyone could answer. Adrenaline drove his legs forward as he crouched low to the ground, his suit jacket tailing behind him in the air.

Cirie grimaced as she leaned against a tree. "That has to be the most pointless structure. Like why do you even need a windmill down here? Not like huge gusts of winds are going to be blowing through the cavern."

Shawn shrugged as Jay's head disappeared through the barn door. She was right, but it was just another unknown on Shawn's list.

The area around them was a ghost yard. There didn't seem to be anyone in sight, which rang true for Shawn. All the testing had been completed, and word was that all the hogs had already been slaughtered for meals. Sure enough, a couple of minutes later, Jay's head reappeared, waving them forward. Cirie and Shawn broke from the tree line and beelined it straight for the door.

Inside, the windmill was exactly as Shawn had remembered it; hay littered the floor, but otherwise, the main hub was empty save for some wooden crates in the corner. His eyes drifted to where he'd sat with Q and Maple as they took in their losses. Where he'd told them about Onyx. Now it was just like any other spot on the floor. It had no marker or sign, but it drew Shawn forward until he was standing on it.

Cirie stood over a dark spot in the hay. "What happened here?"

"Pigs' blood," Jay said as if that explained everything.

"During our test," Shawn jumped in, "part of the evaluation for our job was whether or not we killed a pig."

Cirie knelt down, sliding a piece of hay with dried blood between her fingers. "Hope no one was vegetarian."

"It's already dark. We should make beds of some sort," Jay said, looking for anything that could be of use.

The beds ended up being piles of hay with burlap sacks of rice as pillows. Shawn examined the pitiful layout. "These look—"

"Like something the homeless wouldn't even use?" Jay said.

"I was actually going to say like something out of a five-star hotel." Shawn sat down and tested out the makeshift bed. "Oh, I see we got the 5000-count threaded sheets."

Cirie got down too. "Wow, with memory foam pillows!" Their laughter echoed through the empty space and quickly died out. "I wish I had my sleeping bag," Cirie added.

Jay remained standing. "We should take turns keeping watch. I'll take the first shift." And with that, he left the main room to climb the stairs to the top of the windmill.

After he was out of earshot, Cirie spoke up. "What's his deal?"

"What do you mean?"

"Well, does he ever smile? I mean, you'd think *he* was the one with the name written on that little piece of paper."

Did Jay ever smile? Shawn had only seen it a couple of times, but mostly Jay was his grumpy, moody self. "He's mostly pretty serious. Been like that in the little time I've known him. I don't know the details, but he's stuck by my side through everything so far. That's all I need to know."

"Seems like he's carrying some heavy stuff."

Shawn looked at the door to the spiral stairs and wondered if she was right. Waking up in a death- riddled job does that to a person. Both of them had heavy burdens just being reapers. But was Jay holding onto something more?

"Let's get some rest," Shawn said.

Sleeping on top of a makeshift hay bed with burlap sacks as pillows was about as comfortable as they thought. And not being able to sleep on his stomach delayed Shawn's dreamless slumber too, so he wasn't exactly sure when he fell asleep.

When he awoke, Shawn collected the thoughts that were slowly wafting through the drowsiness in his brain. Nothing moved inside the mill. If there was a mouse, it was fast asleep as well. He had no idea what time it was, but odds were Jay should've already clocked out of his shift. Yet his pile of hay remained untouched.

Being careful not to disturb Cirie, Shawn lifted himself from the hay bed. He raised his arms above his head as far as he could, yawning silently as he stretched. He grimaced as his rib pain reappeared. It didn't seem like Jay was going to come down anytime soon, so Shawn started climbing.

Each step he climbed creaked like it was trying to catch a teenager sneaking out of the house, so he was surprised that Jay didn't hear him reach the top. Jay was facing out toward the woods, both feet dangling over the edge of the lookout platform as he sat watching the trees for movement.

"Hey, man. I'll take over now," Shawn said.

"You got a little more time," Jay said in a slightly muffled voice. With his head between the iron bars of the railing, he analyzed each branch shake. The top of the mill was a perfect lookout spot, not just due to it being three stories up, but for its wrap-around balcony. They could see any dangers coming from any direction.

Shawn sat next to him and put his head between the bars as well. Out of the corner of his eye, he could see that Jay's face was flushed. Shawn opened his mouth to say something but knew that Jay would talk only when he wanted.

Shawn had expected some type of resistance to him sitting down, but his partner didn't protest. For a couple of minutes, they both just took in the night.

"I remember," Jay said, his voice cracking on the words.

"Remember what?"

"My death."

No one was supposed to remember their death, or even the week up to it. It was supposed to help protect them, so as not to ruin their new state of mind in this weird afterlife. "How much?"

"All of it."

Offering a faint glow to the night, the crystals in the room of the cave outlined Jay against the iron bars. "Most people grow up to be loving parents, excited to have kids," Jay continued. "That wasn't my case."

"What do you mean?"

"My mother was a drug addict, and my father, well, he died of a drug overdose when I was barely even walking." A soundless tear traced his cheek. "When I was growing up, my mom's priority was always how to get the next fix. I was the mistake she made while off her mind on pills one sleazy night."

Shawn was stunned. He looked at Jay through the bars, actually seeing him for the first time. "Jay, I'm sorry."

"Nothing to be sorry about. That's just life for some people—people who need help. My mother just didn't get hers in time."

"What happened?"

"We were living in this dump of a motel in Indiana, but my mother was so excited. I remember her raving about it having a pool. Meanwhile, I was just trying to pass chemistry and make sure I didn't look or smell homeless in class the next day. The worst part is, she was in one of the phases where she 'swore' off drugs and went on about how she'd turned over a new leaf."

"You don't have to go on."

"It's fine." He took a breath, closing his eyes. "I even believed her. She'd been doing well the last couple of weeks. Had gone through withdrawal a few days before. The whole deal. I thought, *Hey. Maybe this really is a turning point.* Ha! Three hours later, she was getting her next fix from the scumbag who lived near the ice machine."

Shawn felt his eyes well up. He was fortunate to have parents that cared for him. That loved him. Even when they annoyed him and constantly asked him where he was going, it was out of love. Shawn would now do anything for his dad to ask him that now. He couldn't understand what Jay was going through. "What happened next?"

"I confronted her. I watched her go out for 'groceries' and head straight into his room to shoot up. I walked downstairs and waited. The motel had this dingy pool, so I sat down and put my feet in the deep end, waiting for my drug-induced mother. When she came out, her eyes were shifting around like an animal caught in a trap. I should have known better but..." Jay's voice caught in his throat. "But I was so angry. I jumped up and immediately cussed her out, calling her a liar, how she'd never change, how she'd ruined my life. You know what she said in response?"

Shawn shook his head.

"Nothing. She laughed."

He let that sink in before continuing. "Then she added, through laughter, that if she'd ruined my life so much that I should go wash myself of her. And then she pushed me into the pool."

"Jay..." Shawn lay a hand on his shoulder.

"You know how most parents teach their kids to swim at an early age? Well, I never got those lessons. While most kids splashed around in the kiddy pool, I used to help scrounge cans so I could afford some food. I never learned how to swim."

Shawn squeezed Jay's shoulder, trying to convey that it was okay, even when it clearly never would be.

"I drowned that day." Jay looked up at the ceiling, the crystals illuminating another tear clinging to his face. "I drowned with my mother standing over me, high as a kite, laughing. That's how I died, Shawn." He turned his head back to Shawn, not trying to hide his tears. "No one is supposed to remember how they died. But it's been engraved in my brain from the instant I woke up in that carriage."

Jay pushed his forehead against one of the bars, letting the cold metal seep into his skin. They stayed like that for a while, letting the creaks of branches fill the silence.

After a bit, Jay got up and went downstairs to go to bed, finally accepting the sleep that he'd been deprived of.

As soon as Jay left, Shawn felt hollow. How had Jay held that in the whole time? And why could he remember? The last thing Shawn remembered was going to bed after eating a really shitty burger his mom had tried to cook on the stovetop. Why was Jay different?

Nothing moved in the trees the rest of the night—at least, nothing that caught Shawn's attention. He spent the whole night replaying everything from the last twenty-four hours in his head. From saving Cirie to the conversation with Jay. Could there have been a better path? Everything kept playing over and over, until the crystals finally started to brighten.

Taking this as the final bell on his watch, Shawn made his way down to the others. They needed to get up and discuss what was going to happen the rest of the day. They needed a plan. Shawn took a peek at the parchment paper again and read the time: "2 Days; 15 hours; 33 seconds" and it continued to fall. There must be a way to stop the countdown.

Downstairs, Cirie was already up, staring at the ceiling, and Jay awoke at the sound of feet on the steps.

"Those things are creaky," Jay mumbled.

"Yeah, sorry if I woke you."

"Don't be. I need to be up anyway." He stretched, putting on his suit coat that he was using as a blanket. He gave no sign of the conversation from the night before.

Cirie sat down, crossing her legs. "You guys have absolutely zero ideas on how to save me?"

"Technically, he did already save you back in the train station," Jay answered, which drew daggers from Cirie. "We've never had a plan. It was against our job to save you even then."

Cirie raised an eyebrow "What do you mean?"

"He," Jay said, pointing to Shawn, "jumped in to save you. Our job is merely to observe and collect souls for the next stage. I'm not sure anything like this has ever even happened before in history."

Shawn started pacing. He had an idea. "What if we could find out?"

"What do you think we're doing?" Jay scoffed, sleep and annoyance plastered on his face.

"No no. Not about how to save her but if there's ever been something like this before?"

Cirie sensed an opportunity and leaned forward. "Where would we find something like that?"

"At Wayward. There are tons of records in the library," Shawn said.

"You want to go into the Academy? Right now? Are you insane?" Jay asked.

Shawn continued to pace. "There might be information in there, and I know what you're thinking, but I'm sure Maple and Q would help us."

"No. Not worth the risk," Jay said decisively.

Cirie closed her eyes. "How far away is the library?"

"I said no."

"Yeah, well, I don't care what you say. This is *my* life," Cirie snapped.

"*Our* lives. It's all of our lives now, even if we have died once. I'm not looking forward to doing it again," Jay said.

"That's why I'll go alone," Shawn said.

Cirie and Jay both looked at Shawn like he'd hit his head too hard on those rocks.

"Do I have to echo my earlier statement?" Jay asked in disbelief.

“Look, it’s better if only one of us goes.” Shawn put his hand up, shushing Jay before he could chime in. “Yes, I know I’m in a rough state, but we all are.” He turned directly to Jay. “It’s not worth trying to get all three of us there. And if someone comes here, you have the best chance of fighting them off. Not me. So, you can’t go. I may not be the best fighter, but I do have friends who can help us. Plus, I know the hallways better than you.”

Jay started fidgeting with the hay bed, thinking the idea over. “Bring back food and maybe a change of clothes as well,” he said, motioning to his bare chest.

“I should leave now then. That way I can get there before most people are up.” Shawn could see the light under the barn door starting to get brighter as the crystals kept up with the sun above the ground.

All three of them just looked at each other, not sure what to do. “Isn’t splitting up supposed to be the worst thing to do?” Cirie half-joked.

“If I’m not back by nightfall, assume I’m probably not going to be coming back at all.”

Cirie stood up and walked over to Shawn. “Don’t be the guy who tries to save me and ends up dying in the process. Okay, Stripes?” She threw her arms around him. “Be quick.”

“I’ll do my best.” He released her and nodded at Jay. He walked past the pig blood stained with memories, out of the mill, and into the woods.

Chapter 43

Walking back to Wayward felt eerily normal. This was something that shouldn't have been out of the norm for Shawn. His dirt-stained skin and torn clothing aside, he felt like walking into the dining circle and grabbing some breakfast. Even if he did that, it was too early. There wouldn't be any hot bacon waiting for him on the tables yet.

At the slightest noise, Shawn would hide behind a tree. His head was on a swivel, looking for a reaper that could appear at any moment. Thankfully, the stone ostriches were peeking through the tree line; he was getting close to the gates. With each step, his ribs were pulsing with pain. He would kill for some meds, but he could only handle one crisis at a time.

When he was about thirty feet from the gate, he heard the unmistakable click-clack of a carriage coming down the cobblestone. Rushing, Shawn found a large tree trunk to hide behind. Sure enough, a carriage appeared right before him. The horses trotted up to the gate, stopping to let a familiar passenger out: Trevor.

"Shit," he whispered. He figured that Trevor wouldn't stay tied up forever in the train station. Besides Adriana, Trevor was the last person he wanted to run into.

His mentor looked exhausted as he bit his fingernails. He paced the outside of the gate, waiting. Shawn thought about running, but he couldn't risk making any noise. Instead, he stayed rooted to the spot, gluing his back against the bark of the tree trunk.

Trevor stopped pacing and waved to someone walking up from the Academy side of the gate. Shawn squinted, just able to make out Mac as he approached the iron bars, scythe in hand. Double shit.

Couldn't Shawn catch a break? Nothing like running into the two reapers most likely to instantly decapitate him. No way could he outrun or outfight two of the best reapers in the Academy. Trevor was thrashing his hands around, agitated at whatever was being said.

Against his better judgment, Shawn moved forward. He needed to hear what they were talking about. Tree by tree, he moved up like a checker piece. If his heart had a beat, it would've been loud enough to give him away.

" –isn't working, I told you!" Trevor said.

Mac's eyes narrowed. His anger bubbled beneath the surface. "That isn't possible. You know that."

"Here. You take a look at the stupid thing then!" Trevor threw him a piece of parchment. Shawn knew it had to be another tracker.

Mac scanned the parchment for information. "How is it possible that all three don't have locations?"

"That's what I'd really like to know. How the hell are we going to find them?"

Mac ignored Trevor's question. "The Council is *not* going to be happy about this new development."

"You're one of the heads of the council. Can't you smooth them over?"

"Not the Wayward council, idiot. I had to get permission from the capital for both Turner and Musters' locators."

"Oh, crap."

"Indeed. Let's get back to the Academy. The hospital reaper is waiting to give more information. What a fucking shit show you've led us into Trevor."

Shawn unclenched his hands from the trunk of the tree as the two reapers got into the carriage. The arguing faded as the carriage took off to the Academy. He waited just long enough for it to be out of sight before slipping through the gate. Step one accomplished.

Not wanting to draw attention to himself, he walked in the woods next to the path to the Academy. Due to the pain in his ribs, each step caused him to wheeze like he was having an asthma attack. Or maybe he was hyperventilating from Mac's conversation. They could track reapers. Not only that, but the capital knew of the situation. This was way worse than Shawn had imagined. He needed to find Q or Maple fast.

The center tower greeted him like an unwanted visitor as he approached. Most people were still in bed, so there wasn't anyone around the front door. Still, Shawn knew better than to go into the highest area of traffic. Instead, he made his way over to the side of the building that housed the first and second-year dorms.

A couple of second years he recognized were leaving, but Shawn knew that they were early risers who trained in the tower. He waited for them to enter before ignoring his pain level and sprinting to the door. Just like in the hospital, he prayed that no one was on the other side. The hallway was empty as he slipped through. Lady luck was still on his side.

He worked his way past closed doors, certain that one would open at any moment. Each room he passed made his nerves spike. The staircase he needed was in the corner of the building, which meant passing by every single room in the hallway. Would anyone even be in their room when he got there? Maybe he should've gone straight to the library. He shook his head. Too late to think about that.

From behind him, a door creaked open. The sound was distant, like it was in the middle of the hallway. Would the reaper notice him? His clothes were a giveaway that something was wrong, and Shawn didn't have a good explanation if someone asked. That's if they weren't aware of the situation already. The council was aware, so it was a good chance the rest of Wayward knew. It took everything in him not to run the last couple feet to the stairwell. He felt imaginary eyes drill into the back of his head. Yet, no one called out his name. No-one yelled "Stop!" He slipped into the stairwell.

In such a confined space, Shawn knew he couldn't risk running into someone. He needed to move fast. Taking the steps three at a time, he abandoned normality for speed. Not that there was anything normal about him at the moment, but he managed to get to the third floor unscathed.

He got to Room 324 and grasped the knob. He made it. Then his heart sank into his gut. All hopes were being denied by a lock. No. Someone had to be inside. Were they still sleeping? Were they on their assignment? Shawn was about to pound on the door but hesitated. He didn't want any of the neighbors to think it was *their* door and find his disheveled self standing there. He needed to know if someone was inside though. Ever so lightly, he tapped his knuckles against the door, looking left and right to see if someone else opened up. Nothing. He tapped again. *Please answer.* That's when the thought of a trap filtered through his head. What if the reapers knew he'd seek out Maple and Q? Was this room a trap? Footsteps sounded from the other side. He was either screwed or saved.

The door opened.

"What in the actual hell?" Maple stood in front of him, still in her nightwear and hair frantic with bedhead. Sleep crowded in the corners of her eyes, but Shawn was betting she was a lot more awake than she'd been a few seconds ago.

Shawn couldn't help but smile. "Hey, Maple. Mind letting me in for a second?"

CHAPTER 44

Two steps into the room and Maple quickly shut the door, turning the lock. "What the hell is going on?" She bearhugged Shawn, causing him to whimper in pain. "Oh god, I'm sorry. Are you okay? Where's Jay? Did anyone see you come in?"

They sat on the edge of her bed. "One question at a time, okay? We don't have a lot of time."

It felt odd to be back at Wayward. For a place he'd woken up terrified in for weeks, he was almost grateful to be there again. Shawn sped through an abbreviated telling of the events as Maple sat soaking in every word. At the end she got up, grabbed a pillow, and stuffed her face into it.

She shook her head before the pillow released her face. "Had to go play hero, huh? God, Shawn. You have no idea how crazy things are right now."

"I'm guessing word about us got out?"

"Actually, no."

If Shawn hadn't been sitting on a bed, he was pretty sure he would have collapsed. "What? Really?"

"The council members know, but almost none of the students do. They're keeping it very hush hush. The only reason I even knew something was up because Mac came in and interrogated me about you. He didn't let any details slip, but it doesn't take a detective to figure out something had happened."

"He interrogated you? Why?"

"I'm sure he'll do the same with Q when he gets back from his mustang training. But yeah, the council is freaking out. A couple of hours ago, over a hundred cardinals were released. I'm betting they were carrying your trackers."

Their little tunnel stunt would only buy them so much time. "Well, it's a good thing those don't work down here."

"You guys took a guess and got lucky. Scratch that. Jay took a guess and got it right." Maple sighed, looking away from him. "Why did you get yourself caught up in this? What is it about this girl?"

Shawn blushed, then reached over and grabbed her hand, needing her to understand. "I couldn't just do nothing, Maple. I needed to try, even if I end up being sliced up because of it." He squeezed her fingers. "She could see me. How could I leave someone who needed help when they were staring me right in the face?"

She raised her head, letting herself make eye contact with him. "You can't." She released his hand and went over to rummage through Q's dresser. She tossed him a spare pullover and pants. "Here. Can't have you stand out like a penny among dimes now, can we?"

"Is that even a saying?" Shawn asked, carefully unbuttoning his shirt.

"Uh, yeah." Maple said. Now it was her turn to blush. "My dad used to say it all the time."

Putting on new clothes made Shawn feel better. He tossed the rags he was wearing into the trash. There wasn't anything he could do about the cuts and dirt from the fall though; it wasn't like he had time to take a shower.

"Okay, I'm ready."

Maple rolled her eyes and picked up his tattered clothes. "Knucklehead, we can't leave your suit jacket in my trash can. We'll toss it on the way to the tower." She threw the clothes inside a messenger bag with more spares for the others.

"Do you think there's actually a chance of finding something in the library?"

Maple thought it over. "Normally, no. But when we were researching the girl—I mean Cirie—I ran across a small section that may be of use."

"What about the chance of me coming out of this alive?"

Maple poked her head out of the door, checking both ends of the hallway like she was trying not to be hit by a car. "Come on. We need to get a move on." Outside, reapers were starting to go about their morning: some heading for breakfast, others just milling around. A few headed toward the tower.

"Remember," Maple said, "no one but the council and senior reapers know. As long as it's only students, we're good."

With each step, Shawn's feet felt the urge to carry him into the woods. It felt like everyone was glancing at him as they walked toward the tower. Yet the young reapers were minding their own business. He might actually make it back to Jay and Cirie.

"Woah! Rough first reaping, huh champ!" The voice belonged to the only person Shawn knew with an eye patch.

"Oh, hey Rupert." Maple spoke for Shawn since his voice didn't seem to be working. "Marvin," she said nodding. Rupert never seemed to be far away from his lapdog.

"What happened?" Rupert asked while Marvin stared at Shawn like he was examining a painting on display.

Swallowing his tongue wasn't the best option for keeping a low profile, so he quickly recovered. "Oh, the bruises? Maple and I sparred yesterday: she kicked my ass clearly." He laughed. "I would rather go on another reaping right now than fight her again. At least that went a lot easier." He threw in the last part to try and sound smooth, but the only thing smooth about Shawn was his new clothes.

"Good for you, girl! Girl power and all that!" Rupert playfully punched Maple. His lapdog, meanwhile, just looked on.

"Well, good seeing you guys!" Maple didn't hide the annoyance straining her voice as she tried to end the conversation.

"Okay, weirdos," Rupert said as a cardinal started descending toward him.

As the wings flapped down, Shawn's anxiety rose. This was it. He would be found out by freaking Rupert. Marvin would probably kill him with his bare hands. Rupert grabbed the parchment as the cardinal flew off, taking Shawn's hope with it. Rupert's one eye squinted as he read it, and then he looked up at Shawn.

"Never seen a reaper get his next assignment? Jesus. Come on, Marvin. Let's get out of here."

Both Maple and Shawn let out a collective breath. "Let's go before someone else sees you."

Assignment. No wanted poster or tracking coordinates for him. He was safe again. For now.

Squeezing past a couple of students who looked like they'd been caught making out, they landed on the library floor. Most reapers didn't use it too often; hence, the couple shamelessly walking down the stairs with messy hair.

"Where do we start?" Shawn asked as he stared at the rows of books.

Stack by stack, they went through them. Maple picked out a couple of books she remembered reading last time. "It was in one of these three books."

"Are you sure?"

"Do you have any other books you'd like to check out?" Maple asked.

Touché. They started diving in, flipping pages in a hurry and trying to find just one bit of useful information to help Cirie. A couple of hours later, they still didn't have anything. Only a few people came in and out of the library. Many couples, after pretending to browse for twenty seconds, left quickly after finding someone in their "spot". Maple had chosen a table in the back corner, hidden from view, but Shawn still winced every time someone new came up the stairs.

Page by page, they flipped through each book Maple chose. But with zero results. Tiny paper cuts were starting to appear on Shawn's fingers.

"Oooouch!" Shawn said as he gained another cut. He stuck his finger in his mouth, trying to calm the throbbing. "We've been at it for hours. This is going nowhere." He didn't know what he was going to do if he didn't come back with new information.

"Something has to be here. I remember reading a short blurb about someone."

While she focused on finding that blurb, Shawn went to look for anything else that may be of use. They'd been at it so long that lunch had come and gone. "What am I going to do if I don't find anything?" He whispered to himself.

Maple was scrounging over the book, going line by line, most likely risking her head just to help him. She pulled her hair back into a ponytail, diving deeper into whatever her book was about.

"What?" she asked, catching him staring at her.

"Nothing, sorry. Just thinking."

She pointed to a row of shelves on the other side of the library. "While you're thinking, do you mind grabbing a couple of the books on the bottom shelf over there?"

"Sure thing."

The bottom row of the shelf had some books on the town, several on fighting techniques, and one about the creation of the mill. Shawn wasn't sure which ones she wanted, so he grabbed a few, carrying over as many as he could.

His thoughts jumped to how Jay and Cirie were doing. He hoped that they were safe, and that the countdown was still ticking. Twisting back between the aisles, he almost didn't hear another voice weave its way through the stacks of books.

“Ms. Collins, I thought I might find you here.”

Shawn ducked down where he was. He couldn’t make out the voice entirely, but it wasn’t a student.

Maple, thrown off, took a moment to respond. “Well, of course. Where else would I be? You know, since I’m not allowed to leave Wayward. You guys didn’t expect me to sit in my room like it’s a jail cell, did you?”

“Actually, when I saw you didn’t come to lunch, I got worried, so I brought you some food.”

The smell of pot roast wafted through the library. The saliva building in Shawn’s cheek didn’t have to remind him of the hunger void inside. He didn’t even know the last time he ate; they’d been go go go. Only one person would be kind enough to take food to her. Shawn risked a glance through the stacks to make sure he saw the blue tweed jacket beside the table.

Sure enough, Franklin stood beside Maple holding a plate of food from lunch. He set the food down on the table. “Doing some more research?”

“Yep. Figured I might as well learn more about our history.” Maple shifted uncomfortably in her chair.

Franklin sat on the edge of the table. “Funny how we only have this small library available to students.”

Shawn perked up.

“Available to students?” Maple asked, echoing Shawn’s thoughts.

“Is Mr. Prodit back?” Franklin asked, as he picked up the book Shawn had been looking through. Shawn had left his chair slightly askew. His spine shivered as he started looking for exit paths. Franklin was between him and the stairs. One option was to try to rush the councilmen. Pass. The window loomed nearby, but that was out of the question. He was scarred enough from the results of the previous jumper.

“Not that I’m aware, although I hope he is soon. Maybe he can convince you how ridiculous this whole witch hunt is.”

Franklin fiddled with the corner of a page. “Maybe so.” He let go of the book. “But we have rules for a reason.” He got up off the table and headed toward the staircase.

Shawn slowly released the muscles he didn’t know he’d been tensing.

Franklin paused before the first step. "Maybe one day I'll be able to show you my private collection in my office. I think your appetite for knowledge may be satisfied by reading some early biographies of our founders or maybe even the gargoyles. But alas, I'm afraid you're stuck here in this tree of life we call the library. Have a good night Ms. Collins." He descended the staircase, leaving Maple to the lunch delivery.

Jumping up, Maple raised a hand to ensure Shawn didn't move or talk yet. She ran to the window and didn't give him an all-clear sign until she saw the tweed jacket blowing in the wind.

"That was strange," Shawn said, appearing from behind the shelves.

"Too close."

Shawn dropped the books on the table and eyed the plate of food.

"Eat. I can get more later."

Shawn started scarfing down the pot roast and mashed potatoes. Which seemed like an odd choice for lunch, but neither he nor his stomach was going to complain.

As Shawn soothed his gut, Maple looked around. "I don't know how much time we have, but we aren't going to find what we're looking for in here."

"Do you think he knew I was here?"

"Not 100%, but I think he may have guessed it."

"Why wouldn't he raise the alarm or yell then?" Shawn asked with a mouthful of meat hanging partially out.

"I don't know. Could be going for help now." Her eyes lit up at the sight of one of the book covers. "Wait: that one!" She snatched *An Expanded History of Allen Oak* from Shawn's stack. She furiously started flipping pages. "Ah, here it is!"

"What is it?" As soon as the words left his mouth, a bell started ringing at the Academy, echoing across the fields. They both perked their heads up. Dinner had already passed so it couldn't have been for that. Whatever that bell was, it wasn't good.

Tearing out the page, Maple folded it and handed it to Shawn. He could read it later. "We need to get you out of here. Now."

Not inclined to argue this point, Shawn grabbed his bag of extra clothes Maple had packed, and they started toward the staircase. He almost passed over the object lying at the top of the stairs.

Thankfully, the shiny metal stood out to him like a torch in the night. “Maybe he was trying to help us?”

“Maybe,” Mapled agreed, because sitting at the top of the steps was a brass office key.

Chapter 45

Everyone outside the tower was startled by the bell. Two senior reapers were telling everyone to meet at the stadium, their expressions giving away their confusion.

Maple and Shawn waited until the tower appeared to have cleared out and then took the stairs two at a time. As they passed the training area, empty mats confirmed that there weren't any stragglers left. They made sure to go down the staircase leading the opposite way from the stadium pit.

Looking both ways out of the door, Maple gave a thumbs-up, and they sprinted toward the side door of the Academy. Not wanting to risk running into someone, they crossed the grass as quickly as possible. Maple held the door open as Shawn dipped inside. He got a couple of steps before noticing that she wasn't following. Maple stood at the door looking down.

"What are you doing? Come on. We need to get to Franklin's office."

Maple pulled her ponytail tighter, straightened her posture, and locked eyes with Shawn. "No, you do. I need to get to the pit. Can't risk anyone noticing me missing; otherwise, everything escalates."

She had a point. Shawn knew it, but this meant going their separate ways. Maple would be safe, and that's what mattered. Even if he was discovered, at least she wouldn't be connected to him. He'd make sure to keep her name out of it.

"Make sure Q doesn't drive you too crazy while I'm gone," Shawn said. The last part tasted like acid. The odds of him coming out alive were shrinking.

"He'll be lucky if I don't smother his snoring ass in his sleep," she joked, looking over her shoulder in the direction of the pit.

"I'll see you later Maple." Shawn started turning around and then thought better of it. He ran over to her and gave her a hug that probably lasted a little too long—although she held on just as tight.

"Go save her, you idiot."

And with that, Shawn was racing down the empty hallways.

Unlike Headmaster Tyflin's office, Franklin's was on the fifth floor next to the other council members. The only one on the council that didn't have their office up here was Mac, who insisted that the training tower was his office.

Turning the corner carefully, Shawn peeked out into the hallway to make sure no one from the council was staying behind. Even though the bell had rung, he didn't want to run into any stragglers. Thankfully, not even a cardinal was flapping its wings.

Fingering the brass key, Shawn stood in front of Franklin's door. He took a deep breath and inserted the key. Except it didn't fit. Shit. Why would Franklin give them this key if it didn't open his door? Was this the trap? Would he be caught standing out in the hallway, fake key in hand? He was about to give up and make his way back to the mill when he tried the knob for grins. The handle turned easily, and the door swung open. It was unlocked.

He snuck into the office. Sweat dripped down his back. Shawn felt that someone could come down the hallway at any second. He locked the door for good measure. The bolt sliding into place calmed his nerves a bit.

A giant map of the reaper regions hung on the wall behind the historian's desk. The rest of the walls were left bare, waiting for Franklin to make his mark on them. Bookcases were built into the desk and the wall behind it. A globe sat like an oversized paperweight on top of the notes which spilled across the cherry wood desk. Two worn brown leather chairs sat in front of the desk, giving the room a breath of personality. Also, unlike the headmaster, there were no alcohol decanters. Instead, Franklin opted to display a cardinal skeletal frame below the map of the region.

Looking around, Shawn felt overwhelmed. Here he was again, surrounded by books that may help, with no idea where to start. He clenched his fist, the key imprinting itself into his skin. "Where do you go?" He murmured.

There was nothing on the bookshelves or near the chairs, so Shawn started scrambling. He flipped to the other side of the desk, desperately aware that he didn't have a lot of time to fool around. There! On the right side was a drawer that contained a small keyhole. There wasn't anything else in the room that had a lock. This had to be it. Shawn put the key into the slot, expecting it to go in perfectly. It didn't. Alarms started sounding in his head. He needed to get out. But he forced himself to try again. This time, he slammed the key into the lock. It grinded into place, hugging the inside of the lock. It fit.

Maybe the key was bent or the locking mechanism was slightly askew. Whatever the reason, Shawn didn't care. He was in. Within the drawer were a couple of stacks of papers, a box of coins, and then five books. What did he say again? Biographies of founders? Shawn scanned the titles, yet no biographies were there. A book on gargoyles? None there either. He was about to grab a few random ones, figuring having some was better than none, when one cover stood out to him.

It was a green leather-bound book, with a large tree on it. The roots spread to the corners of the cover. Pages were yellowed from the years, but it was in pristine condition.

The Tree of Life We Call the Library

It was odd phrasing when Franklin said it, but Shawn had thought nothing more of it. That was until he saw the cover of this book.

Not wasting any more time, Shawn threw the book in his messenger bag and closed the door to the built-in safe. He thought about keeping the key, but he didn't need it anymore. So, he lay it on the chair, where Franklin would either see it or feel it. He took one last look around the office and then bolted for the exit.

A normal person under these circumstances would have gone straight back to the mill, but when Shawn entered the forest, he hesitated. Even with a death clock hanging over his head, Shawn had to know what they were saying in the pit. His body started moving before his mind could process his actions.

Keeping a couple of rows back, Shawn maneuvered among the fallen branches until he was on the outskirts of the stadium. He peered down from his vantage point to see that the crowd had already filled up the stone benches.

"This is not a normal circumstance by any means, let me assure you," Tyflin said. She stood in the center, addressing all levels of reapers. The pit wasn't built to handle this size of a crowd. Many had to sit on the steps or stand at the back.

Shawn couldn't help but think that having a meeting of this size was overkill. Did everyone really need to be brought up to speed? Being on the run hadn't allowed the reality of the situation to sink in. Then he thought about the gargoyle, the hospital reaper, a missing assignment, and the person who sat in the front row with their head hung: Trevor.

"As of right now, we don't know their location. Their trackers are malfunctioning and can't provide an accurate position." Tyflin let that sink in as she circled the stage. "Something we've never seen before."

Immediately, murmurs rippled through the crowd. Trackers not working? Something the headmaster had never seen? Everyone was confused.

Shawn found it interesting how Tyflin had left out the part about Jay and Shawn's trackers were also malfunctioning. Guess she didn't want to reveal everything.

Ignoring the crowd rumbles, Tyflin powered on. "This is why we've called you all here today." All noise was squeezed out the arena as she spoke. "Many of us believe that they've made their way back to the Academy... or at least past the gates."

Oh, no.

"We believe they are here, close by, hiding."

This time, the crowd could not contain themselves. Their murmurs turned to shouts. In the fourth row, Shawn spotted the bob of a familiar ponytail as Maple put her head in her hands.

"The gargoyles would know!" Someone said.

"Wouldn't someone have seen them?" Another asked.

Shawn automatically took a step back. He scanned the pit until he found a boy sitting cross-legged on one of the steps. Marvin couldn't speak, but that didn't mean the second year would remain silent.

Raising her hand, Tyflin silenced them. "We've spoken with the gargoyles, and they've assured us that none of our entrances have been compromised."

The reapers started glancing around suspiciously, as if the outlaws were hiding amongst them.

"But" she shouted. "We believe that they've found another way down here. That's why we need you all to be our eyes and ears. If a grounder has made their way here, it could prove to be disastrous for us all."

Their one advantage was gone. They knew they were down here. Shawn had had enough of this. He needed to alert Jay and Cirie.

The headmaster's fierce voice carried as he put trees between him and the pit. "If found, the grounder needs to be reaped immediately. If a reaper gets in the way... don't hesitate to use whatever means necessary."

Shawn didn't need to stick around and hear the rest. He moved quickly through the woods. If Maple saw what he was doing, she wouldn't be happy. Because he wasn't heading toward the mill. Not yet, at least. If they wanted to use whatever means necessary, he was going to need one more thing from the Academy.

Inside the door, he went into a full-out sprint. Why try to hide now that everyone knew him as Public Enemy Number One? Yet again, time wasn't his friend. He raced down hallway after hallway. Where was it? Past the ravens' room? Before the courtyard? That's when he saw the double-arched doors and burst through them without a second thought. The chandeliers glittered off the familiar metal. Fine. They wanted to send people after them? Two could play at that game. Shawn stared at his reflection in the scythe.

Chapter 46

Getting back to the mill went much faster than he expected. Shawn wasn't afraid of bumping into anyone; they were all at the pit. Instead of creeping through the woods, he pumped his legs like a gargoyle was chasing him. He ran full out until the mill doors were in sight.

Absolutely gassed, he entered through one of the chipped doors. If his fellow outlaws weren't already aware of his entrance, the creaking of the door hinges made sure to alert them. "It's me," Shawn called out.

Nothing was out of place inside, but there was no sign of Jay or Cirie. Where were they? Had search parties gone out and already found them? Was Cirie already dead? Her countdown flashed in the back of his mind.

"Were you followed?" Jay called out from an unknown spot.

There were only so many places to hide inside the mill. Looking around, Shawn wasn't sure what door Jay was behind. "Not that I'm aware. The whole Academy was in the pit when I left. I have a lot to tell you both."

Two doors opened simultaneously from opposite sides of the mill. Relief flooded through Shawn at the sight of his two friends. Cirie was still alive, which meant the trip wasn't wasted.

"Please tell me you brought food," Jay said.

Thankfully, Maple had thrown in a random assortment of food with the new clothes. A couple of apples, sticks of beef jerky, and a chocolate bar sat at the bottom of the bag.

"Come and get it," Shawn said. He threw Maple's water canteen over to Jay, who quickly started to deplete its contents. Shawn lay the spread in the middle of the floor like they were on a picnic at the gallows.

"Bring any smokes with you by chance?" Cirie asked, to their bewilderment "What? I'm stressed. Ya know, kind of dying here."

"What did you find out?" Jay asked as a bite of apple disappeared into his mouth.

Shawn ran through his story, informing them of his library experience and his escapades in Franklin's office as they scarfed down the food.

"Our secret's out," Shawn said. "Tyflin called the whole Academy to the pit to tell them to be on the lookout for us three."

Cirie looked over to the scythe. "They know we're down here?"

"Doesn't make a difference," Jay reminded them. "We already know we can't get caught. Nothing has changed. Now, what book did you retrieve from his office?"

Shawn pulled the green leather-bound cover from the bag. "Not sure, actually. Didn't have time to flip through it. But I think this is the one he wanted me to find." He opened the front cover so everyone could see. On the first page was a handwritten inscription that said, "The proper way to introduce reapers into this world".

Jay grabbed the book. "This is about the procedures for securing reapers on their first day. I'm betting every council member has one." Jay started flipping through the pages, searching for anything that could be of use. "There's a whole chapter on how to keep them calm when they wake up and how to break the news of their death." He tossed the book back to Shawn.

Shawn's sails deflated. The whole book was an onboarding manual. "There has to be something in here."

"It's a of couple hundred pages long. You can start reading if you want." Jay picked up Cirie's apple that she'd put down and placed it back into her hands. "You need to eat," he said.

She took the apple from him but put it down to grab a book. "There's got to be something here we could use. What else do you have?" She said each word with confidence only matched by Jay's clenched fist.

Did Shawn grab the wrong book? He could have sworn that Franklin was giving him a hint with that phrase. Maybe it was just a wild goose chase. No. This book had to be useful. He just needed to figure out what he was looking for.

Shawn removed the jagged piece of paper. "Maple tore this page out of one of the books in the library. She said it had stuck out to her and thought it could be useful."

This caught Cirie's attention. "What does it say?"

Shawn uncurled the paper and looked at what appeared to be an Allen Oak news clipping. There was a small paragraph that had a story from eighty years ago:

Current Senior Reaper Sylvia is stepping down from running for the Council of Wayward Academy. Following the incident involving her family member, and a full investigation, punishment has been recorded as time served.

The short paragraph barely gave them any information, but it did give them a name. One that Shawn recognized. "I think we have to stop by Drop Tailors for a fitting."

"Let's get some answers then." Cirie grabbed the spare clothes and slipped inside one of the barn doors to change, leaving the boys to themselves.

"You think Sylvia will help us?" Jay asked as he threw on his own sweatshirt and pants.

Shawn had no idea. But during his strange encounter with her in Allen Oak, she'd told him to follow his gut. Well, his gut was pointing directly to her shop. "Don't really think we have a choice. But if we did, I'd still try it. Something about her tells me she wouldn't turn us in."

Jay nodded as he scrounged through the reaping manual. "Hope you're right. We don't have any other options." He flipped another page. "Now why would old Mr. Franklin have kept this copy of a book locked in a vault?"

"I would've thought it would be in the library," Shawn said. "There had to be a reason for locking it away from the students." Shawn needed there to be something in it. Otherwise, he'd taken an unnecessary risk for nothing. Time was something that they couldn't waste. Time, which, according to the tracker, showed only two days and seven hours.

"The town is going to be busy," Jay said.

Shawn knew visiting the town was dangerous, but what else were they going to do? Wait around for the tracker to hit zero? "Like you said, not like we have a choice. Just can't slip up."

"Fair enough." Jay double-checked the bag to make sure they had everything. "How was Q after his reaping?"

"Not sure. I only saw Maple. Q hadn't made it back. Why?" Shawn asked, a bit taken aback.

Jay shrugged. "I saw how he got after his first observation. Just checking."

Cirie burst through the mill door. "If this Sylvia doesn't kill us, do you think she'll give me a fitting? I want to be flashy like you and Stripes over here."

"Come on. It's a long walk," Jay said unamused as Cirie rolled her eyes. They threw their stuff together and split the necessities. The bag of books went to Shawn, while Jay held onto the tracker and scythe.

"You know how to use that thing?" she asked, eyeing the blade.

Jay twirled the weapon through the air, slicing the space ahead of him like the scythe was an extension of his hand.

Cirie cocked her head to the side. "Well, points to us for having you on our team then."

"I had a friend who used to fence," Jay explained. "I couldn't afford to do it, but he'd lend me equipment after school so I could help him train. Got free lessons out of it." Jay smiled at the memory.

They brushed off as much dirt as they could, but they all could've benefited from a shower. "We're going to stick out like my haircut from 6th grade." Cirie said as both boys stared at her. "Believe me you don't want to know."

Jay held the mill door open. "We might be okay walking into town. You'd be surprised what people ignore when they don't want to be bothered."

They walked far enough alongside the cobblestone path to see it but not to be seen. Each snap from a branch sent the group scrambling behind trees. No one talked for the hour it took to get to the village. Upon seeing the blue, red, and white pennants dancing across the building, Shawn felt the air grow heavier around them. They'd arrived.

"Welcome to Allen Oak," Jay said, mimicking Trevor upon their entrance such a short time ago.

The town was starting to die down from the hustle and bustle of the day. Stores were starting to close. Shawn could see reapers coming and going from a few, not recognizing any. But they would be on the lookout for him.

Cirie poked her head out from around a tree. "Which one is it?"

"Over there," Jay said, pointing. "The white brick building."

The gold letters of Drop Tailors greeted them from afar like a finishing line for exhausted runners. They just had to cross it. The building was near the middle of the square–only the busiest part of town.

"Go in the back?" Shawn suggested.

"Probably be locked," Jay said.

Cirie looked at both of them. "Or I could just walk in." Without waiting for a response, she got up from her crouch and started forward. Shawn caught her arm just before she stepped out of the tree line.

"What?"She asked, as if Shawn should've known her plan.

"Walk in? Are you nuts? You're the most wanted person in the Academy. Possibly ever!"

She shook off his grip. "They only have a description of me."

"She's right," Jay said. "They know what she looks like, but they've never seen her. No one will suspect her walking out into the open. Let alone in the town square. She'll be hiding in plain sight."

Shawn shook his head in disbelief. "They'll still be looking for her."

"They're looking for three people. Not one. Besides, we're more likely to be recognized than her." Jay turned to Cirie. "We'll go to the back. Unlock the door as quickly as you can."

"Will do, captain." She smirked and then sashayed off into the town like it was the most normal thing in the world.

While she made her way across the cobblestones, Shawn pictured reapers flowing into the street after her. But Jay was right. No mob was waiting to snatch her. A simple Academy sweatshirt worked as a perfect camouflage, and she slipped through without raising any red flags. People didn't want to be bothered.

Shawn and Jay walked along the edge of the town until they reached the side streets behind the shop. Attempting to hide their faces, they threw up their hoods and pointed their heads to the ground. It took everything in Shawn to not look around as they made their way closer to the back door. It was only when they were standing in front of it that he allowed himself to look up. Jay checked the door, but as they thought, it was locked. They'd just have to wait.

Down a couple of store fronts, a group of teenage welders were marking up a building. They created their own type of graffiti, using their flames to stain the brick black wherever they pointed. They were halfway through a poorly drawn hourglass before the shop owner finally noticed and started yelling.

"Split!" One welder yelled as the owner stormed out. The three ran off in different directions as the owner screamed after them. He tried to stop them from running but quickly admitted defeat before heading back into his shop. The one who'd been doing the so-called "artwork" had dipped into the back area of Drop Tailors, trying to stay out of eyesight of the street.

At first, the artist didn't notice the two reapers. He was too busy peering his head around the corner to confirm the shop owner was staying inside. After confirming he was in the clear, he turned to see both of them standing at the back door.

"You two didn't see anything," the welder warned with eyes that were lit with the same fire that had been pouring out of his hands. He was a tall, lanky teenager, a few years younger than them, with a gold hoop that pierced the bridge of his nose.

"Didn't see what?" Jay said, leaning the scythe against the wall. He'd suddenly developed an interest in his fingernails.

The welder scoffed as he pulled his long white hair into a bun. Would he recognize them? Shawn felt secure, knowing that tensions were high between the welders and reapers. They were more likely to have fire hurled their way than have the kid turn them in.

No one seemed sure what to say next, but thankfully, no one had to say anything. The back door swung out, opening to a smiling Cirie.

"There you two are. You know I said no more breaks today," Cirie ad-libbed, recognizing the unwanted company.

"Reapers," the kid said, with disgust drooling out of his voice. He turned his attention away from the trio, peeking his head into the street one more time before heading off.

With the welder out of sight, Cirie hurried them both inside. "Quickly," she said as if Shawn needed to be reminded.

The familiar plush green chairs were the first thing Shawn saw. The second was the round pendant hanging around the neck of the person standing next to the chairs.

Sylvia's yellow smile greeted them. "Hello, my little troublemakers."

Chapter 47

Shawn's eyes flickered around the room, making sure that there weren't any other unexpected members in the greeting party. Cirie plopped into one of the green chairs, looking relaxed. Had they talked? Sylvia wasn't running to alert other reapers, and there hadn't been any birds to leave the shop.

"Hi Sylvia," Shawn said.

"Now now, what have you boys gotten into?" She asked, not waiting for a response as she moved past them to relock the back door.

Shawn and Jay looked at each other puzzled. "What? Haven't you heard?" Shawn asked.

"Word travels faster than a cardinal in this town. Believe me, we're all aware of the situation. You three have caused the most amount of gossip in the last decade. Take a seat over there while I lock up." Sylvia walked back to the front of the shop.

When Sylvia was out of earshot, Shawn asked Cirie, "What's going on?"

"Honestly, I have no idea. As soon as I walked in, she shooed the last two people out of the door. Then just asked how I was doing and if I wanted food or anything."

Jay stared at Cirie like she'd grown another set of ears. If Shawn's first interaction with Sylvia was anything to go by, it seemed that she was a wild card.

"She did ask about you two, so I told her that you were both out the back. And now, here we are." Small particles of dust rose as she leaned forward in the armchair.

"Would you three like a little tea and some food?" Sylvia came over carrying a tray of mini sandwiches.

Shawn grabbed one and, remembering his manners, thanked her before stuffing it into his mouth. Cirie followed suit, but Jay was a little more skeptical.

"It's chai, dear," Sylvia insisted as she poured the tea.

"Thank you, Ma'am." Jay took the mug of tea, and his fingers twitched above a sandwich before his stomach forced one into his hands.

Sylvia hiked up the bottom of her dress as she dragged over another armchair. "Now, what can I help you three with?"

"You're not going to turn us in?" Shawn asked in disbelief. Here were three wanted reapers walking into her shop, and instead of putting chains on their hands, she was putting sandwiches into them.

Sylvia shook her head, causing her pearl earrings to swing from side to side. "I don't see any criminals here. And before you get into any tales of your adventures, the less I know the better. So, I'll ask again. What can I do for you three?"

Flabbergasted that this woman was helping them, Jay hadn't even realized that the middle of his sandwich had dropped out from between the bread.

There wasn't a point to beat around the bush any longer. Now that they knew she wasn't turning them in, Shawn reached into his pocket and took out the torn piece of paper. "We came here because we were wondering if you could tell us more about this." He handed it over to her.

A small smile crept onto Sylvia's face. Her eyes looked sad as she read the paper. "Have you two heard of the selection process for reapers?"

Shawn shook his head yes. It was a question that had plagued him since he woke up in the carriage. They knew a bit about it.

"Isn't there a list sent out every year from the capital?" Jay asked.

Sylvia nodded. "Correct, Mr. Musters. Every year, a list of names is sent over to the academies, containing the potential new reapers to be enrolled. Whoever dies on selection day is taken to become a reaper. No one but the Four Horsemen knows how it's done." She took a sip of her tea. "It's the busiest time of the year for reapers. Even those in retirement are called upon to help out."

"What does that have to do with your situation or mine?" Cirie asked.

Sylvia patted Cirie's leg the way a grandmother pats an eager grandchild on the head. "Patience. I'm getting there." She brought the tea to her lips again. "During my time as a reaper, I was doing well. As I reached the end of my contract, there were rumors that I might even have a shot at being the next head talon. I hadn't ruffled any feathers at that stage."

"Why did you resign then?" Shawn asked.

Sylvia toyed with her locket. "Oh, that wasn't by choice. I was forced out."

The way the blurb was written, Shawn wasn't shocked. Then again, he couldn't imagine what someone like Sylvia must have done to be forced to quit.

"When I was in the reading room," Sylvia continued, "one of the other talons had just gotten a namesake. At the time, I was one of the recorders and yet, she refused to tell me. This set alarm bells off in my head."

Cirie pulled her legs into her chest. "What did you do?"

"I argued with her in front of a dozen or so other talons. She was a second year, refusing to let me do my job, and I was up for head talon. I couldn't let that happen. I really called her out. I should have known better. Then the girl told me the name."

"You knew it," Shawn said, remembering his disbelief when he read Cirie's name.

"My father," she said, opening her locket to reveal a family photo. A woman in a floral dress was sitting down holding a baby—presumably Sylvia. Behind them, a short skinny man smiled into the camera as he rested his hand on the woman's shoulder.

"They told you that your father was dying?" Cirie asked, putting her hand over her mouth.

"I wasn't supposed to find out. It's against the rules. I still feel bad for reaming out that second-year..." Sylvia paused, offering everyone another mini sandwich before continuing. "This sent me into a tailspin. I had no idea how to react. In all of my hysterics, I actually ended up thanking the girl as I rushed out the door." Sylvia's voice cracked as she laughed. "Nuts, isn't it?"

"What did you do then?" Shawn wanted to know the end of this story, but, more importantly, he needed to know how it was going to help Cirie.

"After finding out my father was going to die? I did what any reasonable person would. I went to try and save him." She leaned back in the chair as if trying to remember part of a dream after just waking up. "There's a reason they never tell you a family member is being reaped until after it's done. Protocol is in place to prevent instances such as mine."

Every word Sylvia spoke came with a bit of hope. Shawn wasn't the first reaper that wanted to save someone, and he probably wouldn't be the last. "You wanted to save someone from the reaping as well... How did you stop it?"

“I’m sorry.” Sylvia turned to Cirie. “Unfortunately, once your timer starts ticking down, there isn’t a way to stop it.”

The ground beneath Shawn felt wobbly. No way to stop it. He’d been told this countless times, yet he hadn’t accepted it. Now here was the answer to the questions he needed, and he was still trying to find a way out. He rubbed his temples and looked over at Cirie. She sat stone faced, but a quick gulp told Shawn everything he needed to know. He had let her down.

“A worthless mission wouldn’t get you forced out,” Jay pointed out.

Sylvia threw Jay a yellow toothy smile in response. “Correct. Which is why, instead of smuggling a grounder in here like a crazy old bat, I went to make my father a reaper.”

Shawn pulled his hands away from his head. “I’m sorry. Make your father a reaper?”

“You can make me a reaper?” Cirie leaned forward at the possibility of a new life.

“But the list comes from the capital?” Jay asked.

The locket on Sylvia’s chain rattled as she shook her head. “The list from the capital informs us of who’s slated to become a reaper. Not how to make one. Every year on enrollment, we’re given specific scythes to use from the capital. What most people don’t know is that they’ve been dipped in a mixture that binds to the soul we reap.”

A mixture that can create reapers. It was a solution Shawn hadn’t even considered. “That means anyone could technically become a reaper,” he whispered.

“Almost, Mr. Turner. I failed. I was caught creating the mixture, and the next day my father was reaped.”

Cirie put her hand out to Sylvia, who squeezed onto it as she tried to finish.

“The staff were sympathetic at the time and kept it pretty hush-hush. It was only after word got out to one of the Four Horsemen that I was forced out of the position.”

“Lucky that they were sympathetic,” Jay snorted.

This was it. Cirie’s way out. Instead of delaying the inevitable, they could have her become a reaper. It would at least extend her life and if they were able to turn her into one before she signed the contract, she wouldn’t have to suffer with them. They just needed to know how. Thank you, Maple.

"How do we make a reaper?" Shawn asked.

Sylvia slowly lowered her tea. "After they found out about my little scheme, they wiped my last couple of days from my memory. I'm sorry, but I don't remember everything that went into the mixture."

"They can take away your memory?" Cirie asked, bewildered.

"They can only take a couple of days. Reapers have the memory of their death wiped before waking up. I can't remember the last week before I died."

Shawn looked over at Jay. Was this all for nothing? Shawn could sniff the finish line. There just happened to be a moat between him and it.

Jay remained calm. His fist was unclenched. "What do you mean you don't remember *everything*?"

Sylvia picked up the empty tray of sandwiches and walked over to her office. In the corner of the room, she dug her fingernails under the trim. The carpet lifted to reveal old, hard floor panels. Sylvia wiggled one of the now exposed boards before it popped up.

"There it is!" Sylvia exclaimed as she reached into the hole she created. "Always have a hiding spot."

Carrying a glass vial with blue liquid, Sylvia went straight over to Cirie. "Now, I said I was caught before I was able to make the mixture. Just like here, my room at Wayward also had a little hiding spot I liked to use. So, when I woke up with no memory, I went straight to that spot. That's where I found this little guy." She held up the vial. "Even if I didn't remember what I was mixing, I knew where I kept the ingredients."

"Is this it?" Cirie asked as Sylvia placed the vial into her hands.

"Not the complete mixture, no. But one of the ingredients. If I knew the rest of the recipe, I'd tell you. Unfortunately, I don't even remember where I found it."

Shawn's hand shot towards his messenger bag. He fumbled around until he pulled out the green leather-bound book. "Have you ever seen a book like this?"

"That looks familiar." Sylvia cocked her head to the side before taking the book from Shawn. She ran her hand over the cover, tracing the gold tree from branches to roots. Her fingers then flipped open the cover and started rifling through the pages. "Here it is!"

The group leaned forward to examine the page. Printed on it was the process for creating new reapers: the Hades Elixir.

Chapter 48

Light from the wall sconce reflected off the glass vial, illuminating the clear blue liquid inside. Blood of a gargoyle. What had she done to get it? Whatever it was, Shawn was happy that they wouldn't have to repeat the process.

"What else do we need?" Cirie asked.

Sylvia's finger traced the page. "There are only two other ingredients. And they should be easier to get than the blood. Let's see here. You need an unbroken crystal from the cavern and the fire from a welder."

"Excuse me?" Shawn clutched the back of his neck. Welder fire? Obtaining the crystal wouldn't be hard, they might even be able to snag that on the way back to the mill. But getting a welder's fire? Shawn had a better chance of winning a sparring match against Mac.

"Is that it?" Jay asked with a dark chuckle.

"That's it." Sylvia handed the book to Jay just in case he didn't want to take her word for it. "Now I know you're all antsy, but my little birds have informed me that they're doing sweeps throughout the town and woods tonight. Your best bet would to be stay here tonight and get a move on early in the morning."

The two young reapers turned to the one person with a countdown still hanging above her head. Cirie rolled her eyes and rubbed the palm of her hand along the armchair. "Oh, now I get a say in what we do."

"If you don't want to wait, we can try to make our way back to the mill," Shawn said, ignoring the look he was getting from Jay. Shawn knew that they'd run the risk of being found by the sweeps, but it wasn't his time to be spending. For all they knew, Cirie could die in the next minute.

"Let's get some rest. We all know we need it," Shawn said.

Sylvia, satisfied with that answer, pulled pillows and blankets into her office. "You three can stay here. Best to be out of sight. I'll lock both doors, and we should be good as long as we're quiet. They aren't sweeping inside the buildings."

Shawn went and took a blanket from Sylvia as the others went into the office. "Thank you for everything you're doing."

"Not everyone is against you three. Remember that."

The office was small for three people, so they had to huddle together in their makeshift bedroom. Sylvia reminded them that she was upstairs in her studio if they needed anything. Shawn didn't think he'd ever miss the hay bed, but it beat the hardwood floors and blanket.

"Got any cards?" Jay joked.

Shawn flinched, thinking of Trevor.

"Ah, yes. I remembered to pack them in my going-to-die bag," Cirie said.

Jay ignored the remark. "Are you sure you want to stay the night?"

Cirie put her head down and flattened her blanket. "The way I see it, I'm going to die sometime within the next what? Day and a half?"

Shawn checked the tracker. "Two days and three hours."

"Right. So, the way I look at it, I need to make the safest possible moves while I still have that countdown. Gotta play the long game."

She was right. They shouldn't make any unnecessary moves. Yes, her clock was ticking down, but that was only the first countdown. After she passed on, the timer would restart. They'd have a limited window to make her a reaper. They couldn't risk being caught before they had all the ingredients.

"I'd rather avoid getting whacked by some thick-headed stone man again. Once was enough." She ran her hand over the cuts along her injured arm.

Shawn held his ribs. "I'll agree to that. We ran into way too many in the market."

"About that..." Jay said. "There might not have been as many as you think."

"What are you talking about?" It wasn't like Shawn imagined the punch to his ribs.

Both of Jay's shoulders tensed. "When you spotted Cirie in the market, we split up, right?"

"Yeah, you had to lose the gargoyle coming out of the gold statue," Shawn said, thinking back.

Cirie jolted up. "What did you say? Like a gold man in the middle of the market? With a top hat and cane?"

Jay remained silent.

Cirie burst out laughing.

Shawn remained lost in the conversation. "Anyone want to fill me in?"

Jay turned his head away from them both, his ears burning a fire-engine red. Cirie threw an arm over his shoulder. She squeaked out the next sentence between laughing fits. "Your boy ran from a street performer in gold paint."

"He what..." Shawn looked from one face to another. Jay kept his eyes to the floor. A street performer. Shawn burst into laughter which made his chest ache. "Dammit, Jay!"

"It was an easy mistake." He shook his head as the other two continued their fit. A few minutes later, the laughter settled down. Never sure when the next piece of happiness would be their last, the joyful moment hung over the group.

"What happens after I become a reaper?" Cirie asked.

"We should get some sleep. You both can do whatever you want," Jay avoided the question, lying down on his blanket. "After we do this, though, I'm getting the hell out of here."

"Jay, there are people on our side." He thought about Maple, Franklin, and Sylvia. "If we keep running, we'll never stop. Besides, they can track us now. There's nowhere we could go. Maybe we can find some help."

Jay sat up, ears blushing at what Shawn was saying. "We can't just walk over holding hands and say we're sorry. You heard Sylvia. This is one of the biggest stories of the last decade. We're wanted dead or alive."

"Then we make sure we're alive." Jay was wrong. Ever since he'd gotten to Wayward, he had wanted to run. They were still understanding this new world's rules, but not *all* these people were unreasonable.

"Like I said, you guys do what you want." Jay turned over on his stomach, closing his eyes and his part of the conversation.

Darkness stretched into the shop as each candle inside was blown out. Exhaustion had spread through the group like a disease, and no one even mentioned anything about a lookout. One moment Shawn's eyes were open and the next they weren't.

When he opened them again, he had no idea what time it was. The cavern crystals hadn't brightened yet, so he knew he should try to get more sleep. Next to him, Jay was still passed out, but the blankets that were supposed to cover Cirie sat in a clump on the empty spot.

A second or two went by and Shawn allowed the fear to enter his body. After that passed, he crept out of the office. A shadow leaned over near one of the suit racks.

"You'll have to pick one out you know," Shawn said.

Even with her back turned, she didn't jump as he approached. Nerves of steel. She ran her hand along the sleeve of a yellow power suit.

"At least I'll look better in a suit than you, Stripes."

Shawn feigned shock. "How dare you! My blue was electrifying."

"Really? Electrifying?"

Shawn shrugged. "Hey, I'm only running on a couple hours of sleep here. I'm out of my element."

"Whatever you say."

A smile formed across his lips. Halloween seemed like eons ago. "You see anything?"

"Three reapers so far. Headed that way." She pointed toward the center of the square. Outside the front bay windows, the empty street taunted them. Daring them to leave the safety of their shop. "Maybe they don't think we went into town."

"Good. Let's hope it stays that way."

Cirie stayed silent, watching the empty street like a pot she was waiting to boil over.

"Why do you trust us?" Shawn said, his mouth once again moving ahead of his brain.

"Not like I had a lot of options there. Remember when you found me in the alley the other night?"

"How could I forget?"

"Hard to forget your first stalkee?" She winked before continuing. "But do you remember what you said you wanted?"

"Not really."

Cirie's hand reached for a cigarette packet that wasn't there. "You said you wanted to do something meaningful with your life. You've kept your word. You helped me in the train station, the hospital, even here. You saved me. Okay? Remember that."

Outside, the flame of a patrolling reaper flickered off the storefront windows. "Well, we're not done yet."

"Let's get some rest. Might die tomorrow, you know." She laughed then pulled Shawn into a hug, her arms draping over his body like a blanket. "Thank you," she whispered.

“Thank me when it’s over,” Shawn said.

Comforted by the soft glow of the cavern crystals, they were able to fall asleep easily to their natural nightlights. Unfortunately, the sleep didn’t last long.

Someone was shaking him out of a pleasant dream. Shawn woke up with Sylvia standing over them, hand held to her lips. Sunrise must have been close because more light filtered in the bay windows. Cirie and Jay were both already awake, throwing their stuff together.

“You all need to leave now,” Sylvia whispered urgently.

“What’s going on?” Jay asked.

She turned to him and said calmly, “They’re sweeping the buildings.”

Chapter 49

Within minutes everyone had shaken the sleep from their eyes. Whatever dreams they were having were preferable to the nightmare they were waking up in. Shawn knew it was smart on the Academy's part to search the shops so early: they wanted to catch them sleeping.

"All shop owners are being told to come outside while they conduct the search. We're the second-to-last on the street, but they haven't started on the shops behind us yet." Sylvia gave the information at a blistering speed. The only reason they had a few minutes was because another shop owner had sent Sylvia a cardinal, asking if she'd been searched yet.

"Are we clear to go out the back?" Jay asked. The group ducked between the racks, avoiding windows as they moved through the shop.

"There could be someone out there now, so I'll take a look first. I'll do my best to cover for you if there is but be prepared to run."

Cirie took hold of Sylvia before she could open the door. "They'll know you helped us then. You'll need an alibi."

"Oh, honey. I know what I'm getting into. Nothing they can do to this old bat anymore." Her lips brushed Cirie's forehead in a quick peck. She grabbed a trash bag she'd staged by the door. "I'll be right back."

Before long, Sylvia squeezed back through the door. "A few welders and their children are down the block watching the commotion, but otherwise, you're in the clear." She looked over the trio. "A group of three will attract attention."

Split up. Shawn feared that this might happen. He hated being alone when he was at Wayward. But at least then, he didn't have reapers at the doorstep. With no time to argue, it was decided that Jay would go with Cirie. In case they ran into trouble, he was better with the scythe.

"You guys go right when you leave. I'll take the long way around and meet you back at the mill," Shawn said.

"You got it, boss." Cirie said.

Adrenaline pumped through Shawn's system like it was replacing the blood in his veins. This might be the last time he ever saw them. They needed to get past these sweeps and back to the mill unscathed. They had nowhere else to go.

Before Sylvia opened the door, Shawn pulled both Cirie and Jay into a hug. "Don't die yet."

"Think I still have a couple more hours," Cirie said, laughing.

"No promises," Jay responded sarcastically.

The moment of peace was short-lived. They both pulled up their hoods. Shawn hoped they'd blend in with the rest of the sweepers. He didn't need to be reminded what would happen if they didn't. Jay led the way, his scythe in hand. Neither looked back as they left Shawn at the door.

"Wait a minute in case anyone is watching," Sylvia said.

One minute felt like an hour. Shawn was itching to get out of the shop, and every second that passed felt wasted. A pounding at the front door indicated that the waiting time was up.

"Time to go," Sylvia said, opening the door. The reapers had finally arrived at the shop. With an open door in front of him and danger at another, it took everything in Shawn's bones not to bolt out into the street.

"Wait!" he said a little too loudly. Leaning in, Shawn whispered an idea into Sylvia's ear.

She looked at him quizzically before nodding. "I will. Now go," she urged, giving one last tea-stained smile. Throwing his hood up as the door latched shut behind him, Shawn prayed he'd make it to the mill unscathed.

Just as Sylvia had said, the street behind the shop was mostly empty. It wouldn't be the case for long though; with each step Shawn took, more people were waking up. Welders watched in groups as reapers invaded their privacy. They glared at any reaper that walked nearby, which meant they glared at him. Good. Make them think that he was one of the sweepers.

With the tailor shop being near the center of town, he needed to take a few side streets to get back to the woods. Straightening his back, Shawn tried to walk with a purpose. He refused to allow his head to be turned to his feet. He held it straight ahead, hoping to fool himself and anyone else that walked by.

He walked two streets before he saw his first sweeper. Judging by the IV on her shoulder, the Academy had given the students the graveyard shift. Being only a couple of shops away, Shawn waited for her to notice him or for her to call for help. Instead, she passed by without even a glance in his direction. The scowl plastered on her face was a show for the welders throwing dirty looks her way.

So far, so good. Maybe he could pull this off. He wished that he knew how Jay and Cirie were doing. Hopefully, their route had less traffic on it.

"They think they can just come in here and search our things? We owe them nothing!" A voice drifted over from a storefront ahead of him. A large group of welders were gathered outside of it, having a heated conversation.

One woman laughed. "Anex, you *let* them search your place without so much as a protest."

"Shut up, Elaine. What else am I supposed to do? We're lucky they didn't send the gargoyles in."

The one named Elaine scoffed again. "You know gargoyles don't meddle in the village; their territory is above. At least I stood my ground."

"Until you saw the scythe," Anex said.

"This is stupid. We have ways of defending ourselves," a young boy chimed in. Shawn recognized the graffiti vandal from the day before. The boy looked around at his fellow welders, his hands glowing a soft red amber.

Past the group of welders, a line of reapers were sweeping the street, headed straight for them. Deciding that walking past them wasn't his best route, Shawn turned into the nearby alley to cut over one street. He was only a few blocks away from the woods and didn't need to run into trouble now.

Unfortunately, trouble wanted to find him. Three gleaming scythes were making their way down the alley, headed his way.

What to do. Did he risk a close encounter in the alleyway? Or turn back and try to get past the welders before he encountered the other sweepers? At least the alley was private. Shawn was about to take a step into it when he recognized one of the reapers. Kishan Gibson. A second-year reaper, whom Shawn had sparred with twice. Shawn backpedaled into the street, taking his chances with the other group.

Turning back, Shawn discovered his other problem. Sophia's mentor, Hamilton, was leading the group in the street. Whichever way he went, Shawn was going to be recognized. The inside of his chest felt like a trash compactor, slowly squeezing the life out of him. If adrenaline was keeping most of the pain away, Shawn didn't want to find out what he was missing. Panic quickly set in. He was trapped like a lion in a carnival, waiting for the show to start. He needed a way out.

The graffiti guy.

Scrambling, Shawn searched the ground near him, raking the floor until he found exactly what he needed. Looking at both groups, he knew he had no other choice. Like a pitcher throwing a heater, his arm went back and then snapped the object forward. Shawn needed all those years of Little League to pay off.

They did. The stone flew through the air and hit the boy right below the white bun on his head.

"What the FUCK? He screamed.

A woman looked around for the source. Ignoring the fact that the pebble was thrown from the opposite direction, she directed her gaze to the reapers coming toward them. "Oh, is that how it is? Ahhh!" Like she was holding candles inside her palm, her fist grew brighter. With another scream, fire hurled from her hand and into the air. Flames licked at the line of reapers, who were just able to sidestep the attack.

"That's it! No one attacks my son!" Anex raced toward the dispersed reapers with glowing hands, the other welders following his lead. Only the graffiti vandal resisted diving into the chaos, choosing instead to sit back and watch. The reapers were caught off guard, not understanding the anger that they'd suddenly found themselves on the receiving end of. They could only react. The smell of fire spread as fast as the swing of a scythe.

From out of the alley, Kishan and his comrades rushed to provide reinforcements. Shawn peaked out from the trash can he'd hidden behind. They never saw him. Although Shawn was curious to see what the outcome of the fight would be, he wasn't stupid. A large commotion like this was going to draw everyone to him. And also away from Cirie and Jay.

Reapers and welders alike rushed to the flames, passing Shawn without a second glance. Before he knew it, Shawn was weaving through the trees of the forest instead of the streets of Allen Oak. Only war cries followed him as he made his exit.

Chapter 50

It wasn't long before Shawn was back in front of the mill. He approached the barn doors cautiously, not sure if he was the first one back. Just being near the mill brought Shawn's blood pressure down. One of the worst places in his time at Wayward had now become one of the safest. Things can change quickly.

"Get in, Stripes." Poking her head out from behind one of the doors, Cirie beckoned him forward. She was still alive.

Dashing inside, Shawn ran straight into Jay's chest. "You're both alive!"

Jay smirked, brushing off his sweatshirt. "Not one single reaper questioned us. Got out easily. Did you have any trouble?"

"A little bit." He told them about using the welders to create a diversion.

"That'll keep them busy in town for a bit. You're lucky you got out," Cirie said.

The muscles in Shawn's body were aching from lack of rest. He sat down, trying to work out the aches in his calves. "Very. We need to get onto these ingredients now though. Who knows how much time we have?"

"Agreed." Jay made his way over to the book bag. "Let's cook us up a reaper."

As Jay started flipping through the book, Shawn looked around the inside of the mill. Nothing inside was disturbed. A couple of barn doors were slightly ajar from where they had to hide; otherwise, everything seemed to be in place. "You guys checked the whole place, right?"

"We swept the barns and didn't find anyone. Don't think they've hit here yet." Jay flipped through more pages. "Ah, here it is!"

Having a door ajar unnerved Shawn, so he walked over to the closest one. Before he shut it, he hesitated. If they'd swept the windmill, they would have disturbed more than a door. Shawn shook his head. Might as well make sure there was no one in it. Cocking his arm into a fist, he threw open the door.

No one was inside. Just remnants of dried blood on the hay from the testing. It was silly, but everything made Shawn jump now. They hadn't been on the run that long, but his mind may have argued otherwise.

Cirie watched the whole thing. "You good over there?"

"Yeah, I'm goo—" A creak from above stopped him in his tracks. It was an old mill. Old mills make noises, that's all. Yet Shawn knew exactly where that sound came from. Because the staircase wasn't silent. He whipped his head upward to the spiral steps and found two piercing green eyes staring back.

"Cirie, run!" He screamed.

The figure launched himself from the staircase, landing between Shawn and his friends. Marvin. The boy grinned at Cirie; his scythe looked as eager as he was to cut her throat.

Scrambling, Jay positioned himself between Marvin and Cirie. He extended his own scythe, ready to take on their unwanted guest. The anger on Jay's face boiled over into the death grip he had on the shaft of the scythe. He waited, calculating every small movement from Marvin.

"It's three on one, Marvin. You won't win this," Shawn said, eyeing the blade. Shawn had to get that weapon away from him. No one had ever mentioned Marvin's skill with the blade, but he was a second-year. At the very least, he had a full year of training more than they had. Shawn tentatively took a step forward. "Just put down the scythe and let us explain. This doesn't have to get messy."

Marvin cocked his head. No one dared to make the first move. It was a standoff that was only going to be settled one way. The corners of Marvin's lips wormed their way into a smile. Then he swung the scythe. Shawn dove backward, avoiding the arc of the blade by inches. Pain erupted across his ribs, the hay-covered dirt floor doing nothing to cushion the fall. Marvin laughed silently at the spectacle.

"Doesn't look like he's up for talking, Shawn." Jay adjusted his defensive stance. "Cirie, make your way over to Shawn when he charges."

"When he charges?" She asked.

Jay ignored the question and focused solely on the man in front of him.

Marvin looked him up and down. Sensing a true opponent, his smile gained both sets of teeth. Then the space between the two vanished. A sudden clang echoed into the empty mill as Marvin brought his scythe down on top of Jay's. Grimacing, Jay thrust forward, pushing Marvin back as he collected himself.

The second year wasted no time and attacked again. This time, Marvin swung in wide arcs across the air, like he was drawing inspiration from the windmill itself. Jay almost escaped the attack unscathed. Fabric along his arm hung to the side, exposing the small cut. Too close.

After the near hit, Marvin sped up the strikes. Swing, block, swing, block. An extra year of experience might be their downfall, as Jay couldn't get a swing in. Marvin tried coming straight down on top of him again but met resistance when Jay was able to get his scythe up in time.

"That all you got?" Jay screamed after another block.

Continuing to smile like the Cheshire Cat, Marvin didn't let up. While Jay was focused on blocking, Marvin pushed him into a corner. It wasn't long before Jay was up against the wall. Heads inches apart and blades locked in a standstill, Marvin leaned in closer. He rubbed the bridge of his nose against Jay's cheek and inhaled through his nostrils.

"Ahhh!" Jay said, shoving him off. "You're sick. You know that?"

Marvin remained unaffected and charged again. Metal clashed against metal. A swing aimed at Jay's head barely got deflected. One swing later, Jay was late again: the scythe grazed his shoulder. Spots of blood were seeping into the fabric of the sweatshirt.

Cirie took this as her opportunity to act. Bolting from Shawn's side, she ran toward the danger, her grandfather's knife clenched in her palm. Movement slowed down for Shawn at that moment. He could picture the countdown of the tracker above her head. The closer she got to the fight, the closer the countdown got to zero.

"Stop!" Shawn yelled, to no avail.

Like a sixth sense, Marvin turned, arcing his swing toward his new attacker. The blade sliced through the air. Cirie dropped to the floor, losing the knife. The scythe missed her neck by a hair. Marvin grabbed a fistful of her sweatshirt between his fingers. His shoulders bounced in a silent chuckle. Then he shoved Cirie back toward Shawn. With the pocket knife out of reach, he turned his attention back to the only other person with a weapon.

"What are you thinking?" Shawn said, catching Cirie before she hit the dirt. Marvin should've killed her there and then, but he was relishing the chaos. Shawn wanted to jump in but knew that it was useless to get caught between the clashing of blades.

Her hand went to her throat. She grinded her teeth. "Had to get Jay a little more time."

More time: the one thing they were always in desperate need of. By evidence of the enlarging blood spot on his shoulder, Jay was going to need every second. Side-stepping a slice, Jay smiled and went on the offensive. The first, a swing to Marvin's left, was blocked. Taking that in his stride, Jay used the momentum to spin into another attack on Marvin's right side.

Marvin brought his own blade around just in time to block the strike. The smile disappeared on his face as quickly as it had appeared. The second year brought over the middle of the staff to block the next attack from gutting his midsection. This would have blocked Jay's strike if he'd actually gone there. But Jay faked the strike. He adjusted his attack, going low on his swing and delivering the blade to Marvin's feet. Tendons shredded as the blade tore into the back of Marvin's right leg. As the strike sent him down to one knee, a wordless grunt escaped his lips.

Not wasting any time, Jay brought his scythe up and hooked his blade into Marvin's. With one swoop upwards, Marvin was left holding nothing but air. Jay kicked out at Marvin's chest, and he toppled over like a tower of cards. Jay stood with sweat rolling down his face. Panting, bleeding, but victorious.

Chapter 51

Blood pooled underneath Marvin's calf, mixing into the blood-stained hay. Not wanting the weapon to be within the madman's reach, Shawn swooped up the other scythe. The weight of the staff felt good between his hands. There was hope yet; everyone was still alive.

"Let me get some restraints," Cirie said, ruffling through their pile of torn clothing.

Daring him to move, Jay stood above Marvin with the blade ready to swing. "Move and I'll cut your throat like I did that calf." Jay didn't hide the anger in his voice, but he could hide the fear in it. If Shawn hadn't noticed the slight twitch of Jay's thumb as he spoke, he would've believed every word.

Recognizing the situation, Marvin didn't resist. Then again, by becoming as limp as a sack of flour, he didn't help either. Using the strips Cirie made, they bound his arms and legs as tightly as they could with the torn fabric and dragged him to the corner of the room.

"We should gag his mouth," Shawn insisted.

"Is he mute? Or does he willingly not talk?" Cirie asked as she tightened another knot around Marvin's feet. Blood leaked out from under him, creating wet spots in Cirie's jeans as she knelt. The red fluid soaked into the material. Taking what was left of a shirt, she dressed the leg wound.

Finding the wall nearest to him, Jay slid down, wincing the whole way. "From what Q said, the guy cut out his own tongue within the first week at the Academy. He communicates with the senior reapers by writing down messages. He won't be talking anytime soon."

"Doesn't mean he can't make a noise." Shawn eyed their tied-up visitor. "Probably best to gag him. We don't want him to alert anyone that could come nearby."

"Happy to oblige in gagging my would-be murderer." Cirie stuffed a piece of fabric in Marvin's mouth. "What kind of person cuts out their own tongue? Should we put him in one of the barns?"

"No, I want my eyes on him at all times," Jay insisted. As much as Shawn would love not being in the same room as this maniac, he had to agree. Out of sight out of mind, in this case, wasn't a good thing. They couldn't risk him escaping.

They dragged Marvin to one of the corners of the mill. Nothing close to him could be used as a weapon, and it was the farthest possible distance away from the door without putting him on the roof.

Flipping the scythe in his hand, Jay said aloud what they were probably all thinking. "Should we eliminate the problem before it becomes a bigger one?"

"I'm not trading one life for another," said Shawn. "No, we're not going there. Killing won't solve anything; it'll just make things worse." Marvin was a lunatic—Shawn was sure of that. But killing him? He glanced between Cirie and Marvin, finally focusing on Cirie. "We're doing everything we can to save you. But I refuse to achieve that by taking his life. Okay?"

"No offense Shawn, but it's not your opinion I need on this," Jay said, taking Shawn back a little.

"I may have a countdown, but it's all our lives on the line. We aren't 'eliminating the problem,'" Cirie said.

"Just thought we should at least discuss it," Jay released his grip on the scythe. "Good with me."

"What are the odds he came out here without telling anyone?" Shawn asked.

No one said anything. If Marvin had told anyone, it would've been Rupert. Thankfully, Rupert had been called away on assignment before the headmaster's announcement.

"All the more reason to get a move on. We still need to grab the welder's fire," Jay said, the pain from his shoulder showing on his face. "One of you two needs to grab a crystal from the walls of the cave."

Cirie gave Shawn a look. "I'll get the damn rock. There might be some that fell out near the tunnel when we created our little landslide."

"I'll go get the fire then." Jay stood up, a spot of blood falling from his shirt.

Cirie put a hand on Jay's chest. "No, stupid. He's going because you have to make sure bloody thirsty Marvin over here doesn't make any moves."

"No worries. I have the fire covered already," said Shawn, eyeing their attacker. "Plus, I've already made the trip. Just stay here and watch the psycho." Shawn waited for an argument from Jay that never came. "I'll be back as quickly as I can."

"Don't get killed, Stripes," Cirie said, hugging him.

"Be quick," Jay said

"Stay safe, you two," Shawn said. And for the second time in two days, he found himself sprinting through the woods.

Rustling branches still sent Shawn flying at a moment's notice. One person had already found them at the mill, so it was just a matter of time before another reaper would. Thankfully, the Allen Oak distraction seemed to be working, because there wasn't anyone patrolling the woods.

Light from the crystals was dull this early in the morning; their soft glow struggled to illuminate the shadows cast throughout the woods. But this was good for Shawn. If the trio's panic-driven flee from Allen Oak did anything, it helped them get a head start on the morning. Soon the place would be crawling with reapers.

As Shawn moved from tree to tree, he couldn't help but laugh at what the old version of himself would be thinking. It was hard to imagine cringing at a simple camping trip now when he was sleeping in abandoned houses and empty mills. His parents would be shocked. Hell, they wouldn't believe that he was the one breaking the rules. Shawn had been too afraid to sneak out past curfew due to not wanting to disappoint his parents. He wished he could talk to them.

"Oh shit," a voice called out.

Fallen leaves scattered as Shawn dove to the ground. Whose voice was that? Tree bark bit into his back as he tried to locate where the voice had come from. More rustling came from across the cobblestone path. Shawn had been following the road to the Academy, keeping just out of sight. From the other side of the path, another twig snapped.

"Argh, stupid bloody woods," the voice complained loudly.

Shawn quietly made his way over to the other side of the road, checking both ways before he dashed across to the voice. The figure was stumbling his way through the woods, oblivious to Shawn's presence. Moving in closer, Shawn was still out of the reaper's vision.

"I see you got my message," Shawn said.

"Jesus!" Q jumped at the sudden appearance.

"Now I know why you're not part of the search party."

"Shut up, most wanted." Q pulled him into a one-armed hug.

"Ah, careful!" Shawn pulled back, trying not to get burned. "You took the whole goddamn thing?"

"That's what you asked for!"

"I thought you'd just use it to light something else on fire!" Shawn laughed at the stolen object. When Shawn had left Drop Tailors, he wasn't sure if Sylvia had gotten time to send the cardinal out. Now, Q stood in front of him, with his left hand wrapped around the Wayward Academy's everlasting flame.

Q scrunched his eyebrows together. "This is easier to hold. So, you're welcome!" Q said, laughing.

It felt good to have his friend back. They were secretly meeting in the middle of the woods, but it felt normal. Not like they had people hunting them down. Shawn wondered if this was going to be one of the few normal moments he had left. Even if Cirie became a reaper, Shawn wasn't sure if the council would continue to let him be.

Q gave his friend a once-over. "You've been through hell."

"Twice, but I'm still moving."

"Shawn..." Q said, fidgeting as he shifted his weight from foot to foot. "What did you get yourself into?"

"How much do you know?"

"You weren't the only one to send a cardinal my way while I was shadowing Roddick," Q said, smirking. "Maple was able to convince Sophia to use *her* cardinal. She wrote me the gist of the situation. Which looks to be a complete and utter clusterfuck."

"You have no idea, man." The last few days replayed in Shawn's head like a short horror film. "I made a rash decision, Q, but I don't regret it. When it first happened, I convinced myself it was because she was different. She could see us! But I've come to realize that even if it hadn't been for this special circumstance, just giving her just a couple more days was worth it."

"It's hard to look away from someone needing help. I get it." Q's head slumped. "I wish someone had tried to help me. I could've had a few more days with my family."

Shawn was familiar with that wish. "Have they said anything about what they want to do with Jay and me after they catch us?"

"Maple said there are rumors floating around. But nothing concrete."

Of course, no one knew what the punishment would be. The Council would wait until they were caught before they handed him a death sentence. "Figured. Probably won't be anything good." Shawn clenched the handle of the torch until the metal imprinted on his hands. "You have no idea what it means that you brought this. It's going to save Cirie."

"Well, fucking cupcakes, man. Let's get going before someone stumbles upon our little gathering." He walked off in the direction of the mill. Q was willing to sacrifice everything for Cirie, someone he'd never met. That was how unselfish he was. How loyal.

"Q... you can't come."

He spun around. "Nah. See these feet here? That ain't no mirage, they still work."

It would be easy to accept his help. It was another person to help share responsibility, but it was also another person to accept punishment. Shawn sighed, grateful to have met this crazy buffoon. "You can't get involved any more than you already have. I need you to go back."

"I'm coming with."

"No," Shawn said emphatically. He needed to get this through Q's head. "You can't come. It would only alert them that I'm nearby. You've been here for too long anyway. They have Maple in lockdown. I'm surprised they didn't do the same with you."

"There isn't a soul that knows where I am. When I left shadowing, I told Roddick I was needed by Mac in the training tower. Before we even delivered the soul, he let me out of the carriage. Any mustangs in the field haven't been briefed on what's going on yet."

"*Yet* being the keyword. As soon as the soul is delivered, he will be. Then he'll start wondering where the most wanted man's best friend went." Shawn didn't need to drag anyone else into the chaos he created. "And you need to be there for Maple."

"Okay. You have some points." Q gave Shawn a swig of his canteen. "I'll go back and find out everything I can. Let's see them try and lock me up."

"I have." Shawn took a sip. "Twice."

Q feigned shock. "Excuse me? That's false."

"We were locked in the top of the tower together, and we got locked in our rooms."

"Fine. You got me there. But third time is the charm!" Q pulled Shawn into another embrace, letting the silence hang comfortably for a second. "Don't die on me now."

"Everyone keeps telling me that." Shawn squeezed his friend. "I'll be safe, man. I'll introduce you to Cirie at breakfast soon."

"We don't make jokes about food, sir. So, I better see you for some pancakes." Q hesitated before leaving. "Oh, and tell Jay that if he needs any encouragement to get back in one piece, that he can finally take me on that date."

Shawn almost dropped the torch. "Wait. You and Musters? Did I hear that correctly?"

"Well, hopefully," Q said sheepishly.

"I hope so too, man," Shawn smiled, shoving him playfully. "I'll make sure he gets the message."

Q pushed Shawn back. "Go. Get out of here. I'll have the bacon waiting for ya."

"Thanks, Q." Shawn turned in the opposite direction of his friend, flame, and hope, in hand.

Chapter 52

The conversation with Q felt like a firebreak in the bushfire that had become Shawn's life. But the instant he left, all the fear that had dissipated returned. Carrying the torch meant he couldn't sprint through the woods like before. The last thing he wanted to do was trip and snuff out the flame.

Shawn needed the cavern crystals to brighten. Carrying this torch was like carrying around a giant sign for the reapers. He might as well be screaming, "Look at me! I'm over here!" But if his luck could hold out a little longer, they could make Cirie a reaper soon. No more stupid countdown, no more fear of her dying at every turn, no more running. They could plead their case. The main goal Shawn had was to ensure that no one perished because of him.

Until the top of the windmill started poking out over the trees, Shawn didn't feel safe. Trudging his way through the forest this exposed, all his senses were heightened. Any small noise gave his body pins and needles. The walk back was painstakingly long.

Seeing one propeller gave Shawn some relief. It was the sound coming up the cobblestones that took it away. Doing his best to hide the flame, he shielded it behind his body in the tree line. A carriage, pulled by two familiar stallions, trotted up to the outskirts of the mill. Trevor and Mac. The two reapers he wanted to see the least descended out of the carriage, armed with scythes.

"You sure he told you the mill?" Mac asked.

If it wasn't for the heat of the flame Shawn was holding, his blood would have frozen. Marvin must have informed them about his excursion. Shawn frantically looked around. Could he make a distraction? No. They needed this flame. Panic started to set in. Shawn had no idea what to do.

Trevor stopped right before the chipped mill door. "He left me a note, saying to meet him here. Sounded confident that he knew where they were hiding."

"The search team didn't find anything last night," Mac said.

A bead of sweat slid down the back of Trevor's neck. He looked like a little kid being scolded by an adult. Each word was layered with jitters. "I know, but they mentioned the tunnel had collapsed over by Rudy."

"Rudy also said he didn't see anything. It could have been natural. If it wasn't, then either they got away unscathed or are buried under the rubble. We'll only know the latter once their ghosts pop up."

Trevor pointed into the forest. "Rudy could be lying as well. Shouldn't we at least check it out? I don't hear anything inside. If they already swept the place, then let's take a look at the rubble."

"This is true." Mac examined the mill. Squatting down, he took a handful of dirt, and squeezed. "Roddick, you can head on back. I appreciate you taking us out here on such short notice. You can get back to your duties."

From the front seat of the carriage, Roddick saluted. "Ay, ole Cap'n. Good luck to ya both now. Bring those boys back safely!" Roddick waved as both Gracie and Timothy kicked up the dust, speeding their loyal mustang back to the Academy.

"Let's go. I want to see this collapse," Mac said.

The instant the two senior reapers were out of sight, Shawn sprinted toward the mill. His hand moved side to side as he fumbled with the door. While messing with the handle, Shawn hadn't noticed how close the torch had gotten to his body. The smell of burning cloth made its way up into Shawn's nostrils. In the shoulder of his sweatshirt, a small, charred hole had formed. He cursed at his shaky hands. Frustrated, he made his way inside.

"You got it!" Jay was seated in the middle of the mill, digging into the ground.

"We need to leave. Now! Mac and Trevor are here," Shawn spat out.

"Shit." Jay jumped up and threw objects in their bag. "Where are they now?"

"Checking out what remains of Rudy's tunnel. But then, they'll be here." Shawn's mind moved a mile a minute. Run? Hide? Fight? Three options, and Shawn had no idea which way to go.

Jay sensed his indecision and threw their bags at his feet. "We don't have time to run." Option one out. "But I'll hold them off while I can. Grab everything and go into one of the barns. Make her a damn reaper."

"It's Trevor and Mac..." Shawn said.

"Jay they'll kill you," Cirie agreed.

Jay tossed the other scythe to her. "They can fucking try. Now go." He stood facing the door, blade facing out, ready to pounce.

Grabbing the bags, they ran to the furthest barn door. Shawn left the door open a crack, just so they could see what was happening in the main part of the mill. Being inside one of the barn rooms, Shawn couldn't help being reminded of his first time there. Only this time, someone he knew would die instead of a pig.

"Shouldn't we throw the beam across all the doors?" Cirie drew her grandfather's pocket-knife from the security of her pants. She opted for comfort and placed the other blade up against the wall.

"Doesn't matter. There are a few that don't have them. Not each one is used for testing." Shawn started digging through the bag one-handed. "Do you have the crystal?"

"Right here." She tossed him the glowing rock. "Didn't have far to go to get it either. There were tons behind the windmill."

Shawn hadn't even thought about Cirie digging through the collapsed tunnel. Disaster was barely avoided. "Can you read me the process?"

"Put the crystal in the middle of a bowl and then melt it down with the welder's fire." She ran her finger down the page, reading line by line.

Looking around, Shawn noticed one problem with their plan. They had nothing to melt the crystal in. It wasn't like there weren't pots or bowls stored in the windmill. The reapers would be here any minute, and they needed something.

"Uhhh," Shawn said, trying to find an object of use in the room.

Ahead of the game, Cirie was already deep into the dirt. She dug with one hand until the coarse dirt gave way to a smooth, clay-like substance. She held her hand out. "Water."

Trusting she knew what she was doing, Shawn threw her the canteen. Sprinkling water into her makeshift bowl, her hands kneaded the beads of liquid into the clay. The combination quickly formed a useable bowl in the ground. "This is going to have to do." She glanced down at the scythe leaning against the wall. "Shawn..."

Shawn tracked her eyes. *Make her a reaper.* He hadn't fully grasped what they needed to do. Now it was staring him in the face. Or, more accurately, reflecting his face. "It's the last resort. We don't even know if they'll come in here."

Cirie shook her head in agreement but didn't take her eyes off the weapon. "We need to pour in the gargoyle blood after it melts."

Using the everlasting flame, Shawn held the fire against the cavern crystal. Black soot coated the rock. Any light trying to escape ran into a cloud of darkness. With the tips starting to melt, they only needed one last ingredient. "I think we just need the gargoyle blood now."

Cirie ruffled through the messenger bag. She pursed her lips and moved a dreadlock out of her face. Frustration boiled over after another minute of searching, and she promptly dumped the contents of the bag onto the ground. "Not here. I must have left it with Jay when he was digging."

"I'll grab it real quick." Shawn handed her the torch and widened the crack in the door.

Jay snapped his head around before Shawn slipped through. "What are you doing? Get back in there!"

Shawn pointed to the ground near him. "We need the–"

The door to the mill was open, and standing there, scythes in hands, were Mac and Trevor.

Trevor stepped forward. "Well, boys it's been a bit. Let's chat."

Chapter 53

"Not exactly sure what there is to talk about. I can provide directions back to Wayward if that's what you need." Jay positioned himself in front of the vial, blocking it from their sightline.

Being in the same room as Trevor made Shawn's stomach flip. He doubted that his mentor had been pleased when he woke up hog-tied in a janitor's closet. Trevor must have taken a lot of flak for letting it all happen, so Shawn wasn't surprised by the anger radiating off him.

Mac stepped forward, brushing stray hay out of his path. "Let's end this. There isn't any reason for it to go on any longer." The words came out calmly, yet his grip on the scythe tightened.

Had they seen Cirie? Shawn risked a glance back and saw the door to the barn still open, but no Cirie. Good. She hadn't risked trying to close it. They didn't know she was around yet. Shawn had to make sure it stayed that way.

"Don't take another step." Jay readied himself.

Shawn's leg bounced up and down in anticipation. He wasn't sure how Jay kept his composure in times like this.

Mac scrunched his eyebrows. "This isn't a fight you want to pick, Mr. Musters."

"She's not even here," Shawn blurted out. He inched his way toward the vial. He didn't want to draw attention to it but needed to move closer.

"That's a load of bullshit." Trevor steamed.

Mac put a hand up before Trevor had the chance to charge forward. "You tried to fight me once, and it didn't work out so well." The reminder on Jay's eye had now faded into a dull yellow. "And now, what, you want to spar with two of the best? Think, Musters."

Mac turned to Shawn. "Turner, you know this won't end well if you don't give her up. Be a voice of reason."

Hesitantly, Shawn took another step forward until he was beside the hole. The moment he reached down, everything was going to break loose. They knew Cirie was present. They weren't stupid. "We didn't do this because we didn't want to be reapers. I believe in the job." Did he? Really? "It's just that she saw me, Mac.

I'm not talking about a chair moving randomly. She didn't scream about ghosts. She talked to me. Doesn't that mean something?"

"What are you talking about? She saw you. Trevor, you didn't mention this."

"I don't know if that's true. I only saw Shawn save her before I got knocked out by Jay," Trevor lied, the anger in his voice quivering slightly.

In the back of Shawn's head, he made a mental note.

"Can't say I totally regret it now," Jay said, shrugging.

"Stop it. This charade is over." Mac took another step forward, only a couple of feet from Jay. "Where is Ms. Zos?"

Every muscle in Jay's legs tensed. He was ready.

Shawn didn't need a signal from Jay. He knew instinctively that things were about to explode. Bending down, he pretended to stretch. Just that slight movement caused Shawn's chest to tighten like a loose screw. Ever so slowly, he reached over to the hole and palmed the vial.

Only one person in the room hadn't taken his eyes off Shawn the entire time. While Mac and Jay were waiting for the other to flinch first, Trevor had watched the whole sequence. Each stage of emotion was clear on his face: confusion turned to recognition that turned to shock. Getting a glimpse of the blue liquid swirling inside the vial was all he needed to start screaming. "They're making her a reaper!"

That was the spark that set fire to the kindling. Mac followed Trevor's scream to the vial in Shawn's hand. He looked like he couldn't process what he was seeing. Not one to waste an advantage, Jay attacked.

Sprinting toward Mac, Jay raised the blade above his head and made a wide arc. Distracted by the vial, Mac was just able to dodge the blade that would have split his midsection. Tiny strands of fabric hung from the end of Jay's scythe, like ornaments on a tree.

Jay's blade missed the body but made a gaping hole in the middle of Mac's sweatshirt.

"That was your one-shot, Musters. Hope it was worth it." Mac grabbed the bottom portion of the ripped sweatshirt and tore it off. After flinging it to the ground, he charged. Using tiny arcs, he pushed Jay back.

It took everything out of Jay just to block Mac. This fight was completely different from his previous one. At least in that one, Jay could study Marvin's moves, which allowed him to form a plan. There wasn't going to be any planning here. Just pure instinct. Jay bounced from side to side, trying to alter his movements. He didn't want to be caught standing still; he wanted to be unpredictable.

"Cirie!" Shawn used the chaos to reach her barn door. The smell from their mixture started to seep out of the doorway like a thick fog.

"I need more time!" Cirie said, sitting near the makeshift pot, melting the last bits of crystal.

"Catch!" Shawn tossed the glass vial. It was a poor toss. The blood was going to land a few feet short onto the hard ground. Cirie reacted instantly, diving with her outstretched arm. The vial teetered between her fingers, before falling to the ground. Shawn didn't breathe. Was this it?

"Got it!" She held up the intact glass triumphantly. She looked up at Shawn, but her smile faded faster than the color in her cheeks. "Get the scythe!"

Turning around, Shawn found himself in between Trevor and the stall Trevor was trying to get into. Shawn scrambled back, almost tripping over himself.

Trevor took another step forward. "You know we can't let you guys do that."

"Why not?" Shawn gasped. He needed to grab that scythe. "She's seen this world now. Hell, she could see it before. No one here is like her. If anything, she should be a reaper, not me! Why do they get to choose who becomes one or not?" He let the words tumble out, letting his brain go on autopilot. This allowed him to focus on maneuvering to the stall door. "Surely you can see that this isn't right? She shouldn't have to be hunted!"

"You're right, Shawn. She shouldn't have to be hunted. But you ran." Trevor tensed, his knuckles cracking as he squeezed the weapon. "Our job is not to interfere. Yet I get knocked unconscious, and here we are! Don't you remember the dock? We're trying to prevent that from happening everywhere."

"I get it now. Once a tracker is sent out, it's final. Shouldn't we still be allowed to help people if there is a chance?" Shawn's fingertips reached for the weapon. With his hand on the inside of the stall, he searched unnoticed until his fingers interlocked around the staff. "Can't there be exceptions? Ways to extend life?"

"We aren't here to be judge, jury, and executioner. We're here to get them to the next phase." Trevor swiped at the hay with his feet. Straw floated into the air, gently falling its way back to earth. "One where we all go, Shawn, even us reapers. All you'd be doing is making her die twice."

"We don't have to do this." Shawn pulled his scythe from the wall, angling his feet into a defensive stance.

Trevor shook his head. "Actually, Shawn, I think we do."

Behind them, Jay and Mac were still trading blows, with Jay taking a lot more than he was giving. Blood started to soak into his sweatshirt again. The stain circled the wound like a shark in the water. They had to buy more time. Shawn just wished it didn't involve fighting the two best fighters in the Academy.

Trevor and Shawn waited for the other to make the first move. There wasn't a world in which Shawn won going on the offensive, so he was happy to wait. He kept his defensive stance to let his opponent expend his energy. Their standoff didn't last long.

Folding his left arm into a chicken wing over his heart, Trevor brought the scythe behind his back. With his right arm extended behind him, he took off like a starting gun had been shot. Trevor closed the gap instantly. A couple of feet away, he dropped down, swinging the blade as he hit the hay-littered floor.

Shawn jumped, the arc of the blade coming within spitting distance of his feet. Stumbling back, he wheezed from his rib pain. Shawn didn't know Trevor had this kind of speed. At this rate, he was going to be losing a lot more than his balance. He just needed to make sure Trevor stayed away from Cirie.

"Good instincts." Trevor couldn't hide the amusement in his voice. He didn't bother to wipe off the stray pieces of hay attached to his legs when he bounced up. The man had entered another void: the only thing that mattered was the attack. Shawn was finding out quickly why this man was one of the best fighters at Wayward.

Another attack came from above. Vibrations shot up and down Shawn's arms as their staffs collided. He wasn't going to last long against Trevor. He was already having too many close calls. They were locked in a battle, one where Shawn didn't have the strength to push off the attack. Shawn jumped to the side, letting his blade fall like a limp noodle in his hands. Trevor's blade pierced the dirt Shawn had been standing in. Carrying his momentum, Trevor pulled his blade from the soil, swiping upwards at Shawn's chest. Metal clashed against metal.

"Is that all you got?" Shawn screamed. Adrenaline poured through his veins. But he soon regretted his last move. Trevor had been testing him. That had been the bunny slope for Shawn, and the double black diamond was on its way next.

After that miss, Trevor came down on top of his head. Shawn brought his scythe up for a block, but the blade whiffed at his left. Trevor's foot, on the other hand, found its mark in Shawn's gut. The damage burst through Shawn's nerves. The pain consumed everything in that second. Shawn hadn't even realized he was hunched over. Using the non-bladed side, Trevor jammed the staff into Shawn's temple.

The whole attack happened in an instant. Shawn wobbled out of range, wheezing for air. Black spots appeared in his vision, only this time they weren't going to be cavern crystals. The side of Shawn's head was already swelling like a cake in an oven. If adrenaline was keeping the pain at bay, Shawn didn't want to know what it felt like once it wore off.

"Enough. Let me through, Shawn. This needs to end." Trevor stood with sweat slowly tracing the upper edge of his cheek. Shawn had no idea how far along Cirie was in the process or if Jay had survived Mac. But he couldn't stop.

Black spots danced their way out of Shawn's vision. Had Cirie created the Hades Elixir? They needed more time. Jay was leaking blood along his arms and legs. Yet he was still getting blocks up. Jay wouldn't stop. Shawn couldn't stop.

There wouldn't be another block. Shawn wasn't going to survive another attack. Trevor smelled the victory and rushed forward to finish the job. Shawn used the only move he had left. The scythe flew from his hand, propelling through the air like a javelin. Right at Trevor.

A bull in a China shop. That's how his dad described him playing sports; well, Shawn was going to channel that inner bull. It didn't matter if the blade connected with Trevor. He didn't expect it to. He had heaved it with all his strength and then charged.

The scythe tumbled into the dirt, deflected with ease. Trevor was unamused with the feeble attempt before he realized what was happening. Shawn had learned from his training sessions. He rammed his shoulder directly into Trevor's chest.

An audible "Oof" left Trevor's mouth. The force lifted him off his feet and propelled him backward. Trevor landed hard; his head snapped back, crashing into the ground. Shawn untangled himself from Trevor, rolling off the senior reaper. He took short shallow breaths. He was absolutely spent. Would Trevor get up and finish him off? Shawn glanced at the door, hoping he'd given Cirie enough time.

"Ahhhhhh!" Jay screamed from somewhere above him. Shawn had no energy to see what had happened. It was a full-time job just keeping his eyes open. Metal clanks filled Shawn's ears. Where was Cirie? After a few more clangs, a body thumped to the ground.

"You idiot." The voice didn't belong to Shawn's roommate. Mac stood over him, scythe ready. A red film coated the blade. The scythe hovered above him like a guillotine. Was this the last thing Cirie would see? Him dying? His bloodstains would become just another spot in the blood-soaked hay.

"Jay?" Shawn croaked.

Mac ignored him and shook Trevor. "Wake up, Trevor. Dammit, Turner, you knocked him out. I'll go get her then." Out of his peripheral vision, Shawn saw Mac walk over to the other body on the ground that was still moving: Marvin. Two slices of the blade later, he was freed.

"Stay here and watch them," Mac instructed Marvin. Someone with only one working leg wasn't going to make the best guard, but neither Shawn nor Trevor would be going anywhere soon.

Shawn's head throbbed; he couldn't think straight. He needed to move. Was Jay alive? His arm hurt badly. He swallowed the saliva building up in his mouth, and the taste of copper danced across his tastebuds. Where was Cirie?

A shadow filled the doorway of one of the barns. "Heard you boys were looking for me?" A blurry version of Cirie sidestepped one blade and easily dodged the feeble attempt from Marvin.

"Grab her!" Mac yelled at Marvin. But it was too late. She'd already left the mill. Mac took off, leaving Shawn with an unconscious Trevor. Meanwhile, Marvin was limping his way to help Mac.

"It's ready!" Cirie screamed from the outside.

What was ready? Shawn attempted to move his head, with pain pulsing from it. Instead of a view of Cirie, all he had was the image of a scythe. A scythe. A new wave of adrenaline pushed into

Shawn. Summoning his last bit of strength, he crawled over to the weapon. Getting to the scythe took a lot, but now he had to dip it in the Hades Elixir. Black spots floated in front of the barn stall, one that seemed impossibly far away.

1 Day; 14 Hours; 42 Seconds.

The tracker laughed at Shawn from its soil-filled spot beside the scythe. Yet it kept ticking. Waving off the black dots, Shawn stood, pocketing the tracker. Using the scythe as a cane, he moved to the stall. A green mixture bubbled in their makeshift bowl. What next? Grunting, Shawn lifted the blade into the mixture, coating it in the Hades Elixir. He didn't have a chance to read how long it needed to be in there, but he thought a few seconds would do it. Pulling it out, the blade itself looked no different. It had a tinge of green shine to it. That was it. Besides the dripping slime, Shawn wouldn't have been able to distinguish it from any other scythe.

Improvised crutch in hand, Shawn limped his way to the exit. His head was swimming, and pain screamed at him to stop. Following the sound of voices, he didn't have far to limp. Light filtered through the treetops of the woods, illuminating the horrors contained in their foliage. Cirie wove around the trees at a breakneck pace, leading her attacker in a maze of branches.

"You need to stop," Mac called out after her. His torn sweatshirt fluttered in the air after each movement. Besides that tear, he didn't have a scratch on him. Change the torn pit-stained sweatshirt, and he could be teaching class in the next hour. Jay didn't leave a mark on him.

Dragging one leg after them, Marvin made a feeble attempt to catch up. Dry blood was pasted to the wrap on his calf, but the second year didn't care. Hunger filled his eyes.

"Screw you!" Cirie shouted. Her dreadlocks dangled in the air, trailing behind her as she ran. Using a scythe she'd picked up in the barn, she attempted swiping down branches to get in Mac's way. It was no use. Cirie was fast, but Mac was gaining ground. Exhaustion from the last few days played out at the worst time. Her feet dragged from fatigue. Mac was tightening the space between them. Then she locked eyes with Shawn and took her gaze off what was in front of her.

No one else had noticed Shawn yet.

And Cirie hadn't noticed the root protruding out of the ground. One step. She needed one step to get over. Instead, she dragged her feet again. Her toe caught underneath, her balance evaporating along with her chances of escape. With one hand occupied and the other in a sling, she couldn't catch her fall. Cirie dropped the scythe as she tumbled. A scream erupted from her lips.

The blade ripped into her chest.

Confusion quickly turned into fear. Cirie's eyes searched around frantically until they landed on Shawn. She held his gaze in her emerald eyes, silently communicating. A moment later her head drooped and her chest stopped rising.

"I'm sorry it had to be this way," Mac whispered.

Shawn wanted to scream as she crumpled to the ground. He wanted to cry as the blood poured out of the puncture wound. Instead, he stood silently nearby, waiting. Seconds later, he saw his target. Blue light pulsed through Cirie's lifeless body, collecting until a bright blue orb ascended from the middle of her chest. Shawn focused on that as he ran forward against every nerve in his body. His legs didn't want to, and his head was slipping into darkness, but he continued on.

The orb was his only focus. He had to hold back the darkness circling his vision. A few feet away, Shawn lifted his blade, ready to pierce the orb. Ready to bring his friend back. Except he couldn't bring the blade down. A hand held the staff back, preventing his meek attempt. Soon his fingertips were gripping air. The scythe was snatched from his grip. Shawn fell to his knees, looking up at Marvin. The reaper stood behind him, a dirty smirk on his face.

Mac kneeled and put a hand on his shoulder. "It's over, Shawn."

The eyes that held his gaze just a moment before were now vacant. Shawn had failed. Cirie would never sit in Shanowen Park with her friends again. She would never hold her father's money clip. She wouldn't cradle the bow to her violin. In the distance, hooves clattered against the cobblestones leading to the mill. Looking to the top of the cavern, Shawn released everything and let the darkness engulf his vision.

Chapter 54

0 Days; 0 Hours; 0 Seconds

Fold. Crease. Fold. Crease. Shawn worked the parchment until lines spiderwebbed across every inch. The bare mattress they had provided didn't bother him now. The scratchy material reminded him of a weathered quilt, and that was all the comfort he needed. Shawn wasn't expecting pleasantries.

After passing out near the windmill, Shawn had woken up to chains attached to his ankles. Apart from the nurse, who came in to apply ointments to his wounds, there were no other visitors to the cell. Shawn was alone that first night and slept on a metal cot welded to the floor. He'd tried to let the tears flow, had wanted to weep, but nothing came. It was like he'd been trying to empty a bucket with nothing inside.

Only when the door of his concrete prison opened early the next morning did something inside Shawn click back into place. Jay. Their embrace was short, as Jay had been injured worse than Shawn. Wheeled in on a chair, Jay was just now able to walk with a slight limp. If there had been a mirror in the cell, Shawn didn't think they'd recognize themselves.

That had been three days ago.

"Think it will be today?" The voice belonged to the other bed in the cell. Its occupant wished the only bruise was the fading one around his eye. Mac had left his mark. Cuts were starting to scab up and down Jay's body. Where there wasn't a cut, a bruise lay in its spot. Jay looked like someone had smashed all the grapes on a vine and left it there as a warning. But he was alive.

Shawn swallowed the dry mashed potatoes that had come through the metal slot in the door. "At this point, does it matter?" He answered Jay.

Jay sat on the edge of his bed; his knees filled the tight space between the cots. "Shawn..."

"I failed," Shawn said before Jay could finish.

Jay hobbled over and lowered himself next to Shawn. "Yes, we did. But we aren't dead. If you want a life after this, then now's not the time to give up."

"Says the person who planned on running away," Shawn said curtly, remembering Jay's plan.

"You're right. I *was* going to run." Jay folded his hands in his lap. "Still, I didn't. Reapers are needed. I accepted that once I saw the victims on the dock walk. If we can convince them to let us continue training to become reapers, then maybe this wasn't for nothing. Not everyone here is unreasonable, right?"

"Like the guy who tore you to shreds?"

Jay narrowed his eyes until they were only slits. "Mac was strategic with every slice. If he wanted to kill me, it would've been over in a minute. He wanted to teach me a lesson." The hands in his lap folded into fists.

Teach them a lesson. During the fight at the barn, Trevor had plenty of chances to cut Shawn's throat. Instead of using the blade, one of the best to wield a scythe in Wayward had kicked Shawn. And knocked him in the head with a staff. Maybe Jay was right. "Then we keep on fighting."

Jay shrugged in agreement. "No point in stopping now."

"Thanks Jay," Shawn said, coughing, the pain in his ribs subsiding a bit.

"You know, I'm getting real tired of being locked in a room with you." Jay turned his head around the cell. "Sooner or later, I'm going to need one with a pleasant view."

A smile teased its way onto Shawn's lips. "Yeah, I'm sure there's someone you'd much rather be stuck in a room with."

Jay stiffened. His eyes stopped scanning the room. "Plenty of people would have been better than you, Turner."

"Q told me to let you know he's ready for that date whenever you are."

"Uh... thanks," Jay blushed and stumbled through his words. "Good to know."

"You know, at one point I really thought you and Sophia were together"

A nervous chuckle escaped Jay. "She tried to make a move in the training tower once. After I told her I was gay, she backed off a bit."

"Now that's one interaction I would have killed to see." Shawn leaned over and lightly bumped into Jay's shoulder. "Heard he likes sunflowers." He winked.

Shuffling outside the door caught their attention. They snapped back into reality. A clanging of keys later and Headmaster Tyflin stood in front of the open door in her signature black and red suit.

"Good afternoon."

"Is it the afternoon? That's nice to know." Jay's words dripped with sarcasm.

"Hi." Shawn responded flatly to the holder of his fate. He stared into her eyes, wishing they'd been the ones to go vacant instead. Was he going to be the next example?

"Mr. Musters, please come with me." She motioned to the door.

"Not unless you forgot to say Turner's name over there too." Jay refused to move. As if he had a choice.

The headmaster straightened her bowtie. "We are *not* doing this dance again. The council is trying these cases separately. Mr. Turner will get his chance. Now please, it's the last day."

"I–"

Shawn grabbed Jay's forearm. "Go. It's going to be fine."

As usual, two senior reapers followed behind Tyflin. The scythes of her bodyguards gleamed against their black suits. Was Shawn going to be okay? He had no idea.

"Fine. Let's get this damn thing over with." It took a few attempts to get out of bed, but Jay was able to limp over. The two senior reapers escorted him out of the cell, leaving Shawn alone again.

A couple of hours passed as Shawn stared at the ceiling. He never thought he'd miss clocks this much. He used to be annoyed by them. None of the ones he grew up with were ever right. His dad didn't excel in time management and was always running behind to events. That's what gave his mom the brilliant idea to set every clock in the home ten minutes behind. She hated arriving late.

A knock at the door pushed Shawn off Memory Lane.

Tyflin was back. "Let's go," she said, her voice void of any emotion.

For the first time after questioning, Jay wasn't brought back to the cell. Was that the last time he'd seen Jay? He resisted asking where he went, as he knew there'd be no answer. He followed the two escorts into the hallway.

Outside the cell, the hallway had the same color scheme. Gray. Concrete floors, walls, and doors. "Where are we exactly?" Shawn asked, his nerves working his mouth instead of his brain.

"Dante 7. It works as both a court and criminal holding area," Tyflin replied like answering a question on a quiz.

Dante? Like Dante's Inferno? There were times when Shawn didn't know if this was a cruel joke or something someone else had made into a cruel joke. "Are there six others?"

"Yes." She ended the conversation.

The escorts led him through a maze of cell corridors until they came upon a room that other hallways fed into. Two gargoyles stared at the group from behind a stone desk. Shawn gulped, still unsure how much the gargoyle community knew of the circumstances.

On the desk was a small glass sand-timer. One of the gargoyles reached over and flipped it upside down. Sand started tumbling from one chamber to the next. It only seemed out of place to Shawn. Apparently, this was their custom before a meeting. It was used to give respect to the group they were meeting.

When the last grain fell, the two gargoyles waved them to a hallway to their left. This path sloped down until the floor morphed into stairs. It tightened into a spiral until spewing them out into a large, curved room. A wooden table sat in front, with six matching chairs. A gallery of familiar reapers peered down at them from their elevated seats.

Tyflin avoided her usual chair from the other proceedings and sat in the only remaining seat available. The two reaper escorts guided Shawn to the center of the room, where a wooden stool faced the group. A hand went on both of Shawn's shoulders, and he quickly found himself sitting down.

Per usual, in each chair sat a member of the Wayward council. Camren Fidler, Franklin, and the head of the mustangs, Peppertine. Since Mac had been involved in the incident, he wasn't allowed to take part in the deliberation. He testified with Trevor and the rest the day prior. Carlin McLally was the other member missing; she stayed back to take charge of the students. Everyone was in their usual chair from the last couple of days, like an unspoken classroom rule. Everyone but Tyflin. In her seat sat an unknown woman.

The woman had a familiar presence. Her olive-green bowtie hung slightly askew beneath her bob of black hair. She shimmered in her black and gold checkered suit coat. She raised an eyebrow, examining Shawn as he watched her. Without taking her eyes off him, she raised a gavel and pounded on the table.

"I, Ivy Chan, am calling to order the case of Mr. Shawn Turner. This council will use the information provided from the last couple of days to determine what actions are needed. Before we conclude, Mr. Turner will answer any lingering questions. We will give him respect and listen to his answers. Are there any objections?"

"No." The filled seats sounded in unison.

Paper shuffled in front of the woman. She licked her finger before flipping a page. "Well, let us get started then."

Shawn's knee bounced up and down, sending shockwaves of pain through his damaged body. Why did this woman seem vaguely familiar? He was trying to think through a fog. Steel spheres dangled from the woman's ears, swinging in a hypnotic-like state. The fog cleared from Shawn's mind as he watched the earrings sway. There was a good reason he recognized her. Any reaper would. She had her bust back in Wayward. Not just council members were deciding his fate: one of the Four Horsemen was.

Chapter 55

Stale air filled Shawn's lungs with every breath. Was he going to be spending the rest of his time in this depressing brick building? Every wall was barren. Whoever had designed the place made sure that no relief for the defendants could be found hanging on the walls. The only light filtered in from the three circular windows behind the council members. The cavern light shone straight into Shawn's face. It was like they'd designed the chamber so that a spotlight fell directly on the stool.

"Shawn Harlan Turner. You've caused quite the uproar around here." She licked her finger again before flipping to the next page. She held complete control of the room. Tyflin and the rest of the council members deferred to her. "Have to say, this is a first for me. I've been briefed on your... situation. I'm sorry we haven't been able to be introduced before now. I'm sure you're confused as to why I'm here."

"You're one of the Four Horsemen, Your Honor." His mouth moved without prompt. Shawn had never been in a courtroom, let alone on trial, but he had watched enough television to know that you had to respect the judge. He tensed, waiting for her response.

A flicker of surprise registered on Judge Chan's face, but she appeared to quickly squash it. "They did warn me you were a bit sporadic."

Shawn decided to push his luck. "Yes, Ma'am, and I apologize for interrupting again, but I need to know if Jay is okay."

"Mr. Musters was interviewed, and the court has already made a ruling. The time I have is very limited, Mr. Turner. So please let *me* ask the questions." She shuffled her notes some more before locking onto Shawn. "Start from the beginning."

From the first carriage ride into Wayward Academy to being locked in the cell, Shawn went through it all again. He'd told the story so many times the last few days that he could turn his brain on autopilot as his lips formed a detailed account of the events. Unlike previous times, no one interrupted Shawn over small details. If a council member wanted to ask a question, they'd only be doing it after the Horseman asked one. And she was perfectly content sitting back and listening.

"Hmmm..." The rider lifted another eyebrow. "Before opening it up to the rest of the council, I first have a question of my own."

"Yes, Ma'am," Shawn replied, racking his brain for possible questions.

"Why?"

Shawn glanced at the other members of the council, who gave him blank faces in return. Only Franklin gave an encouraging smile. "Why what, Ma'am?"

"Why did you disobey your senior reaper, the council, the laws of our world? Why?"

Shawn hesitated. He could give a cookie-cutter answer—one that might satisfy them—or he could follow his gut. He took Sylvia's advice.

"With all due respect, just because they're the laws doesn't mean they're right, Ma'am." A murmur went through the Council, but Shawn continued. "I went along at first. Even after being locked in a room. After being buried alive. After watching people close to me die." Shawn flashed back to the graveyard, sitting over Onyx's body. He felt the heat inside him rising. "Yes, I did my observations and went to the trainings. Reapers are the journey people for those who perish. I get it! But a girl looked me in the eyes as she was dying. Grounders can't escape death. Seven days. That's all they might have left. Shouldn't we be doing everything we can to try and help extend that time? If day three comes and we see a car coming, shouldn't we push them out of the way? Yes, they might die the next day. But they gain one more. That's why. Wouldn't we all want one more day above ground?"

If the members of the council were surprised by Shawn's words, it didn't show. He never broke eye contact with the Horseman. He knew who was deciding things here. They probably thought of him as arrogant. Here he was challenging their way of life. Questioning their processes, and their beliefs. Jay told Shawn not to give up. He hadn't. He told them the truth. Should he have begged for forgiveness? It might've been the only way he walked out of the room with his neck, but he wouldn't have done right by Cirie. She'd deserved those extra moments of life.

Ivy Chan slid a strand of hair out of her face. "We have enough to make our decision. Guards, please take him into the east hallway." The pounding of the gavel burrowed around the sparsely filled chamber.

The guards ripped him from his seat so fast that Shawn thought his pants might still be attached to the stool. As the reapers ushered him out, he tried to gauge the reactions of those deciding his fate. Everyone had their heads down, and even Franklin refused to look up from the wood surface. The only one willing to meet his gaze was Ivy. She had an empty smile fastened to her face. Her lips may have been turned upward, but she was analyzing every movement of Shawn's.

An hour passed as Shawn sat on a bench in the hall. Inside, it felt like the last birthday candle had just been blown out; the singing and excitement were over, and now he had to eat his cake. He wasn't sure what they were deliberating over. He didn't care anymore; he'd grown used to being left in the dark.

"Any idea what's in store for me?" Shawn asked his cell guards. The only reply Shawn received was silence. Reapers here made great guards. But crap conversationalists.

The sound of the gavel signaled Shawn's return. The guards led him back to the center of the room but didn't force him to sit. Shawn remained standing and held his head high. Time to pay the piper. Everyone waited for Horseman Chan to speak. Shawn followed their lead and waited for her to deliver his fate.

"Mr. Turner, we thank you for your time here today. Headmaster Tyflin, you may lead him to the carriage now."

Carriage? He was leaving, but going where?

The headmaster took the steps one at a time as she made her way down from the jury platform. She stood in front of Shawn, emotionless. "Follow me, Mr. Turner."

"Where am I going?" He asked, standing his ground. What else could they do to him?

"Just follow me first, Mr. Turner."

Turn after turn, Tyflin led him through the hallways of the jail. Shawn tried to memorize the layout and figure out where they were headed, but it was impossible. It was like being lost with a compass that couldn't point north.

A series of hallways later, they arrived at the entrance of the building. Four gargoyles stood at the entryway of the jail. When Shawn's group approached, the stone men stepped to the side to let them out. Shawn was instantly blinded by the light. Squinting, he tried to find a dimmer cavern crystal to focus on. Except there were no cavern crystals. There was no cavern ceiling. The light searing into his corneas was from the sun. They were above ground.

"Get in, please."

A soft breeze lifted the cuffs of Shawn's sweatshirt. He disobeyed the request and walked to the side of the road. The paved path could fit two carriages passing each other, but nothing else. If one carriage was a little larger, then the fall would let the other reach a new destination.

Where the pavement ended, the ground ended as well. A drop of a couple hundred feet bookended the road into the building. The entire thing acted as a cliff walk out to the jail, where it sat with the water crashing below. Shawn inhaled, the scent of the water flowing over his senses. "I deserve to know where I'm going."

"We both do," a voice said from inside the carriage.

Shawn rushed to the carriage. "Jay!"

"In the flesh. For now," he responded in all his bandaged glory.

"Please move to the side." Tyflin shooed Shawn inside and knocked on the mustang door.

"Where to Ma'am?"

Roddick. Of course, Shawn's journey would end with Roddick at the helm.

"Graveyard 11. We're on a tight schedule."

Shawn and Jay exchanged a glance. Whatever decision had been made behind those closed doors had them leaving a prison and heading to a graveyard.

"Will do! Come on, Gracie. You heard her, Timothy! Let's get a going!" A whip of the reigns later and they were off.

Red wings soared past their carriage. Cardinals clutched messages in their feet as they flapped to their destination. Shawn hadn't even had a chance to send a message with his bird. He wondered what would happen to Mojo. Maybe Maple would think of that, though. She could take care of him or at least find a new home. Shawn just wished he could send one last message.

"Is there a reason you're keeping us in the dark?" Jay asked.

"The council thought it best for the punishment to be read at the graveyard," Tyflin said.

Shawn was tired of talking, and it seemed Jay was too. Those were the last words either of them uttered during the ride. Shawn leaned into Jay and fell into a sleep-like state. Maple, Quintin, Onyx, Jay, Cirie. Names drifted in and out of his head. He didn't dream or totally fall asleep. Occasionally, he'd wake up and listen for changes, only to fall asleep again before he realized if there had been any. Before long, headstones were visible from the carriage.

"Wooooaaahhhh, Gracie. I told you to slow her!" Roddick knocked twice. "Ma'am, we're here."

The headmaster opened the door and stepped out. Shawn didn't want to follow. He wanted to stay in this carriage and pretend nothing was happening. His legs didn't listen to his head, because he found himself standing on the ground of the graveyard.

The cemetery remained quiet, accepting these new visitors like it had accepted its previous ones. Overgrown weeds dotted the grass between the headstones. Shawn wasn't sure if this was the same graveyard he'd been buried in already. If so, the second time would be the charm. Without a word, Roddick turned and high-tailed it as soon as Jay hobbled out.

Mac watched from across the graveyard, his scythe reflecting Shawn's fears. To his right, a gargoyle kept a watchful eye. The three gold dots stitched into his tunic brought Shawn back to the first time he was standing over an open grave. No one had helped them there either.

"Come take a seat with me, boys." Tyflin sat them down on a stone bench near two empty graves. They sat, reluctantly, gazing at the holes dug before them. "Almost everyone ends up in a graveyard. We start our journey as reapers here and it is also where many end their lives as grounders. Birth in death."

"Let me guess. Our deaths will be the births of better reapers." Jay's ears burned a nuclear red with each passing word.

"Do I really need to go through the list you two checked? Knocked out a senior member of the reaping community. Attacked a gargoyle. Disrupted a medical blade on duty. Started a riot in town. Injured a fellow student. And lest we forget, alerted a grounder to our presence." After each point, she held up a different finger until she had to switch to a new hand. "So no, you do not get off scot-free. The council has decided that both of you need to be punished and that you'll be made examples of."

Shawn tightened his knuckles around the edge of the bench and zeroed in on the scythe in Mac's hand. Here it was. Do something meaningful in his life? He had two chances to do so and still couldn't. Everything had been for nothing. Shawn laughed at himself.

“It’s been determined that both of you will be assigned to Dante 2. You’ll clean out cells, scoop food for prisoners, and perform any other tasks required. This will only be during the period between years at Wayward. And while you’ll be able to leave the prison, you will live there while punishment is served. Is that clear?”

“What?” they both replied.

“I thought I was good as dead.” Shawn rubbed his temples, stress shedding off his body.

“Your case was full of unforeseen circumstances that the council and Horseman Chan considered. A grounder being aware of us without interaction is an unusual instance. Not that your case didn’t have merit, but if this had happened a year earlier, your bodies would be filling those two graves before you.”

“We get to live,” Shawn exclaimed. A tear rolled down Jay’s face, and Shawn realized his own cheeks were wet too.

“By a stroke of dumb freaking luck, yes, you both will live. Don’t get us wrong. There was strong consideration to putting you two into retirement.”

“What changed then?” Shawn asked.

“I’ll be honest. Ivy Chan is a new Horseman. She was only elected last year, so she’s looking to gain favor with the other horsemen. She took your situation as an opportunity to propose a new rule mandate.” Tyflin stopped abruptly and then regained her composure. “There are more consequences to come, but we will get into that. First, you should appreciate that you’re *not* in one of these graves.”

Alive. Shawn would see his friends again. He would see Maple again. His eyes drifted from grave to grave, thinking of the ones that he wouldn’t see. The ones that wouldn’t be coming back. Thankfully, a lot of empty graves filled the area. And luckily, neither Shawn nor Jay would need their headstones today.

“An executive decision was made by council members Franklin and Mac after you both succumbed to your injuries at the mill. It was approved quickly by the Four Horsemen.”

Mac had stayed rooted in his spot on the other side of the graveyard, but Shawn finally noticed he wasn’t watching them. Instead, Mac’s focus was on a grave in front of him. One full of dirt. Shawn gasped.

“Wayward Academy isn’t always what it appears to be.”

In the middle of the grave, the earth started cracking. Dirt spilled over into the grass, attempting to settle into a new resting place. Then, as if a bolt of lightning had struck the ground, it opened up. A black hand shot up into the air a pocketknife in its clutches.

Acknowledgments

Book 1 is complete! Those are words I thought I might never be able to write. None of this could have been possible without the amazing support from my friends and family.

I first want to give a huge shoutout to the first person to ever read my book and who wouldn't stop bothering me until she read it, Jess Martell. You helped push me to complete it and I will be forever thankful for that.

Thank you to my cover artist Emily Farr for designing a book cover that captured the essence of the story. The effort you made to make sure I was getting what I wanted didn't go unnoticed!

To my first readers, Gail, Alex, Collen, Megan, Monica, Mackenzie, Anthony, and Jess W, thank you for helping polish it up and going through this wild journey with me.

Finally, I have to give a shoutout to all three of my sisters for always believing in me and encouraging me to write.

Now, on to book 2.